# fairy Tale comics

First Second
New York

**First Second**
New York

Compilation copyright © 2013 by First Second
Editor's Note copyright © 2013 by Chris Duffy

Published by First Second
First Second is an imprint of Roaring Brook Press,
a division of Holtzbrinck Publishing Holdings Limited Partnership
175 Fifth Avenue, New York, New York 10010
All rights reserved

Edited by Chris Duffy
Book design by Colleen AF Venable

Cataloging-in-Publication Data is on file at the Library of Congress.

ISBN: 978-1-59643-823-1

First Second books are available for special promotions and premiums.
For details, contact: Director of Special Markets, Holtzbrinck Publishers.

First edition 2013
Printed in China by South China Printing Co. Ltd., Dongguan City, Guangdong Province

10 9 8 7 6 5 4 3 2 1

# Contents

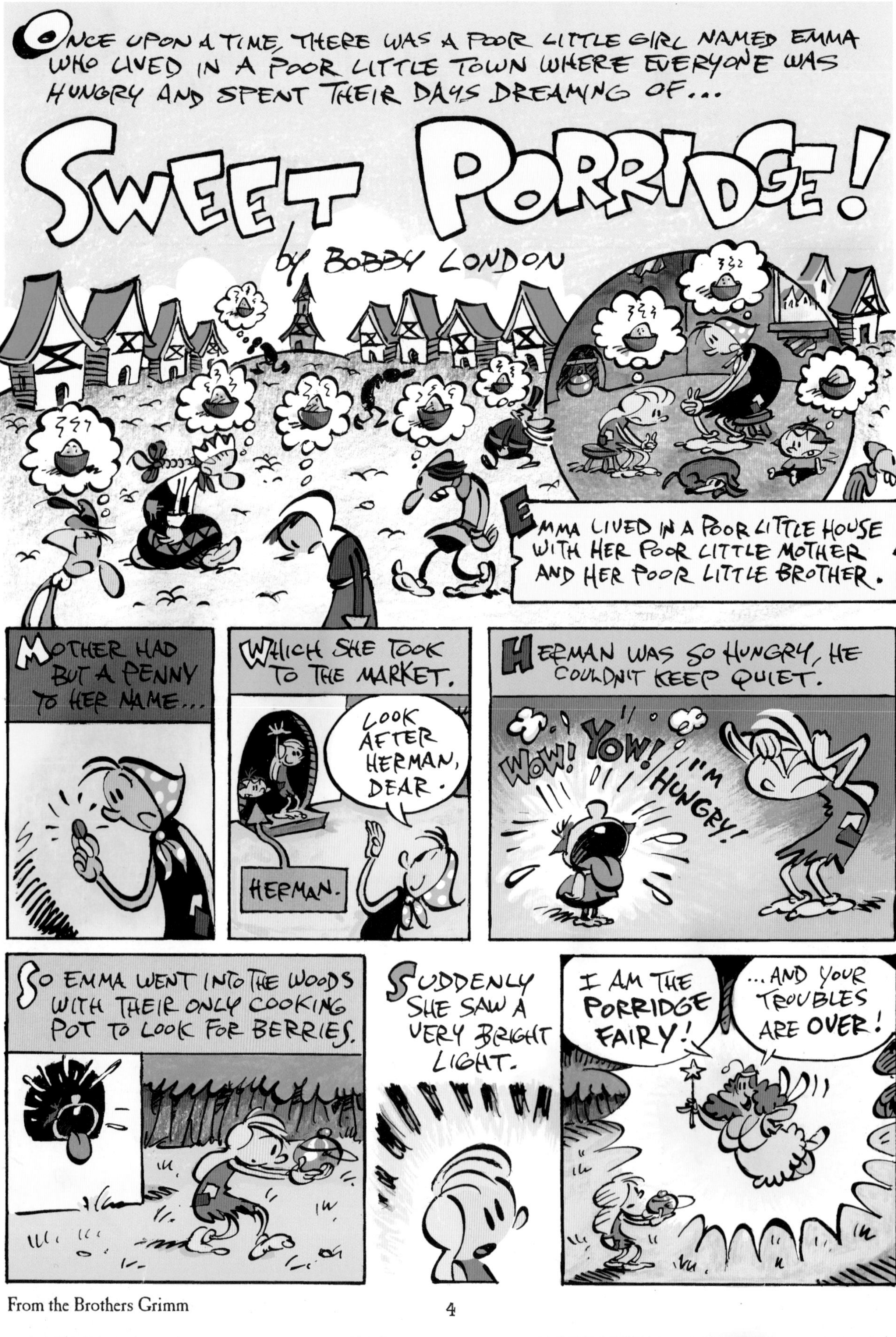

ONCE UPON A TIME, THERE WAS A POOR LITTLE GIRL NAMED EMMA WHO LIVED IN A POOR LITTLE TOWN WHERE EVERYONE WAS HUNGRY AND SPENT THEIR DAYS DREAMING OF...
SWEET PORRIDGE!
by BOBBY LONDON
EMMA LIVED IN A POOR LITTLE HOUSE WITH HER POOR LITTLE MOTHER AND HER POOR LITTLE BROTHER.
MOTHER HAD BUT A PENNY TO HER NAME...
WHICH SHE TOOK TO THE MARKET.
LOOK AFTER HERMAN, DEAR.
HERMAN.
HERMAN WAS SO HUNGRY, HE COULDN'T KEEP QUIET.
WOW! YOW!
I'M HUNGRY!
SO EMMA WENT INTO THE WOODS WITH THEIR ONLY COOKING POT TO LOOK FOR BERRIES.
SUDDENLY SHE SAW A VERY BRIGHT LIGHT.
I AM THE PORRIDGE FAIRY!
...AND YOUR TROUBLES ARE OVER!


Color by Mark Martin

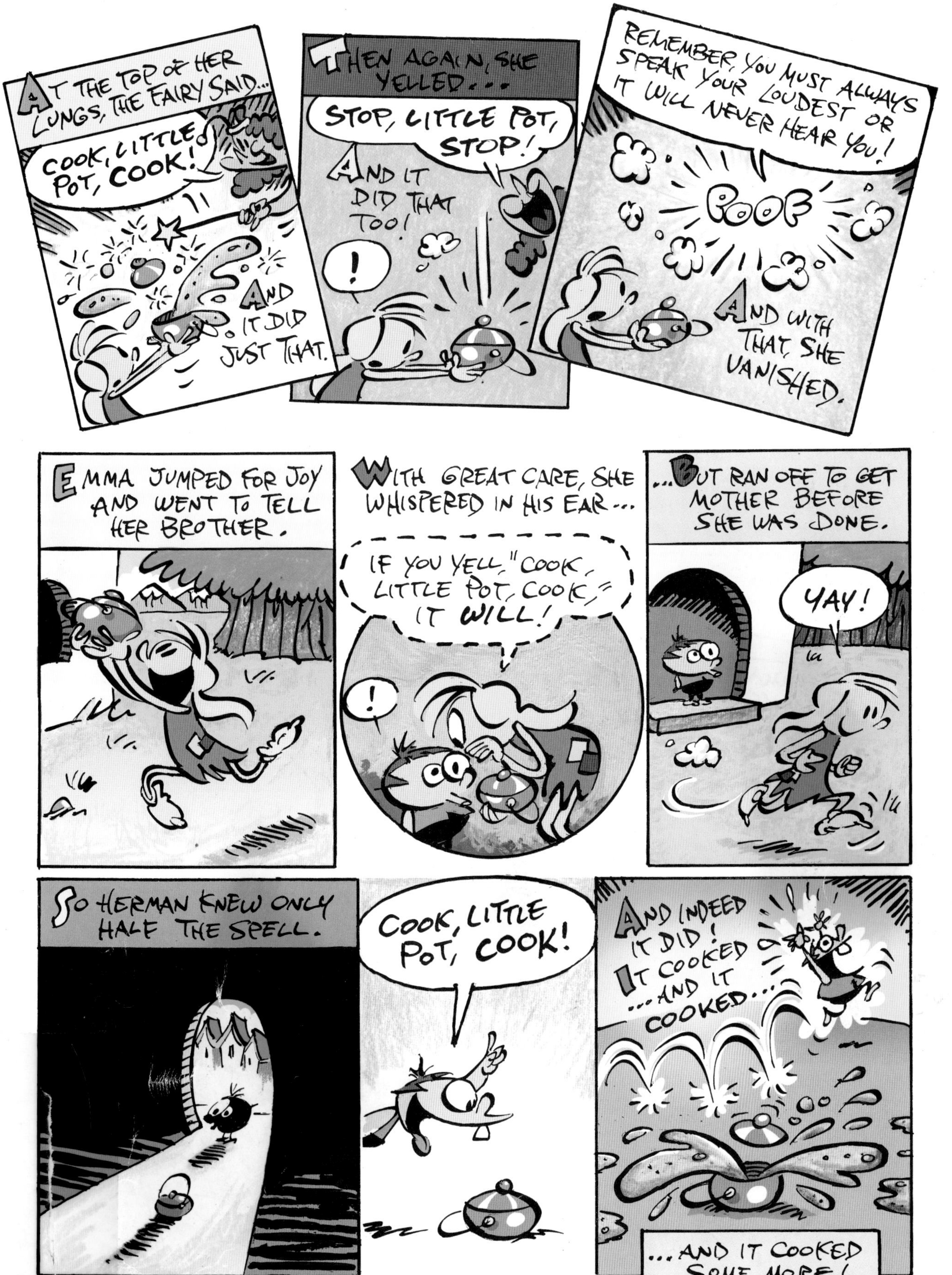

AT THE TOP OF HER LUNGS, THE FAIRY SAID...
COOK, LITTLE POT, COOK!
AND IT DID JUST THAT.
THEN AGAIN, SHE YELLED...
STOP, LITTLE POT, STOP!
AND IT DID THAT TOO!
!
REMEMBER, YOU MUST ALWAYS SPEAK YOUR LOUDEST OR IT WILL NEVER HEAR YOU!
POOF
AND WITH THAT, SHE VANISHED.
EMMA JUMPED FOR JOY AND WENT TO TELL HER BROTHER.
WITH GREAT CARE, SHE WHISPERED IN HIS EAR...
IF YOU YELL "COOK, LITTLE POT, COOK," IT WILL!
!
...BUT RAN OFF TO GET MOTHER BEFORE SHE WAS DONE.
YAY!
SO HERMAN KNEW ONLY HALF THE SPELL.
COOK, LITTLE POT, COOK!
AND INDEED IT DID! IT COOKED ...AND IT COOKED...
...AND IT COOKED SOME MORE!

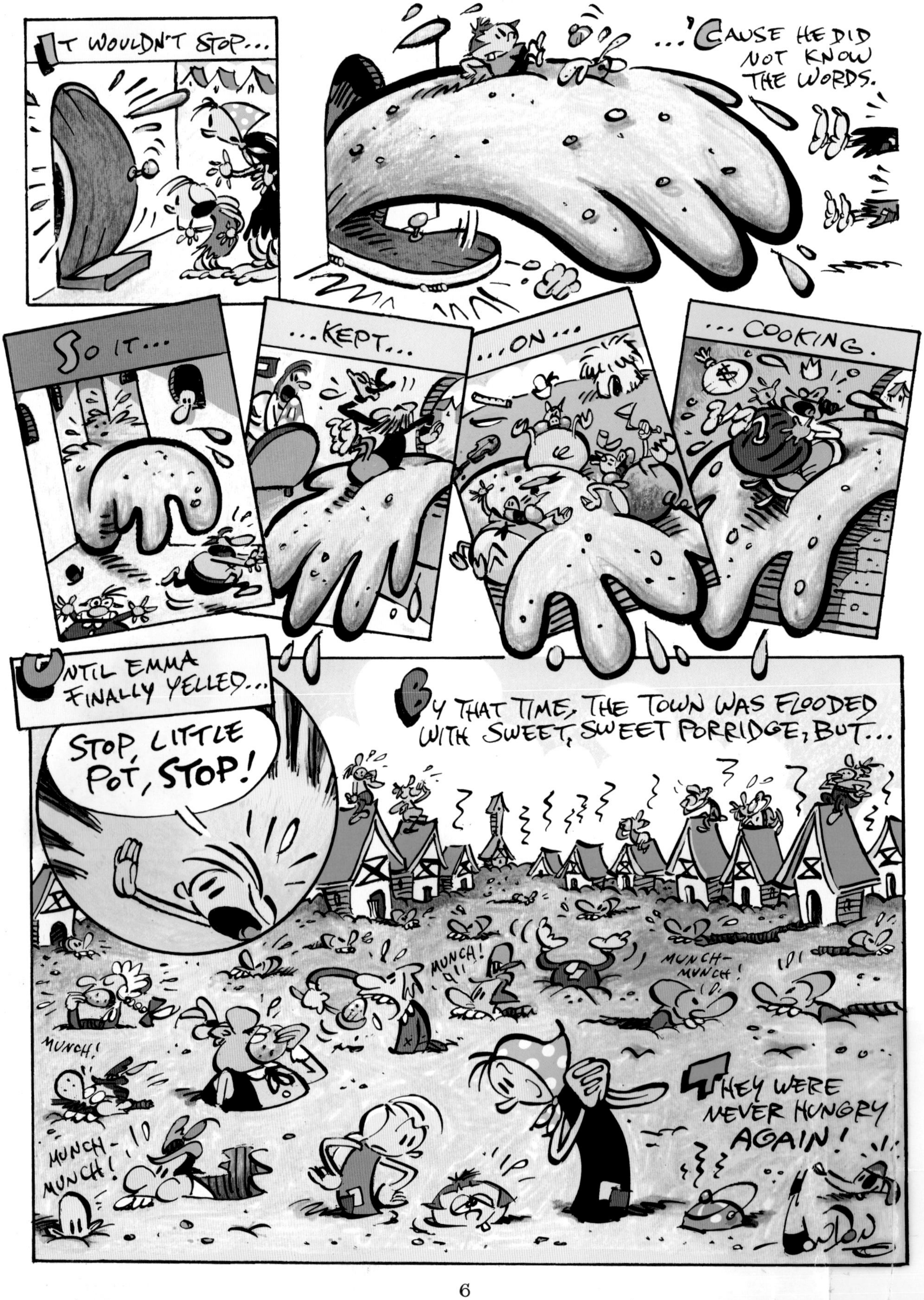
IT WOULDN'T STOP...
...'CAUSE HE DID NOT KNOW THE WORDS.
SO IT...
...KEPT...
...ON...
...COOKING.
UNTIL EMMA FINALLY YELLED...
STOP, LITTLE POT, STOP!
BY THAT TIME, THE TOWN WAS FLOODED WITH SWEET, SWEET PORRIDGE, BUT...
MUNCH!
MUNCH-MUNCH!
MUNCH!
MUNCH-MUNCH!
THEY WERE NEVER HUNGRY AGAIN!

# the 12 DANCING princesses

adapted by
EMILY CARROLL

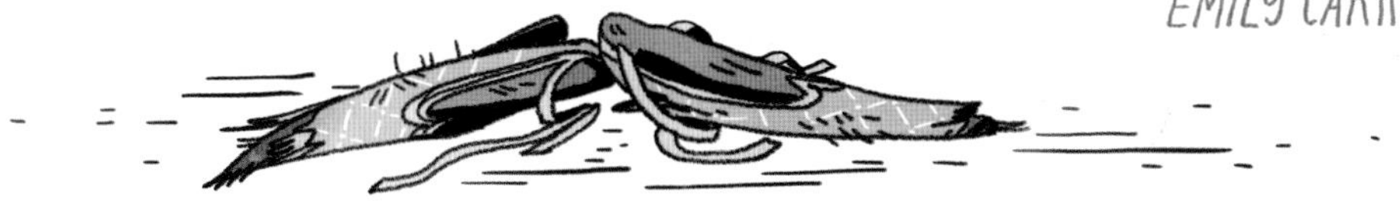

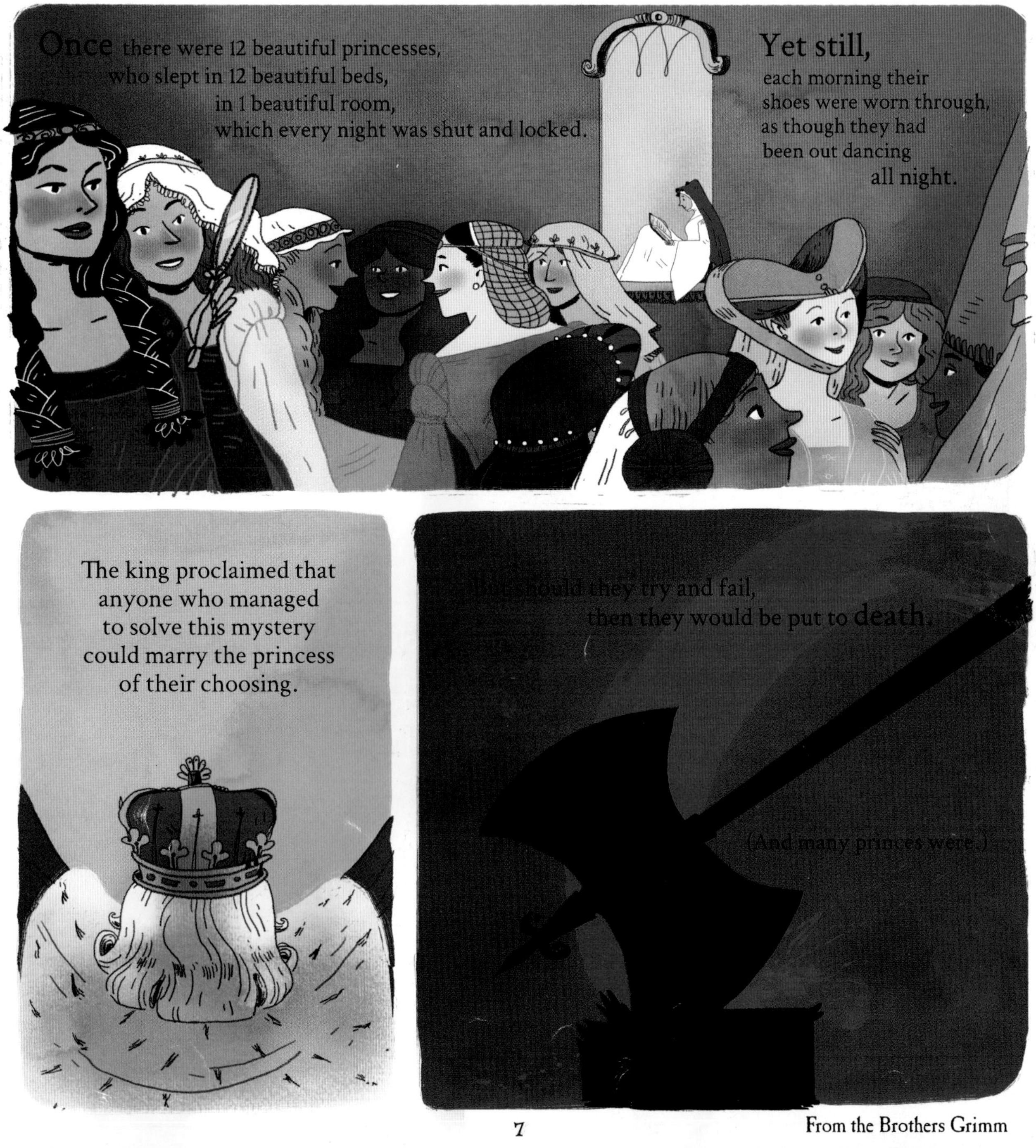
Once there were 12 beautiful princesses,
who slept in 12 beautiful beds,
in 1 beautiful room,
which every night was shut and locked.
Yet still,
each morning their shoes were worn through,
as though they had been out dancing all night.
The king proclaimed that anyone who managed to solve this mystery could marry the princess of their choosing.
But should they try and fail,
then they would be put to death.
(And many princes were.)



From the Brothers Grimm

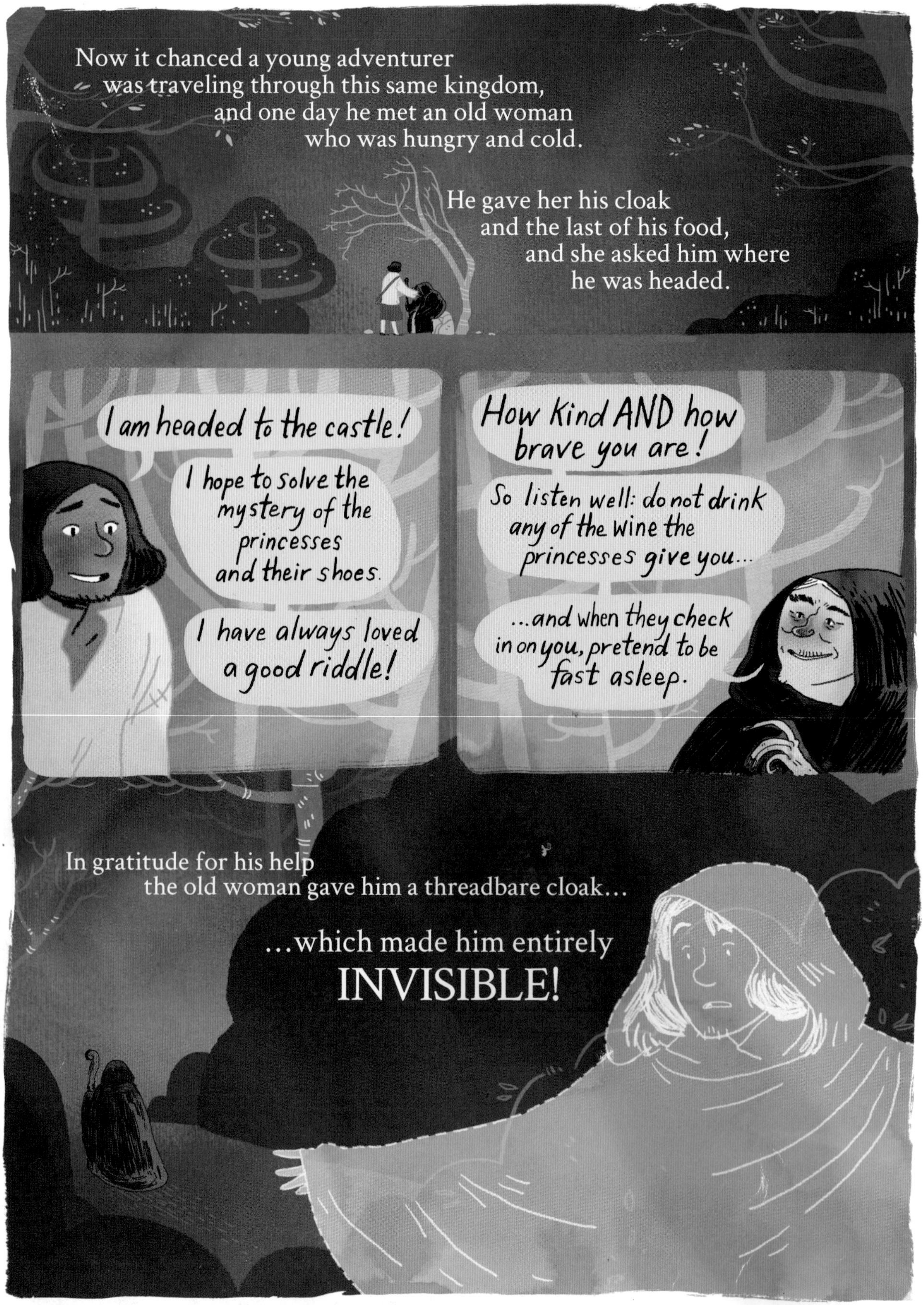
Now it chanced a young adventurer was traveling through this same kingdom, and one day he met an old woman who was hungry and cold.
He gave her his cloak and the last of his food, and she asked him where he was headed.
I am headed to the castle!
I hope to solve the mystery of the princesses and their shoes.
I have always loved a good riddle!
How kind AND how brave you are!
So listen well: do not drink any of the wine the princesses give you...
...and when they check in on you, pretend to be fast asleep.
In gratitude for his help the old woman gave him a threadbare cloak...
...which made him entirely INVISIBLE!

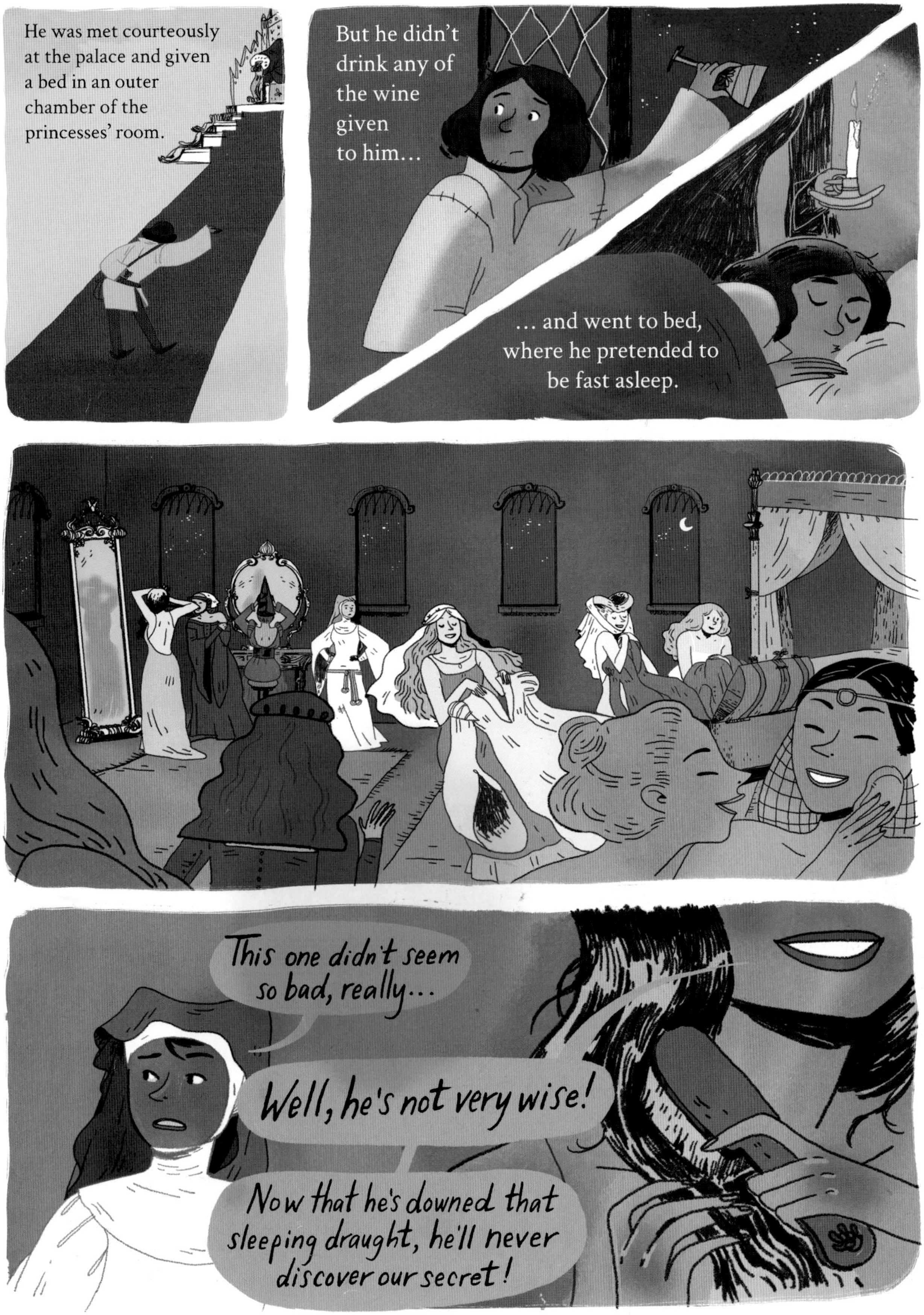
He was met courteously at the palace and given a bed in an outer chamber of the princesses' room.
But he didn't drink any of the wine given to him...
... and went to bed, where he pretended to be fast asleep.
This one didn't seem so bad, really...
Well, he's not very wise!
Now that he's downed that sleeping draught, he'll never discover our secret!

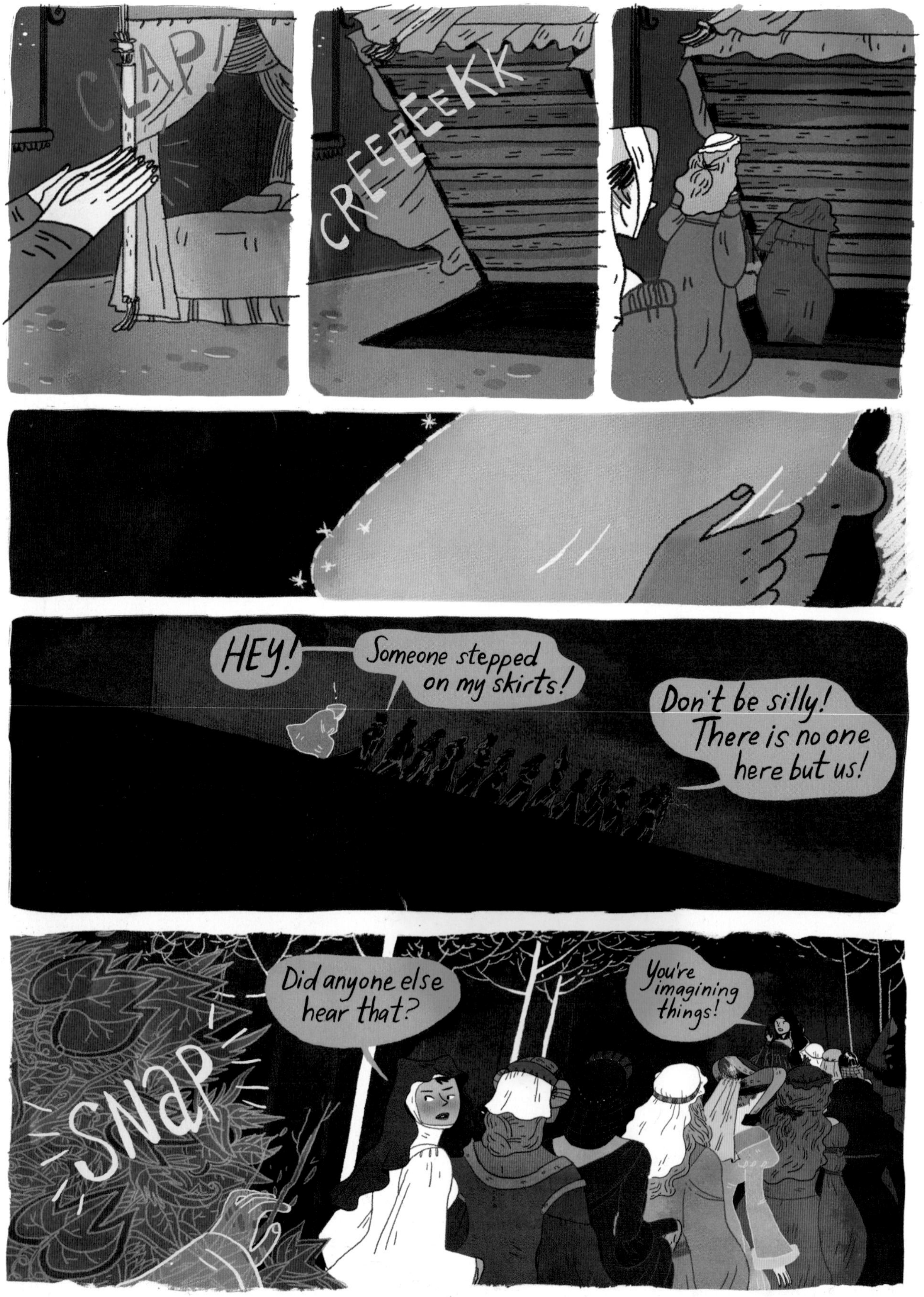
CLAP!
CREEEEEKK
HEY!
Someone stepped on my skirts!
Don't be silly! There is no one here but us!
SNAP
Did anyone else hear that?
You're imagining things!

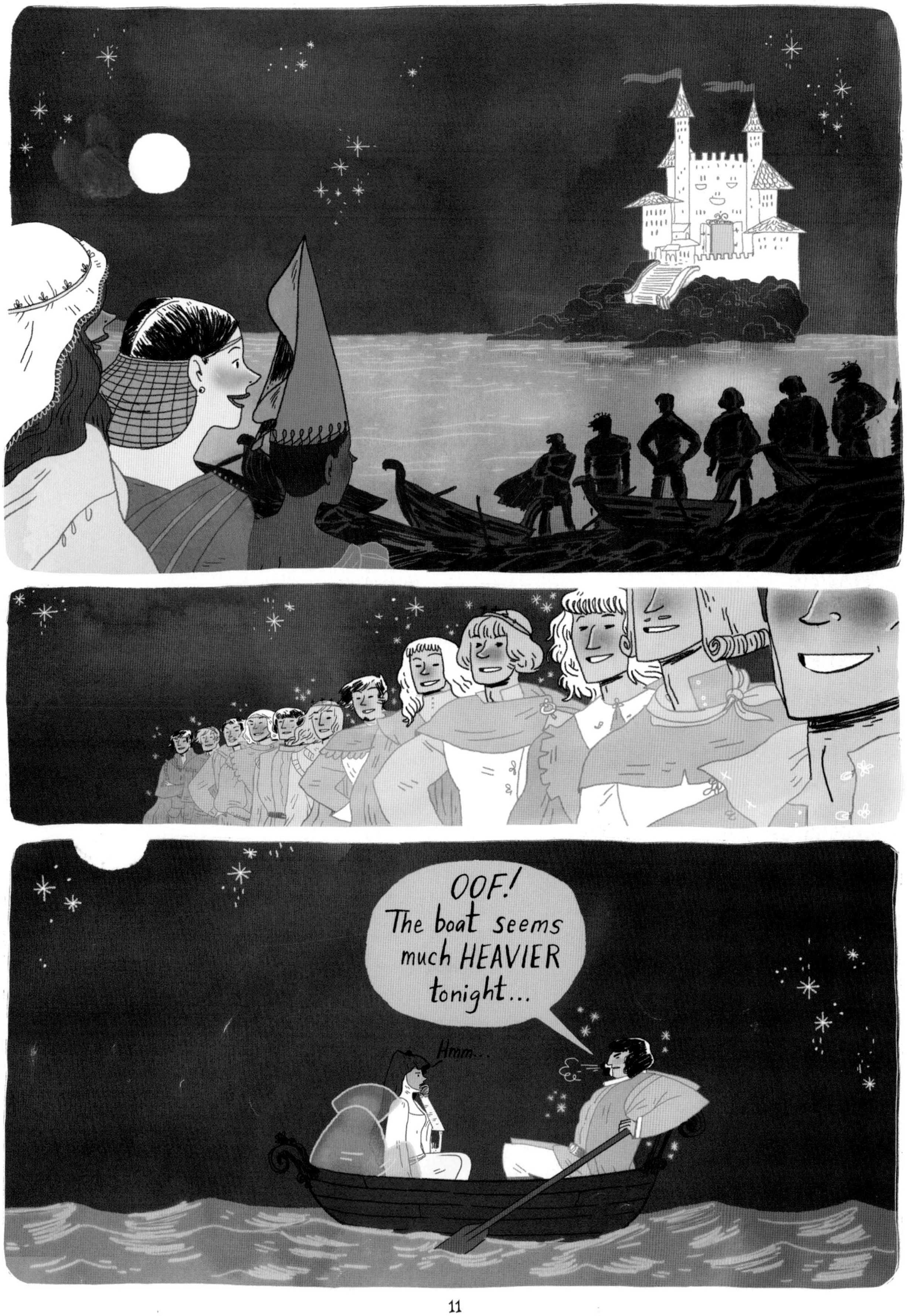
OOF!
The boat seems much HEAVIER tonight...
Hmm...

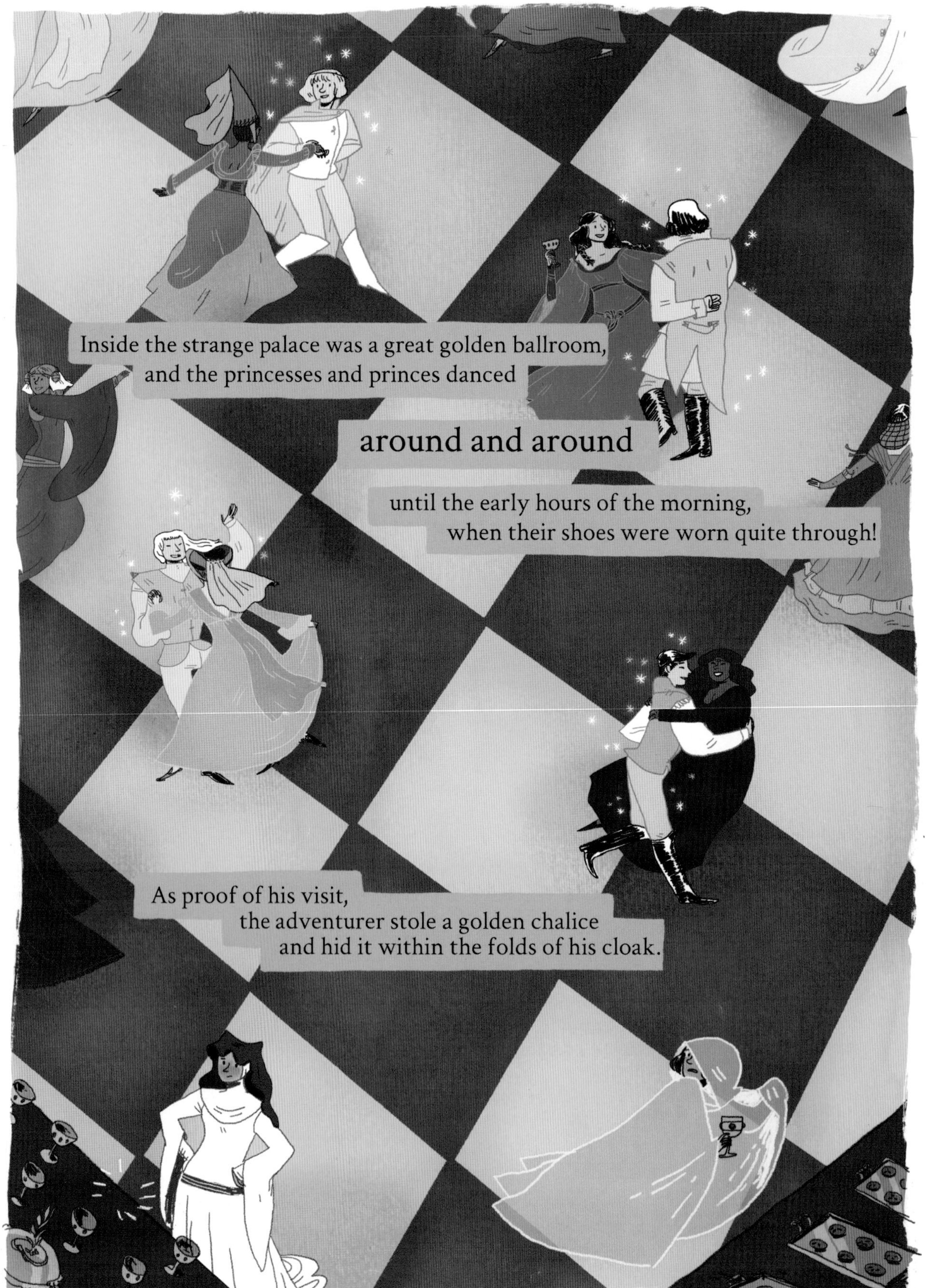
Inside the strange palace was a great golden ballroom,
and the princesses and princes danced
around and around
until the early hours of the morning,
when their shoes were worn quite through!
As proof of his visit,
the adventurer stole a golden chalice
and hid it within the folds of his cloak.

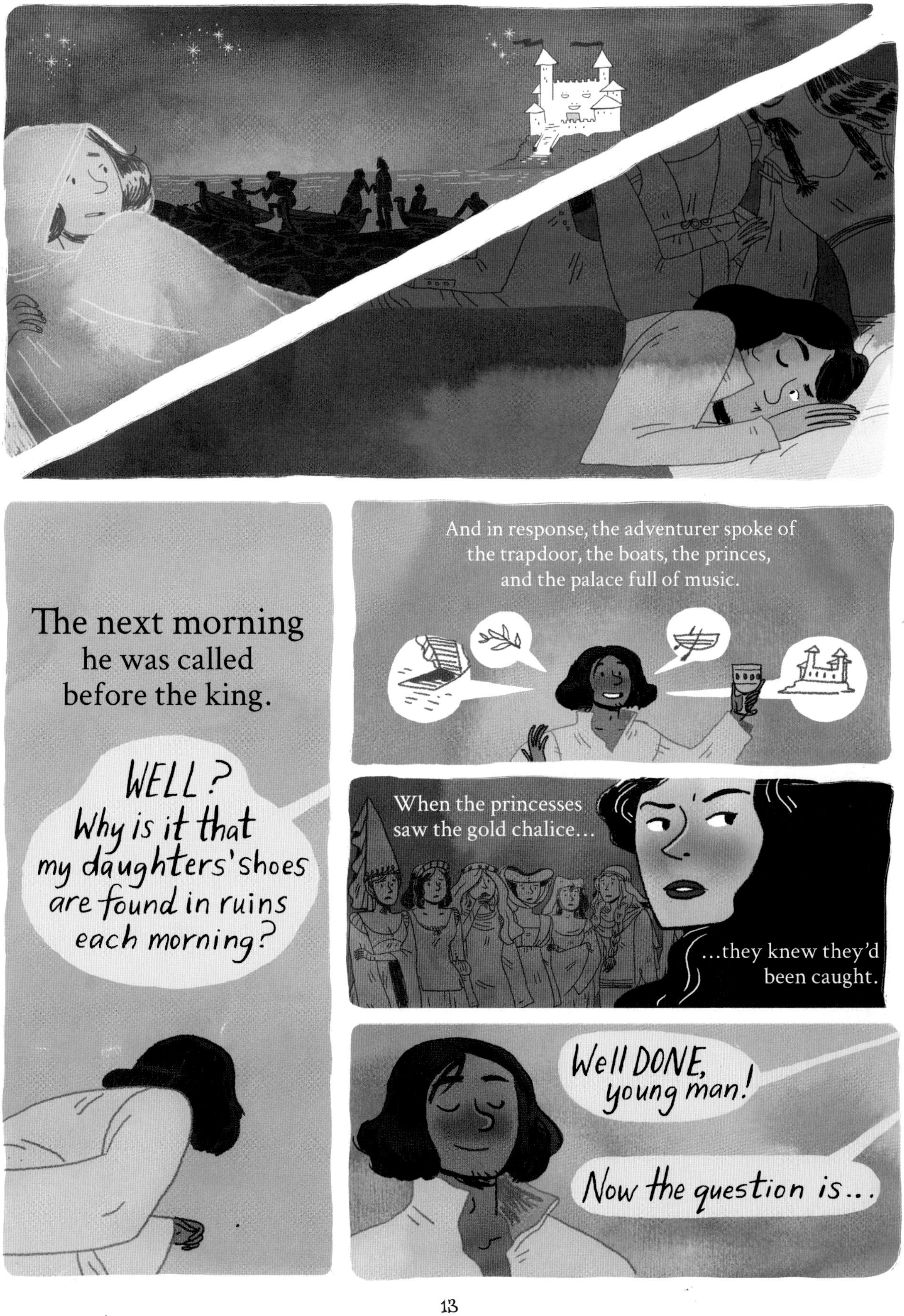
The next morning he was called before the king.
WELL? Why is it that my daughters' shoes are found in ruins each morning?
And in response, the adventurer spoke of the trapdoor, the boats, the princes, and the palace full of music.
When the princesses saw the gold chalice...
...they knew they'd been caught.
Well DONE, young man!
Now the question is...

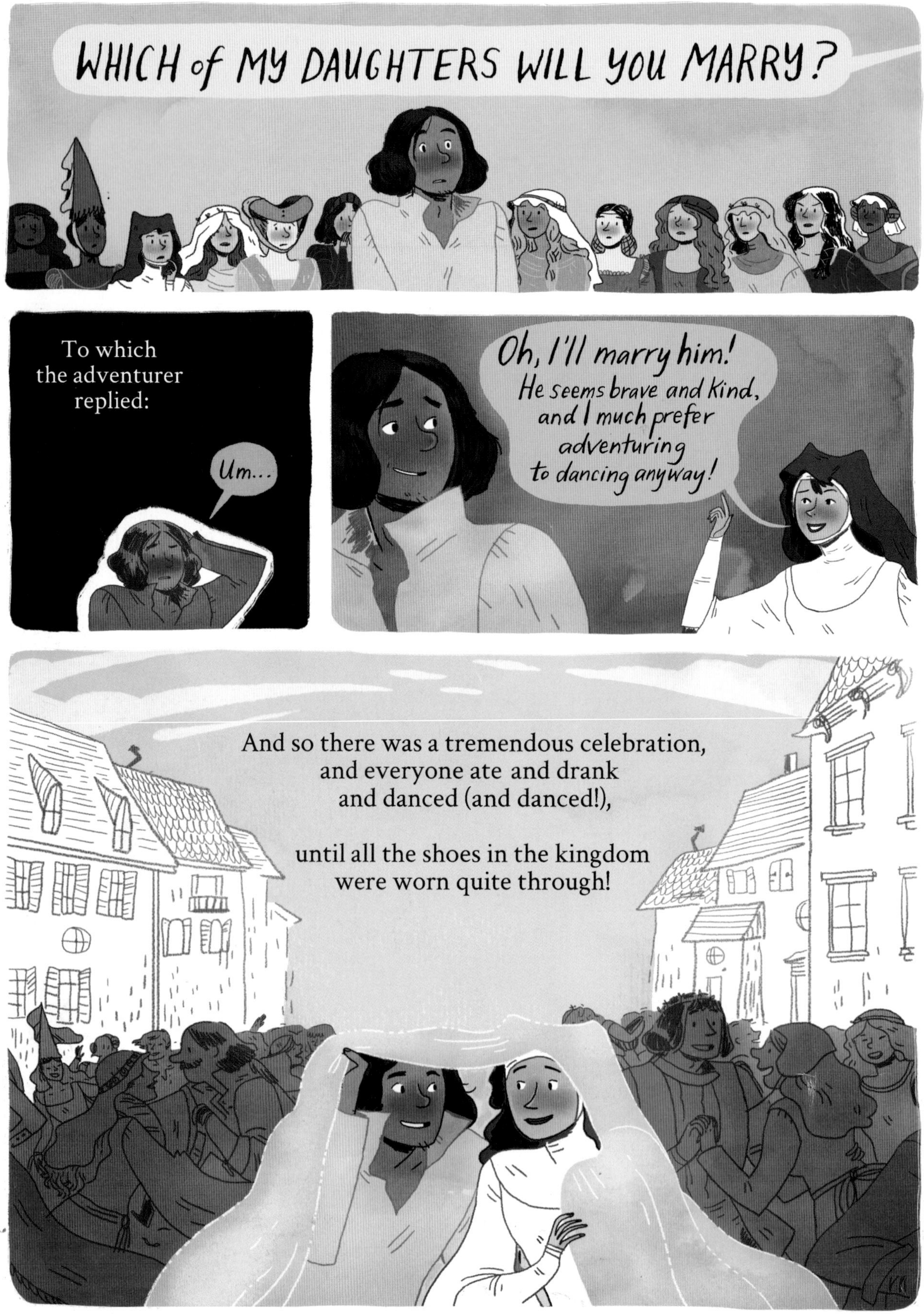
WHICH of MY DAUGHTERS WILL YOU MARRY?
To which the adventurer replied:
Um...
Oh, I'll marry him! He seems brave and kind, and I much prefer adventuring to dancing anyway!
And so there was a tremendous celebration, and everyone ate and drank and danced (and danced!),
until all the shoes in the kingdom were worn quite through!

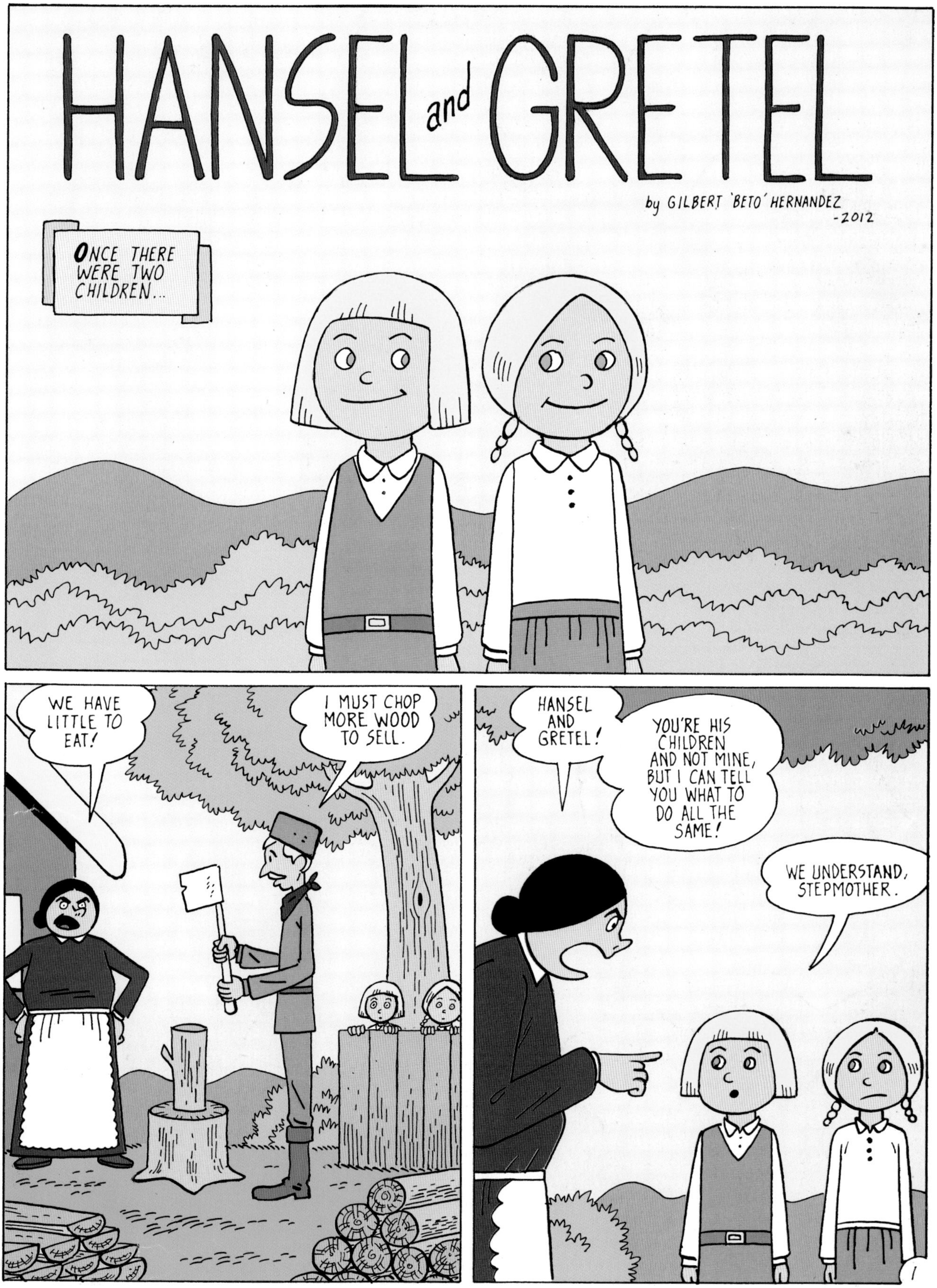
HANSEL and GRETEL
by GILBERT 'BETO' HERNANDEZ -2012
ONCE THERE WERE TWO CHILDREN...
WE HAVE LITTLE TO EAT!
I MUST CHOP MORE WOOD TO SELL.
HANSEL AND GRETEL!
YOU'RE HIS CHILDREN AND NOT MINE, BUT I CAN TELL YOU WHAT TO DO ALL THE SAME!
WE UNDERSTAND, STEPMOTHER.
1

Color by Joanne Bagge

From the Brothers Grimm

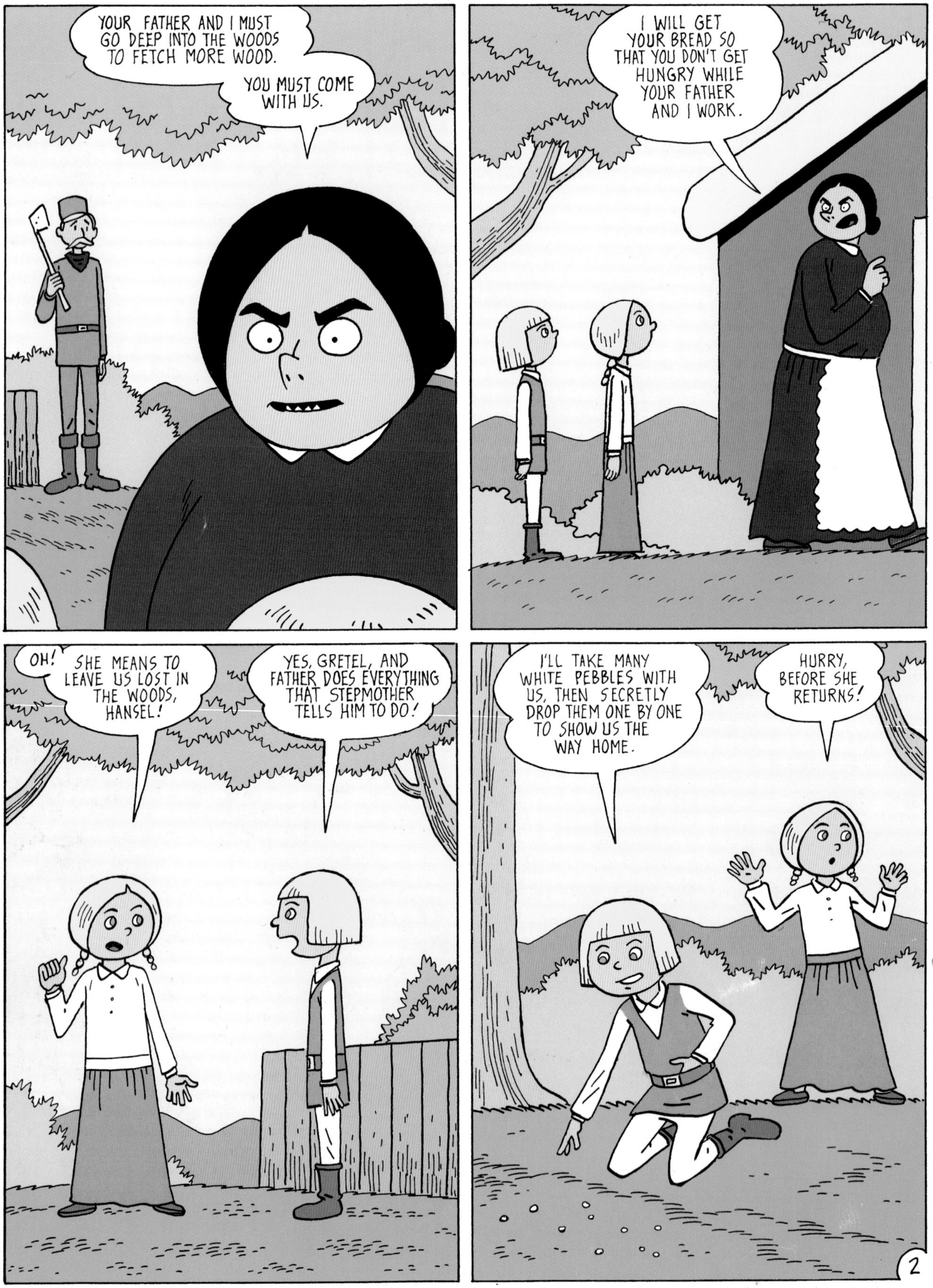
YOUR FATHER AND I MUST GO DEEP INTO THE WOODS TO FETCH MORE WOOD.
YOU MUST COME WITH US.
I WILL GET YOUR BREAD SO THAT YOU DON'T GET HUNGRY WHILE YOUR FATHER AND I WORK.
OH!
SHE MEANS TO LEAVE US LOST IN THE WOODS, HANSEL!
YES, GRETEL, AND FATHER DOES EVERYTHING THAT STEPMOTHER TELLS HIM TO DO!
I'LL TAKE MANY WHITE PEBBLES WITH US, THEN SECRETLY DROP THEM ONE BY ONE TO SHOW US THE WAY HOME.
HURRY, BEFORE SHE RETURNS!
2

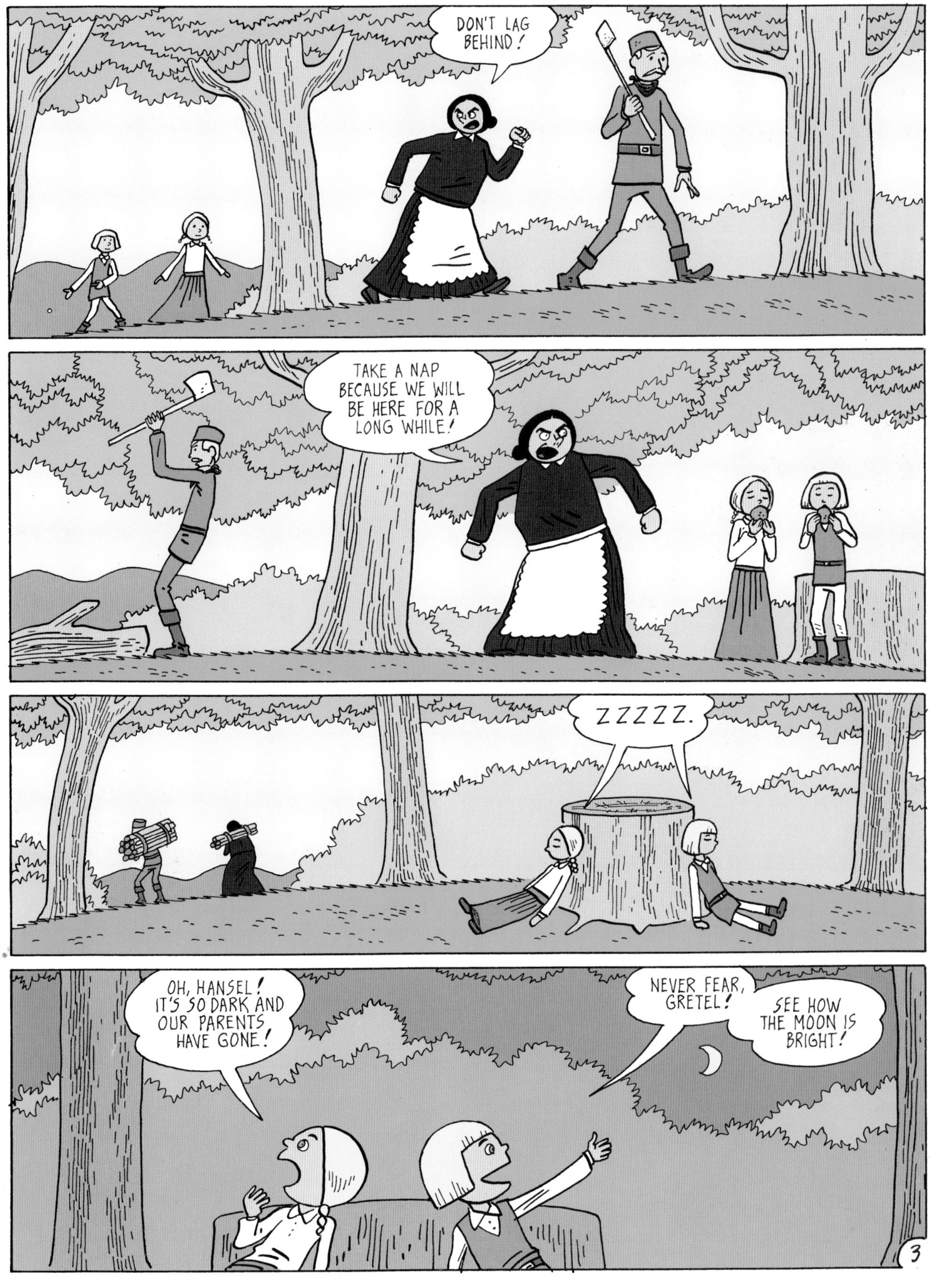
DON'T LAG BEHIND!
TAKE A NAP BECAUSE WE WILL BE HERE FOR A LONG WHILE!
ZZZZZ.
OH, HANSEL! IT'S SO DARK AND OUR PARENTS HAVE GONE!
NEVER FEAR, GRETEL!
SEE HOW THE MOON IS BRIGHT!
3

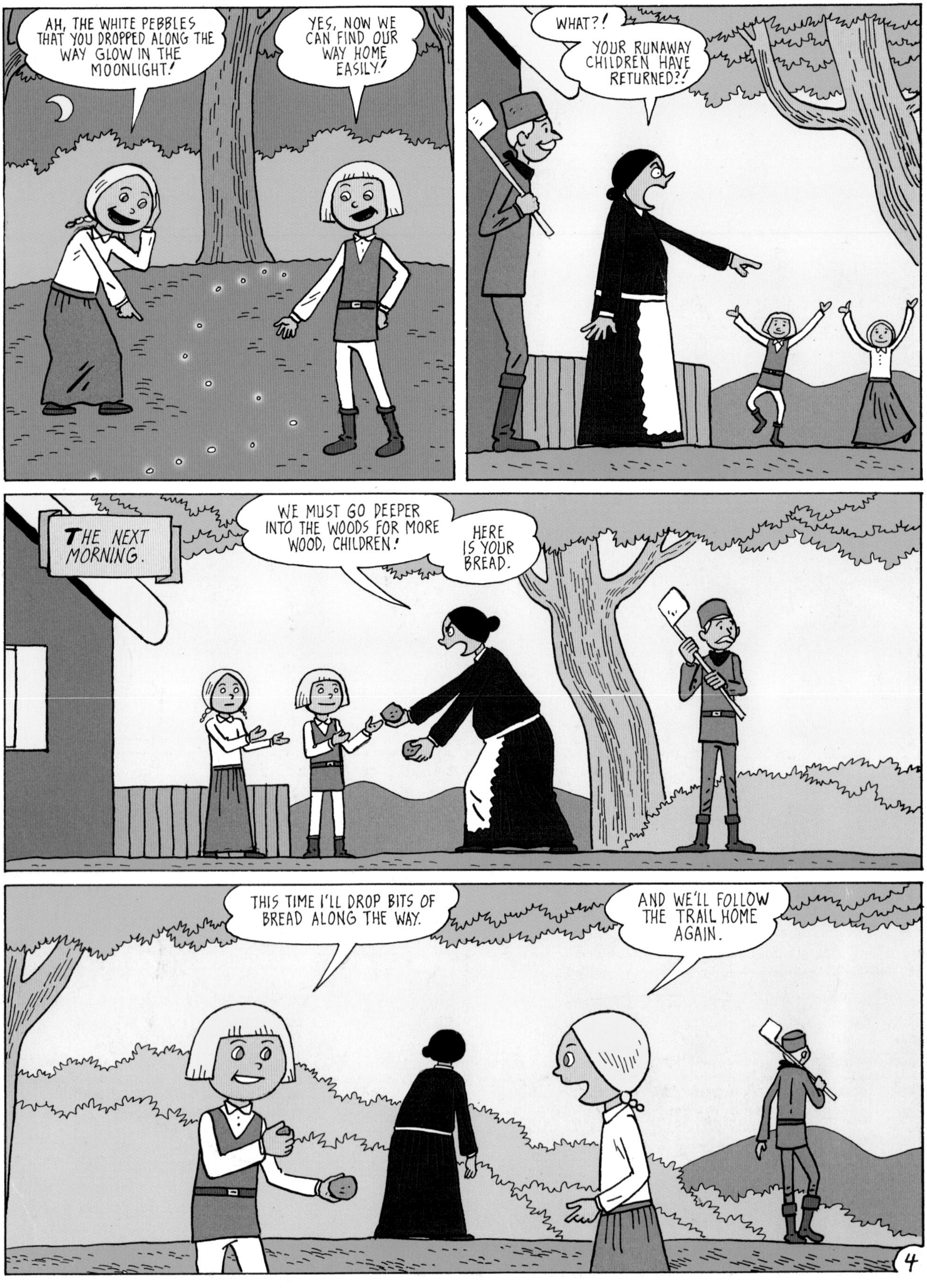
AH, THE WHITE PEBBLES THAT YOU DROPPED ALONG THE WAY GLOW IN THE MOONLIGHT!
YES, NOW WE CAN FIND OUR WAY HOME EASILY!
WHAT?!
YOUR RUNAWAY CHILDREN HAVE RETURNED?!
THE NEXT MORNING.
WE MUST GO DEEPER INTO THE WOODS FOR MORE WOOD, CHILDREN!
HERE IS YOUR BREAD.
THIS TIME I'LL DROP BITS OF BREAD ALONG THE WAY.
AND WE'LL FOLLOW THE TRAIL HOME AGAIN.
4

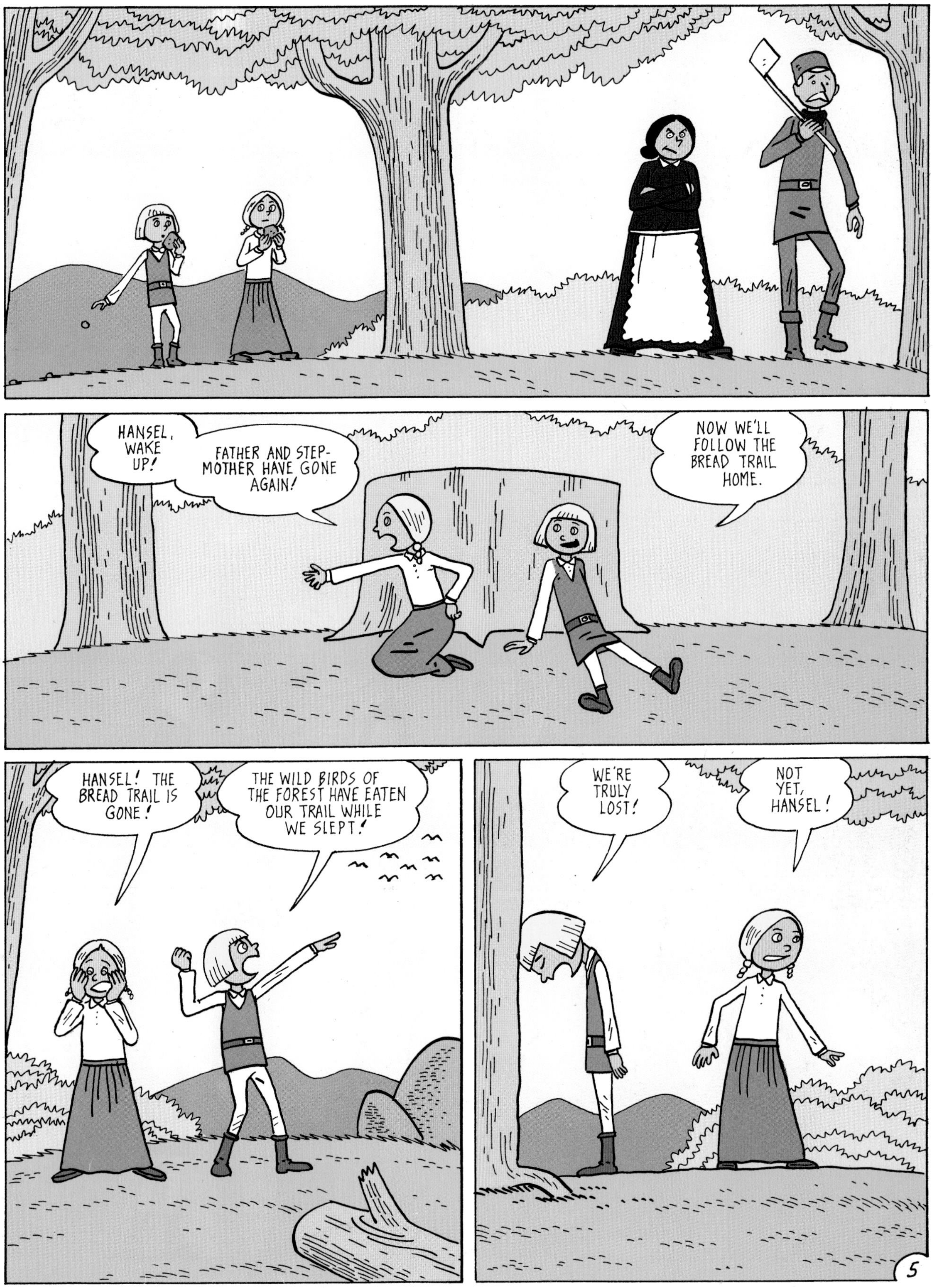
HANSEL, WAKE UP!
FATHER AND STEP-MOTHER HAVE GONE AGAIN!
NOW WE'LL FOLLOW THE BREAD TRAIL HOME.
HANSEL! THE BREAD TRAIL IS GONE!
THE WILD BIRDS OF THE FOREST HAVE EATEN OUR TRAIL WHILE WE SLEPT!
WE'RE TRULY LOST!
NOT YET, HANSEL!
5

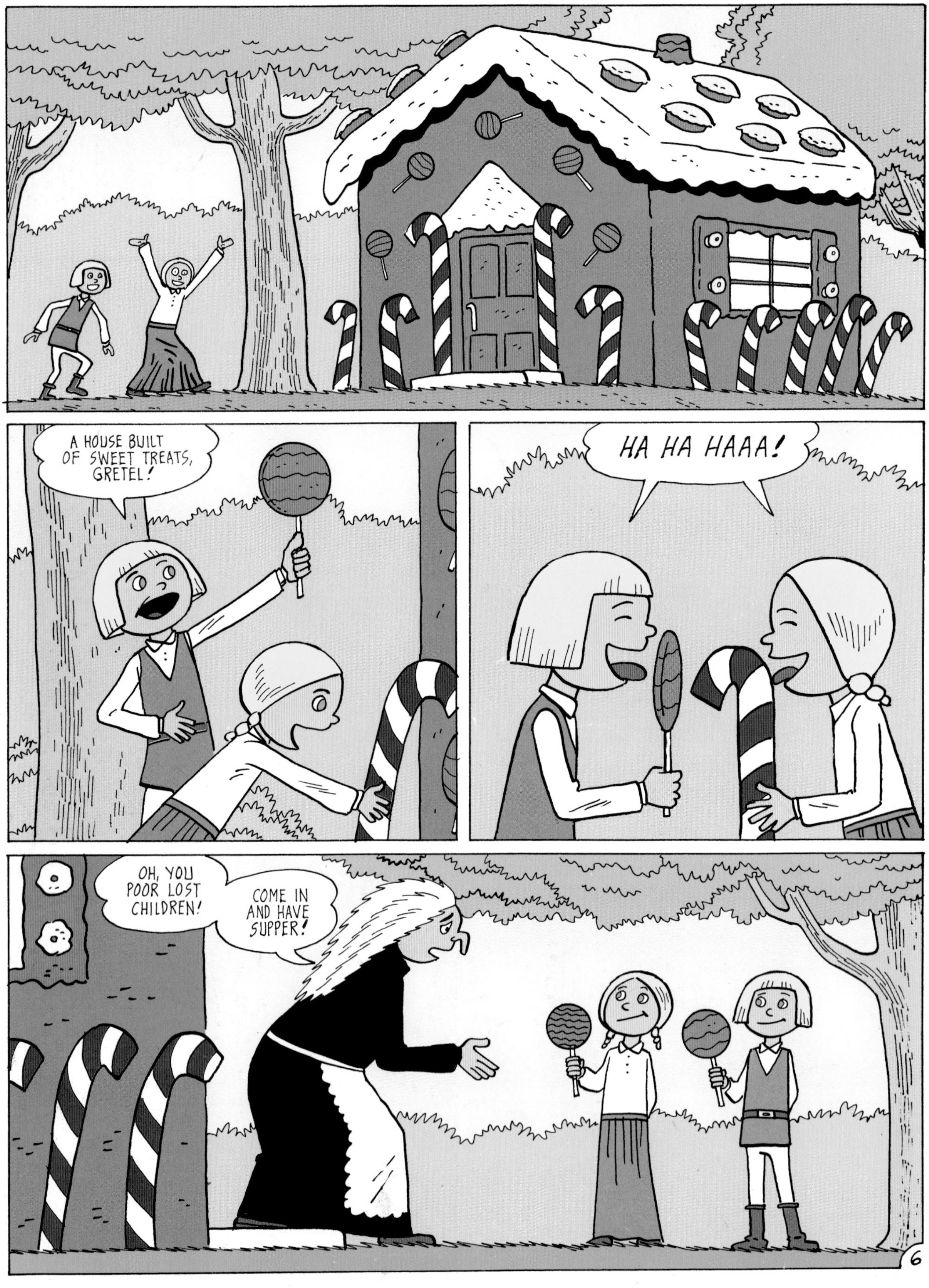
A HOUSE BUILT OF SWEET TREATS, GRETEL!
HA HA HAAA!
OH, YOU POOR LOST CHILDREN!
COME IN AND HAVE SUPPER!
6

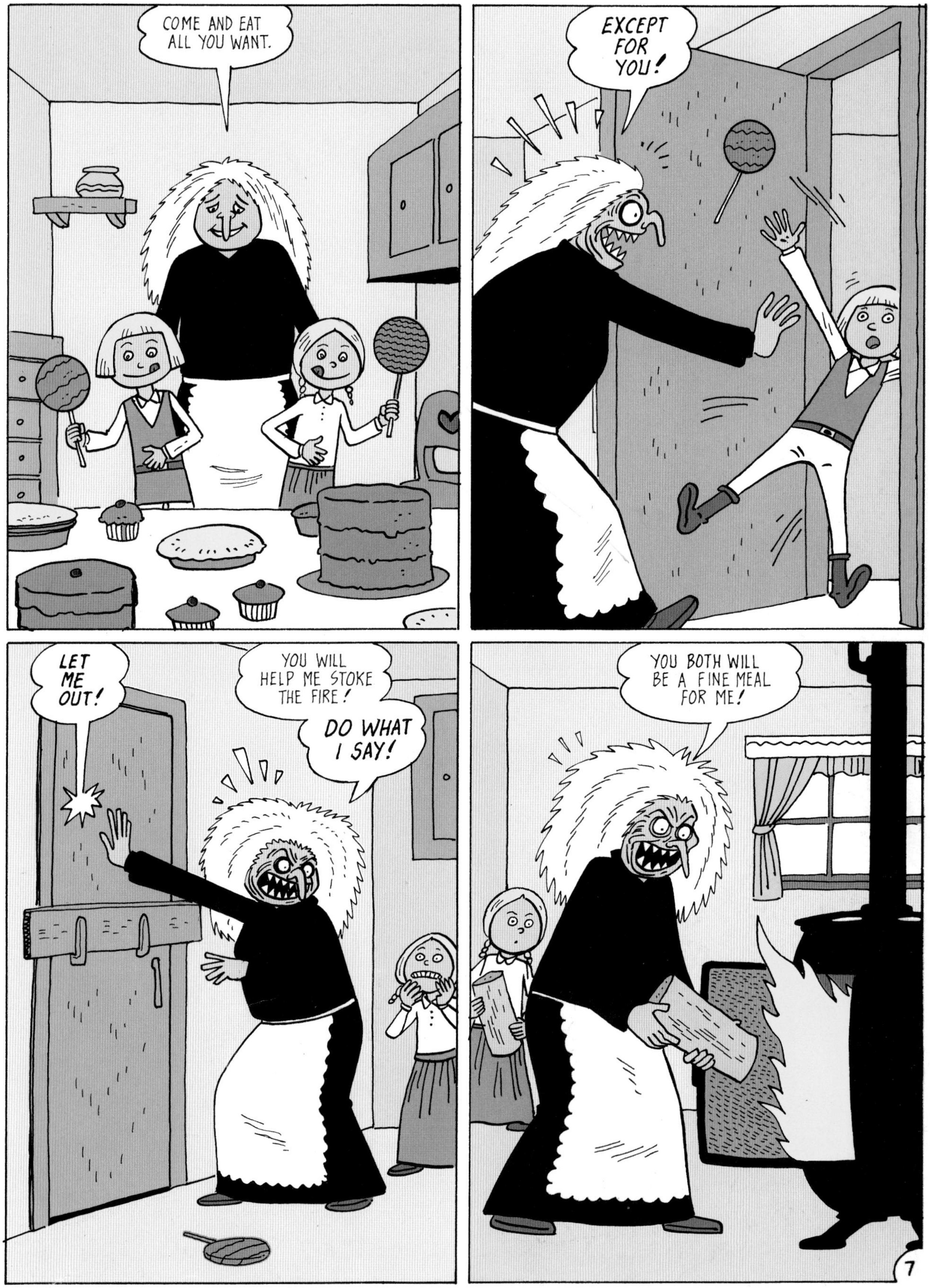
COME AND EAT ALL YOU WANT.
EXCEPT FOR YOU!
LET ME OUT!
YOU WILL HELP ME STOKE THE FIRE!
DO WHAT I SAY!
YOU BOTH WILL BE A FINE MEAL FOR ME!
7

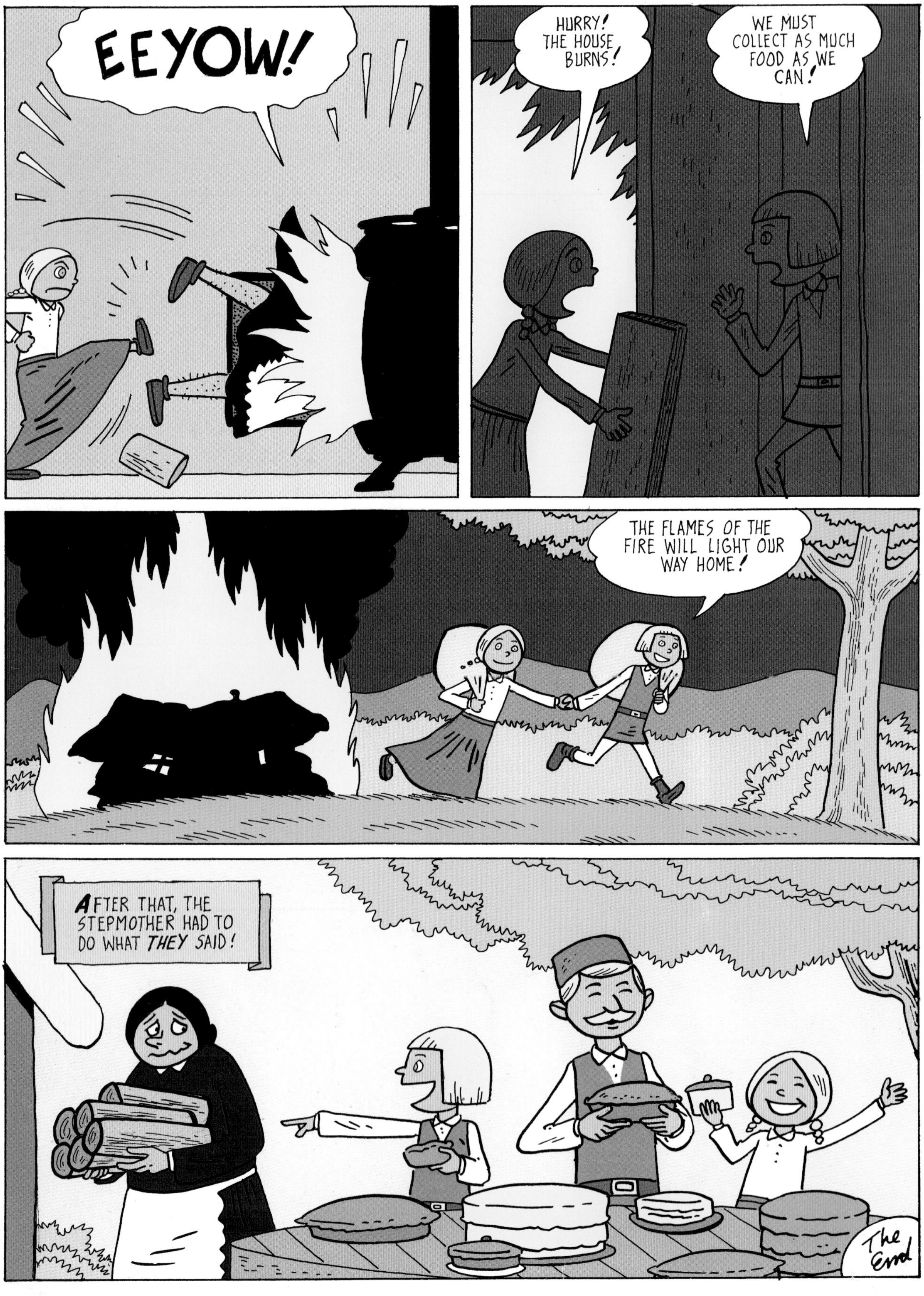
EEYOW!
HURRY! THE HOUSE BURNS!
WE MUST COLLECT AS MUCH FOOD AS WE CAN!
THE FLAMES OF THE FIRE WILL LIGHT OUR WAY HOME!
AFTER THAT, THE STEPMOTHER HAD TO DO WHAT THEY SAID!
The End

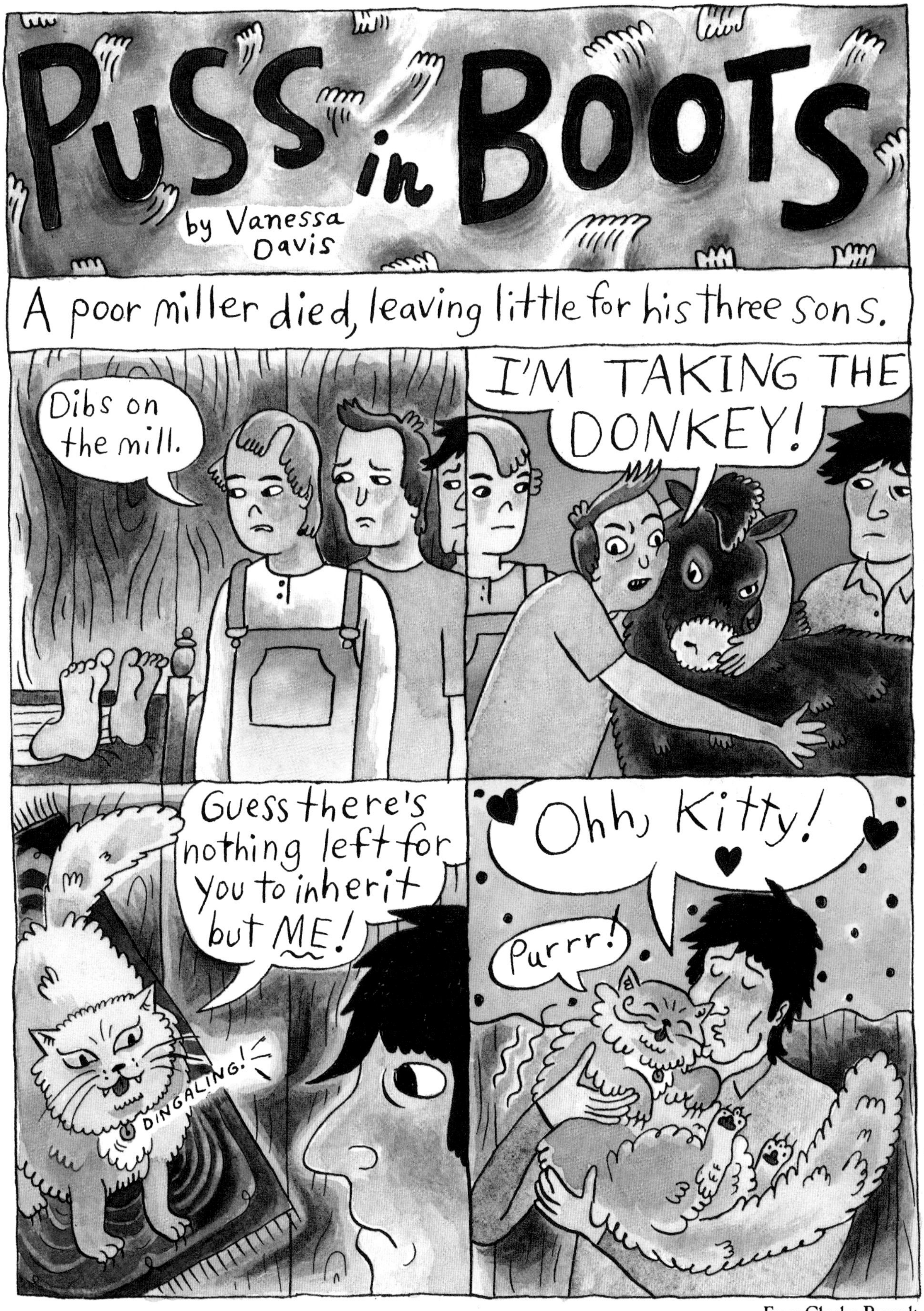
PUSS in BOOTS
by Vanessa Davis
A poor miller died, leaving little for his three sons.
Dibs on the mill.
I'M TAKING THE DONKEY!
Guess there's nothing left for you to inherit but ME!
DINGALING!
Ohh, Kitty!
Purrr!



From Charles Perrault

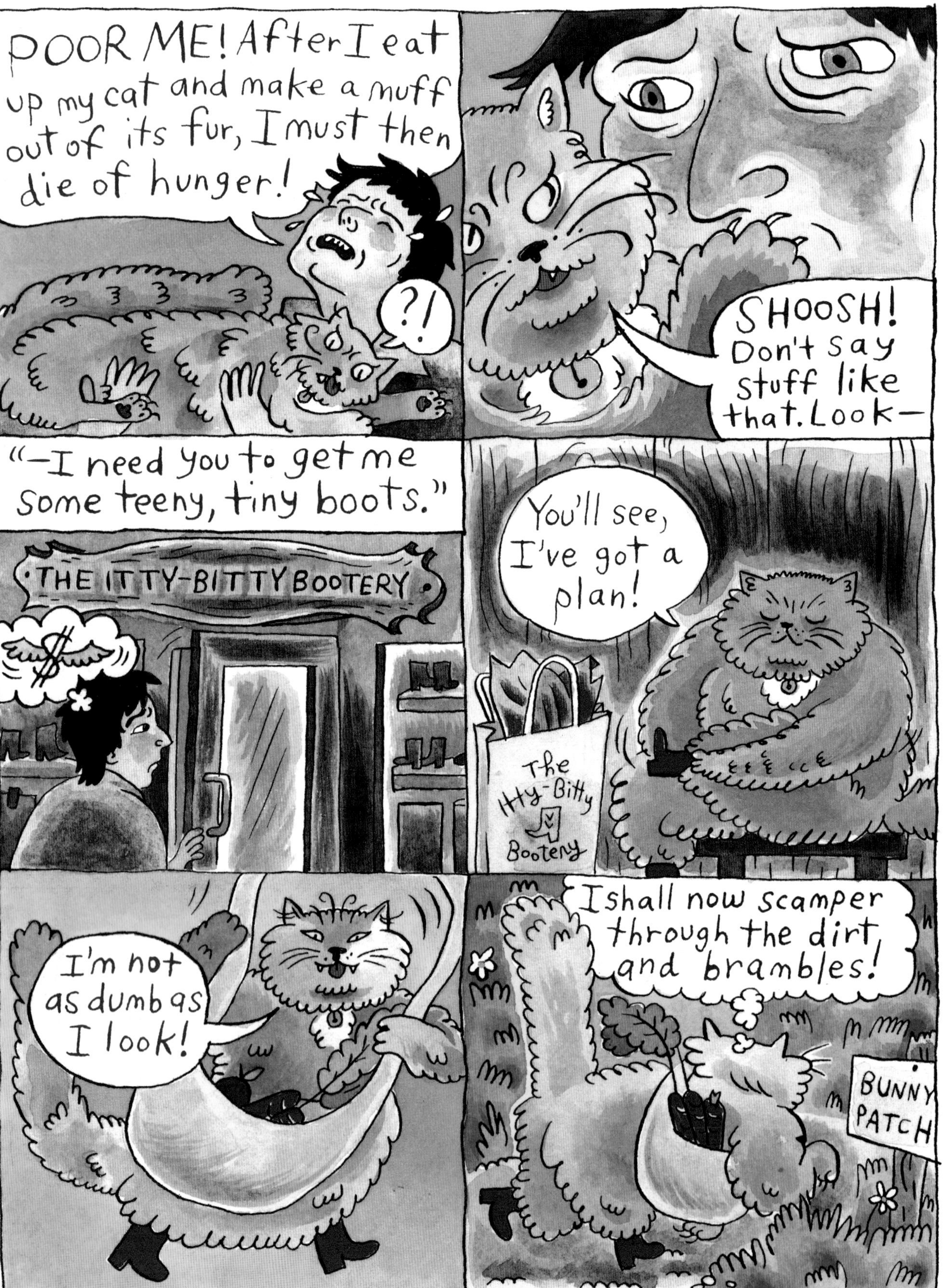
POOR ME! After I eat up my cat and make a muff out of its fur, I must then die of hunger!
?!
SHOOSH! Don't say stuff like that. Look—
"—I need you to get me some teeny, tiny boots."
THE ITTY-BITTY BOOTERY
You'll see, I've got a plan!
The Itty-Bitty Bootery
I'm not as dumb as I look!
I shall now scamper through the dirt and brambles!
BUNNY PATCH

!
SNATCH!
The cat then went to visit the king.
♪
yes, Kitty. Please follow me.
for you, your Highness!
BUNNY.
A gift from my master, LORD Pistachio!
And with this exchange, the cat's plan went into effect.

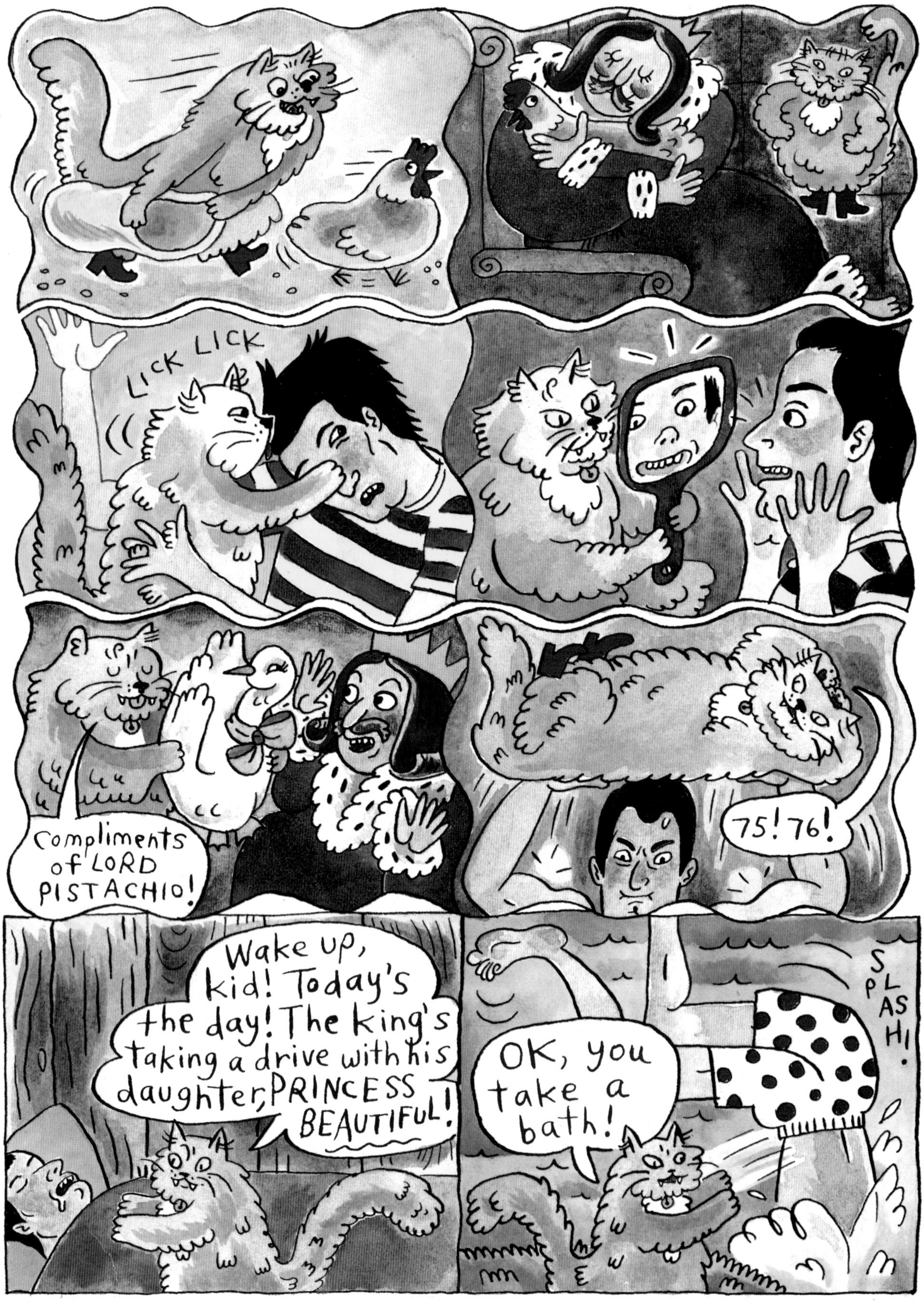
LICK LICK
Compliments of LORD PISTACHIO!
75! 76!
Wake up, kid! Today's the day! The king's taking a drive with his daughter, PRINCESS BEAUTIFUL!
OK, you take a bath!
SPLASH!

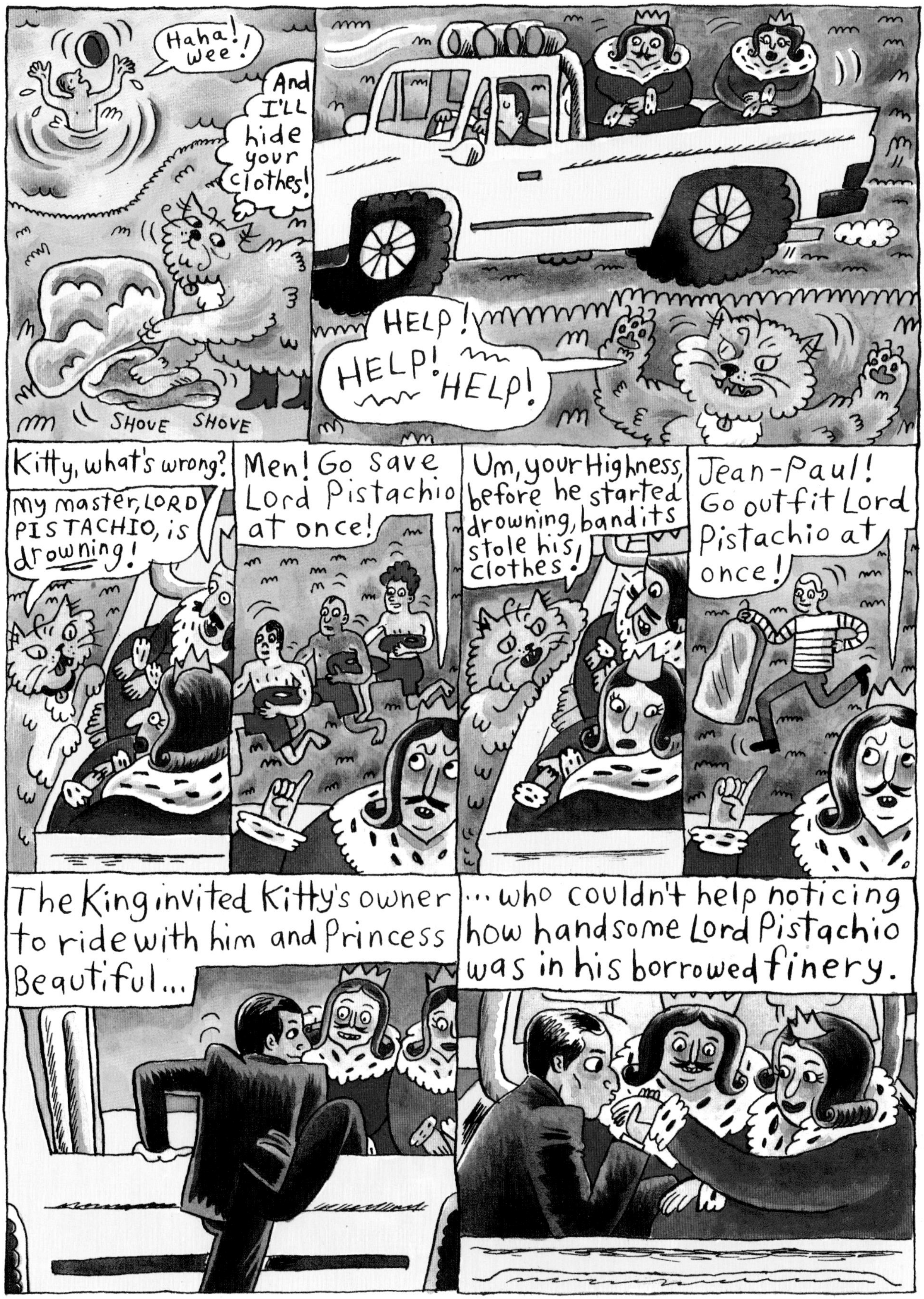
Haha! wee!
And I'LL hide your clothes!
SHOVE SHOVE
HELP! HELP! HELP!
Kitty, what's wrong?
my master, LORD PISTACHIO, is drowning!
Men! Go save Lord Pistachio at once!
Um, your Highness, before he started drowning, bandits stole his clothes!
Jean-Paul! Go outfit Lord Pistachio at once!
The King invited Kitty's owner to ride with him and Princess Beautiful...
... who couldn't help noticing how handsome Lord Pistachio was in his borrowed finery.

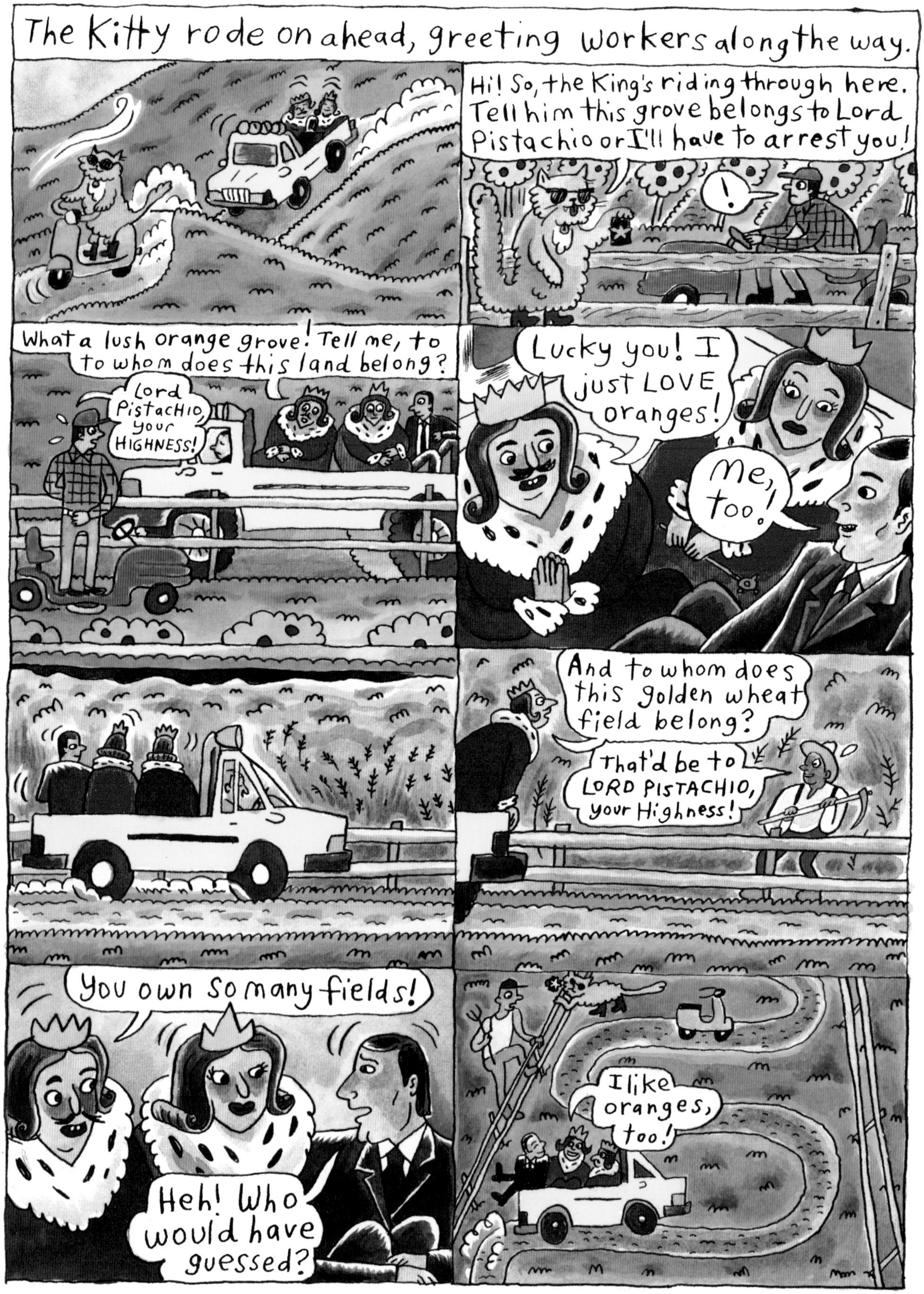
The Kitty rode on ahead, greeting workers along the way.
Hi! So, the King's riding through here. Tell him this grove belongs to Lord Pistachio or I'll have to arrest you!
!
What a lush orange grove! Tell me, to to whom does this land belong?
Lord Pistachio, your HIGHNESS!
Lucky you! I just LOVE oranges!
Me, too!
And to whom does this golden wheat field belong?
That'd be to LORD PISTACHIO, your Highness!
You own so many fields!
Heh! Who would have guessed?
I like oranges, too!

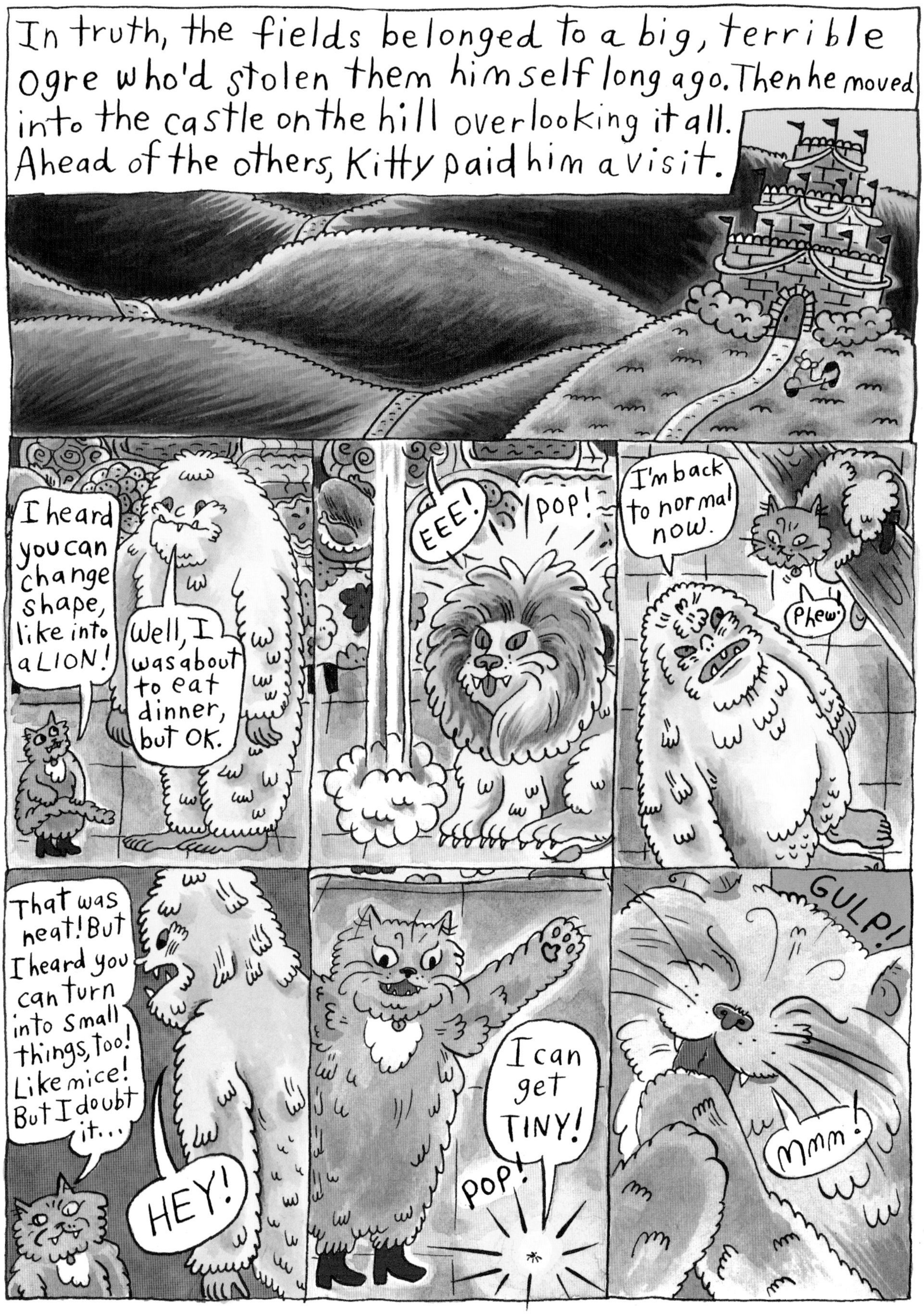
In truth, the fields belonged to a big, terrible ogre who'd stolen them himself long ago. Then he moved into the castle on the hill overlooking it all. Ahead of the others, Kitty paid him a visit.
I heard you can change shape, like into a LION!
Well, I was about to eat dinner, but OK.
EEE!
POP!
I'm back to normal now.
Phew.
That was neat! But I heard you can turn into small things, too! Like mice! But I doubt it...
HEY!
I can get TINY!
POP!
GULP!
Mmm!

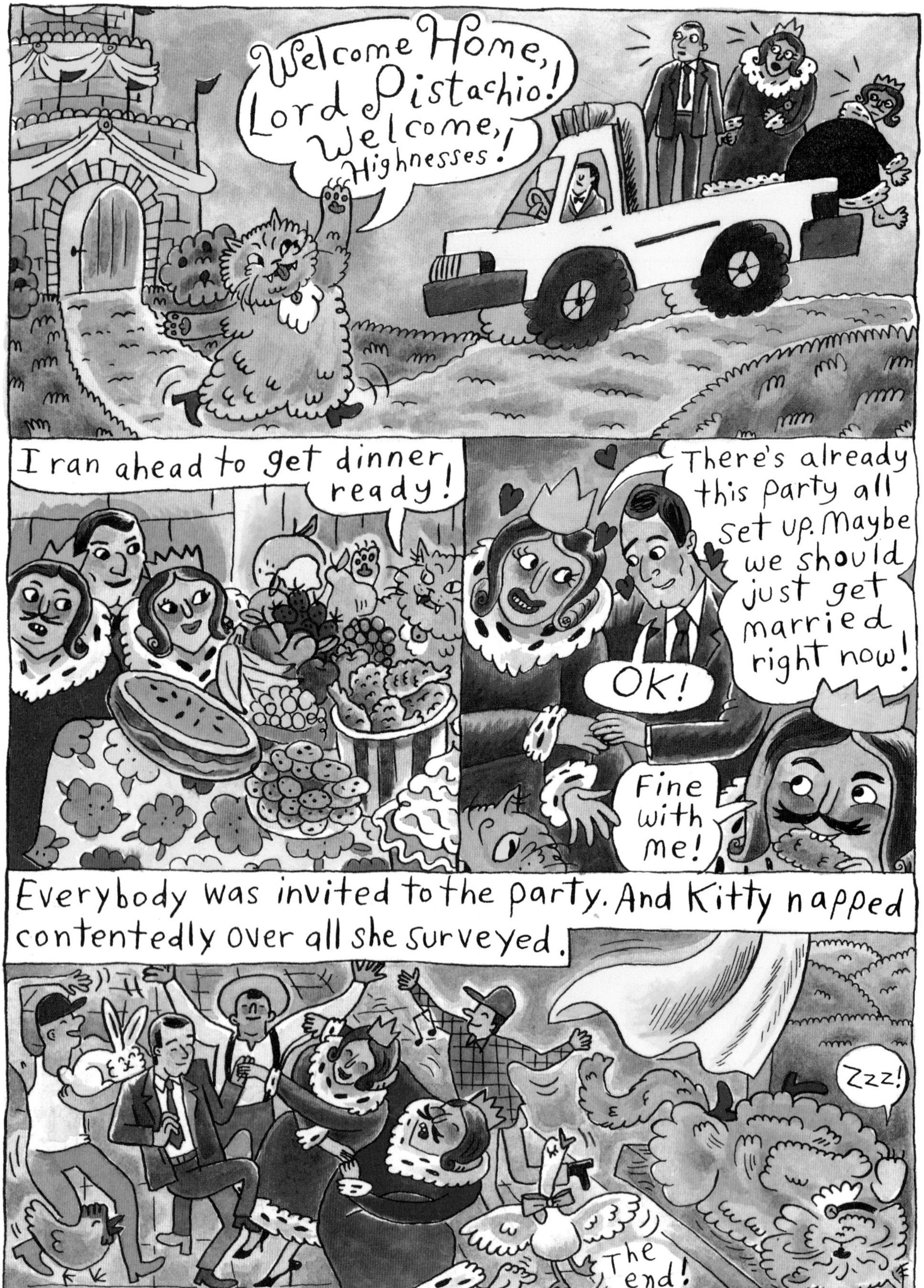
Welcome Home, Lord Pistachio! Welcome, Highnesses!
I ran ahead to get dinner ready!
There's already this party all set up. Maybe we should just get married right now!
OK!
Fine with me!
Everybody was invited to the party. And Kitty napped contentedly over all she surveyed.
Zzz!
The end!

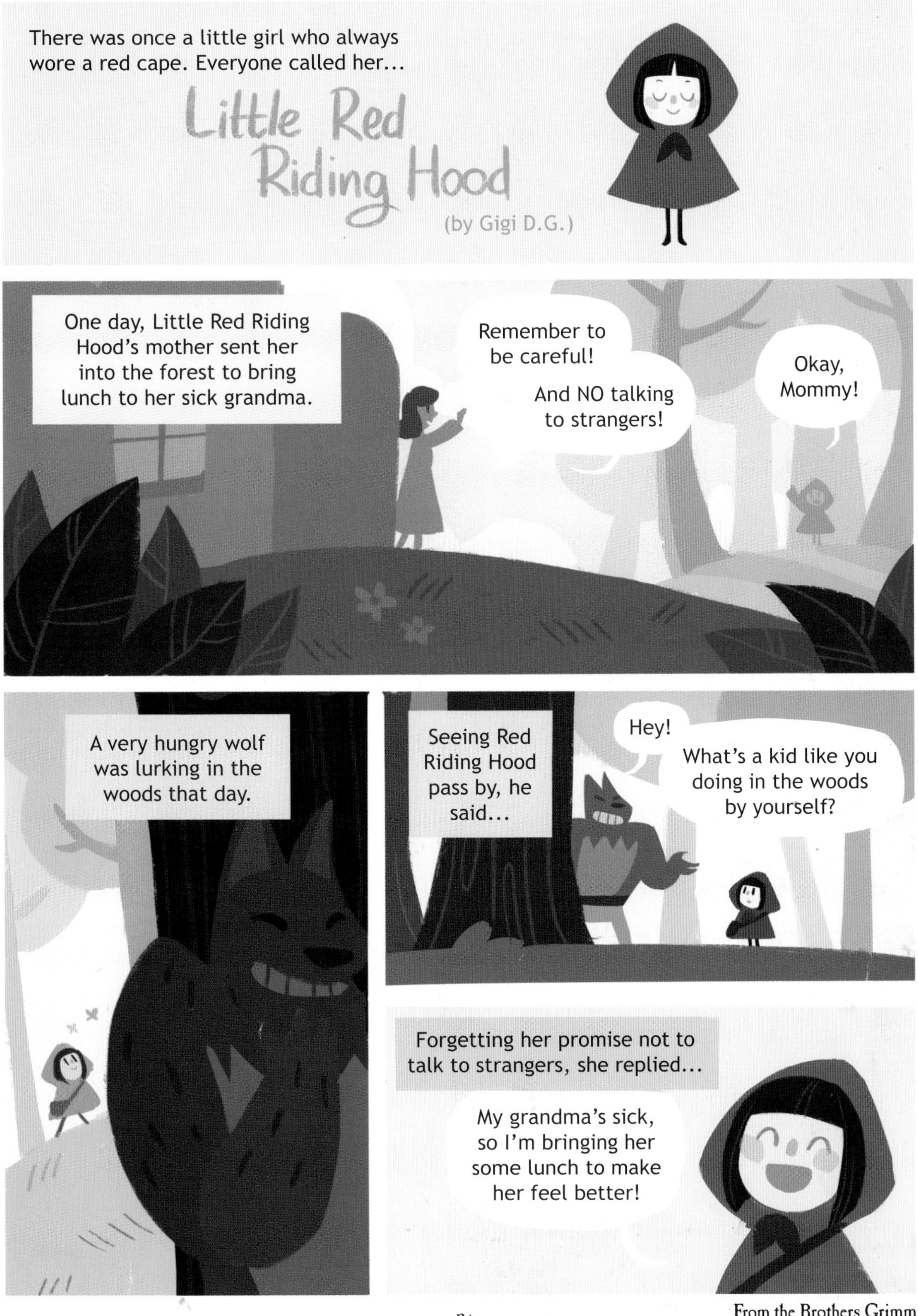
There was once a little girl who always wore a red cape. Everyone called her...
Little Red Riding Hood
(by Gigi D.G.)
One day, Little Red Riding Hood's mother sent her into the forest to bring lunch to her sick grandma.
Remember to be careful!
And NO talking to strangers!
Okay, Mommy!
A very hungry wolf was lurking in the woods that day.
Seeing Red Riding Hood pass by, he said...
Hey!
What's a kid like you doing in the woods by yourself?
Forgetting her promise not to talk to strangers, she replied...
My grandma's sick, so I'm bringing her some lunch to make her feel better!



From the Brothers Grimm

Lunch, huh? Sounds great.

So where's your grandma live, kiddo?

Just that way!

Really!

Well, why don't you stop and pick a few flowers for her? I bet she'd love that.

Hmm...

Okay!

As Red Riding Hood sat and picked flowers...

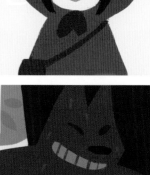

...the wolf sneaked off ahead of her.

And once she'd spent enough time in the flower patch, she finally continued on to her grandma's house.

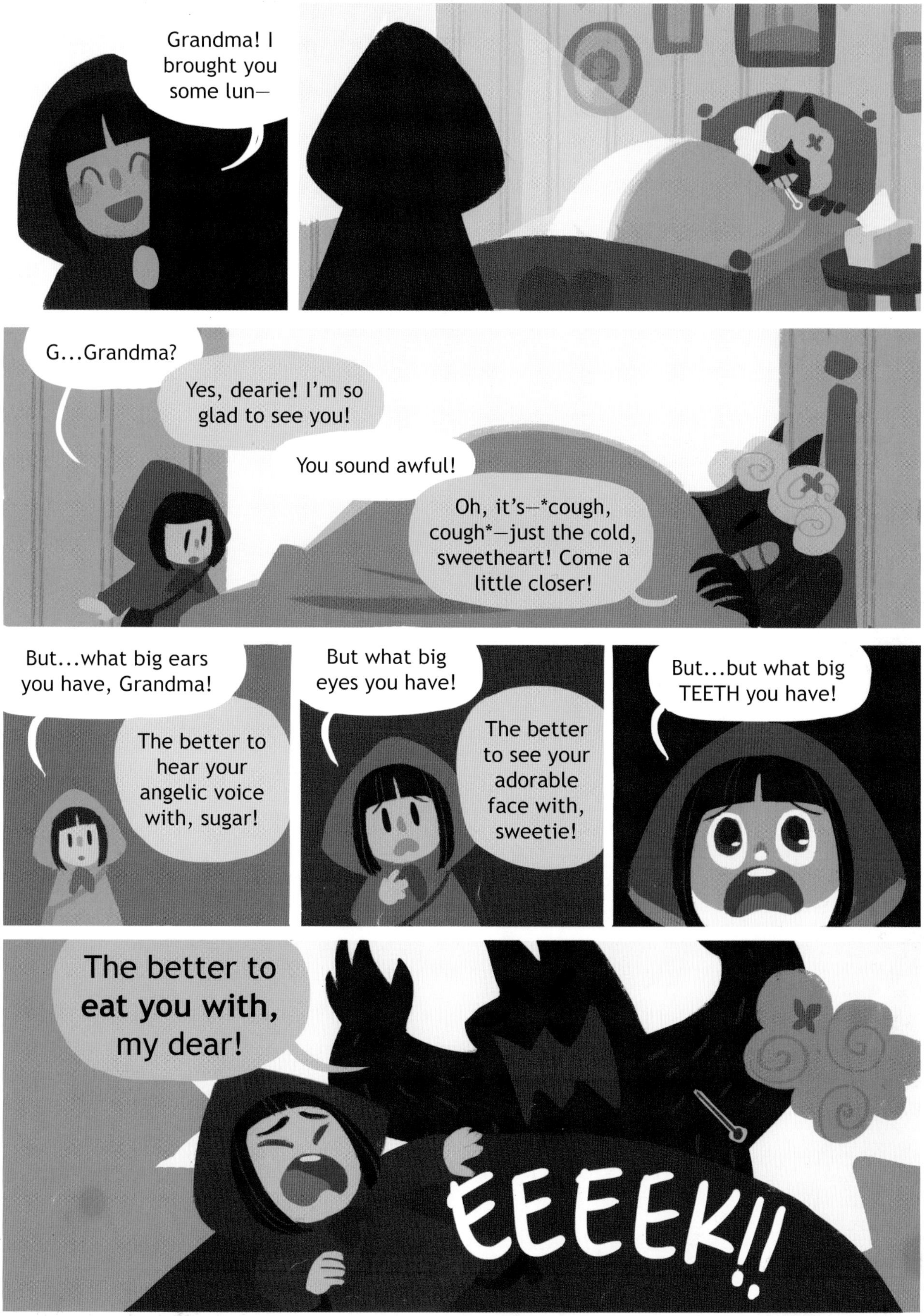

Grandma! I brought you some lun—
G...Grandma?
Yes, dearie! I'm so glad to see you!
You sound awful!
Oh, it's—*cough, cough*—just the cold, sweetheart! Come a little closer!
But...what big ears you have, Grandma!
The better to hear your angelic voice with, sugar!
But what big eyes you have!
The better to see your adorable face with, sweetie!
But...but what big TEETH you have!
The better to **eat you with,** my dear!
EEEEK!!

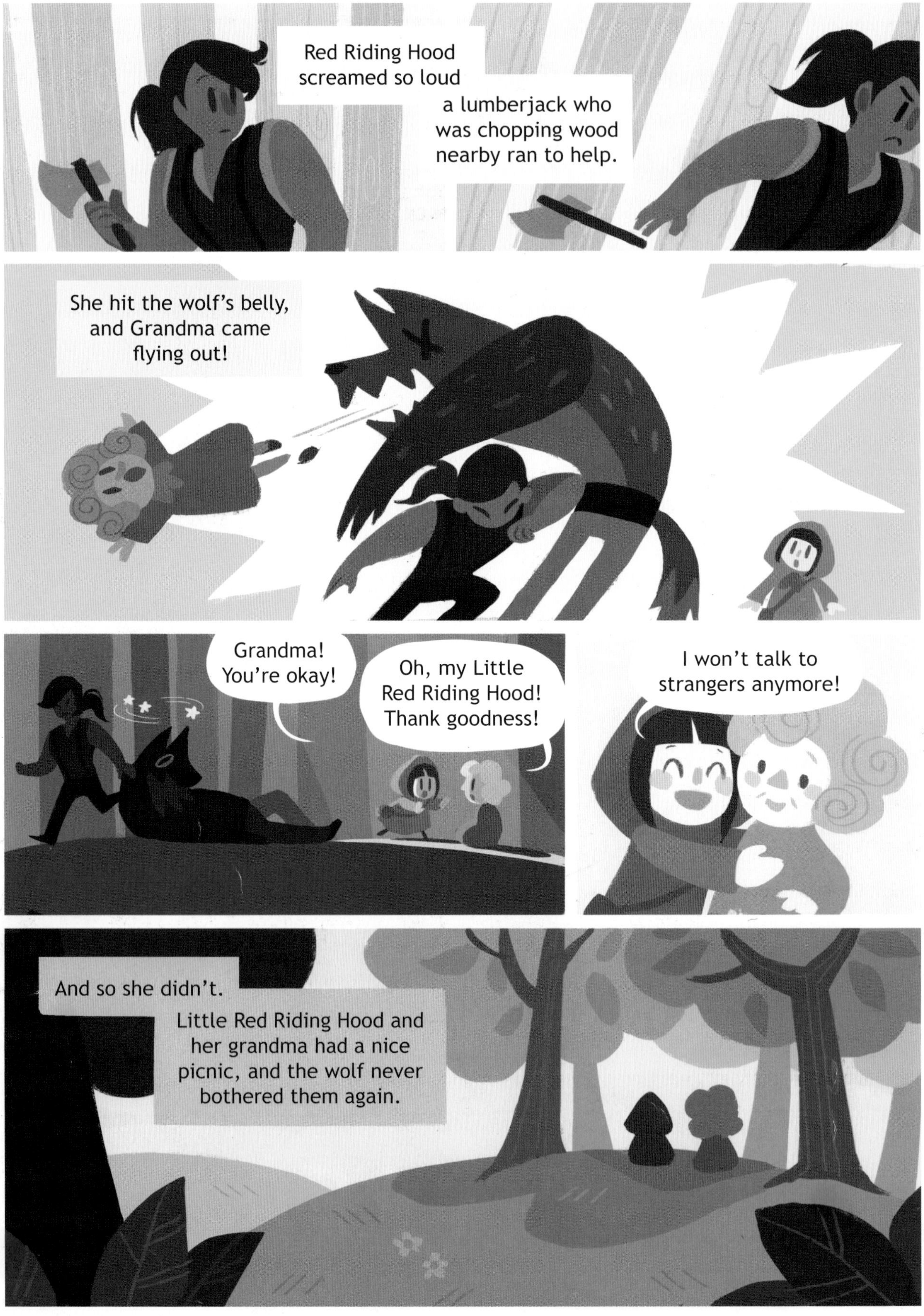
Red Riding Hood screamed so loud
a lumberjack who was chopping wood nearby ran to help.
She hit the wolf's belly, and Grandma came flying out!
Grandma! You're okay!
Oh, my Little Red Riding Hood! Thank goodness!
I won't talk to strangers anymore!
And so she didn't.
Little Red Riding Hood and her grandma had a nice picnic, and the wolf never bothered them again.

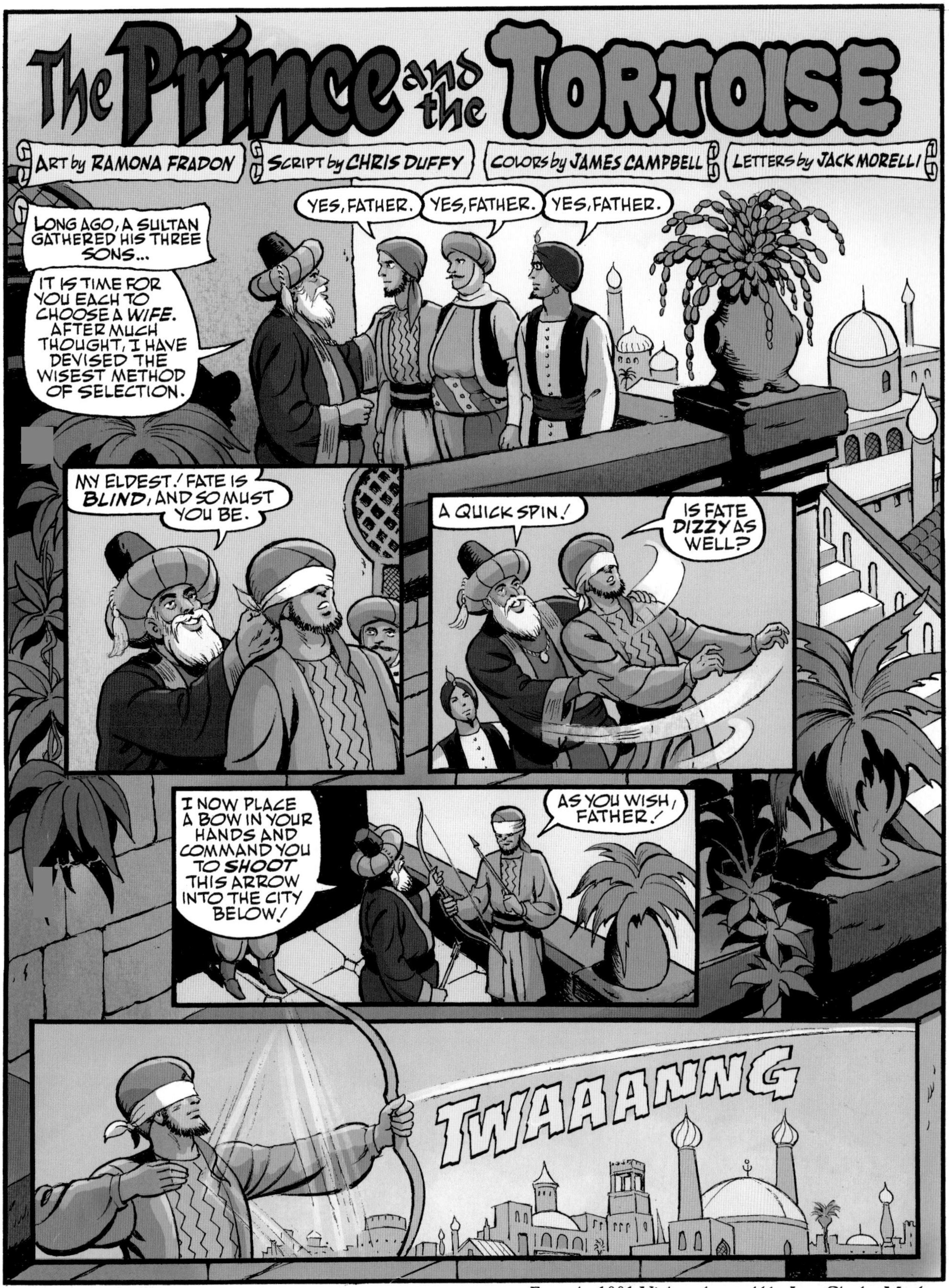
The Prince and the Tortoise
Art by Ramona Fradon
Script by Chris Duffy
Colors by James Campbell
Letters by Jack Morelli
Long ago, a sultan gathered his three sons...
It is time for you each to choose a wife. After much thought, I have devised the wisest method of selection.
Yes, father.
Yes, father.
Yes, father.
My eldest! Fate is blind, and so must you be.
A quick spin!
Is fate dizzy as well?
I now place a bow in your hands and command you to shoot this arrow into the city below!
As you wish, father!
TWAAANNG

From the 1001 Nights tale as told by Jean-Charles Mardrus

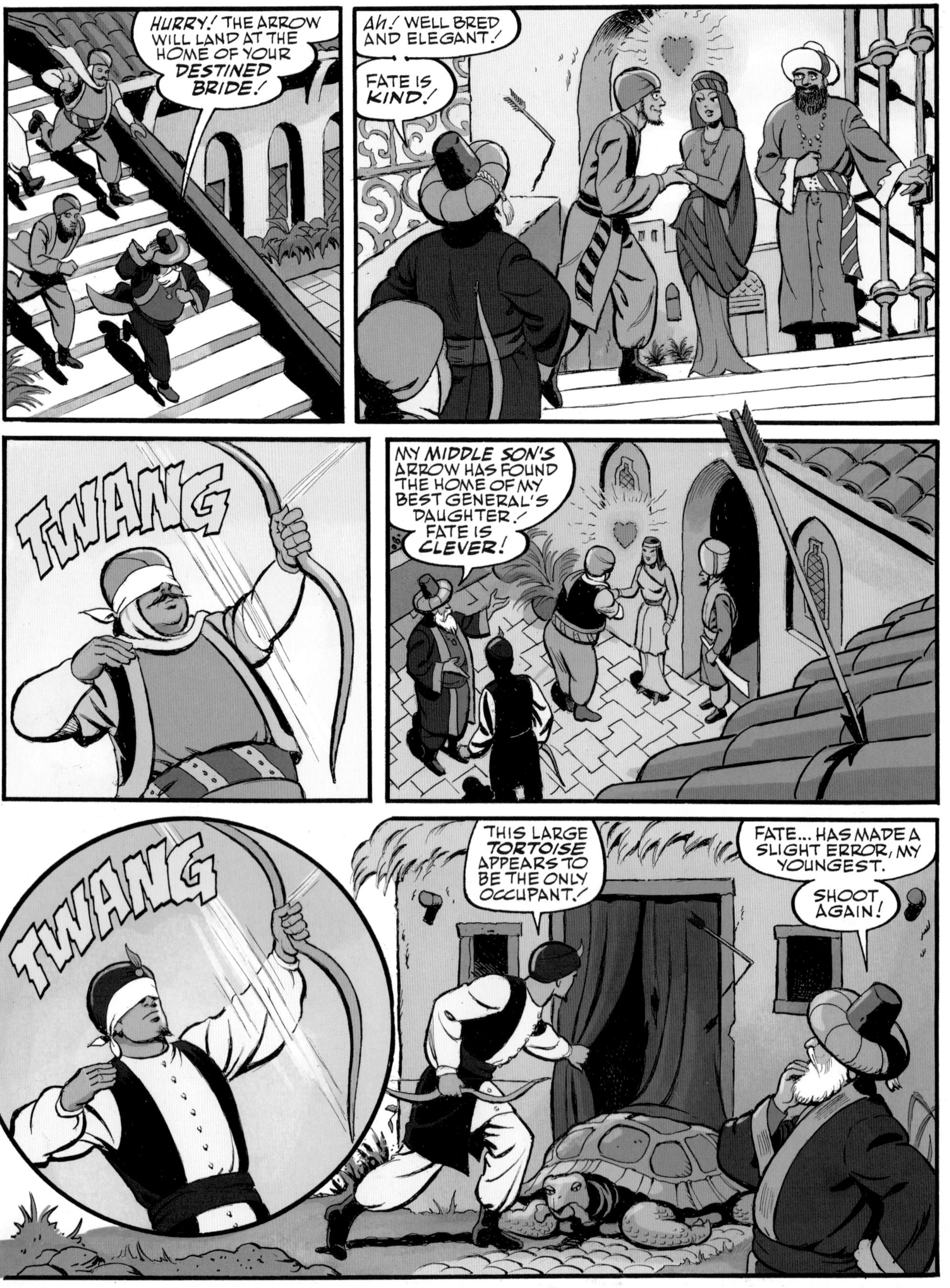
HURRY! THE ARROW WILL LAND AT THE HOME OF YOUR DESTINED BRIDE!
Ah! WELL BRED AND ELEGANT!
FATE IS KIND!
TWANG
MY MIDDLE SON'S ARROW HAS FOUND THE HOME OF MY BEST GENERAL'S DAUGHTER! FATE IS CLEVER!
TWANG
THIS LARGE TORTOISE APPEARS TO BE THE ONLY OCCUPANT!
FATE... HAS MADE A SLIGHT ERROR, MY YOUNGEST.
SHOOT AGAIN!

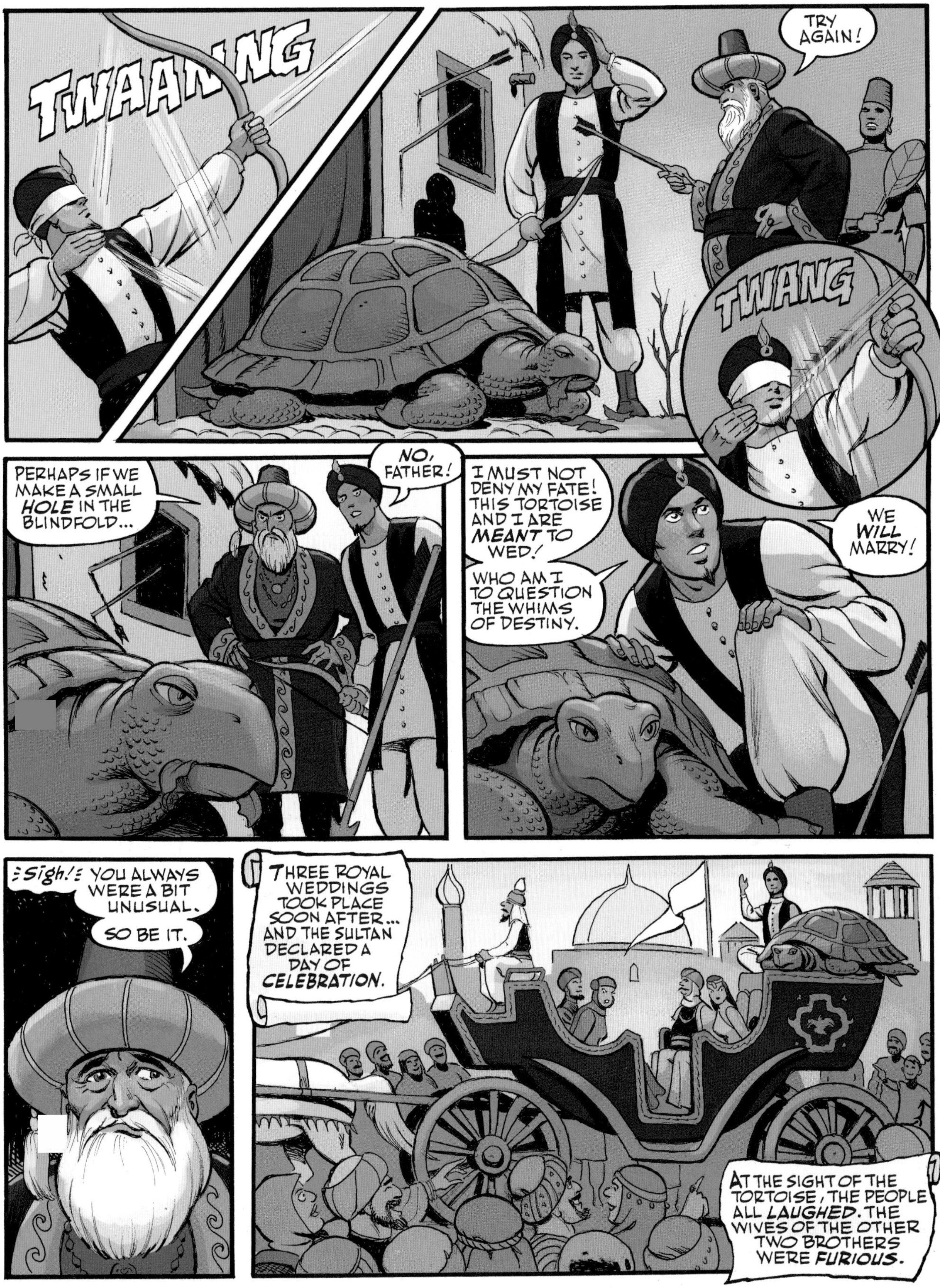
TWAANNG
TRY AGAIN!
TWANG
PERHAPS IF WE MAKE A SMALL HOLE IN THE BLINDFOLD...
NO, FATHER!
I MUST NOT DENY MY FATE! THIS TORTOISE AND I ARE MEANT TO WED!
WHO AM I TO QUESTION THE WHIMS OF DESTINY.
WE WILL MARRY!
Sigh!
YOU ALWAYS WERE A BIT UNUSUAL.
SO BE IT.
THREE ROYAL WEDDINGS TOOK PLACE SOON AFTER... AND THE SULTAN DECLARED A DAY OF CELEBRATION.
AT THE SIGHT OF THE TORTOISE, THE PEOPLE ALL LAUGHED. THE WIVES OF THE OTHER TWO BROTHERS WERE FURIOUS.

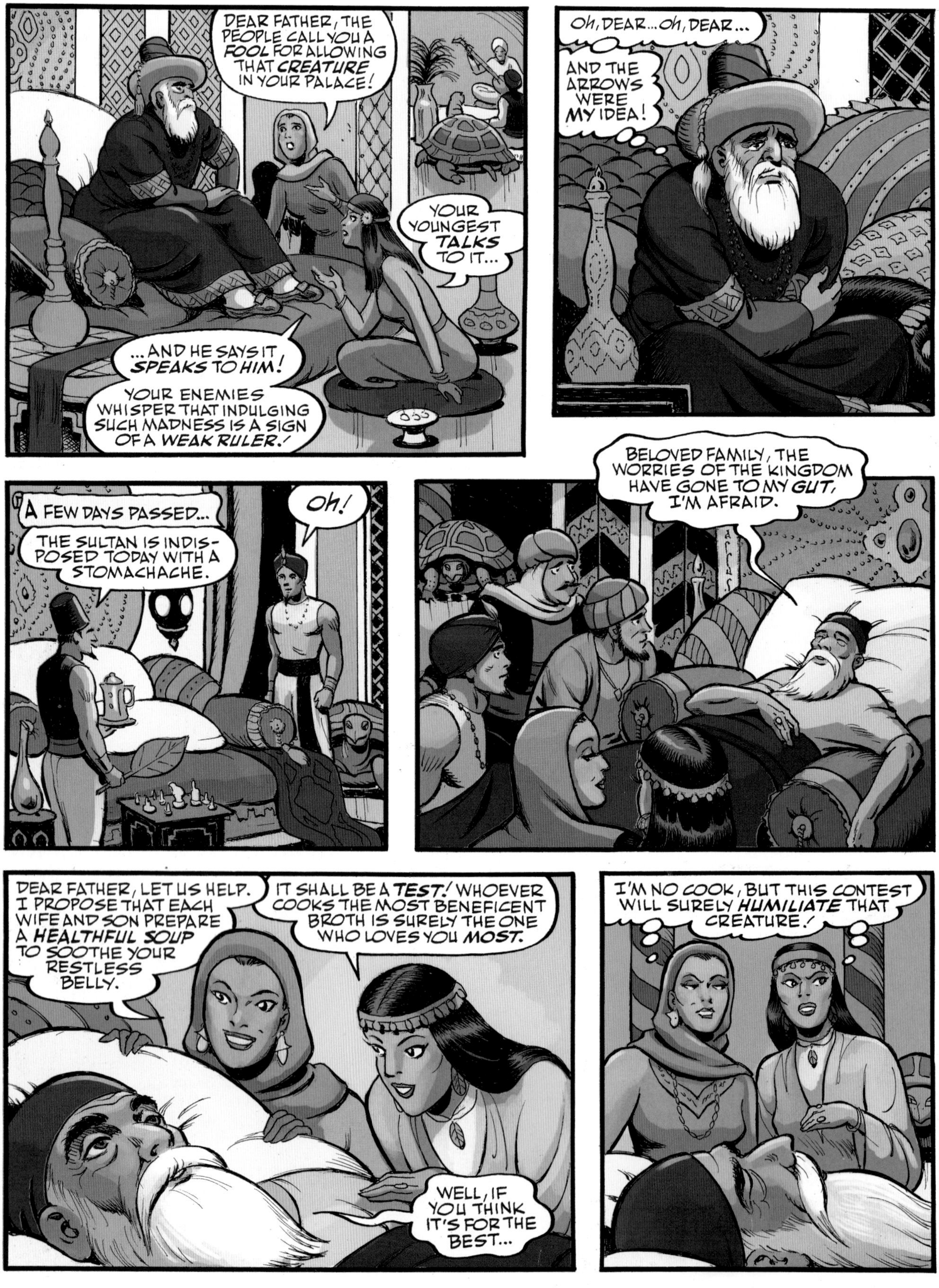
DEAR FATHER, THE PEOPLE CALL YOU A FOOL FOR ALLOWING THAT CREATURE IN YOUR PALACE!
YOUR YOUNGEST TALKS TO IT...
...AND HE SAYS IT SPEAKS TO HIM!
YOUR ENEMIES WHISPER THAT INDULGING SUCH MADNESS IS A SIGN OF A WEAK RULER!
Oh, DEAR... Oh, DEAR...
AND THE ARROWS WERE MY IDEA!
A FEW DAYS PASSED...
THE SULTAN IS INDISPOSED TODAY WITH A STOMACHACHE.
Oh!
BELOVED FAMILY, THE WORRIES OF THE KINGDOM HAVE GONE TO MY GUT, I'M AFRAID.
DEAR FATHER, LET US HELP. I PROPOSE THAT EACH WIFE AND SON PREPARE A HEALTHFUL SOUP TO SOOTHE YOUR RESTLESS BELLY.
IT SHALL BE A TEST! WHOEVER COOKS THE MOST BENEFICENT BROTH IS SURELY THE ONE WHO LOVES YOU MOST.
WELL, IF YOU THINK IT'S FOR THE BEST...
I'M NO COOK, BUT THIS CONTEST WILL SURELY HUMILIATE THAT CREATURE!

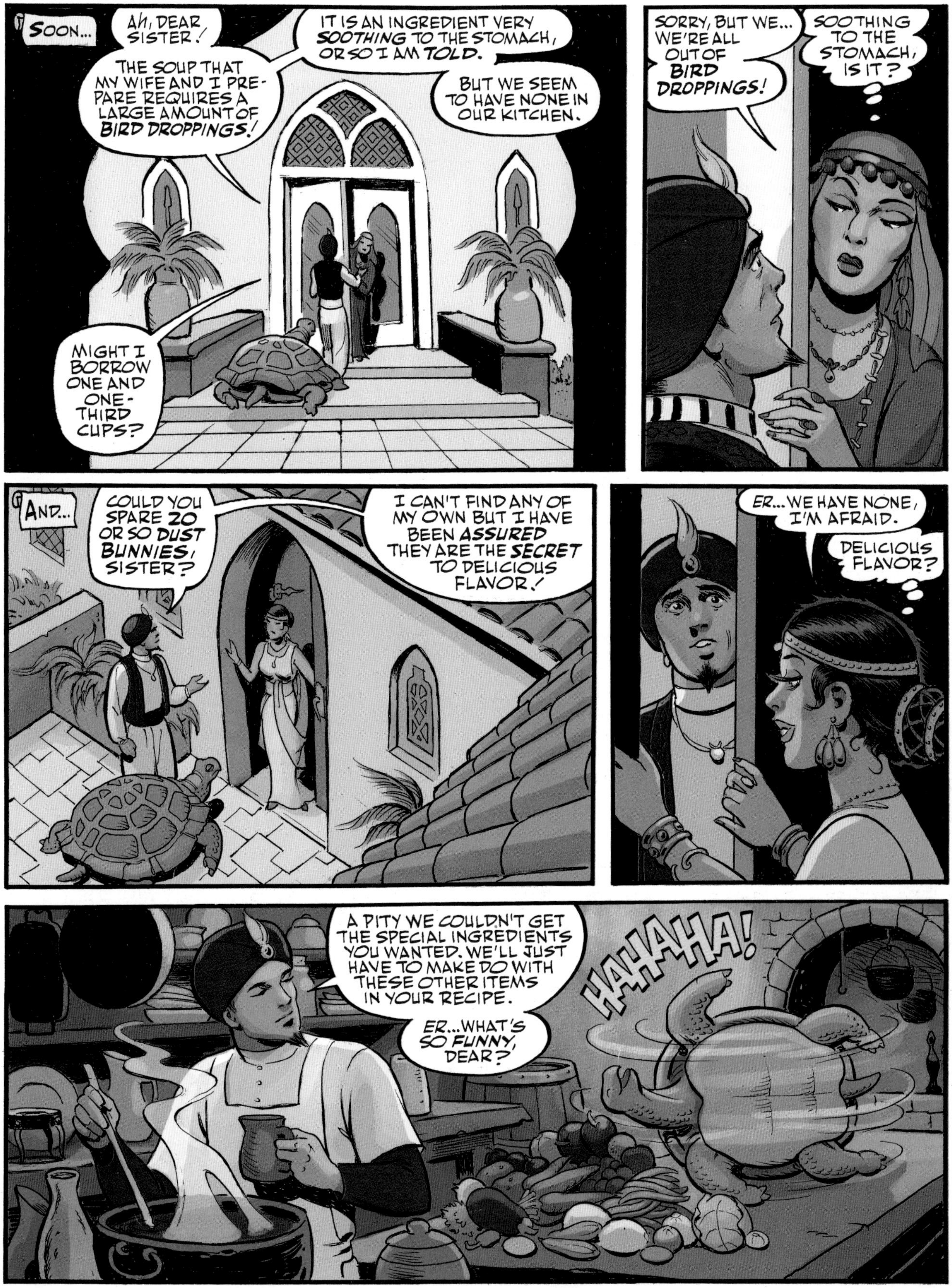

SOON...
AH, DEAR SISTER!
THE SOUP THAT MY WIFE AND I PREPARE REQUIRES A LARGE AMOUNT OF BIRD DROPPINGS!
IT IS AN INGREDIENT VERY SOOTHING TO THE STOMACH, OR SO I AM TOLD.
BUT WE SEEM TO HAVE NONE IN OUR KITCHEN.
MIGHT I BORROW ONE AND ONE-THIRD CUPS?
SORRY, BUT WE... WE'RE ALL OUT OF BIRD DROPPINGS!
SOOTHING TO THE STOMACH, IS IT?
AND...
COULD YOU SPARE 20 OR SO DUST BUNNIES, SISTER?
I CAN'T FIND ANY OF MY OWN BUT I HAVE BEEN ASSURED THEY ARE THE SECRET TO DELICIOUS FLAVOR!
ER...WE HAVE NONE, I'M AFRAID.
DELICIOUS FLAVOR?
A PITY WE COULDN'T GET THE SPECIAL INGREDIENTS YOU WANTED. WE'LL JUST HAVE TO MAKE DO WITH THESE OTHER ITEMS IN YOUR RECIPE.
HAHAHA!
ER...WHAT'S SO FUNNY, DEAR?

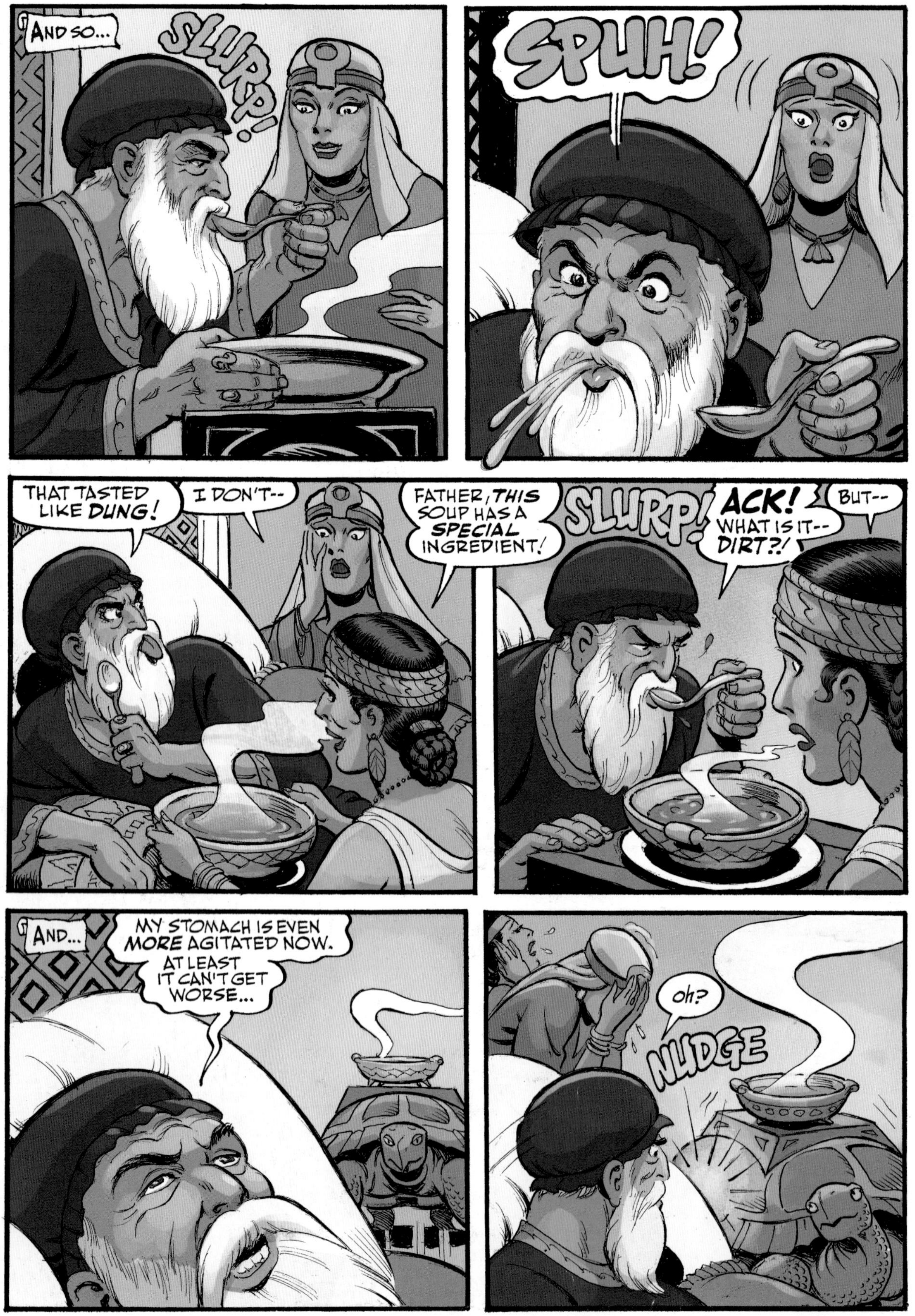
AND SO...
SLURP!
SPUH!
THAT TASTED LIKE DUNG!
I DON'T--
FATHER, THIS SOUP HAS A SPECIAL INGREDIENT!
SLURP!
ACK! WHAT IS IT-- DIRT?!
BUT--
AND...
MY STOMACH IS EVEN MORE AGITATED NOW. AT LEAST IT CAN'T GET WORSE...
oh?
NUDGE

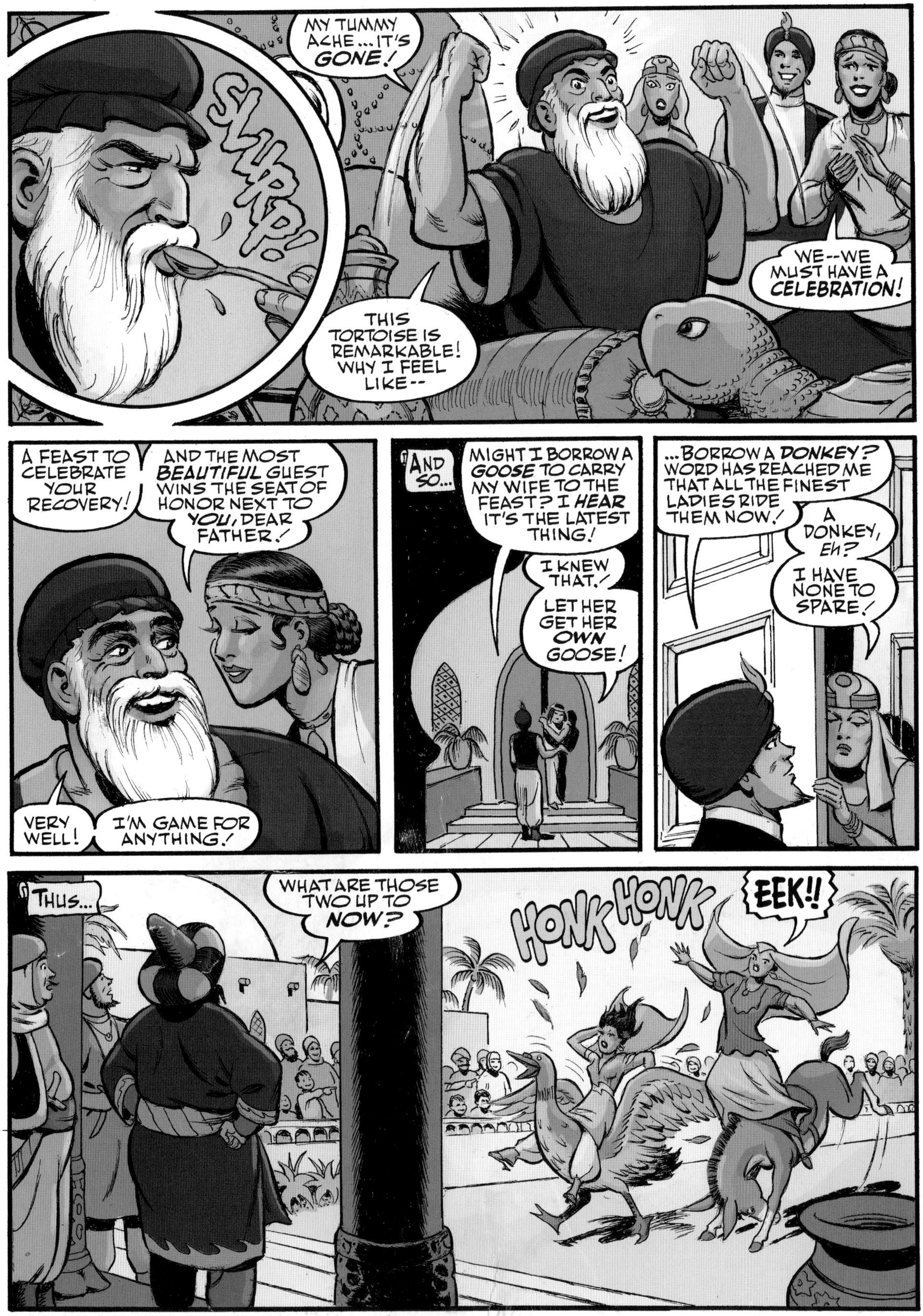
SLURP!
MY TUMMY ACHE... IT'S GONE!
THIS TORTOISE IS REMARKABLE! WHY I FEEL LIKE--
WE--WE MUST HAVE A CELEBRATION!
A FEAST TO CELEBRATE YOUR RECOVERY!
AND THE MOST BEAUTIFUL GUEST WINS THE SEAT OF HONOR NEXT TO YOU, DEAR FATHER!
VERY WELL!
I'M GAME FOR ANYTHING!
AND SO...
MIGHT I BORROW A GOOSE TO CARRY MY WIFE TO THE FEAST? I HEAR IT'S THE LATEST THING!
I KNEW THAT.
LET HER GET HER OWN GOOSE!
...BORROW A DONKEY? WORD HAS REACHED ME THAT ALL THE FINEST LADIES RIDE THEM NOW!
A DONKEY, Eh?
I HAVE NONE TO SPARE!
THUS...
WHAT ARE THOSE TWO UP TO NOW?
HONK HONK
EEK!!

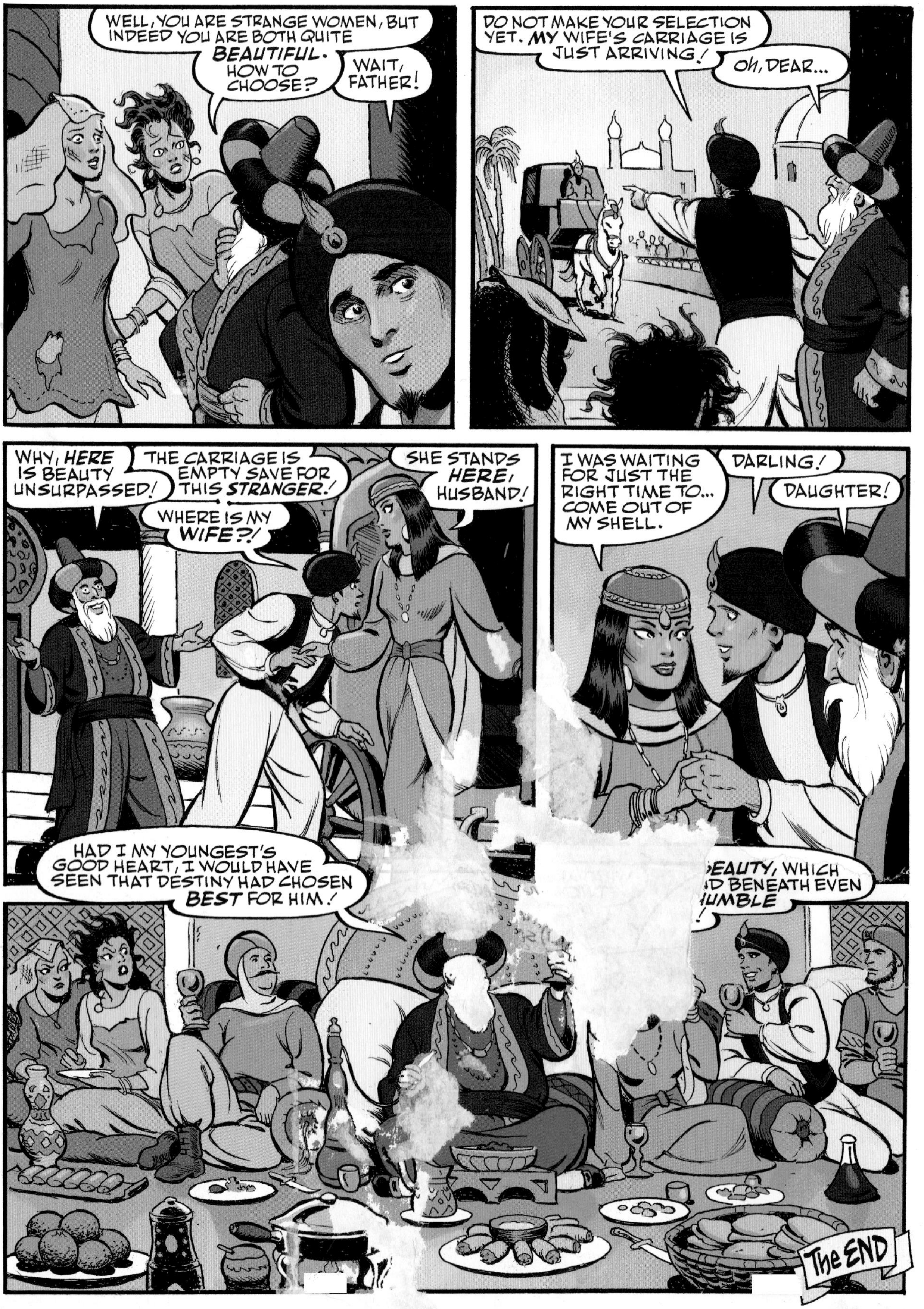
WELL, YOU ARE STRANGE WOMEN, BUT INDEED YOU ARE BOTH QUITE BEAUTIFUL. HOW TO CHOOSE?
WAIT, FATHER!
DO NOT MAKE YOUR SELECTION YET. MY WIFE'S CARRIAGE IS JUST ARRIVING!
Oh, DEAR...
WHY, HERE IS BEAUTY UNSURPASSED!
THE CARRIAGE IS EMPTY SAVE FOR THIS STRANGER!
WHERE IS MY WIFE?!
SHE STANDS HERE, HUSBAND!
I WAS WAITING FOR JUST THE RIGHT TIME TO... COME OUT OF MY SHELL.
DARLING!
DAUGHTER!
BEAUTY, WHICH
BENEATH EVEN
HUMBLE
HAD I MY YOUNGEST'S GOOD HEART, I WOULD HAVE SEEN THAT DESTINY HAD CHOSEN BEST FOR HIM!
The END

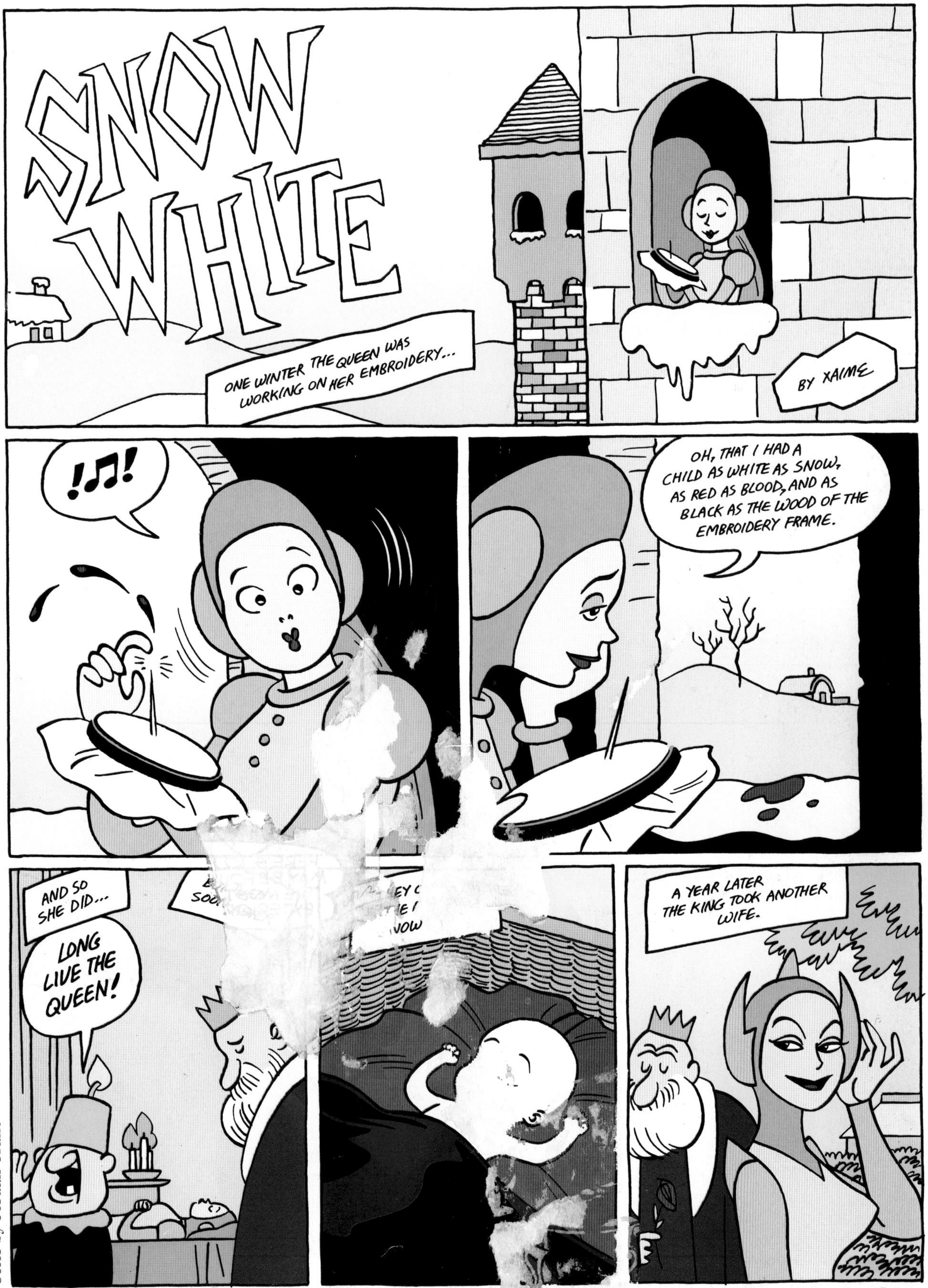
SNOW WHITE
ONE WINTER THE QUEEN WAS WORKING ON HER EMBROIDERY...
BY XAIME
!♫!
OH, THAT I HAD A CHILD AS WHITE AS SNOW, AS RED AS BLOOD, AND AS BLACK AS THE WOOD OF THE EMBROIDERY FRAME.
AND SO SHE DID...
LONG LIVE THE QUEEN!
A YEAR LATER THE KING TOOK ANOTHER WIFE.

Color by Jordan Crane

From the Brothers Grimm

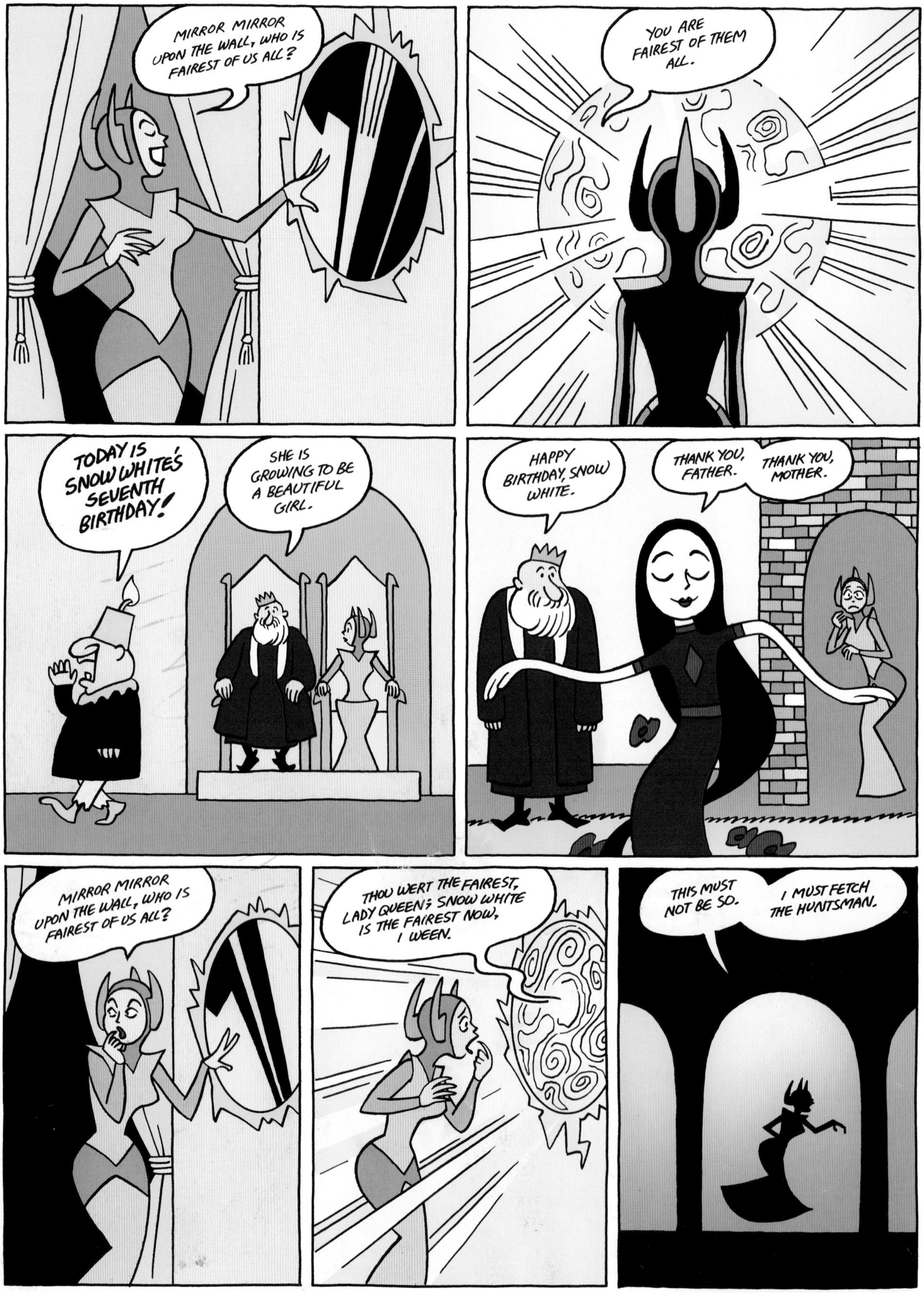
MIRROR MIRROR UPON THE WALL, WHO IS FAIREST OF US ALL?
YOU ARE FAIREST OF THEM ALL.
TODAY IS SNOW WHITE'S SEVENTH BIRTHDAY!
SHE IS GROWING TO BE A BEAUTIFUL GIRL.
HAPPY BIRTHDAY, SNOW WHITE.
THANK YOU, FATHER.
THANK YOU, MOTHER.
MIRROR MIRROR UPON THE WALL, WHO IS FAIREST OF US ALL?
THOU WERT THE FAIREST, LADY QUEEN; SNOW WHITE IS THE FAIREST NOW, I WEEN.
THIS MUST NOT BE SO.
I MUST FETCH THE HUNTSMAN.

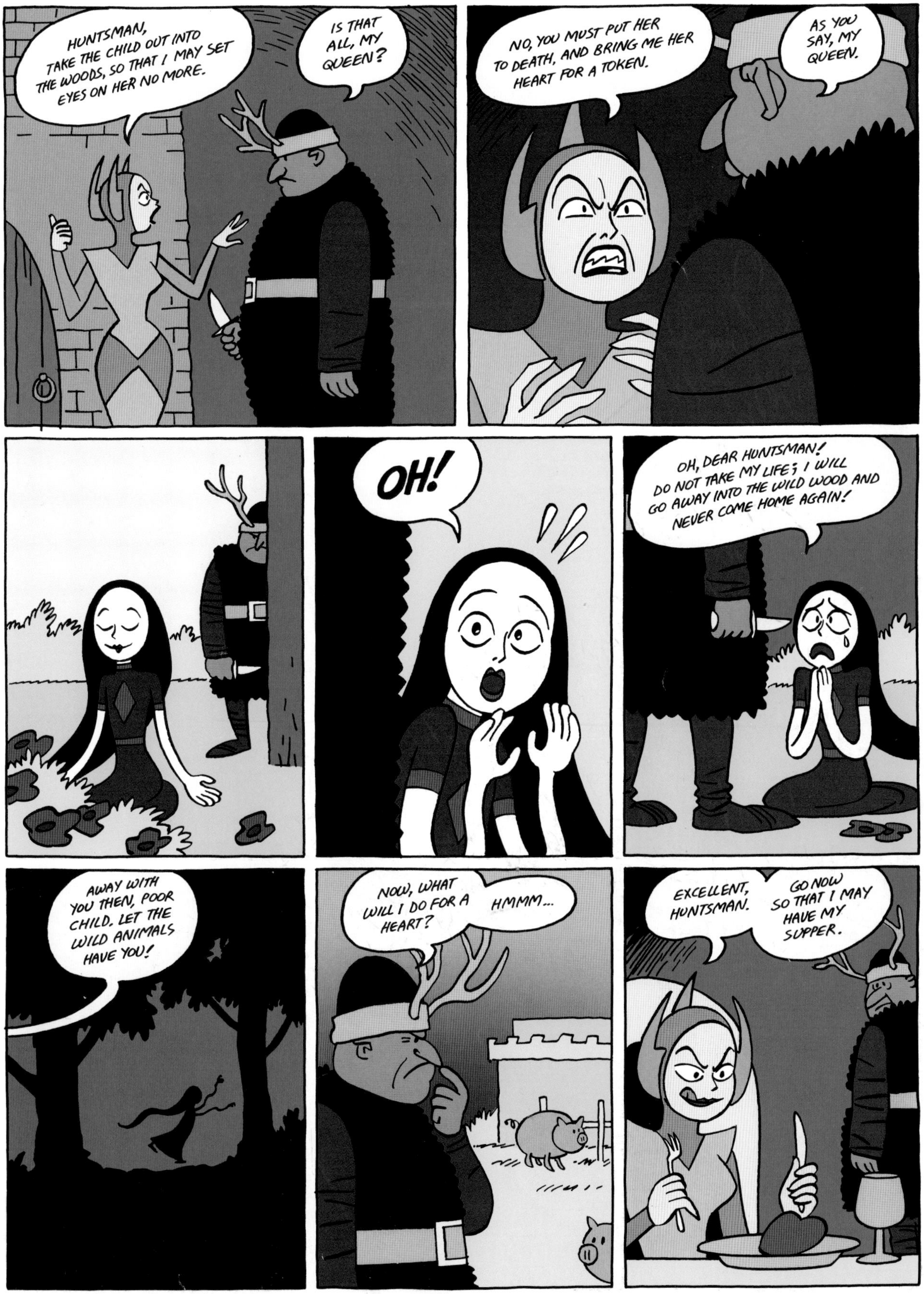
HUNTSMAN, TAKE THE CHILD OUT INTO THE WOODS, SO THAT I MAY SET EYES ON HER NO MORE.
IS THAT ALL, MY QUEEN?
NO, YOU MUST PUT HER TO DEATH, AND BRING ME HER HEART FOR A TOKEN.
AS YOU SAY, MY QUEEN.
OH!
OH, DEAR HUNTSMAN! DO NOT TAKE MY LIFE; I WILL GO AWAY INTO THE WILD WOOD AND NEVER COME HOME AGAIN!
AWAY WITH YOU THEN, POOR CHILD. LET THE WILD ANIMALS HAVE YOU!
NOW, WHAT WILL I DO FOR A HEART?
HMMM...
EXCELLENT, HUNTSMAN.
GO NOW SO THAT I MAY HAVE MY SUPPER.

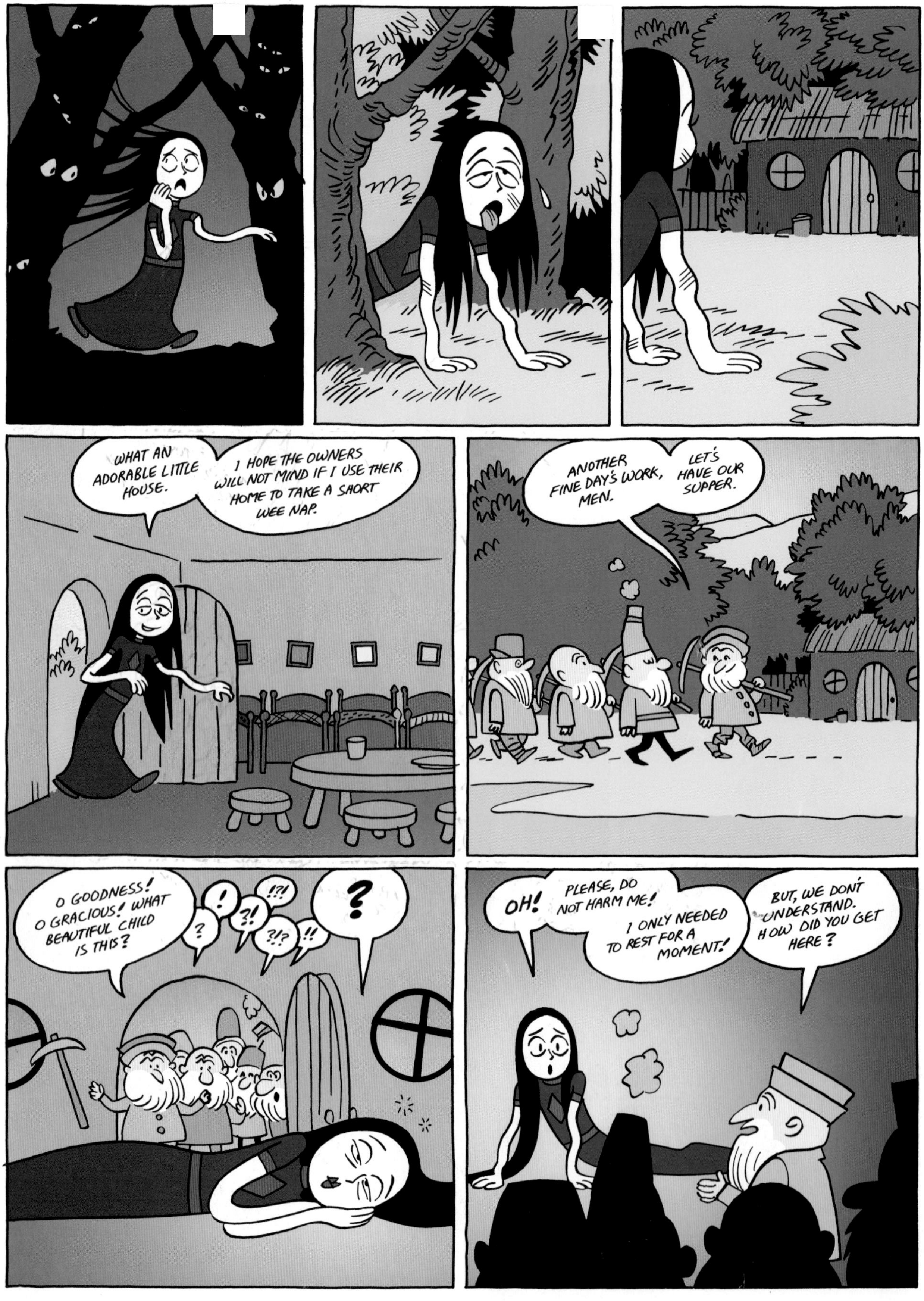
WHAT AN ADORABLE LITTLE HOUSE.
I HOPE THE OWNERS WILL NOT MIND IF I USE THEIR HOME TO TAKE A SHORT WEE NAP.
ANOTHER FINE DAY'S WORK, MEN.
LET'S HAVE OUR SUPPER.
O GOODNESS! O GRACIOUS! WHAT BEAUTIFUL CHILD IS THIS?
!
?
?!
!?!
?!?
!!
?
OH!
PLEASE, DO NOT HARM ME!
I ONLY NEEDED TO REST FOR A MOMENT!
BUT, WE DON'T UNDERSTAND. HOW DID YOU GET HERE?

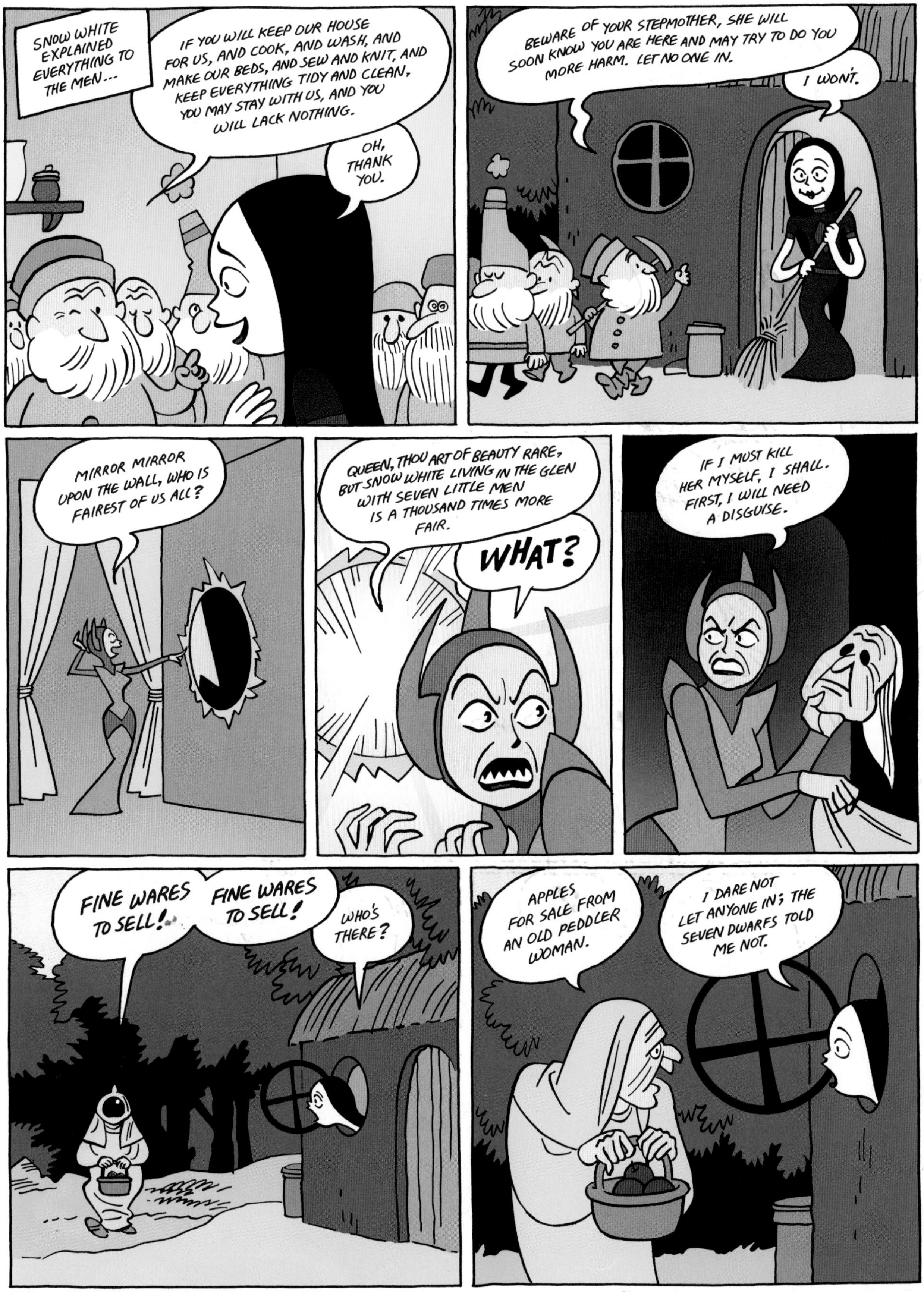

SNOW WHITE EXPLAINED EVERYTHING TO THE MEN...
IF YOU WILL KEEP OUR HOUSE FOR US, AND COOK, AND WASH, AND MAKE OUR BEDS, AND SEW AND KNIT, AND KEEP EVERYTHING TIDY AND CLEAN, YOU MAY STAY WITH US, AND YOU WILL LACK NOTHING.
OH, THANK YOU.
BEWARE OF YOUR STEPMOTHER, SHE WILL SOON KNOW YOU ARE HERE AND MAY TRY TO DO YOU MORE HARM. LET NO ONE IN.
I WON'T.
MIRROR MIRROR UPON THE WALL, WHO IS FAIREST OF US ALL?
QUEEN, THOU ART OF BEAUTY RARE, BUT SNOW WHITE LIVING IN THE GLEN WITH SEVEN LITTLE MEN IS A THOUSAND TIMES MORE FAIR.
WHAT?
IF I MUST KILL HER MYSELF, I SHALL. FIRST, I WILL NEED A DISGUISE.
FINE WARES TO SELL!
FINE WARES TO SELL!
WHO'S THERE?
APPLES FOR SALE FROM AN OLD PEDDLER WOMAN.
I DARE NOT LET ANYONE IN; THE SEVEN DWARFS TOLD ME NOT.

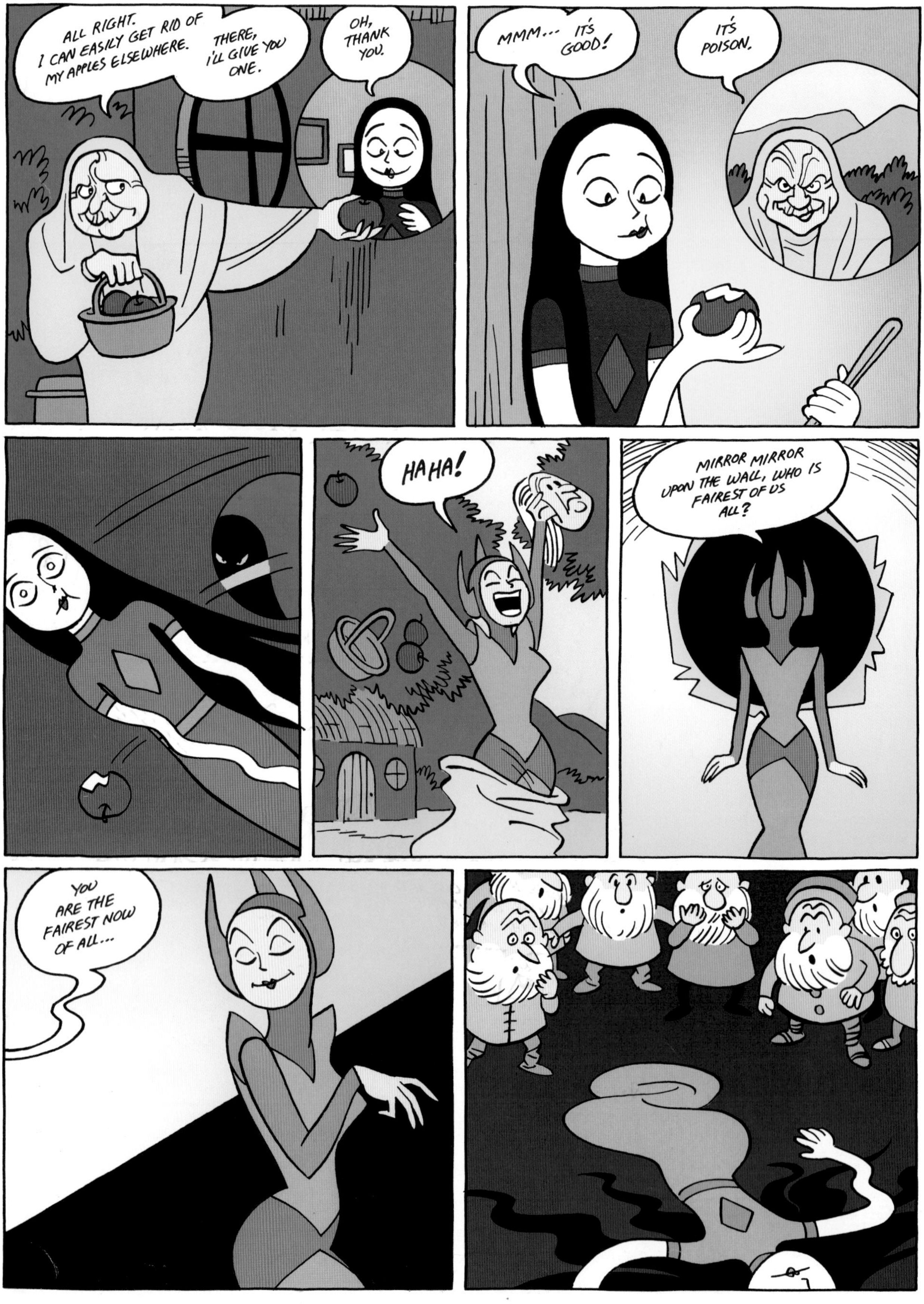
ALL RIGHT. I CAN EASILY GET RID OF MY APPLES ELSEWHERE.
THERE, I'LL GIVE YOU ONE.
OH, THANK YOU.
MMM... IT'S GOOD!
IT'S POISON.
HAHA!
MIRROR MIRROR UPON THE WALL, WHO IS FAIREST OF US ALL?
YOU ARE THE FAIREST NOW OF ALL...

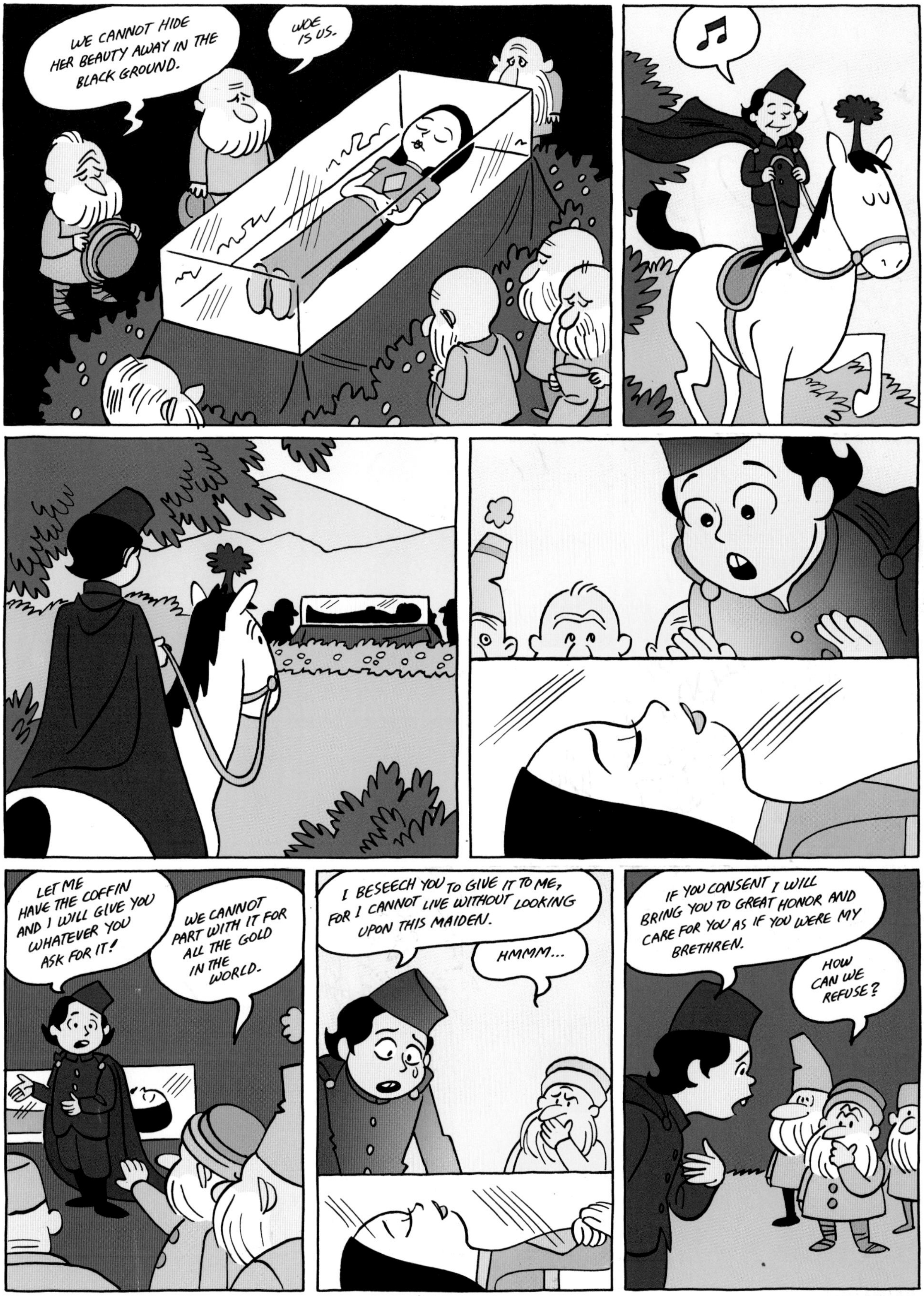
WE CANNOT HIDE HER BEAUTY AWAY IN THE BLACK GROUND.
WOE IS US.
♫
LET ME HAVE THE COFFIN AND I WILL GIVE YOU WHATEVER YOU ASK FOR IT!
WE CANNOT PART WITH IT FOR ALL THE GOLD IN THE WORLD.
I BESEECH YOU TO GIVE IT TO ME, FOR I CANNOT LIVE WITHOUT LOOKING UPON THIS MAIDEN.
HMMM...
IF YOU CONSENT I WILL BRING YOU TO GREAT HONOR AND CARE FOR YOU AS IF YOU WERE MY BRETHREN.
HOW CAN WE REFUSE?

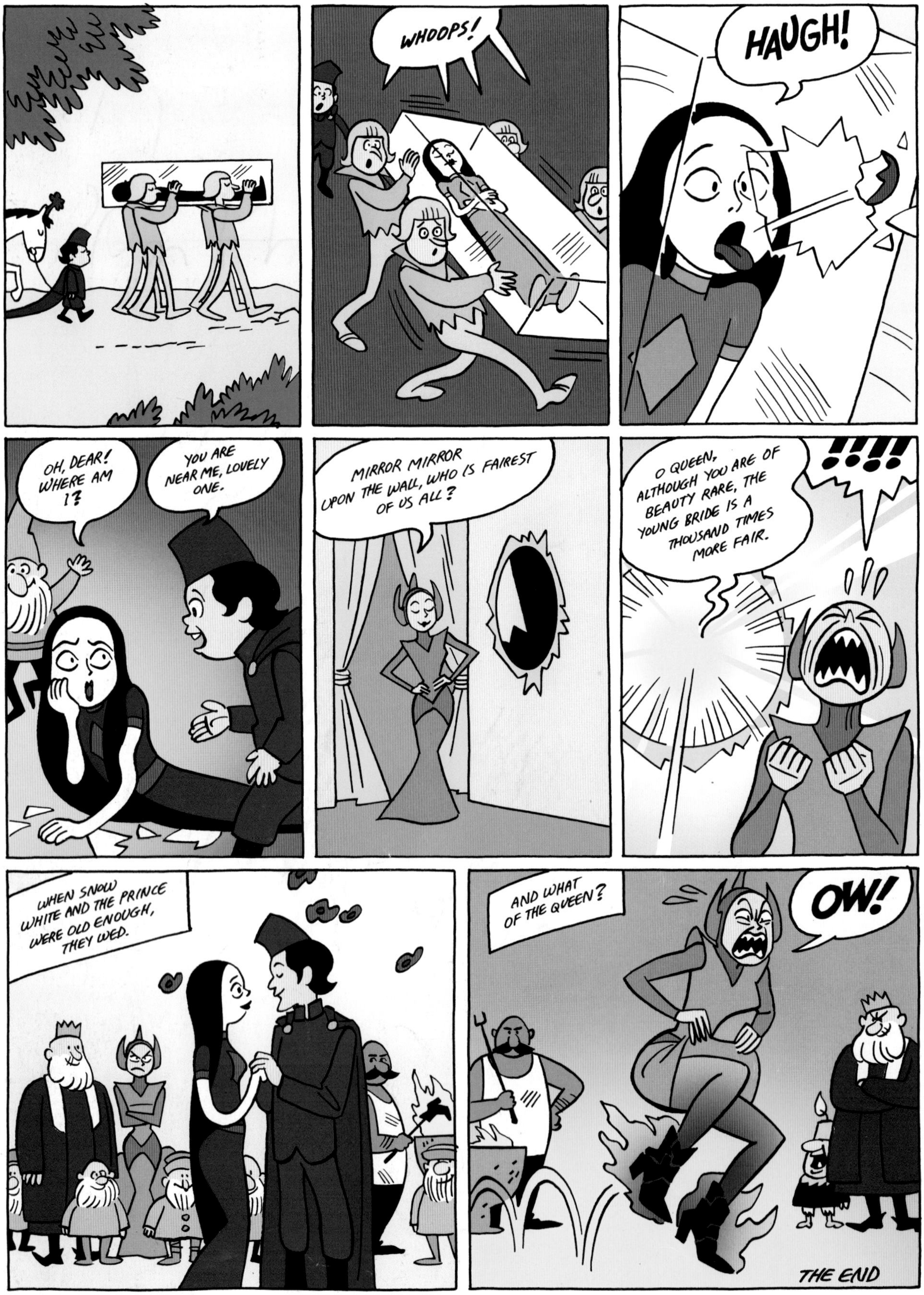
WHOOPS!
HAUGH!
OH, DEAR! WHERE AM I?
YOU ARE NEAR ME, LOVELY ONE.
MIRROR MIRROR UPON THE WALL, WHO IS FAIREST OF US ALL?
O QUEEN, ALTHOUGH YOU ARE OF BEAUTY RARE, THE YOUNG BRIDE IS A THOUSAND TIMES MORE FAIR.
!!!!
WHEN SNOW WHITE AND THE PRINCE WERE OLD ENOUGH, THEY WED.
AND WHAT OF THE QUEEN?
OW!
THE END

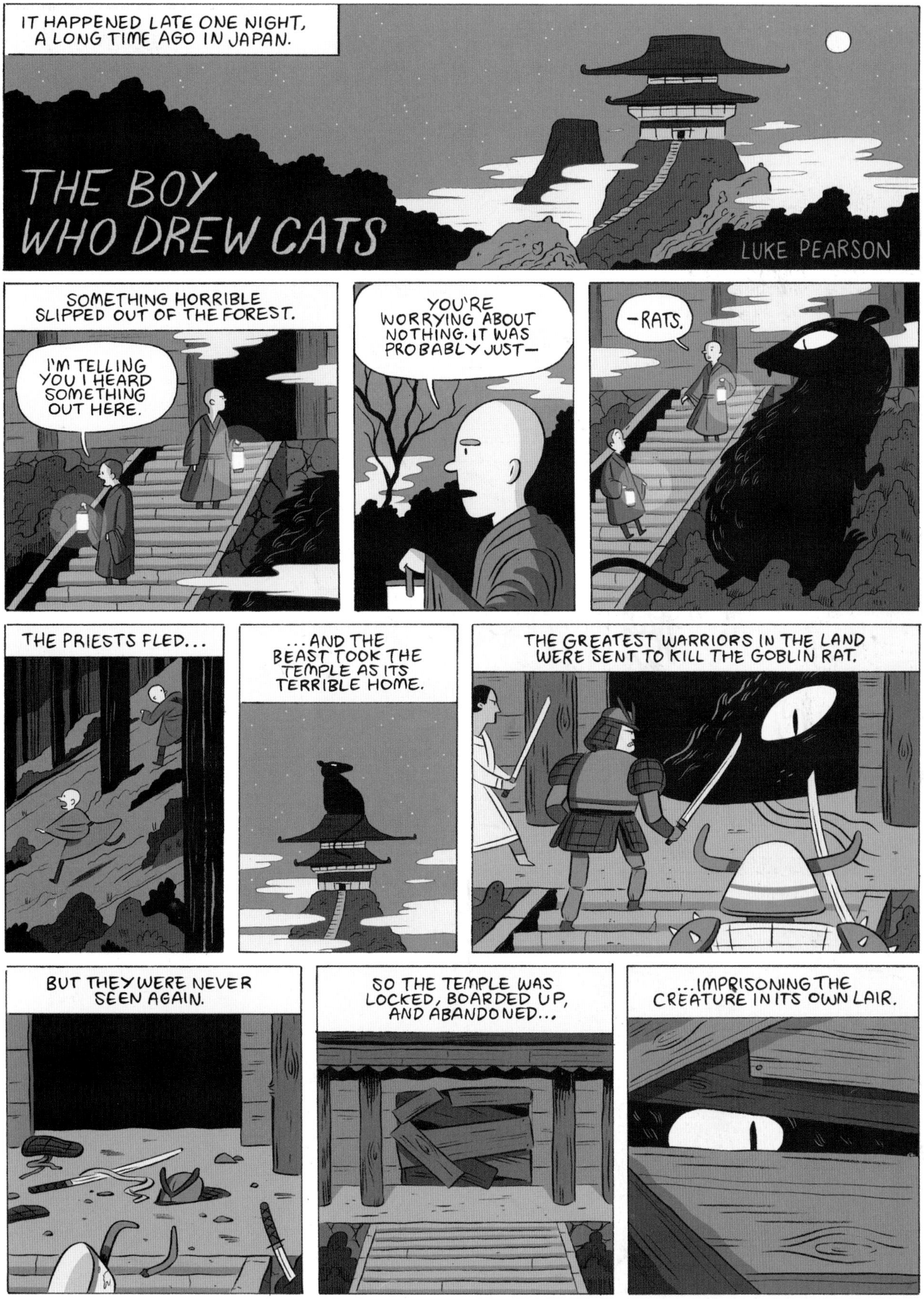
IT HAPPENED LATE ONE NIGHT, A LONG TIME AGO IN JAPAN.
THE BOY WHO DREW CATS
LUKE PEARSON
SOMETHING HORRIBLE SLIPPED OUT OF THE FOREST.
I'M TELLING YOU I HEARD SOMETHING OUT HERE.
YOU'RE WORRYING ABOUT NOTHING. IT WAS PROBABLY JUST—
—RATS.
THE PRIESTS FLED...
...AND THE BEAST TOOK THE TEMPLE AS ITS TERRIBLE HOME.
THE GREATEST WARRIORS IN THE LAND WERE SENT TO KILL THE GOBLIN RAT.
BUT THEY WERE NEVER SEEN AGAIN.
SO THE TEMPLE WAS LOCKED, BOARDED UP, AND ABANDONED...
...IMPRISONING THE CREATURE IN ITS OWN LAIR.

From the Japanese tale as told by Lafcadio Hearn

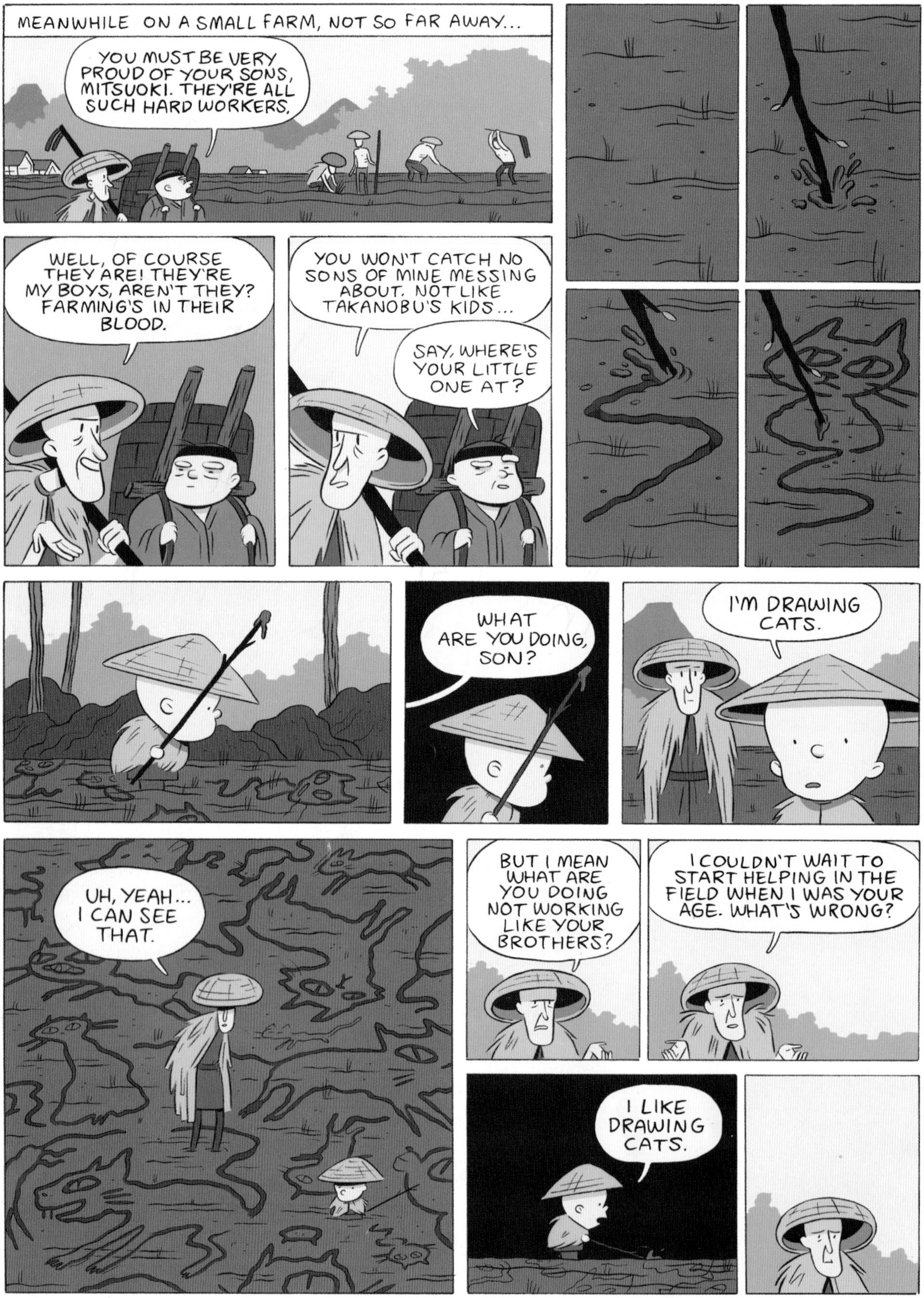
MEANWHILE ON A SMALL FARM, NOT SO FAR AWAY...
YOU MUST BE VERY PROUD OF YOUR SONS, MITSUOKI. THEY'RE ALL SUCH HARD WORKERS.
WELL, OF COURSE THEY ARE! THEY'RE MY BOYS, AREN'T THEY? FARMING'S IN THEIR BLOOD.
YOU WON'T CATCH NO SONS OF MINE MESSING ABOUT. NOT LIKE TAKANOBU'S KIDS...
SAY, WHERE'S YOUR LITTLE ONE AT?
WHAT ARE YOU DOING, SON?
I'M DRAWING CATS.
UH, YEAH... I CAN SEE THAT.
BUT I MEAN WHAT ARE YOU DOING NOT WORKING LIKE YOUR BROTHERS?
I COULDN'T WAIT TO START HELPING IN THE FIELD WHEN I WAS YOUR AGE. WHAT'S WRONG?
I LIKE DRAWING CATS.

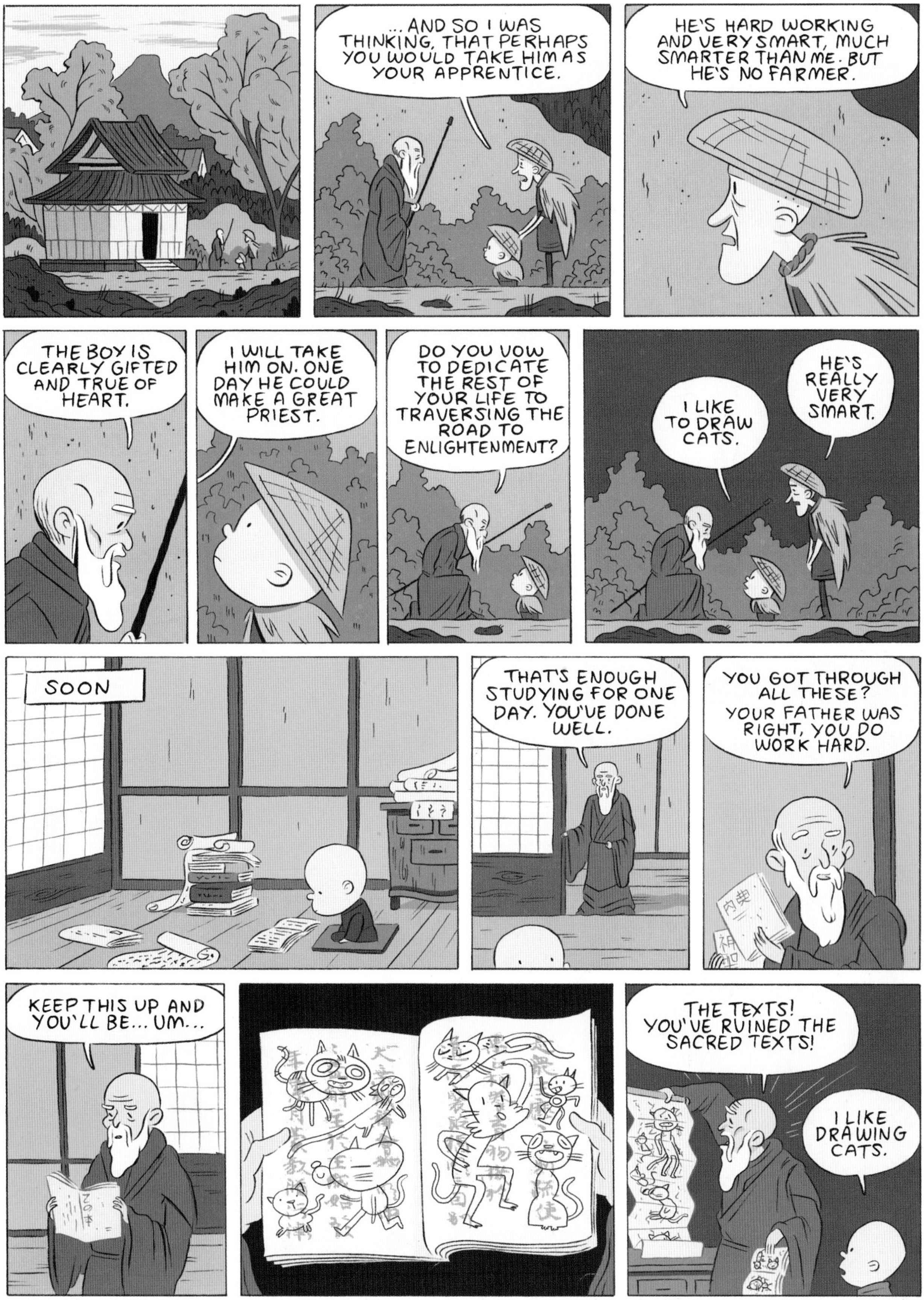
...AND SO I WAS THINKING, THAT PERHAPS YOU WOULD TAKE HIM AS YOUR APPRENTICE.
HE'S HARD WORKING AND VERY SMART, MUCH SMARTER THAN ME. BUT HE'S NO FARMER.
THE BOY IS CLEARLY GIFTED AND TRUE OF HEART.
I WILL TAKE HIM ON. ONE DAY HE COULD MAKE A GREAT PRIEST.
DO YOU VOW TO DEDICATE THE REST OF YOUR LIFE TO TRAVERSING THE ROAD TO ENLIGHTENMENT?
HE'S REALLY VERY SMART.
I LIKE TO DRAW CATS.
SOON
THAT'S ENOUGH STUDYING FOR ONE DAY. YOU'VE DONE WELL.
YOU GOT THROUGH ALL THESE? YOUR FATHER WAS RIGHT, YOU DO WORK HARD.
KEEP THIS UP AND YOU'LL BE... UM...
THE TEXTS! YOU'VE RUINED THE SACRED TEXTS!
I LIKE DRAWING CATS.

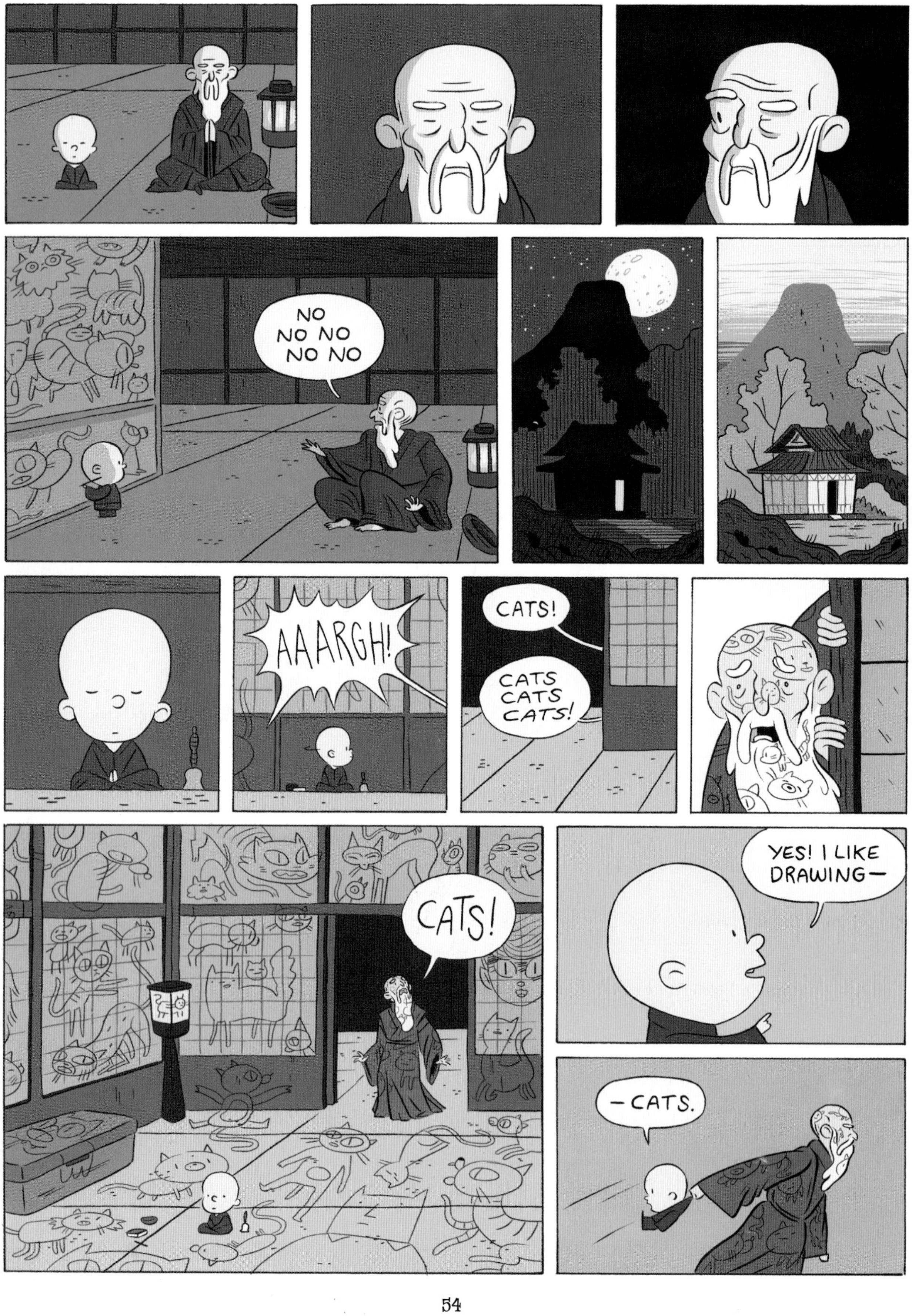
NO
NO NO
NO NO
AAARGH!
CATS!
CATS
CATS
CATS!
CATS!
YES! I LIKE
DRAWING—
—CATS.

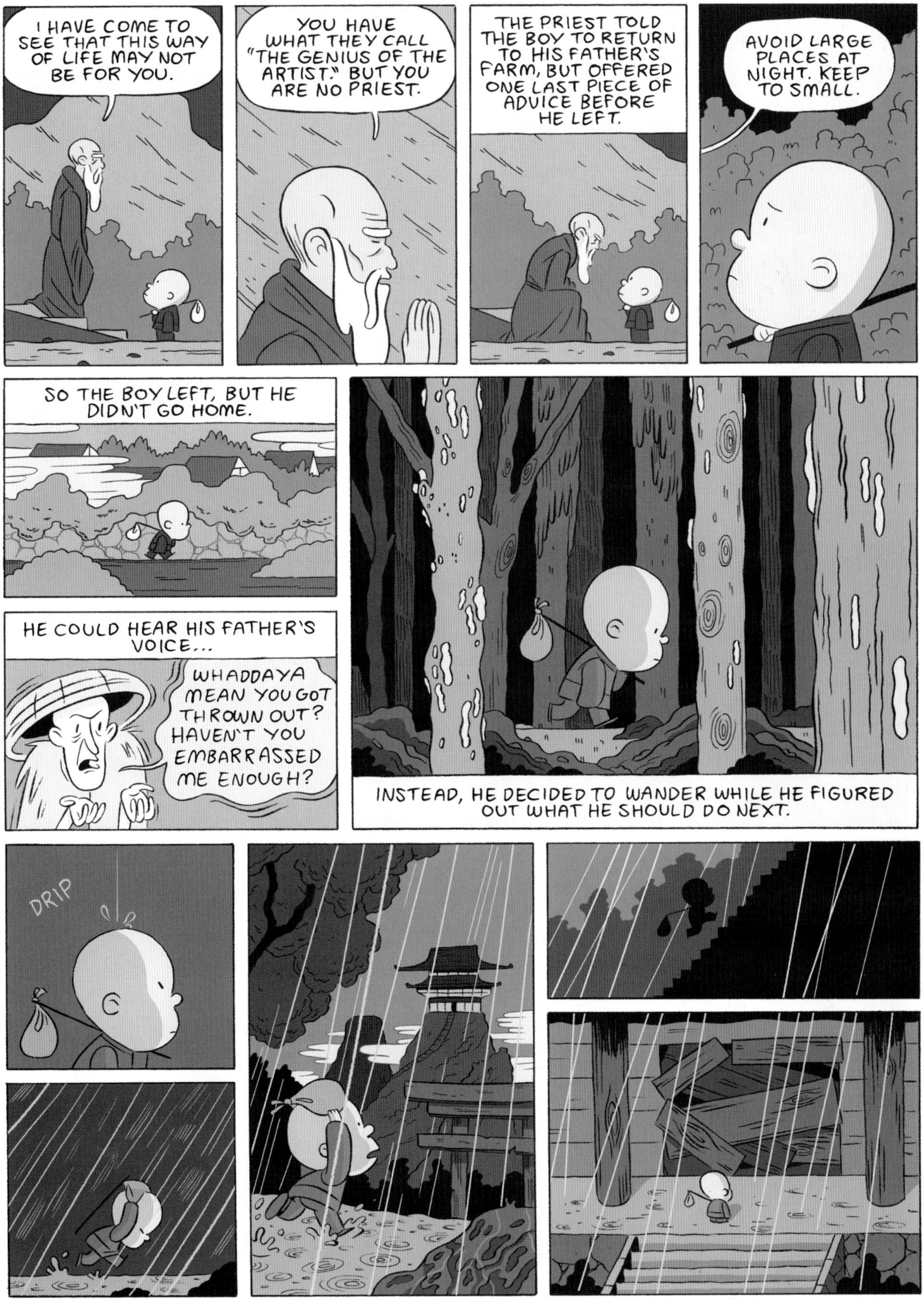
I HAVE COME TO SEE THAT THIS WAY OF LIFE MAY NOT BE FOR YOU.
YOU HAVE WHAT THEY CALL "THE GENIUS OF THE ARTIST." BUT YOU ARE NO PRIEST.
THE PRIEST TOLD THE BOY TO RETURN TO HIS FATHER'S FARM, BUT OFFERED ONE LAST PIECE OF ADVICE BEFORE HE LEFT.
AVOID LARGE PLACES AT NIGHT. KEEP TO SMALL.
SO THE BOY LEFT, BUT HE DIDN'T GO HOME.
HE COULD HEAR HIS FATHER'S VOICE...
WHADDAYA MEAN YOU GOT THROWN OUT? HAVEN'T YOU EMBARRASSED ME ENOUGH?
INSTEAD, HE DECIDED TO WANDER WHILE HE FIGURED OUT WHAT HE SHOULD DO NEXT.
DRIP

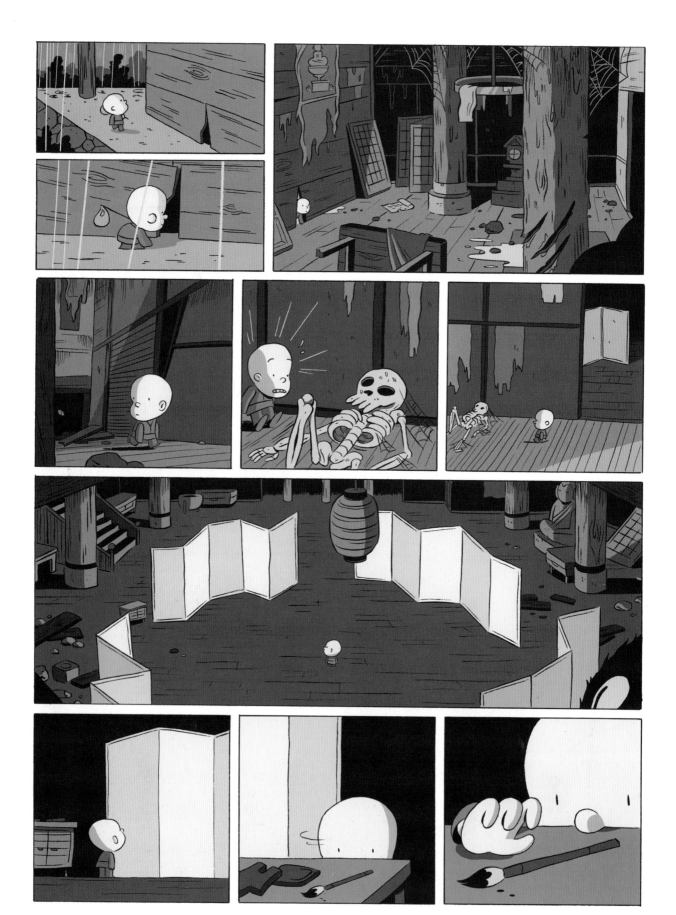

HAVING TIRED HIMSELF OUT WITH DRAWING...

...THE BOY LAY DOWN RIGHT WHERE HE WAS TO GO TO SLEEP.

BUT JUST BEFORE HE DRIFTED OFF...

AVOID LARGE PLACES AT NIGHT. KEEP TO SMALL.

SATISFIED THAT THIS LITTLE CABINET WAS SMALL ENOUGH, HE DOZED OFF RIGHT AWAY.

BUT HE WAS SOON AWOKEN BY THE MOST TERRIFYING SOUNDS HE'D EVER HEARD—

—SOUNDS OF FIGHTING AND SCREAMING, AND THE WHOLE TEMPLE SEEMED TO BE SHAKING.

BRRR!!!

EVENTUALLY THERE WAS SILENCE, BUT THE BOY WAS TOO SCARED TO EVEN LOOK OUTSIDE UNTIL THE MORNING.

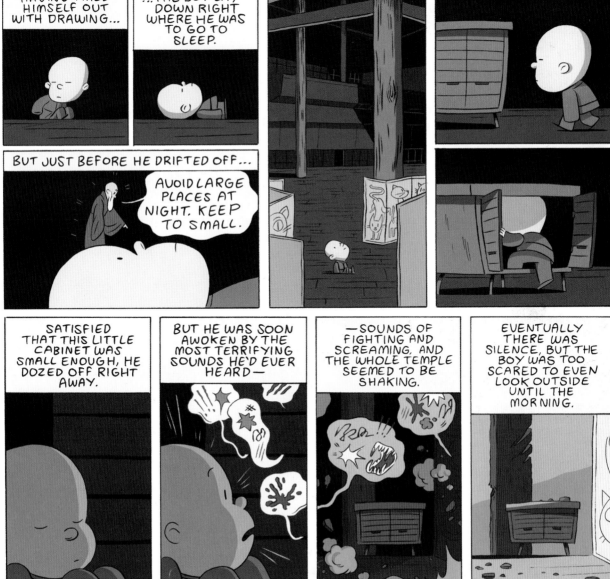

CREAK
LYING IN THE MIDDLE OF THE HALL WAS THE DEAD BODY OF AN ENORMOUS GOBLIN RAT.
AS THE BOY TRIED TO UNDERSTAND WHAT HAD KILLED THE CREATURE...
...HE NOTICED THERE WAS SOMETHING DIFFERENT ABOUT HIS DRAWINGS FROM THE NIGHT BEFORE.
WHEN HE LEFT THE TEMPLE HE WAS HAILED AS A HERO FOR DEFEATING THE MONSTER.
IMPRESSED BY THIS FEAT, A GREAT SAMURAI OFFERED TO TAKE HIM AS AN APPRENTICE.
AND SO THE BOY RODE OFF TOWARD ADVENTURE, SURE TO BECOME A MIGHTY WARRIOR.
I REALLY JUST WANT TO DRAW CATS.

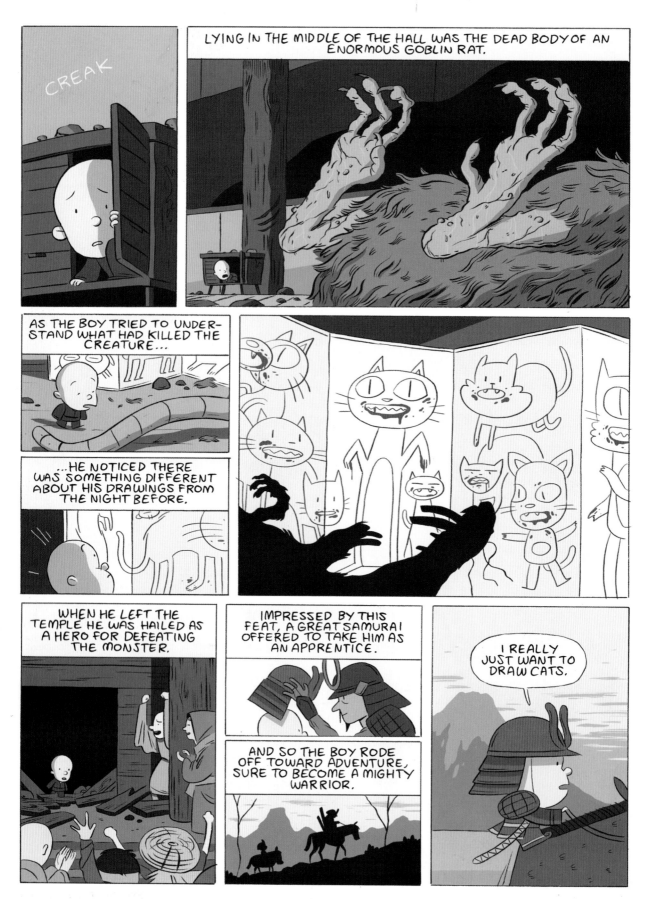

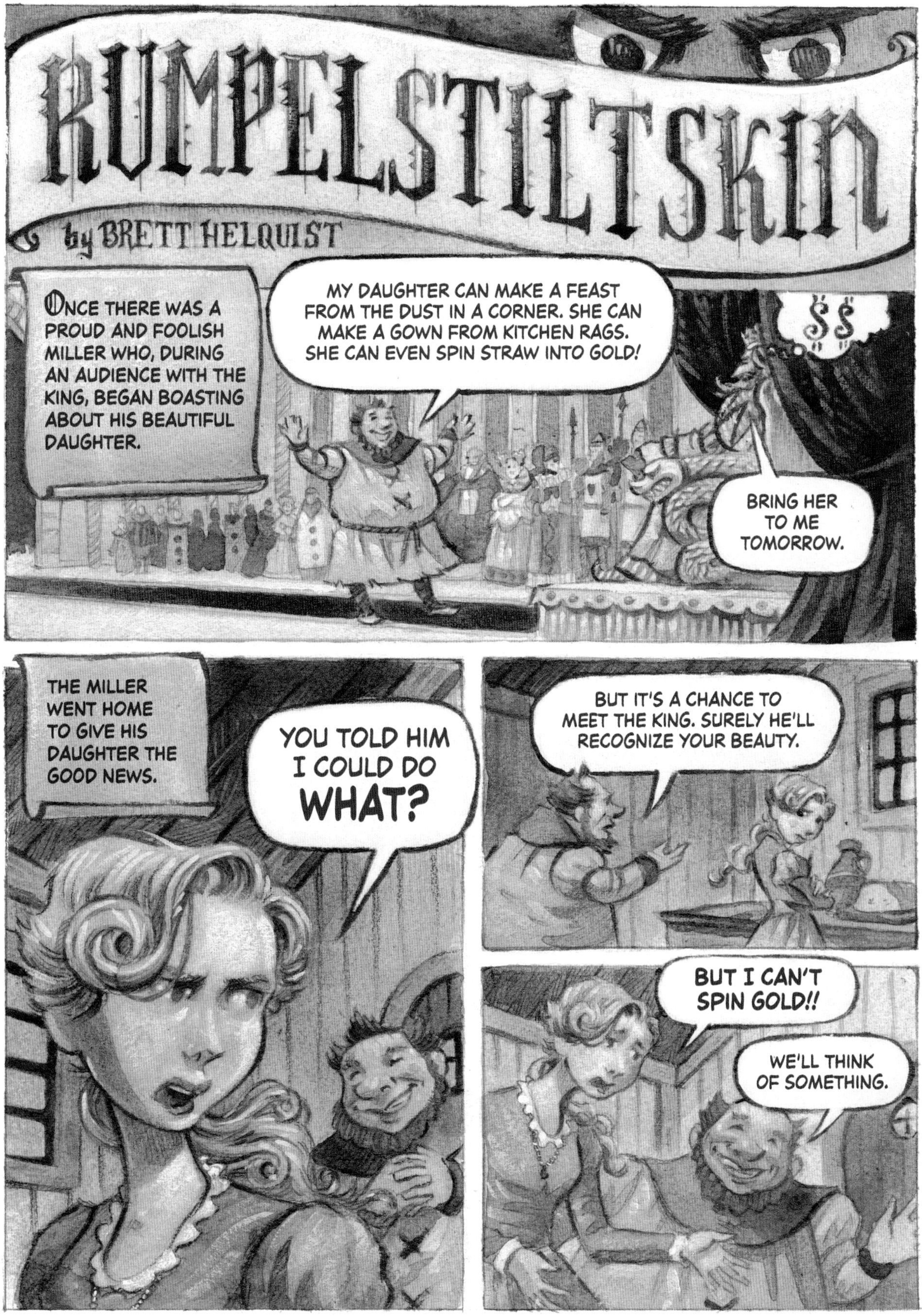
RUMPELSTILTSKIN
by BRETT HELQUIST
ONCE THERE WAS A PROUD AND FOOLISH MILLER WHO, DURING AN AUDIENCE WITH THE KING, BEGAN BOASTING ABOUT HIS BEAUTIFUL DAUGHTER.
MY DAUGHTER CAN MAKE A FEAST FROM THE DUST IN A CORNER. SHE CAN MAKE A GOWN FROM KITCHEN RAGS. SHE CAN EVEN SPIN STRAW INTO GOLD!
$$
BRING HER TO ME TOMORROW.
THE MILLER WENT HOME TO GIVE HIS DAUGHTER THE GOOD NEWS.
YOU TOLD HIM I COULD DO WHAT?
BUT IT'S A CHANCE TO MEET THE KING. SURELY HE'LL RECOGNIZE YOUR BEAUTY.
BUT I CAN'T SPIN GOLD!!
WE'LL THINK OF SOMETHING.

Lettering by John Green

From the Brothers Grimm

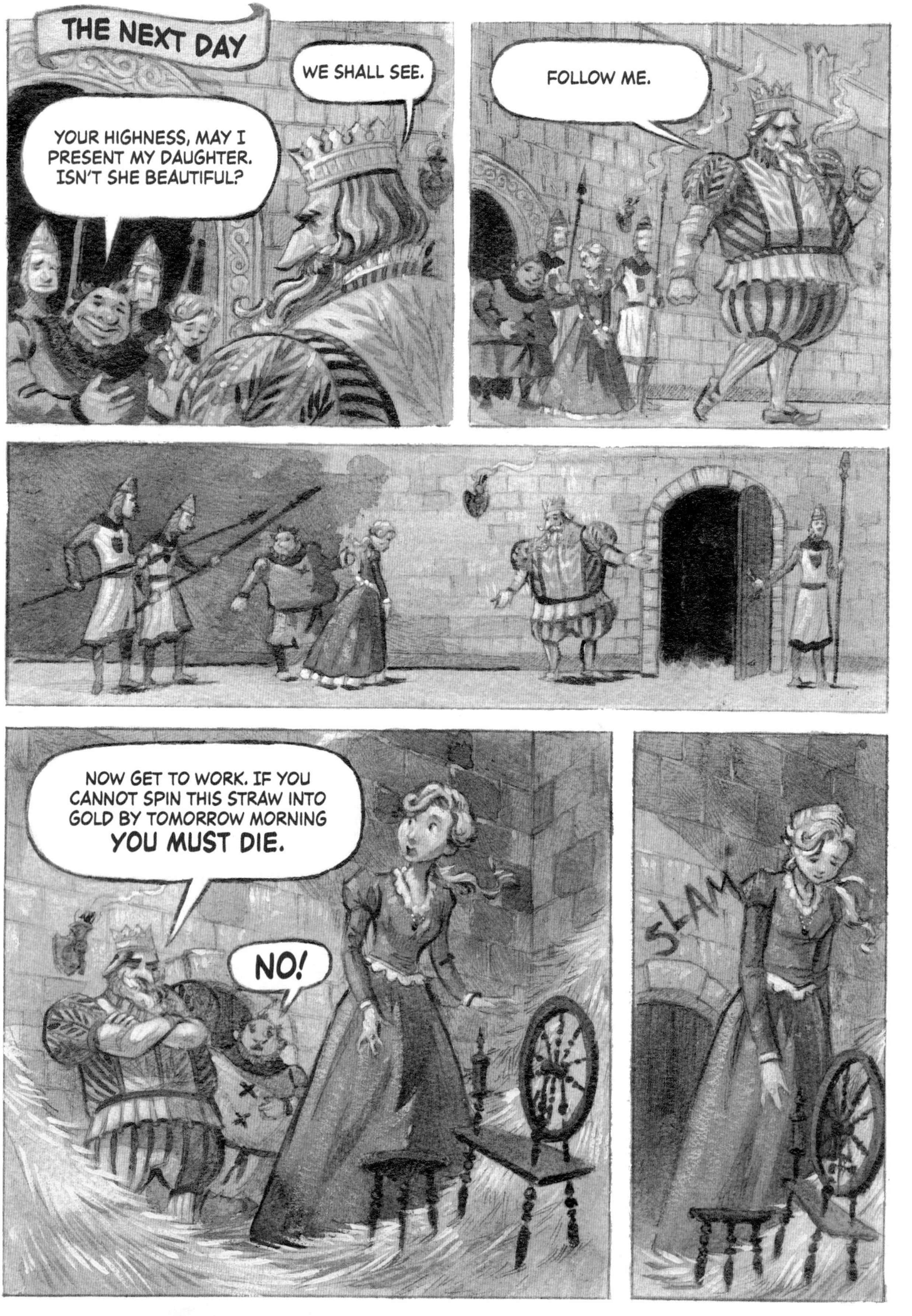
THE NEXT DAY
YOUR HIGHNESS, MAY I PRESENT MY DAUGHTER. ISN'T SHE BEAUTIFUL?
WE SHALL SEE.
FOLLOW ME.
NOW GET TO WORK. IF YOU CANNOT SPIN THIS STRAW INTO GOLD BY TOMORROW MORNING YOU MUST DIE.
NO!
SLAM

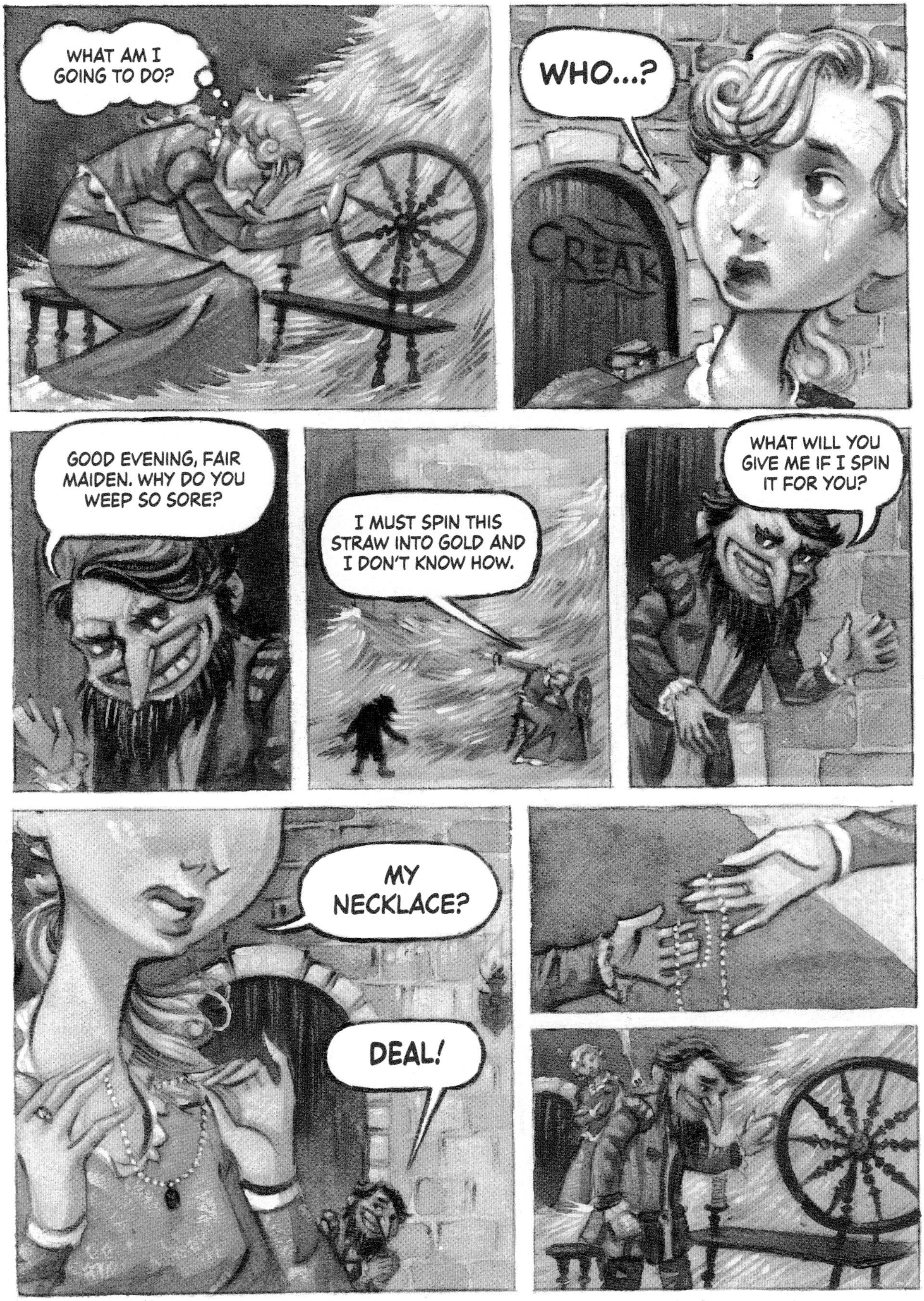
WHAT AM I GOING TO DO?
WHO...?
CREAK
GOOD EVENING, FAIR MAIDEN. WHY DO YOU WEEP SO SORE?
I MUST SPIN THIS STRAW INTO GOLD AND I DON'T KNOW HOW.
WHAT WILL YOU GIVE ME IF I SPIN IT FOR YOU?
MY NECKLACE?
DEAL!

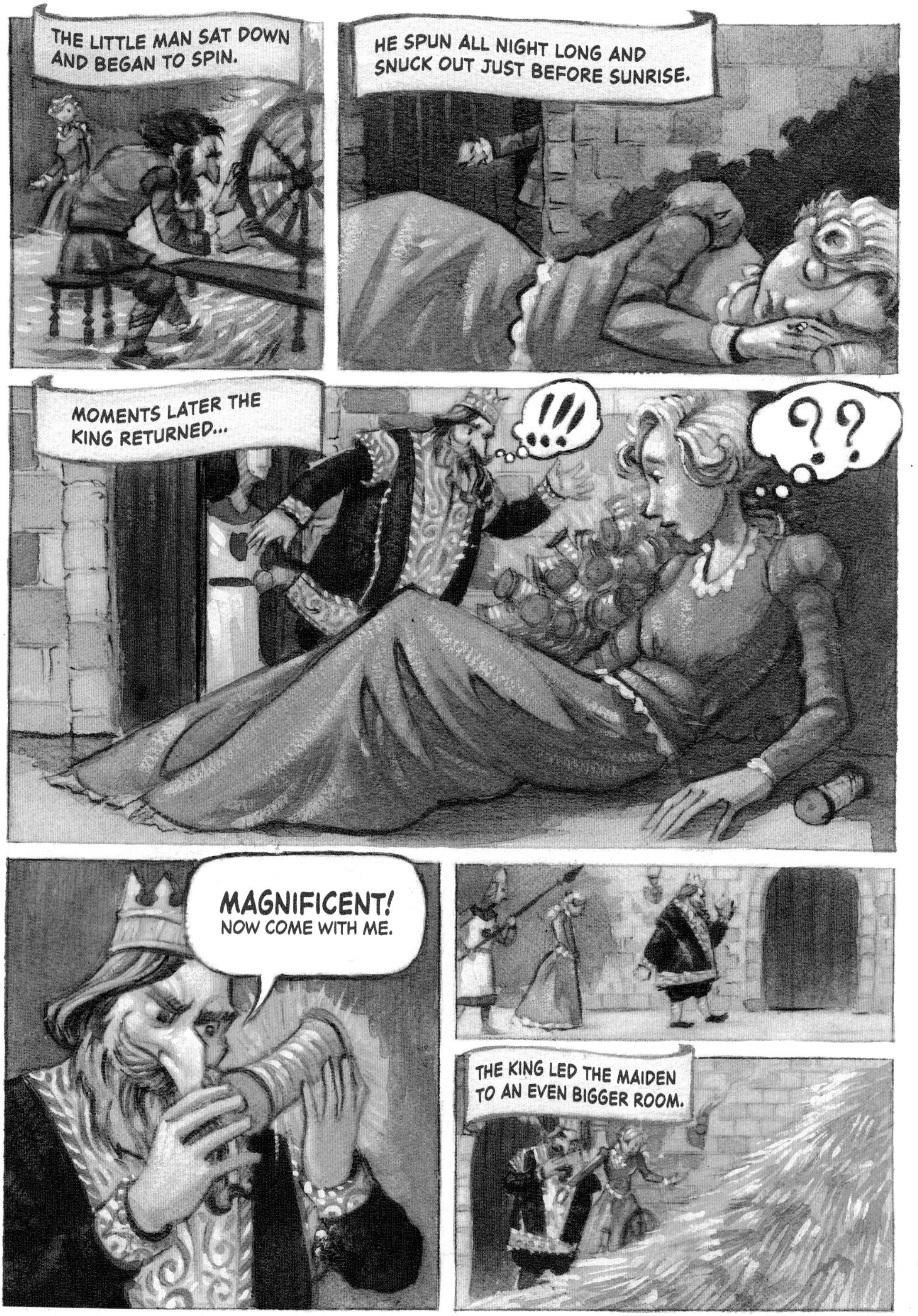
THE LITTLE MAN SAT DOWN AND BEGAN TO SPIN.
HE SPUN ALL NIGHT LONG AND SNUCK OUT JUST BEFORE SUNRISE.
MOMENTS LATER THE KING RETURNED...
!!!
??
MAGNIFICENT! NOW COME WITH ME.
THE KING LED THE MAIDEN TO AN EVEN BIGGER ROOM.

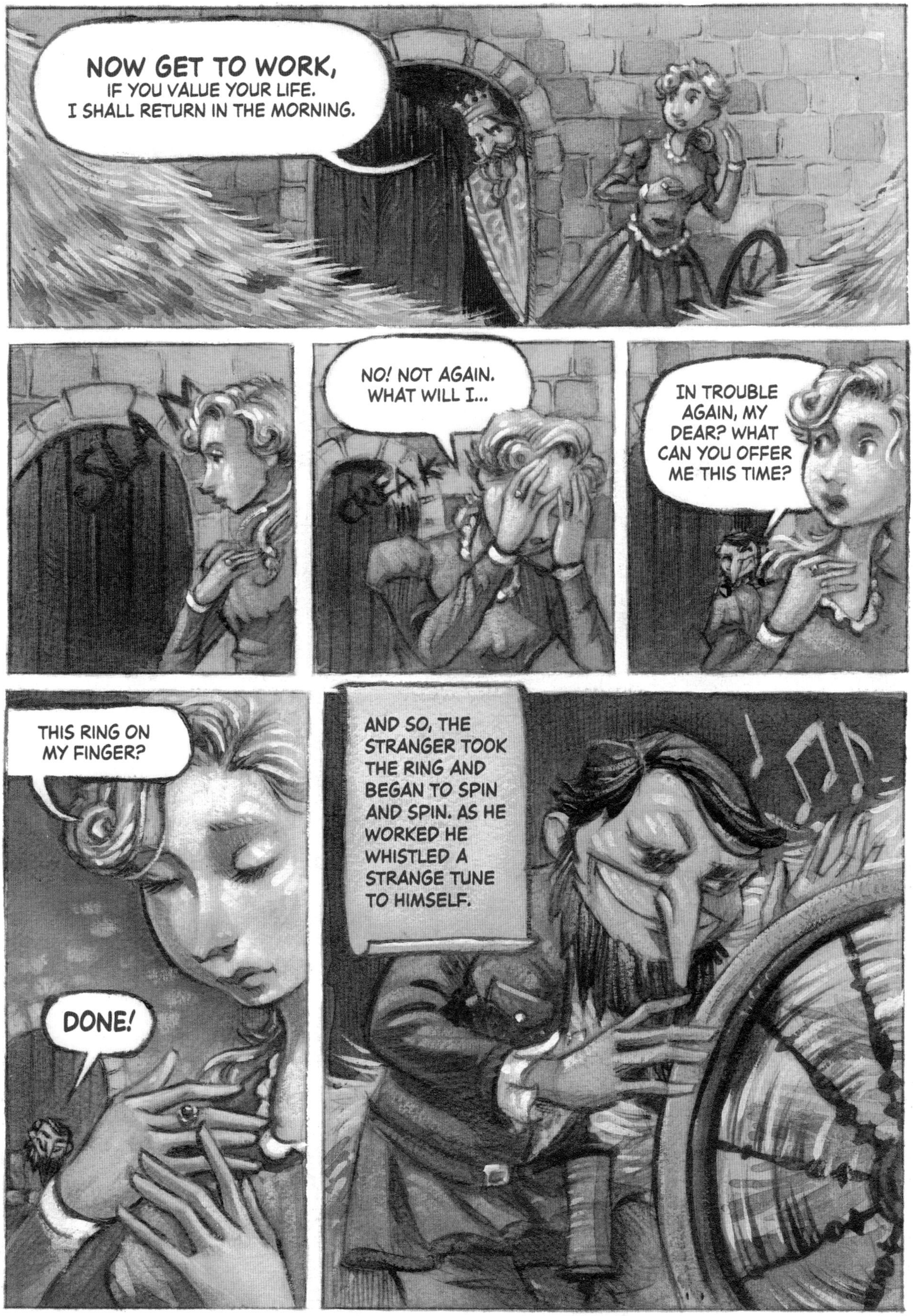
NOW GET TO WORK,
IF YOU VALUE YOUR LIFE.
I SHALL RETURN IN THE MORNING.
NO! NOT AGAIN.
WHAT WILL I...
CREAK
IN TROUBLE AGAIN, MY DEAR? WHAT CAN YOU OFFER ME THIS TIME?
THIS RING ON MY FINGER?
DONE!
AND SO, THE STRANGER TOOK THE RING AND BEGAN TO SPIN AND SPIN. AS HE WORKED HE WHISTLED A STRANGE TUNE TO HIMSELF.

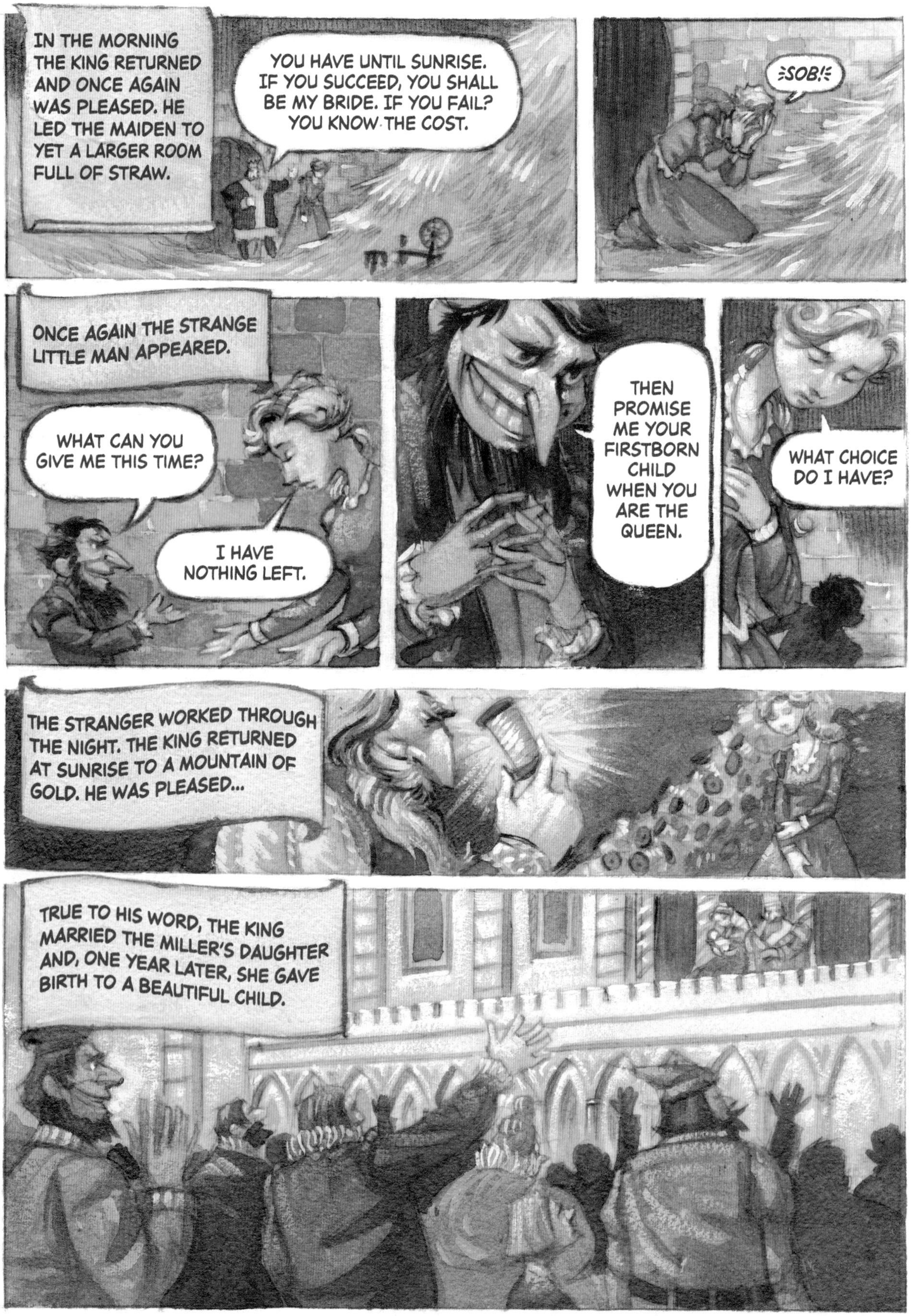
IN THE MORNING THE KING RETURNED AND ONCE AGAIN WAS PLEASED. HE LED THE MAIDEN TO YET A LARGER ROOM FULL OF STRAW.
YOU HAVE UNTIL SUNRISE. IF YOU SUCCEED, YOU SHALL BE MY BRIDE. IF YOU FAIL? YOU KNOW THE COST.
SOB!
ONCE AGAIN THE STRANGE LITTLE MAN APPEARED.
WHAT CAN YOU GIVE ME THIS TIME?
I HAVE NOTHING LEFT.
THEN PROMISE ME YOUR FIRSTBORN CHILD WHEN YOU ARE THE QUEEN.
WHAT CHOICE DO I HAVE?
THE STRANGER WORKED THROUGH THE NIGHT. THE KING RETURNED AT SUNRISE TO A MOUNTAIN OF GOLD. HE WAS PLEASED...
TRUE TO HIS WORD, THE KING MARRIED THE MILLER'S DAUGHTER AND, ONE YEAR LATER, SHE GAVE BIRTH TO A BEAUTIFUL CHILD.

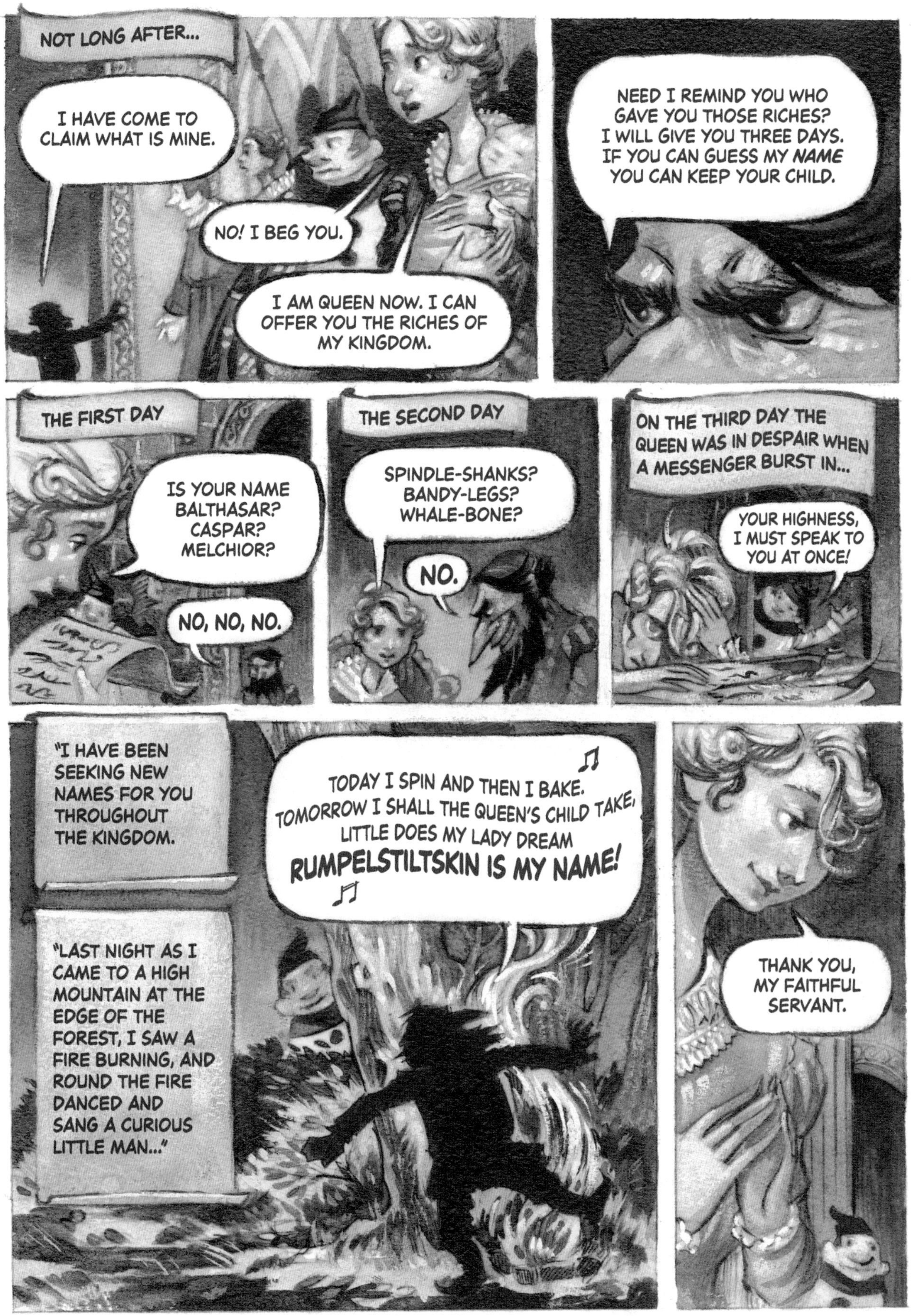
NOT LONG AFTER...
I HAVE COME TO CLAIM WHAT IS MINE.
NO! I BEG YOU.
I AM QUEEN NOW. I CAN OFFER YOU THE RICHES OF MY KINGDOM.
NEED I REMIND YOU WHO GAVE YOU THOSE RICHES? I WILL GIVE YOU THREE DAYS. IF YOU CAN GUESS MY *NAME* YOU CAN KEEP YOUR CHILD.
THE FIRST DAY
IS YOUR NAME BALTHASAR? CASPAR? MELCHIOR?
NO, NO, NO.
THE SECOND DAY
SPINDLE-SHANKS? BANDY-LEGS? WHALE-BONE?
NO.
ON THE THIRD DAY THE QUEEN WAS IN DESPAIR WHEN A MESSENGER BURST IN...
YOUR HIGHNESS, I MUST SPEAK TO YOU AT ONCE!
"I HAVE BEEN SEEKING NEW NAMES FOR YOU THROUGHOUT THE KINGDOM.
"LAST NIGHT AS I CAME TO A HIGH MOUNTAIN AT THE EDGE OF THE FOREST, I SAW A FIRE BURNING, AND ROUND THE FIRE DANCED AND SANG A CURIOUS LITTLE MAN..."
TODAY I SPIN AND THEN I BAKE. TOMORROW I SHALL THE QUEEN'S CHILD TAKE, LITTLE DOES MY LADY DREAM **RUMPELSTILTSKIN IS MY NAME!**
THANK YOU, MY FAITHFUL SERVANT.

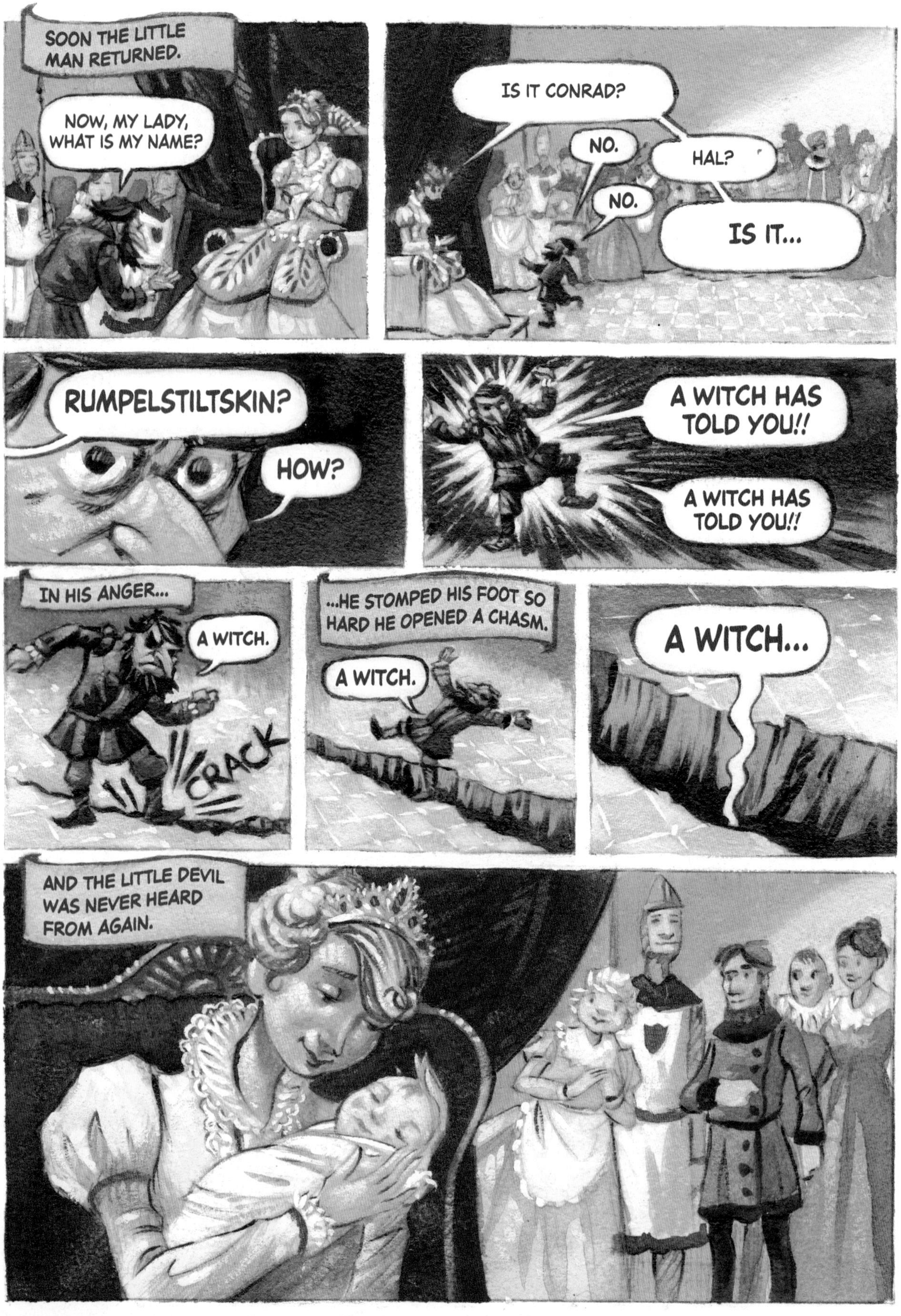
SOON THE LITTLE MAN RETURNED.
NOW, MY LADY, WHAT IS MY NAME?
IS IT CONRAD?
NO.
HAL?
NO.
IS IT...
RUMPELSTILTSKIN?
HOW?
A WITCH HAS TOLD YOU!!
A WITCH HAS TOLD YOU!!
IN HIS ANGER...
A WITCH.
CRACK
...HE STOMPED HIS FOOT SO HARD HE OPENED A CHASM.
A WITCH.
A WITCH...
AND THE LITTLE DEVIL WAS NEVER HEARD FROM AGAIN.

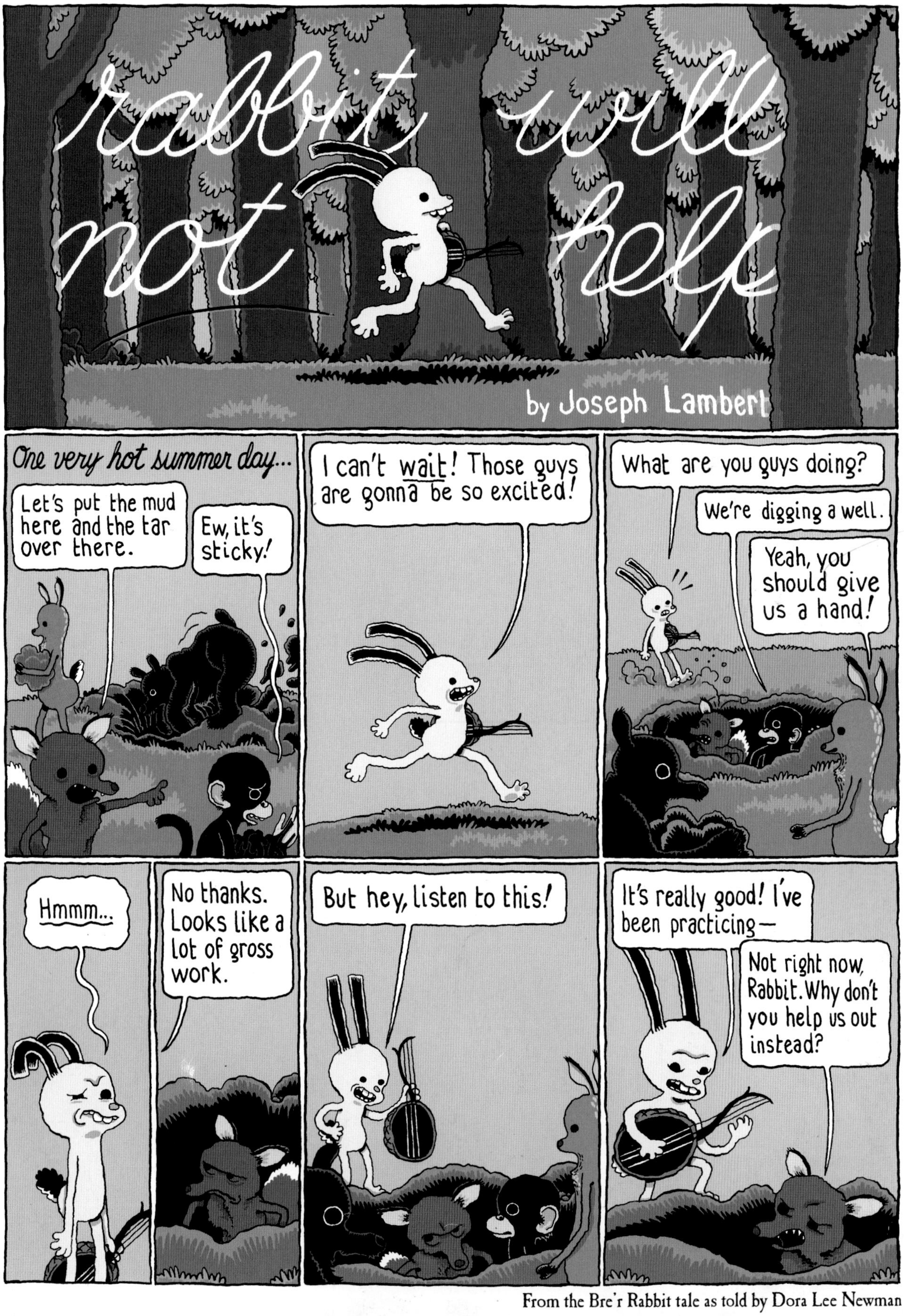
rabbit will not help
by Joseph Lambert
One very hot summer day...
Let's put the mud here and the tar over there.
Ew, it's sticky!
I can't wait! Those guys are gonna be so excited!
What are you guys doing?
We're digging a well.
Yeah, you should give us a hand!
Hmmm...
No thanks. Looks like a lot of gross work.
But hey, listen to this!
It's really good! I've been practicing—
Not right now, Rabbit. Why don't you help us out instead?

From the Bre'r Rabbit tale as told by Dora Lee Newman

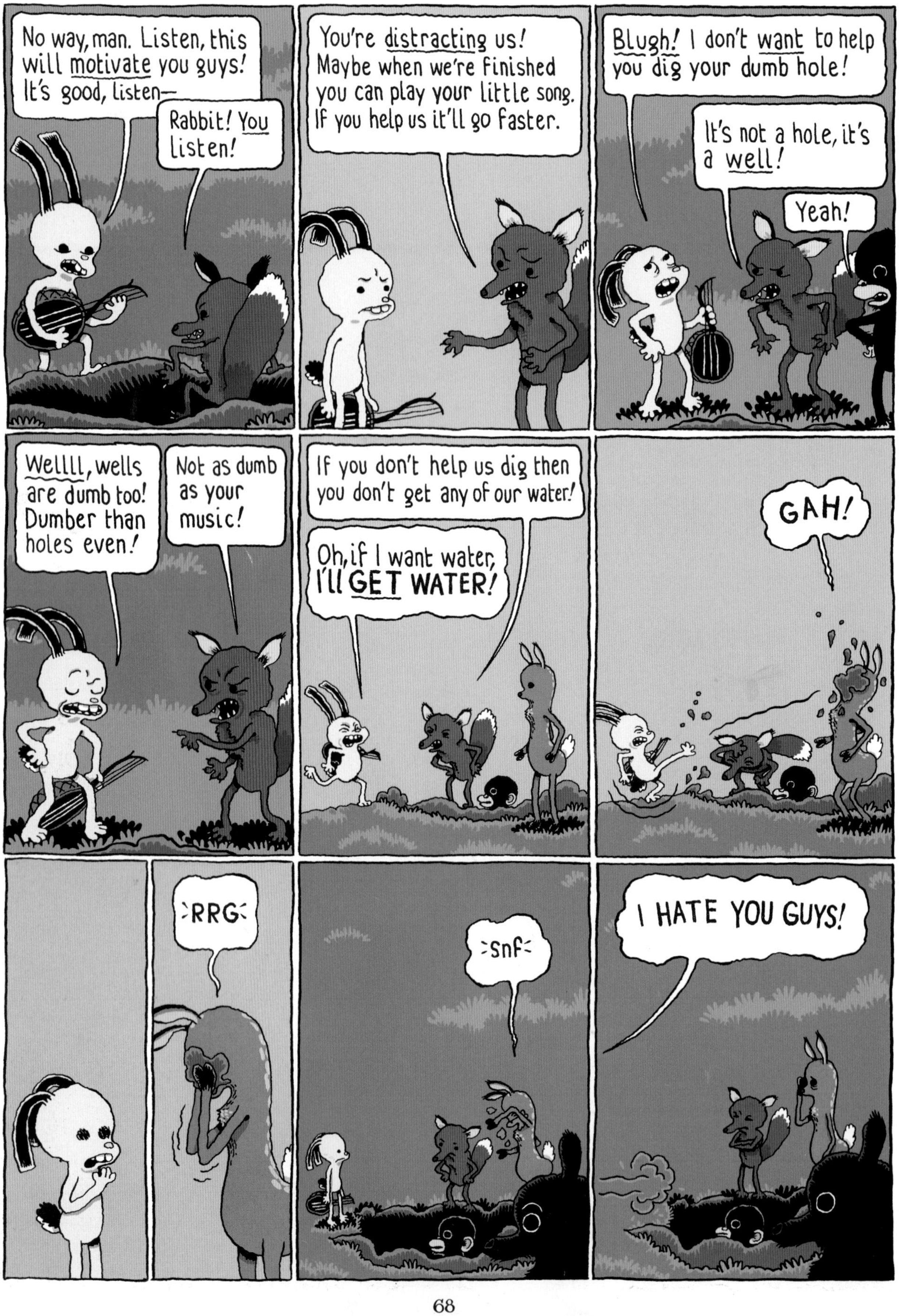
No way, man. Listen, this will motivate you guys! It's good, listen—
Rabbit! You listen!
You're distracting us! Maybe when we're finished you can play your little song. If you help us it'll go faster.
Blugh! I don't want to help you dig your dumb hole!
It's not a hole, it's a well!
Yeah!
Wellll, wells are dumb too! Dumber than holes even!
Not as dumb as your music!
If you don't help us dig then you don't get any of our water!
Oh, if I want water, I'll GET WATER!
GAH!
RRG
snf
I HATE YOU GUYS!

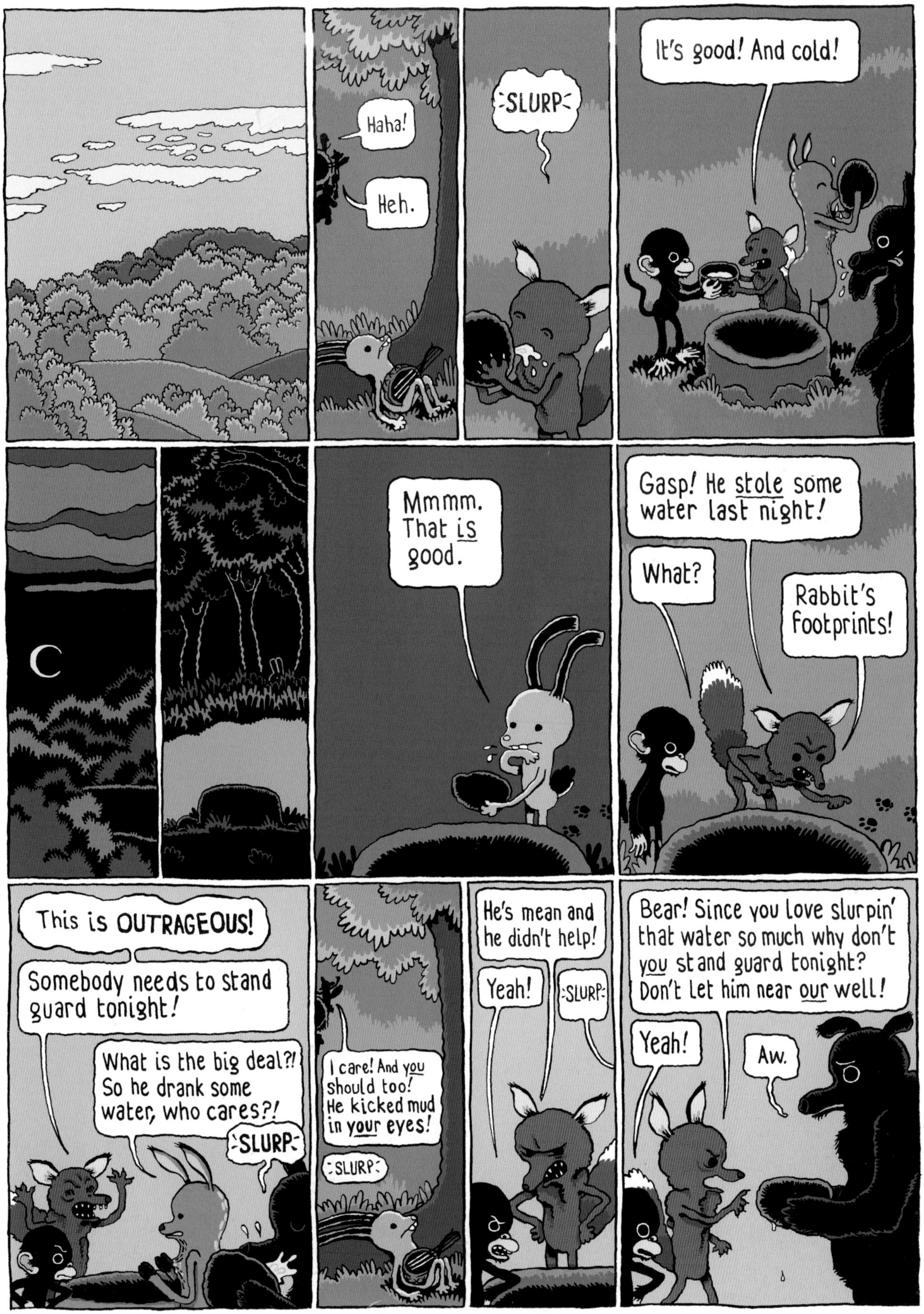

Haha!
Heh.
SLURP
It's good! And cold!
Mmmm. That is good.
Gasp! He stole some water last night!
What?
Rabbit's footprints!
This is OUTRAGEOUS!
Somebody needs to stand guard tonight!
What is the big deal?! So he drank some water, who cares?!
SLURP
I care! And you should too! He kicked mud in your eyes!
SLURP
He's mean and he didn't help!
Yeah!
SLURP
Bear! Since you love slurpin' that water so much why don't you stand guard tonight? Don't let him near our well!
Yeah!
Aw.

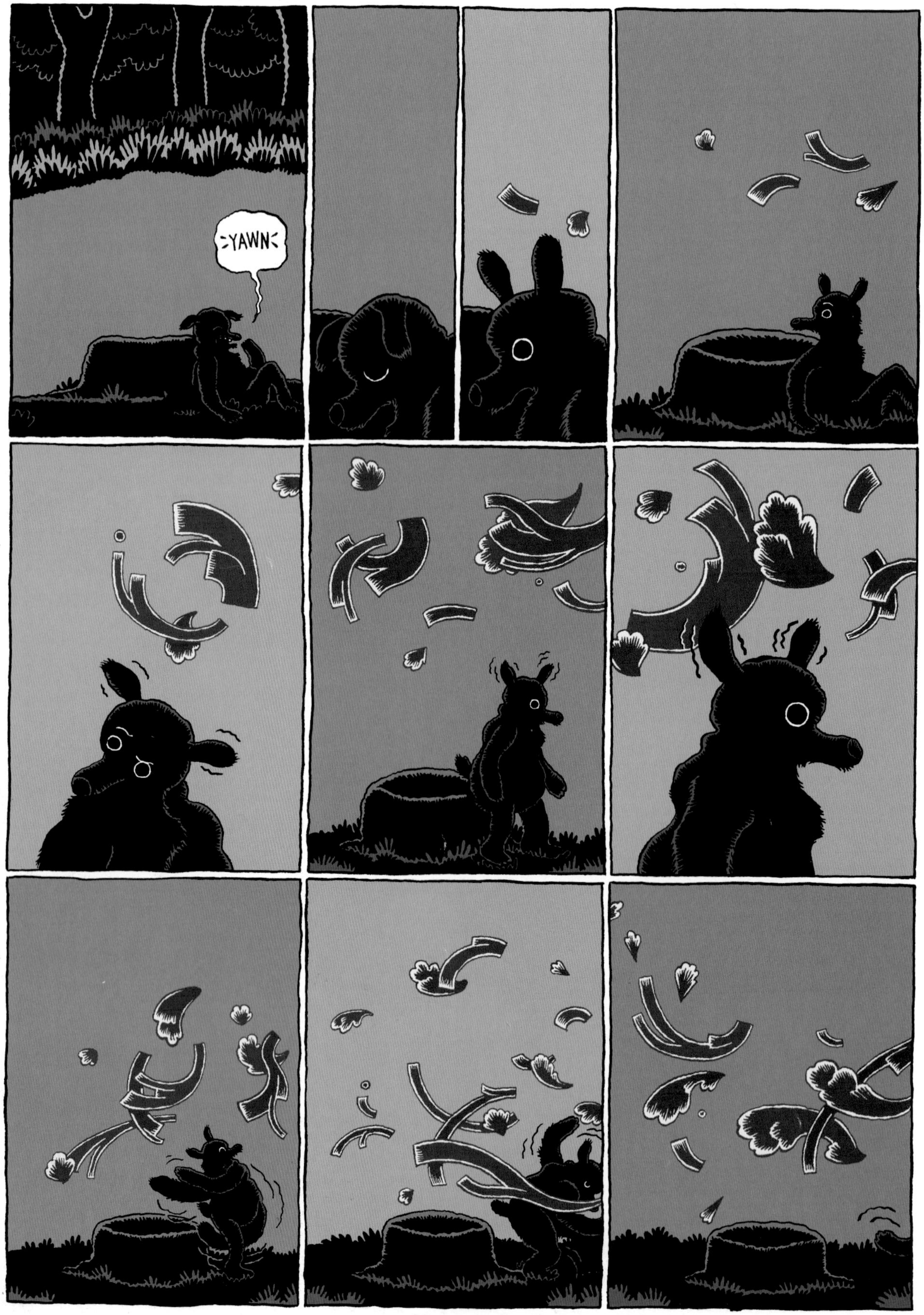
YAWN

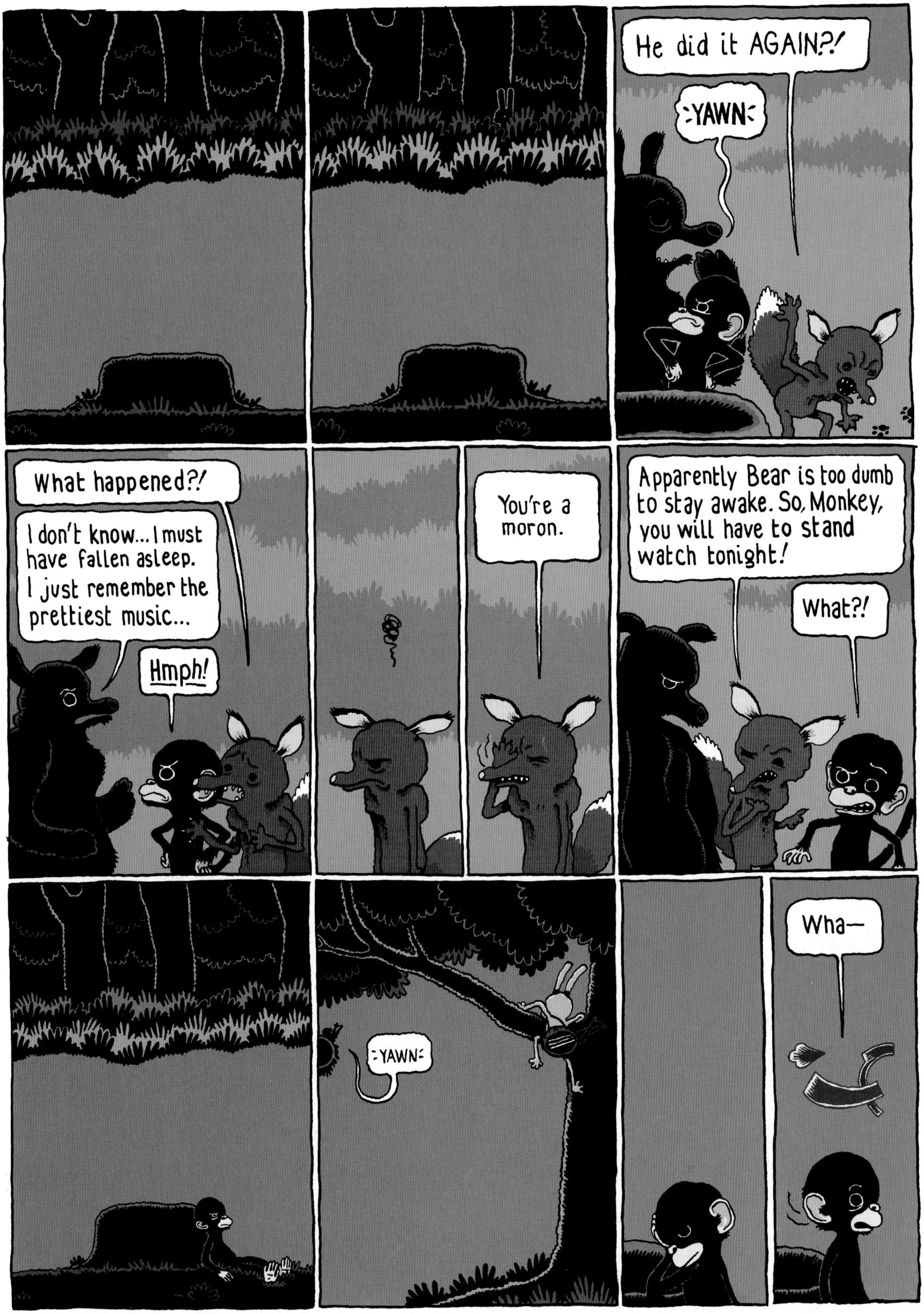
He did it AGAIN?!
YAWN
What happened?!
I don't know... I must have fallen asleep. I just remember the prettiest music...
Hmph!
You're a moron.
Apparently Bear is too dumb to stay awake. So, Monkey, you will have to stand watch tonight!
What?!
YAWN
Wha—

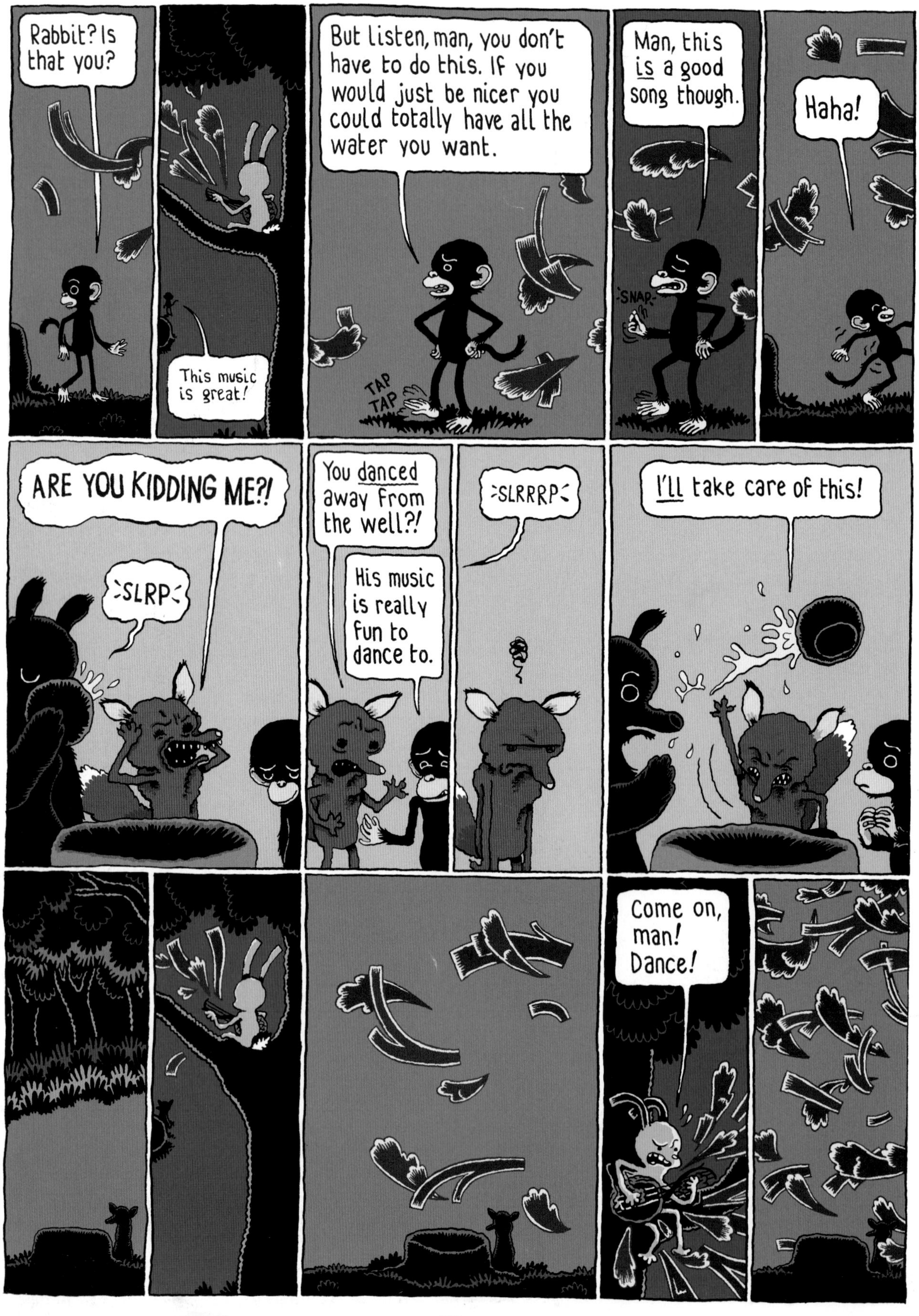
Rabbit? Is that you?
This music is great!
But listen, man, you don't have to do this. If you would just be nicer you could totally have all the water you want.
TAP TAP
Man, this is a good song though.
SNAP
Haha!
ARE YOU KIDDING ME?!
SLRP
You danced away from the well?!
His music is really fun to dance to.
SLRRRP
I'll take care of this!
Come on, man! Dance!

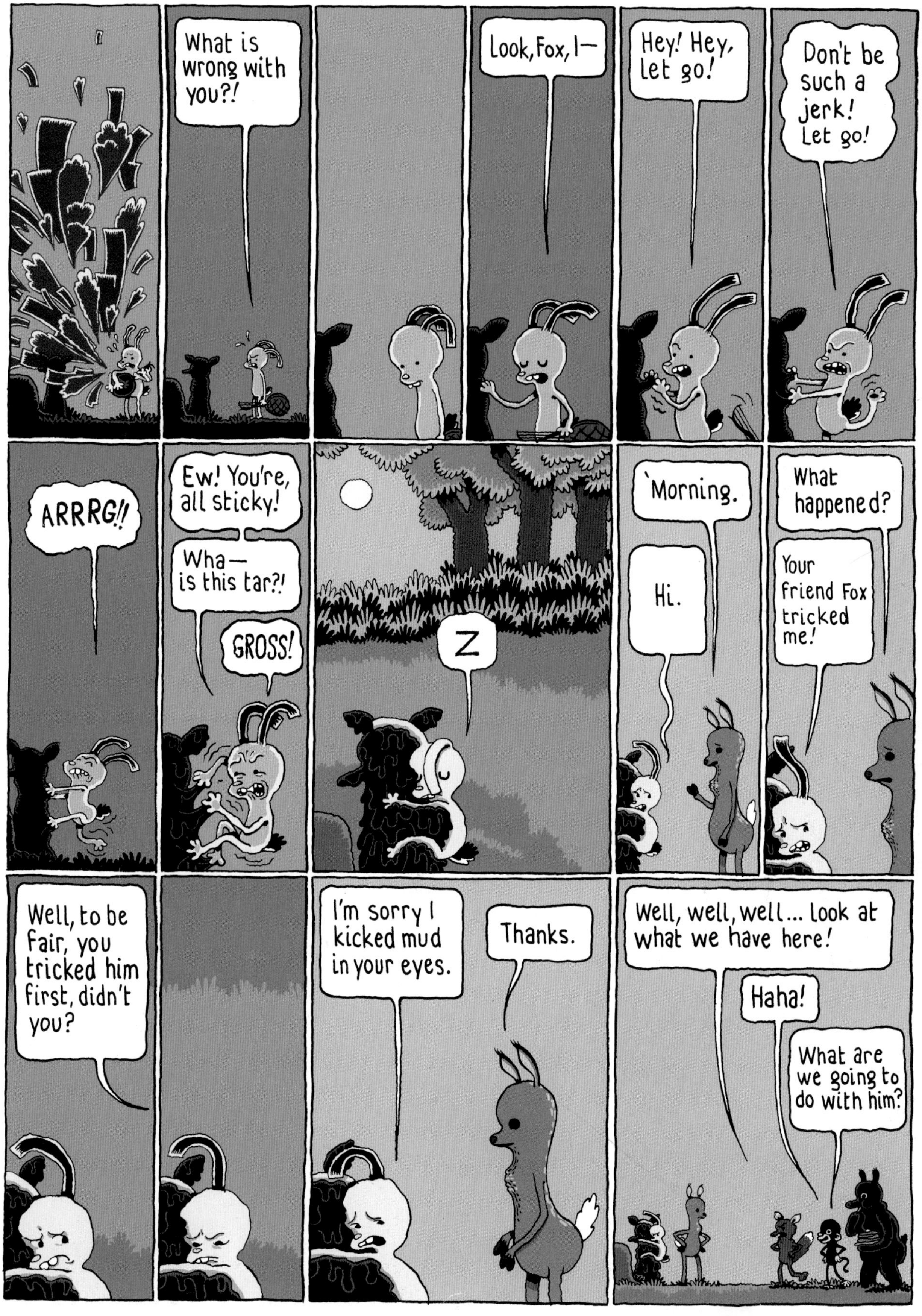
What is wrong with you?!
Look, Fox, I—
Hey! Hey, let go!
Don't be such a jerk! Let go!
ARRRG!!
Ew! You're, all sticky!
Wha— is this tar?!
GROSS!
Z
`Morning.
Hi.
What happened?
Your friend Fox tricked me!
Well, to be fair, you tricked him first, didn't you?
I'm sorry I kicked mud in your eyes.
Thanks.
Well, well, well... look at what we have here!
Haha!
What are we going to do with him?

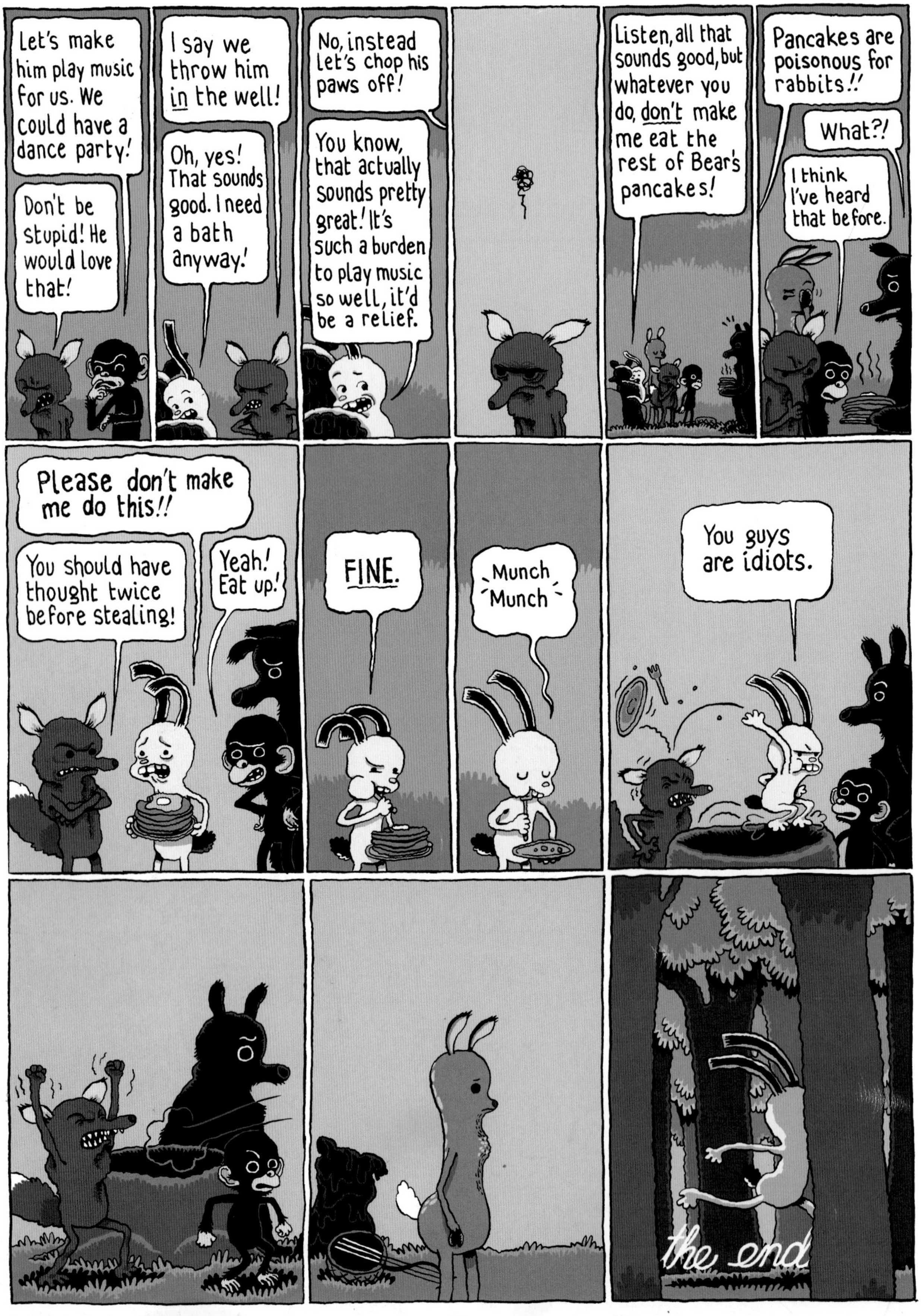
Let's make him play music for us. We could have a dance party!
Don't be stupid! He would love that!
I say we throw him in the well!
Oh, yes! That sounds good. I need a bath anyway!
No, instead let's chop his paws off!
You know, that actually sounds pretty great! It's such a burden to play music so well, it'd be a relief.
Listen, all that sounds good, but whatever you do, don't make me eat the rest of Bear's pancakes!
Pancakes are poisonous for rabbits!!
What?!
I think I've heard that before.
Please don't make me do this!!
You should have thought twice before stealing!
Yeah! Eat up!
FINE.
Munch
Munch
You guys are idiots.
the end

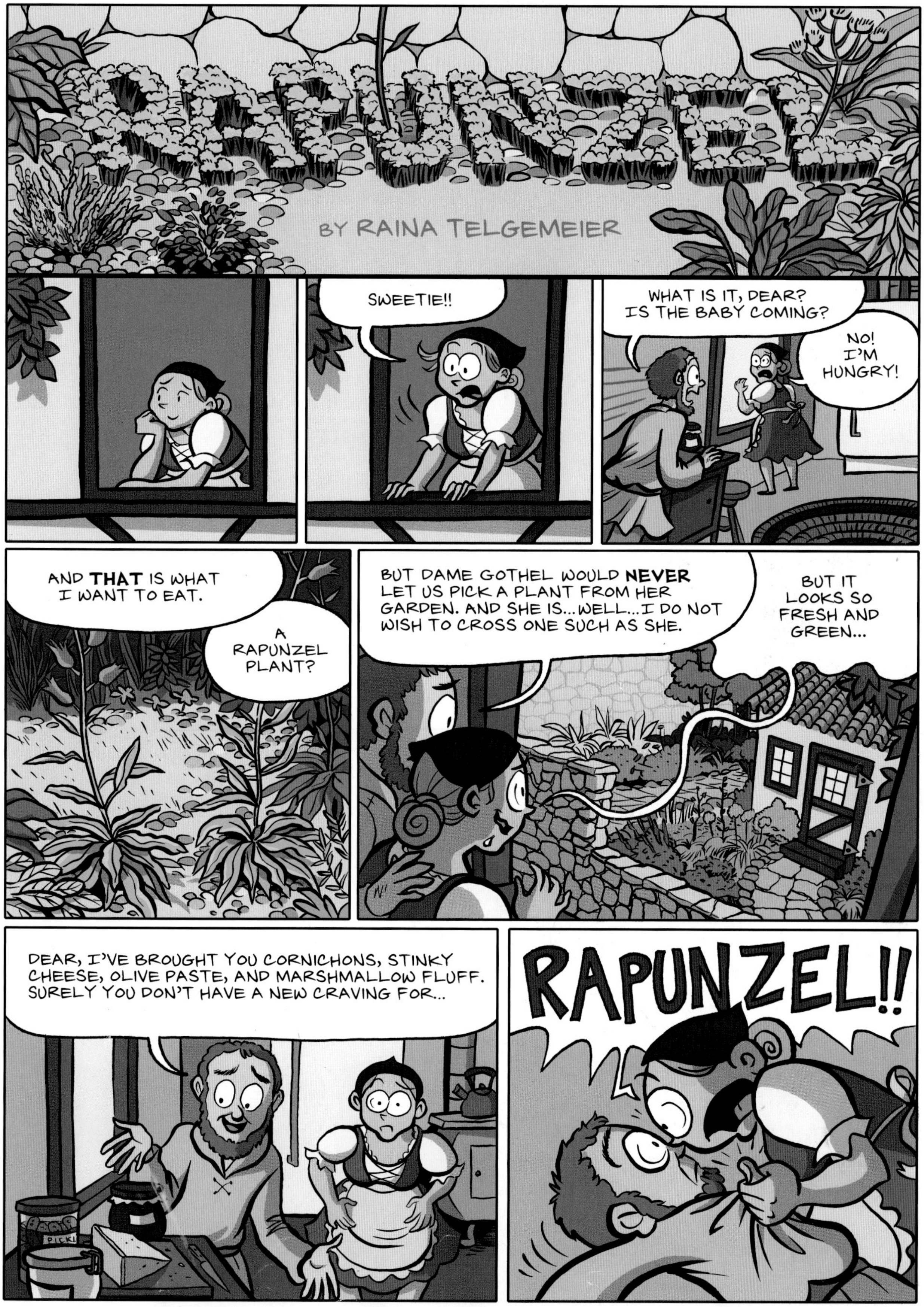
RAPUNZEL
BY RAINA TELGEMEIER
SWEETIE!!
WHAT IS IT, DEAR? IS THE BABY COMING?
NO! I'M HUNGRY!
AND **THAT** IS WHAT I WANT TO EAT.
A RAPUNZEL PLANT?
BUT DAME GOTHEL WOULD **NEVER** LET US PICK A PLANT FROM HER GARDEN. AND SHE IS...WELL...I DO NOT WISH TO CROSS ONE SUCH AS SHE.
BUT IT LOOKS SO FRESH AND GREEN...
DEAR, I'VE BROUGHT YOU CORNICHONS, STINKY CHEESE, OLIVE PASTE, AND MARSHMALLOW FLUFF. SURELY YOU DON'T HAVE A NEW CRAVING FOR...
RAPUNZEL!!



From the Brothers Grimm

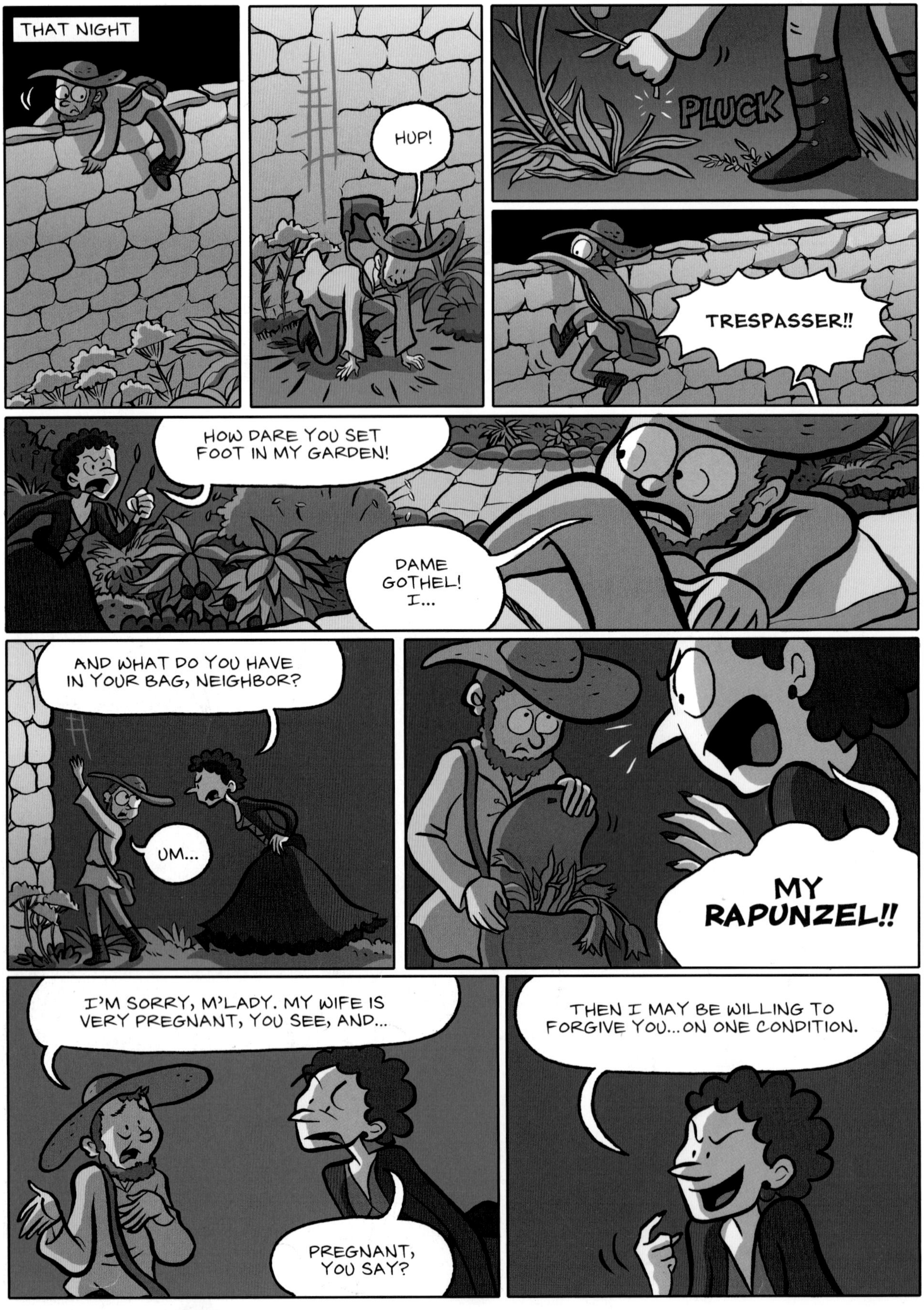
THAT NIGHT
HUP!
PLUCK
TRESPASSER!!
HOW DARE YOU SET FOOT IN MY GARDEN!
DAME GOTHEL! I...
AND WHAT DO YOU HAVE IN YOUR BAG, NEIGHBOR?
UM...
MY RAPUNZEL!!
I'M SORRY, M'LADY. MY WIFE IS VERY PREGNANT, YOU SEE, AND...
PREGNANT, YOU SAY?
THEN I MAY BE WILLING TO FORGIVE YOU...ON ONE CONDITION.

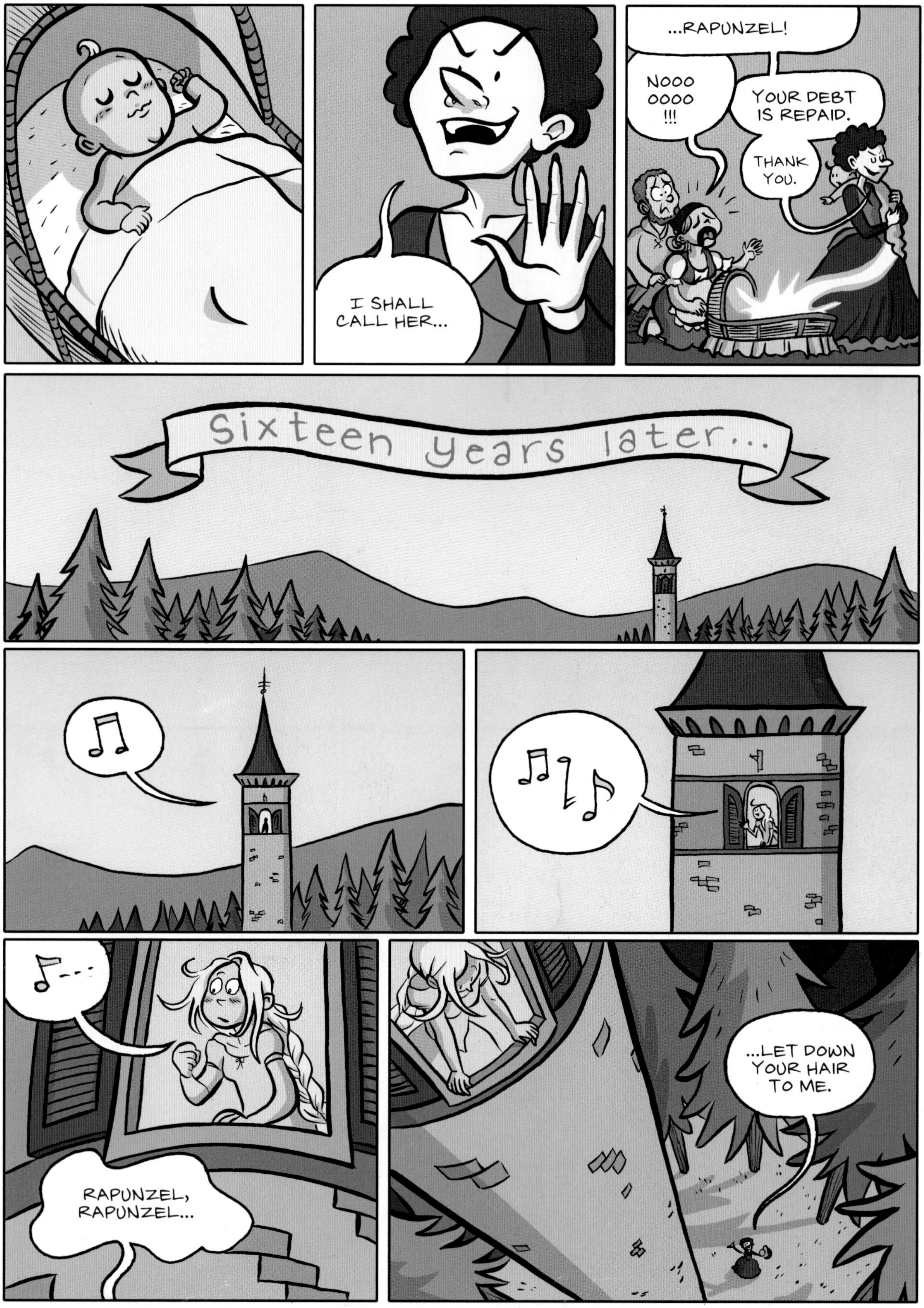
I SHALL CALL HER...
...RAPUNZEL!
NOOO OOOO !!!
YOUR DEBT IS REPAID.
THANK YOU.
Sixteen years later...
RAPUNZEL, RAPUNZEL...
...LET DOWN YOUR HAIR TO ME.

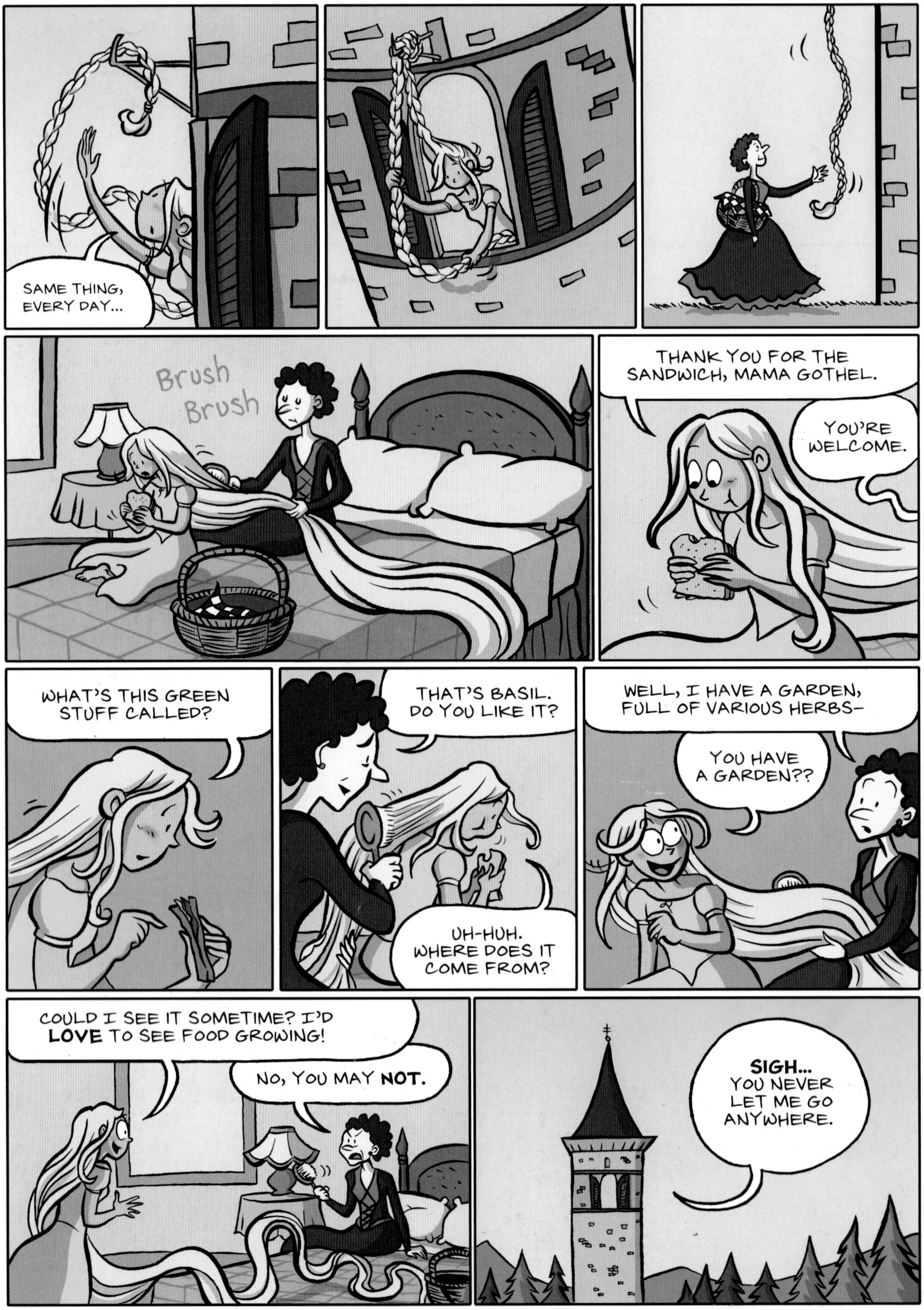

SAME THING, EVERY DAY...
Brush Brush
THANK YOU FOR THE SANDWICH, MAMA GOTHEL.
YOU'RE WELCOME.
WHAT'S THIS GREEN STUFF CALLED?
THAT'S BASIL. DO YOU LIKE IT?
UH-HUH. WHERE DOES IT COME FROM?
WELL, I HAVE A GARDEN, FULL OF VARIOUS HERBS–
YOU HAVE A GARDEN??
COULD I SEE IT SOMETIME? I'D **LOVE** TO SEE FOOD GROWING!
NO, YOU MAY **NOT**.
**SIGH...** YOU NEVER LET ME GO ANYWHERE.

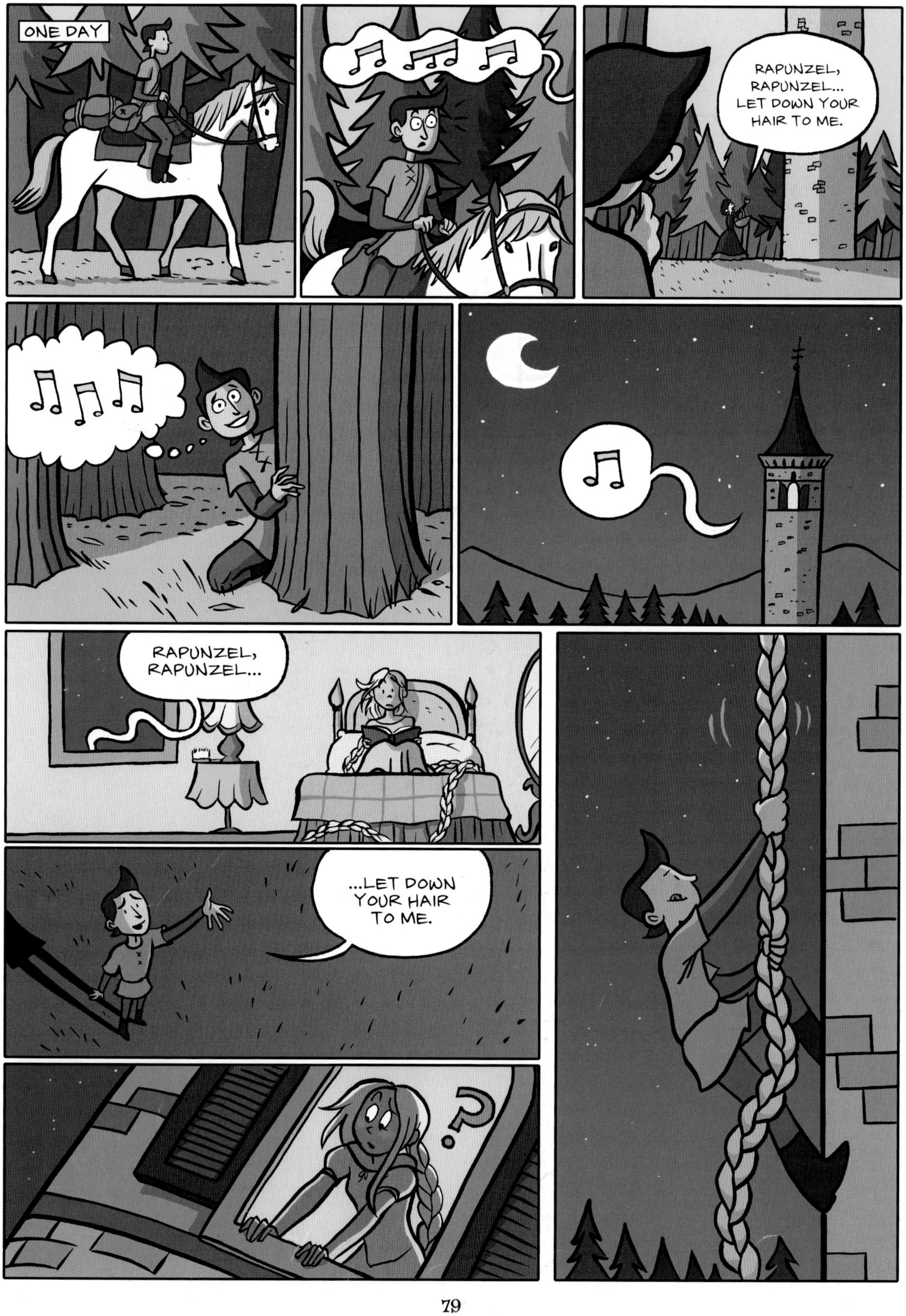
ONE DAY
RAPUNZEL, RAPUNZEL... LET DOWN YOUR HAIR TO ME.
RAPUNZEL, RAPUNZEL...
...LET DOWN YOUR HAIR TO ME.
?

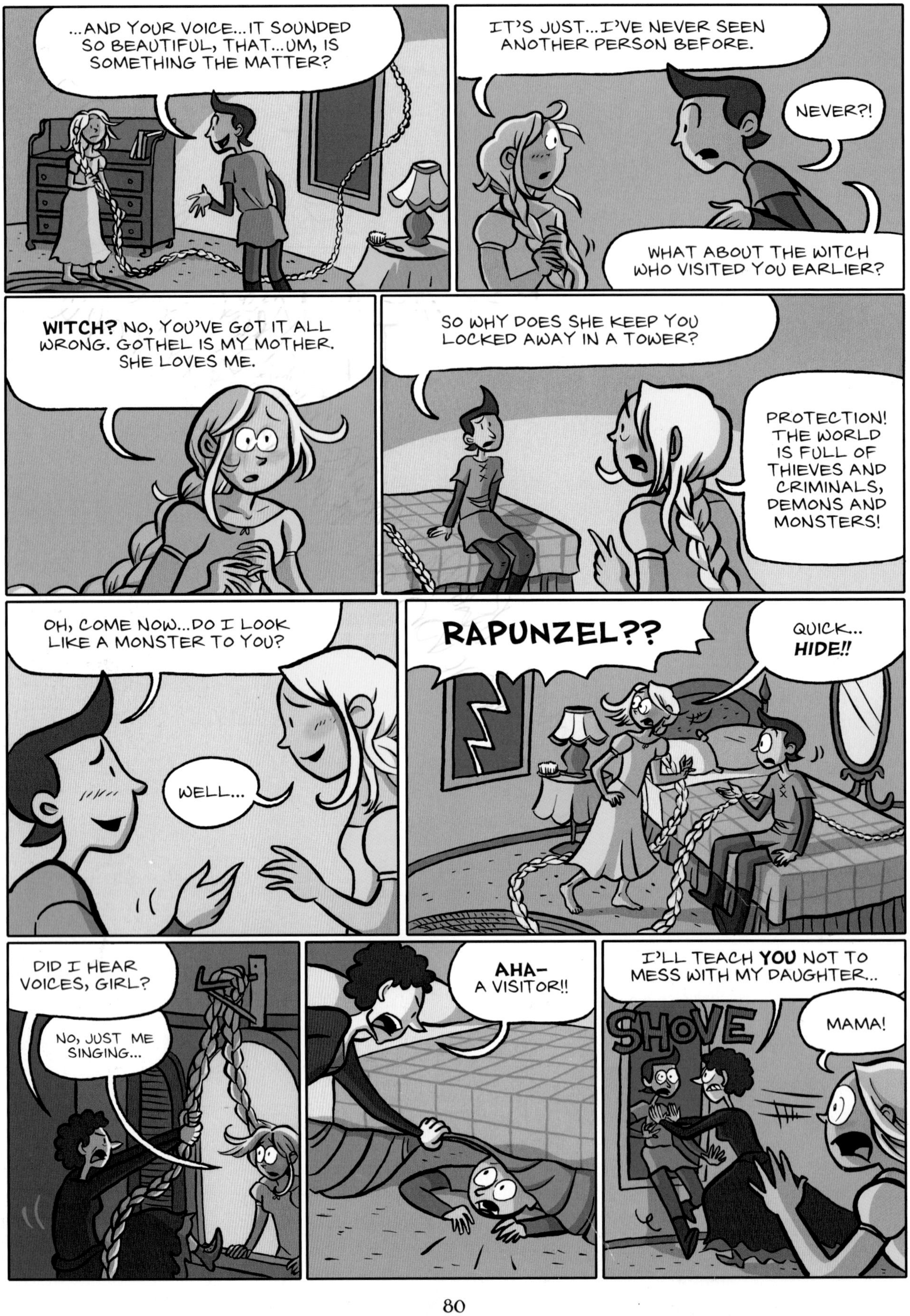

...AND YOUR VOICE...IT SOUNDED SO BEAUTIFUL, THAT...UM, IS SOMETHING THE MATTER?
IT'S JUST...I'VE NEVER SEEN ANOTHER PERSON BEFORE.
NEVER?!
WHAT ABOUT THE WITCH WHO VISITED YOU EARLIER?
WITCH? NO, YOU'VE GOT IT ALL WRONG. GOTHEL IS MY MOTHER. SHE LOVES ME.
SO WHY DOES SHE KEEP YOU LOCKED AWAY IN A TOWER?
PROTECTION! THE WORLD IS FULL OF THIEVES AND CRIMINALS, DEMONS AND MONSTERS!
OH, COME NOW...DO I LOOK LIKE A MONSTER TO YOU?
WELL...
RAPUNZEL??
QUICK... HIDE!!
DID I HEAR VOICES, GIRL?
NO, JUST ME SINGING...
AHA- A VISITOR!!
I'LL TEACH YOU NOT TO MESS WITH MY DAUGHTER...
SHOVE
MAMA!

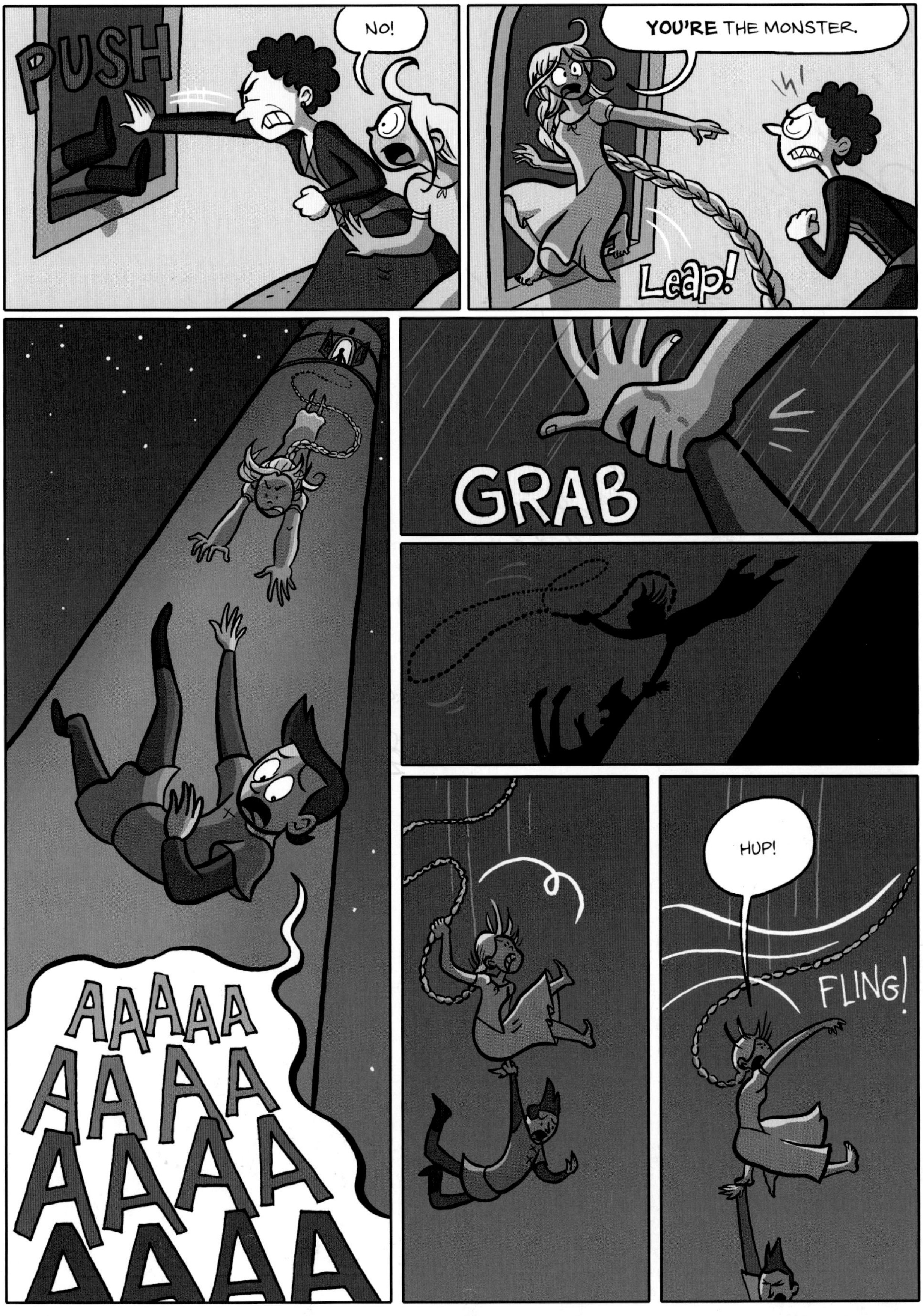
PUSH
NO!
YOU'RE THE MONSTER.
Leap!
GRAB
AAAAA
AAAA
AAAA
AAAA
HUP!
FLING!

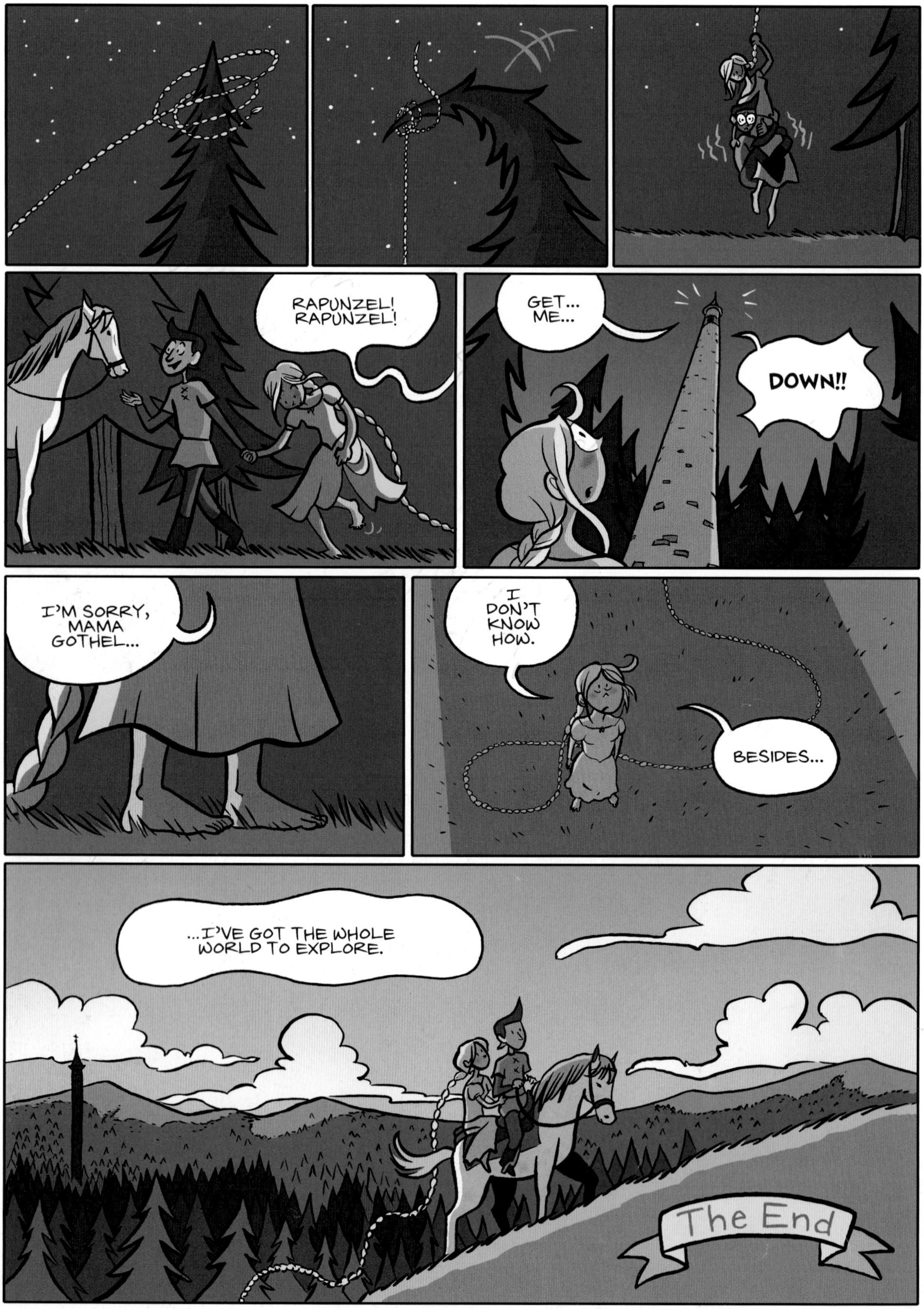
RAPUNZEL! RAPUNZEL!
GET... ME...
DOWN!!
I'M SORRY, MAMA GOTHEL...
I DON'T KNOW HOW.
BESIDES...
...I'VE GOT THE WHOLE WORLD TO EXPLORE.
The End

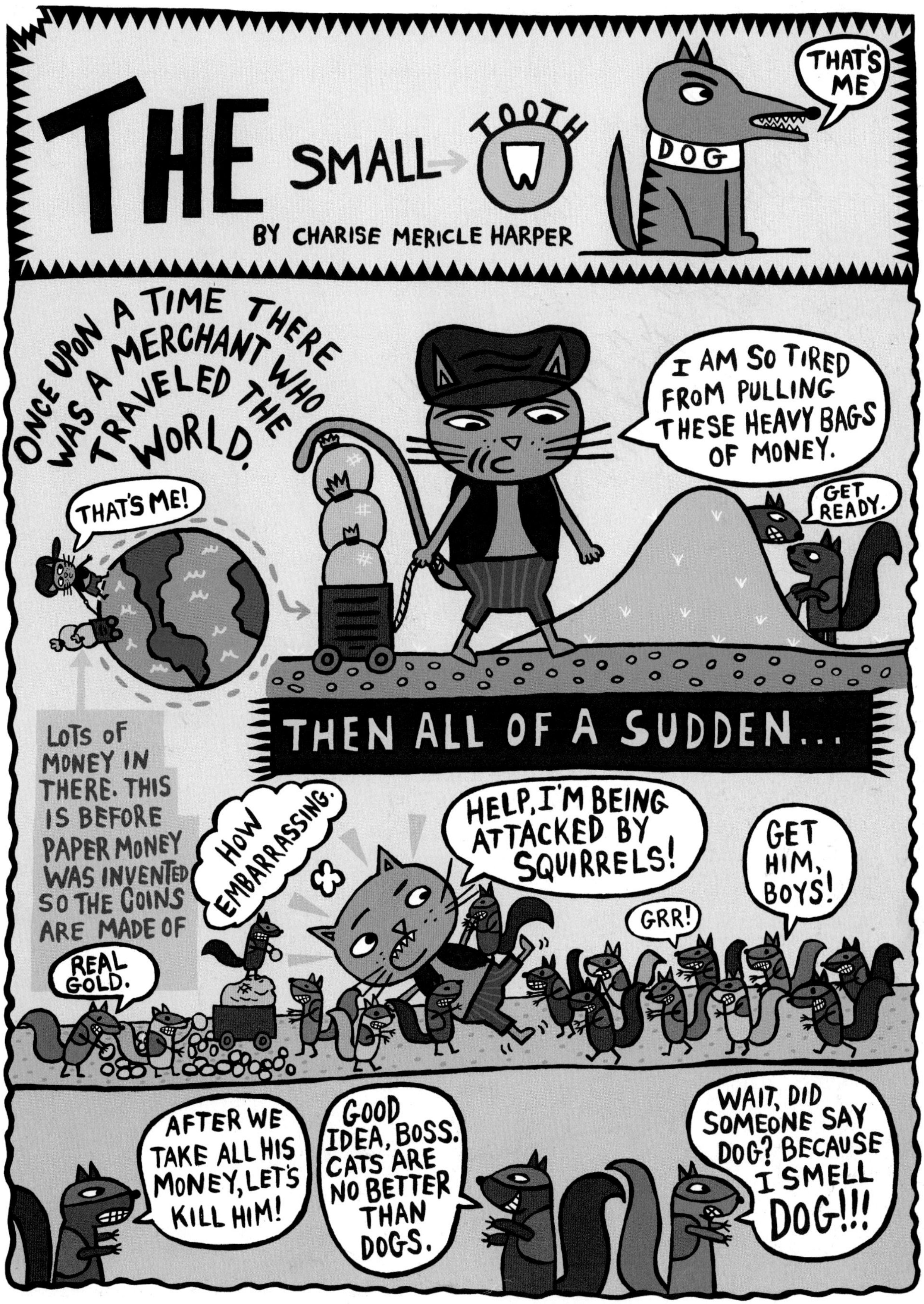

THE SMALL TOOTH DOG
THAT'S ME
BY CHARISE MERICLE HARPER
ONCE UPON A TIME THERE WAS A MERCHANT WHO TRAVELED THE WORLD.
THAT'S ME!
I AM SO TIRED FROM PULLING THESE HEAVY BAGS OF MONEY.
GET READY.
LOTS OF MONEY IN THERE. THIS IS BEFORE PAPER MONEY WAS INVENTED SO THE COINS ARE MADE OF
REAL GOLD.
THEN ALL OF A SUDDEN...
HOW EMBARRASSING.
HELP, I'M BEING ATTACKED BY SQUIRRELS!
GRR!
GET HIM, BOYS!
AFTER WE TAKE ALL HIS MONEY, LET'S KILL HIM!
GOOD IDEA, BOSS. CATS ARE NO BETTER THAN DOGS.
WAIT, DID SOMEONE SAY DOG? BECAUSE I SMELL DOG!!!




From the English tale as told by Sidney Oldall Addy

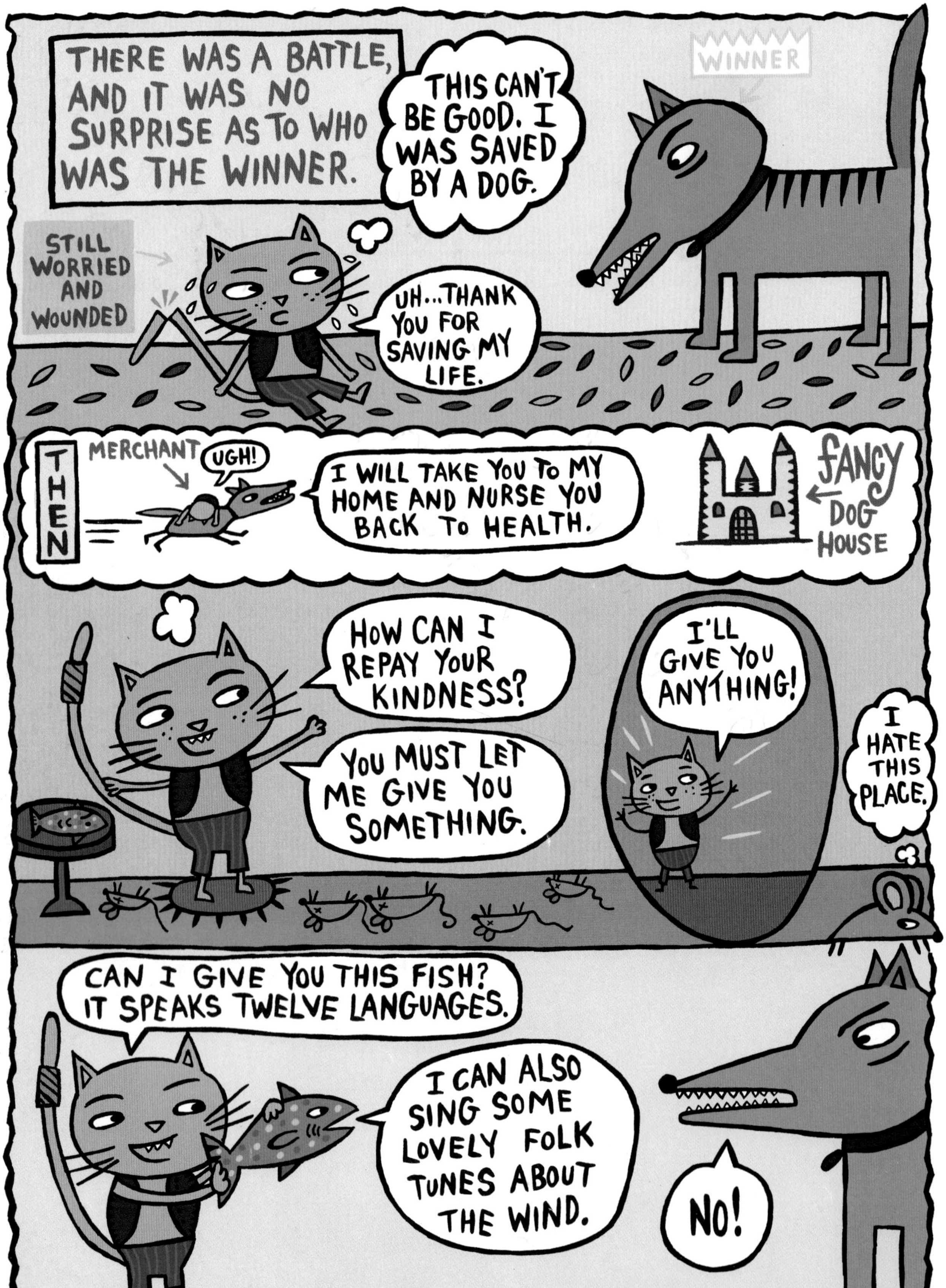

THERE WAS A BATTLE, AND IT WAS NO SURPRISE AS TO WHO WAS THE WINNER.
THIS CAN'T BE GOOD. I WAS SAVED BY A DOG.
WINNER
STILL WORRIED AND WOUNDED
UH...THANK YOU FOR SAVING MY LIFE.
THEN
MERCHANT
UGH!
I WILL TAKE YOU TO MY HOME AND NURSE YOU BACK TO HEALTH.
FANCY DOG HOUSE
HOW CAN I REPAY YOUR KINDNESS?
YOU MUST LET ME GIVE YOU SOMETHING.
I'LL GIVE YOU ANYTHING!
I HATE THIS PLACE.
CAN I GIVE YOU THIS FISH? IT SPEAKS TWELVE LANGUAGES.
I CAN ALSO SING SOME LOVELY FOLK TUNES ABOUT THE WIND.
NO!

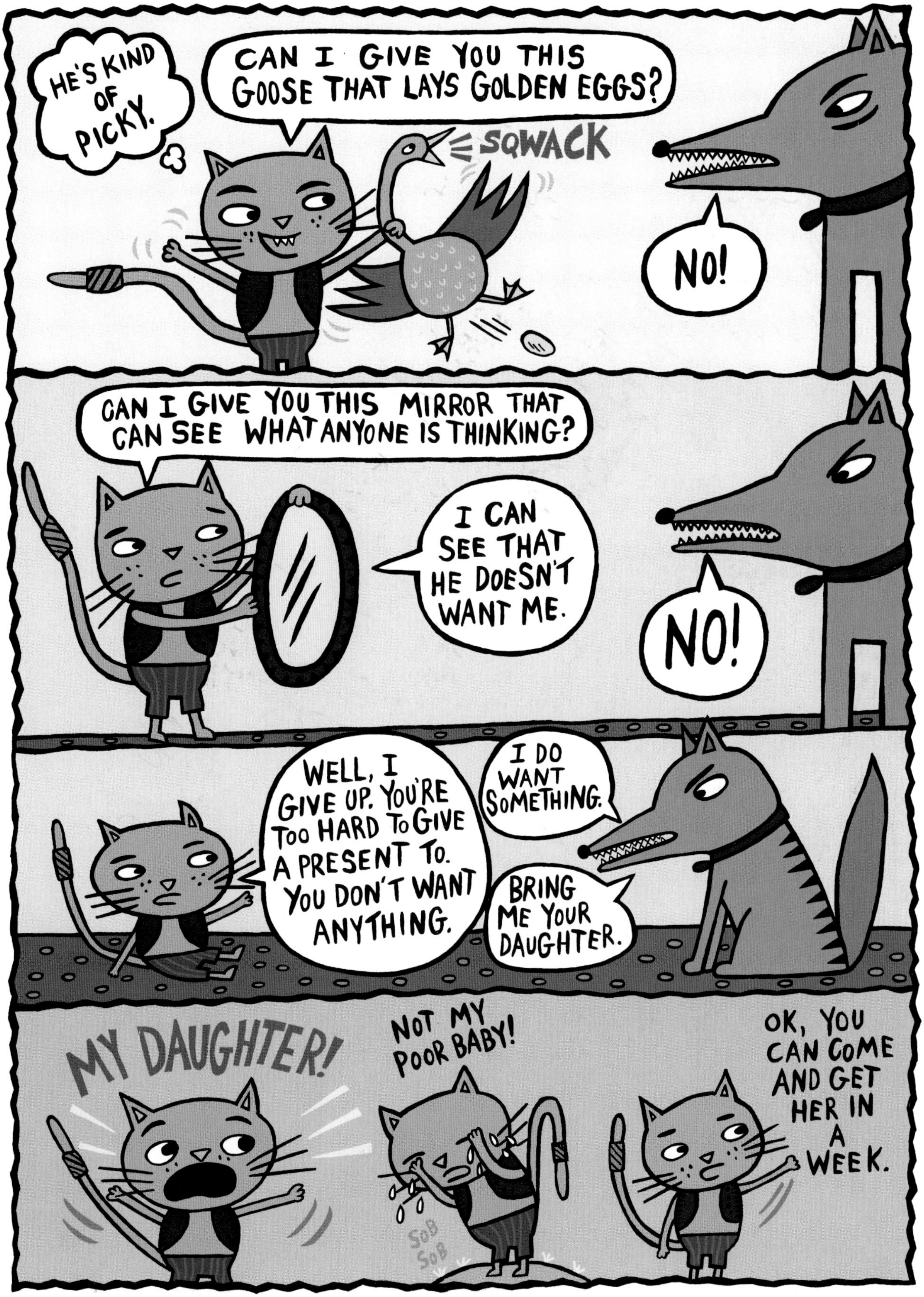
HE'S KIND OF PICKY.
CAN I GIVE YOU THIS GOOSE THAT LAYS GOLDEN EGGS?
SQWACK
NO!
CAN I GIVE YOU THIS MIRROR THAT CAN SEE WHAT ANYONE IS THINKING?
I CAN SEE THAT HE DOESN'T WANT ME.
NO!
WELL, I GIVE UP. YOU'RE TOO HARD TO GIVE A PRESENT TO. YOU DON'T WANT ANYTHING.
I DO WANT SOMETHING.
BRING ME YOUR DAUGHTER.
MY DAUGHTER!
NOT MY POOR BABY!
SOB SOB
OK, YOU CAN COME AND GET HER IN A WEEK.

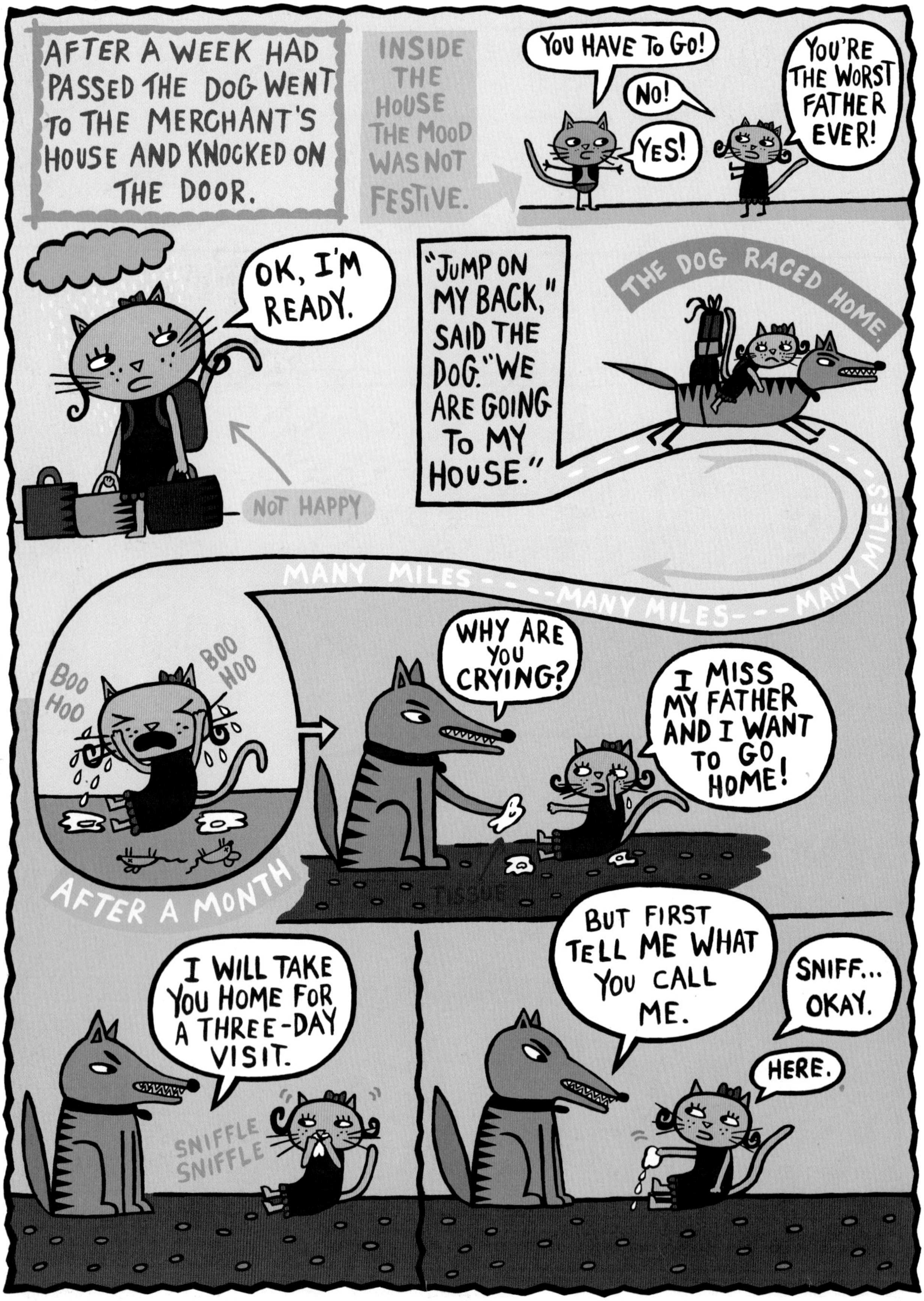
AFTER A WEEK HAD PASSED THE DOG WENT TO THE MERCHANT'S HOUSE AND KNOCKED ON THE DOOR.
INSIDE THE HOUSE THE MOOD WAS NOT FESTIVE.
YOU HAVE TO GO!
NO!
YES!
YOU'RE THE WORST FATHER EVER!
OK, I'M READY.
NOT HAPPY
"JUMP ON MY BACK," SAID THE DOG. "WE ARE GOING TO MY HOUSE."
THE DOG RACED HOME.
MANY MILES - - - MANY MILES - - - MANY MILES - - - MANY MILES
AFTER A MONTH
BOO HOO
BOO HOO
WHY ARE YOU CRYING?
I MISS MY FATHER AND I WANT TO GO HOME!
TISSUE
I WILL TAKE YOU HOME FOR A THREE-DAY VISIT.
SNIFFLE SNIFFLE
BUT FIRST TELL ME WHAT YOU CALL ME.
SNIFF... OKAY.
HERE.

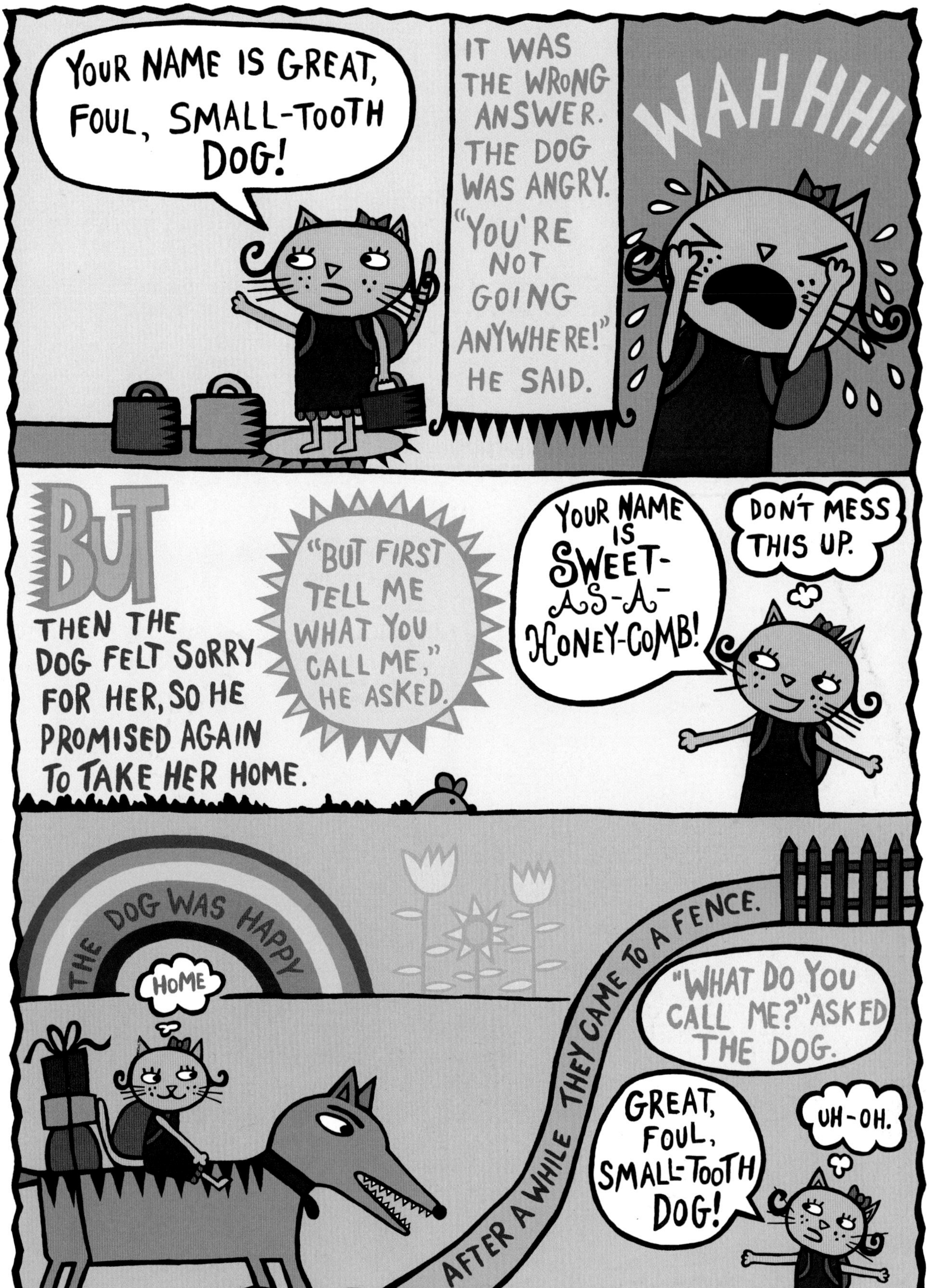
YOUR NAME IS GREAT, FOUL, SMALL-TOOTH DOG!
IT WAS THE WRONG ANSWER. THE DOG WAS ANGRY. "YOU'RE NOT GOING ANYWHERE!" HE SAID.
WAHHH!
BUT THEN THE DOG FELT SORRY FOR HER, SO HE PROMISED AGAIN TO TAKE HER HOME.
"BUT FIRST TELL ME WHAT YOU CALL ME," HE ASKED.
YOUR NAME IS SWEET-AS-A-HONEY-COMB!
DON'T MESS THIS UP.
THE DOG WAS HAPPY
HOME
AFTER A WHILE THEY CAME TO A FENCE.
"WHAT DO YOU CALL ME?" ASKED THE DOG.
GREAT, FOUL, SMALL-TOOTH DOG!
UH-OH.

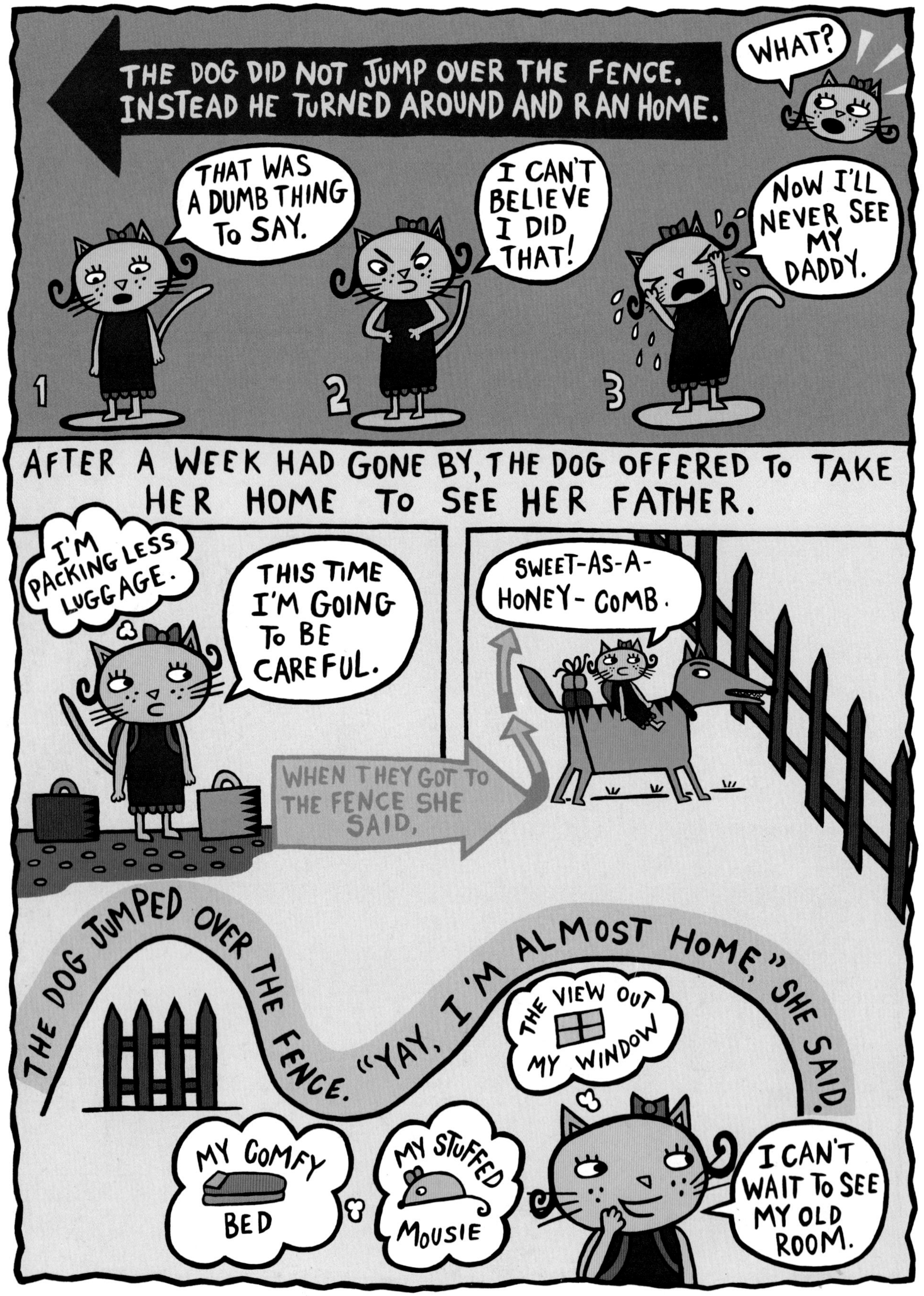
THE DOG DID NOT JUMP OVER THE FENCE. INSTEAD HE TURNED AROUND AND RAN HOME.
WHAT?
THAT WAS A DUMB THING TO SAY.
I CAN'T BELIEVE I DID THAT!
NOW I'LL NEVER SEE MY DADDY.
1
2
3
AFTER A WEEK HAD GONE BY, THE DOG OFFERED TO TAKE HER HOME TO SEE HER FATHER.
I'M PACKING LESS LUGGAGE.
THIS TIME I'M GOING TO BE CAREFUL.
WHEN THEY GOT TO THE FENCE SHE SAID,
SWEET-AS-A-HONEY-COMB.
THE DOG JUMPED OVER THE FENCE. "YAY, I'M ALMOST HOME," SHE SAID.
THE VIEW OUT MY WINDOW
MY COMFY BED
MY STUFFED MOUSIE
I CAN'T WAIT TO SEE MY OLD ROOM.

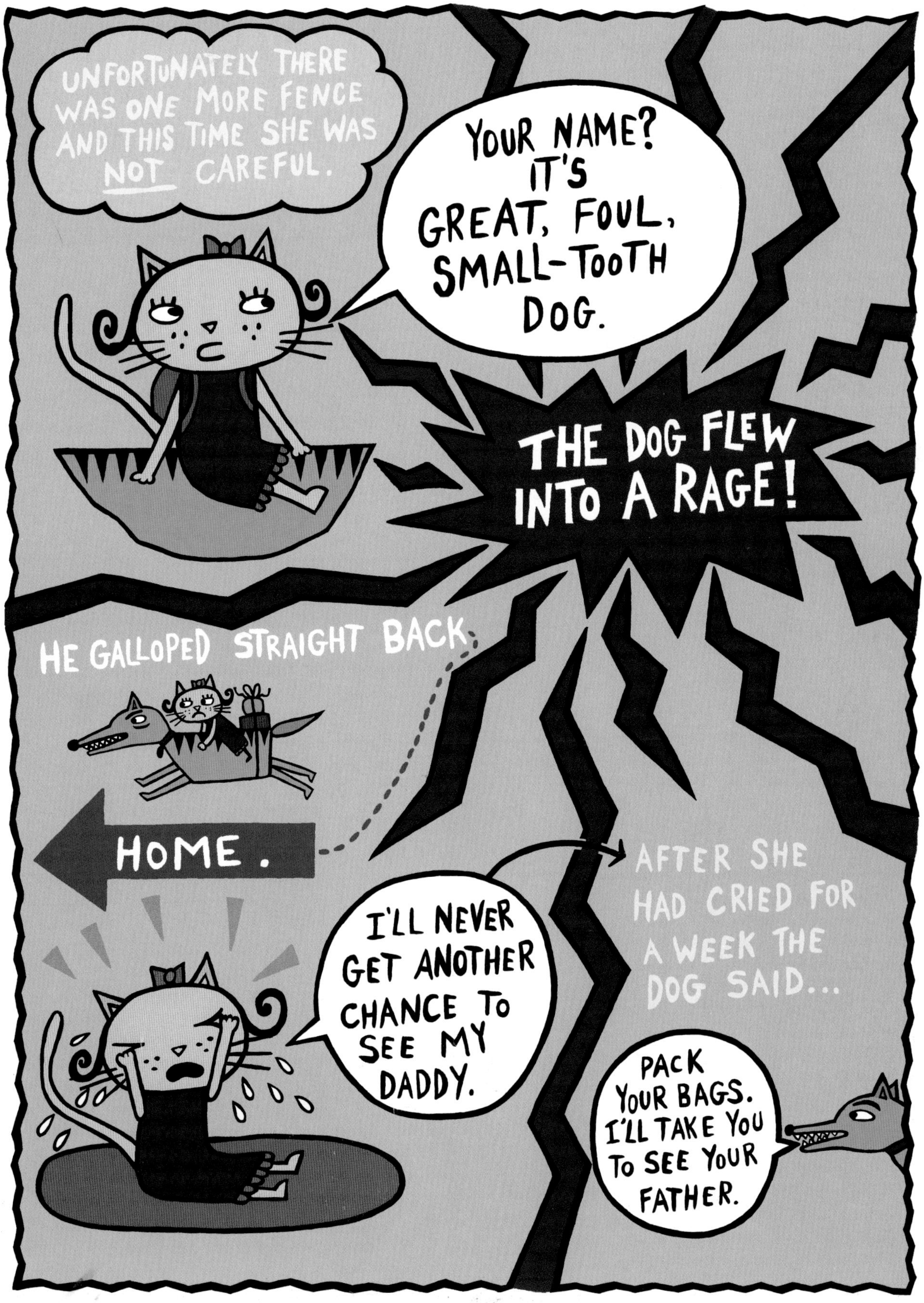
UNFORTUNATELY THERE WAS ONE MORE FENCE AND THIS TIME SHE WAS NOT CAREFUL.
YOUR NAME? IT'S GREAT, FOUL, SMALL-TOOTH DOG.
THE DOG FLEW INTO A RAGE!
HE GALLOPED STRAIGHT BACK
HOME.
I'LL NEVER GET ANOTHER CHANCE TO SEE MY DADDY.
AFTER SHE HAD CRIED FOR A WEEK THE DOG SAID...
PACK YOUR BAGS. I'LL TAKE YOU TO SEE YOUR FATHER.

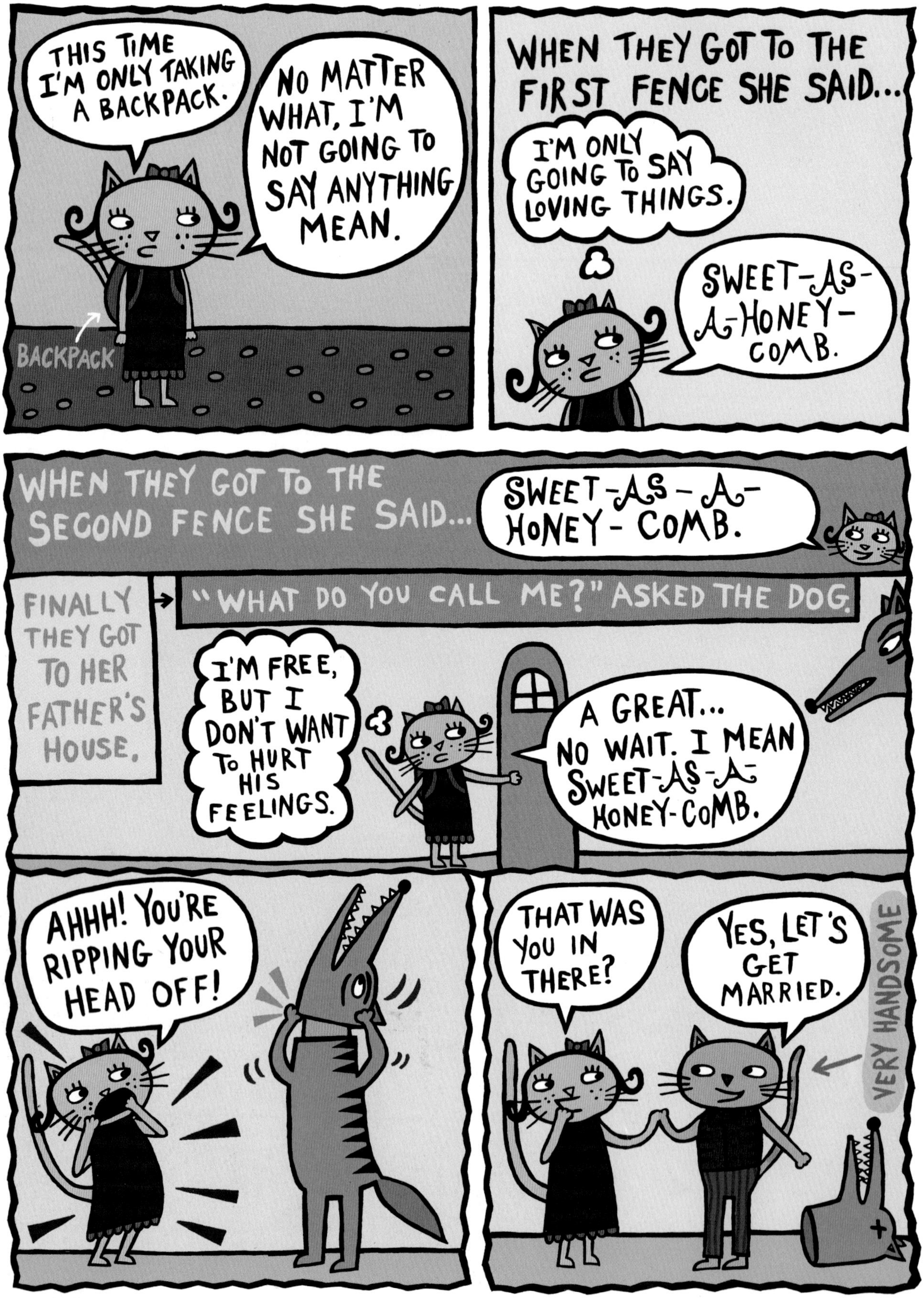
THIS TIME I'M ONLY TAKING A BACKPACK.
NO MATTER WHAT, I'M NOT GOING TO SAY ANYTHING MEAN.
BACKPACK
WHEN THEY GOT TO THE FIRST FENCE SHE SAID...
I'M ONLY GOING TO SAY LOVING THINGS.
SWEET-AS-A-HONEY-COMB.
WHEN THEY GOT TO THE SECOND FENCE SHE SAID...
SWEET-AS-A-HONEY-COMB.
FINALLY THEY GOT TO HER FATHER'S HOUSE.
"WHAT DO YOU CALL ME?" ASKED THE DOG.
I'M FREE, BUT I DON'T WANT TO HURT HIS FEELINGS.
A GREAT... NO WAIT. I MEAN SWEET-AS-A-HONEY-COMB.
AHHH! YOU'RE RIPPING YOUR HEAD OFF!
THAT WAS YOU IN THERE?
YES, LET'S GET MARRIED.
VERY HANDSOME

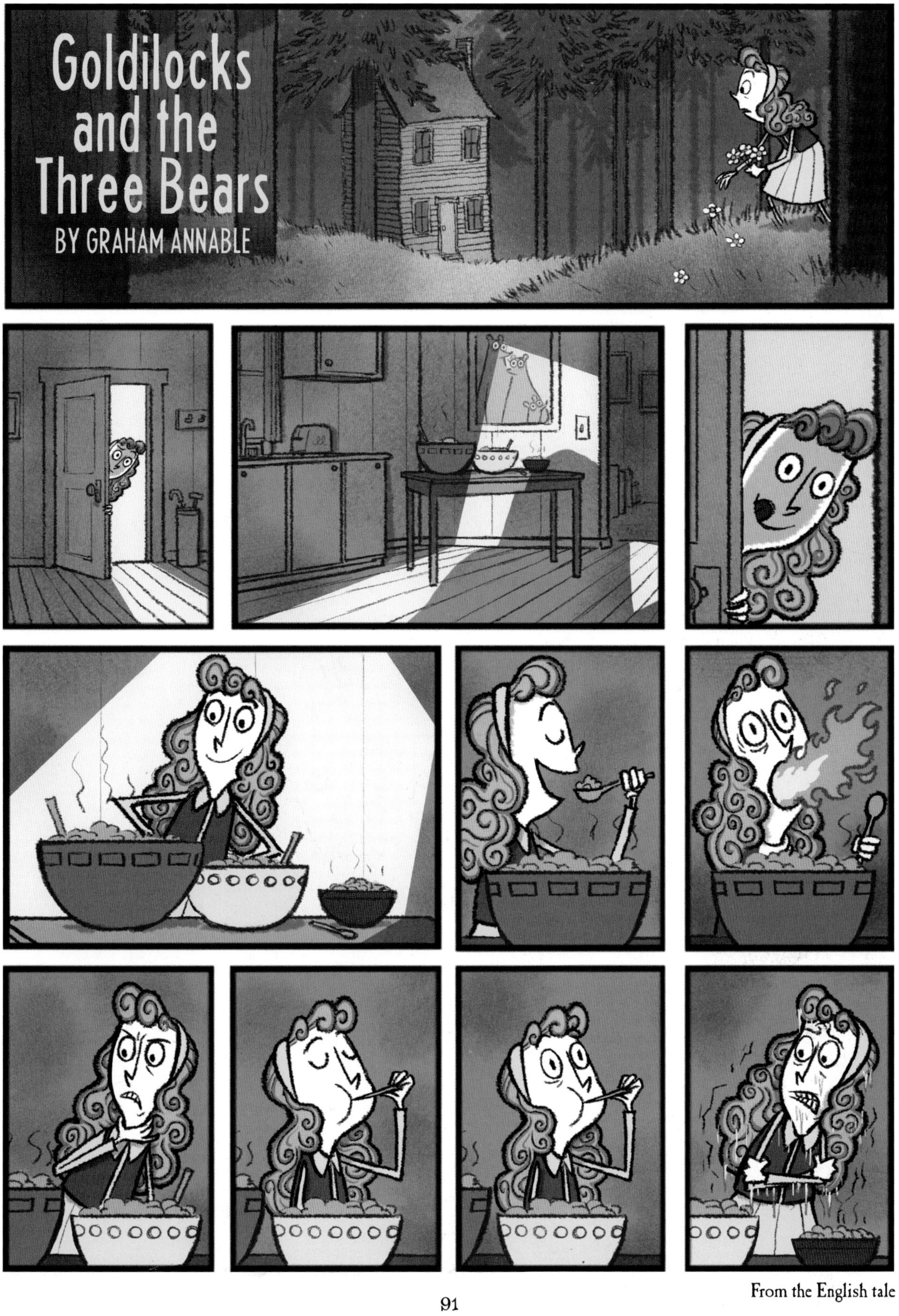
Goldilocks and the Three Bears
BY GRAHAM ANNABLE

From the English tale

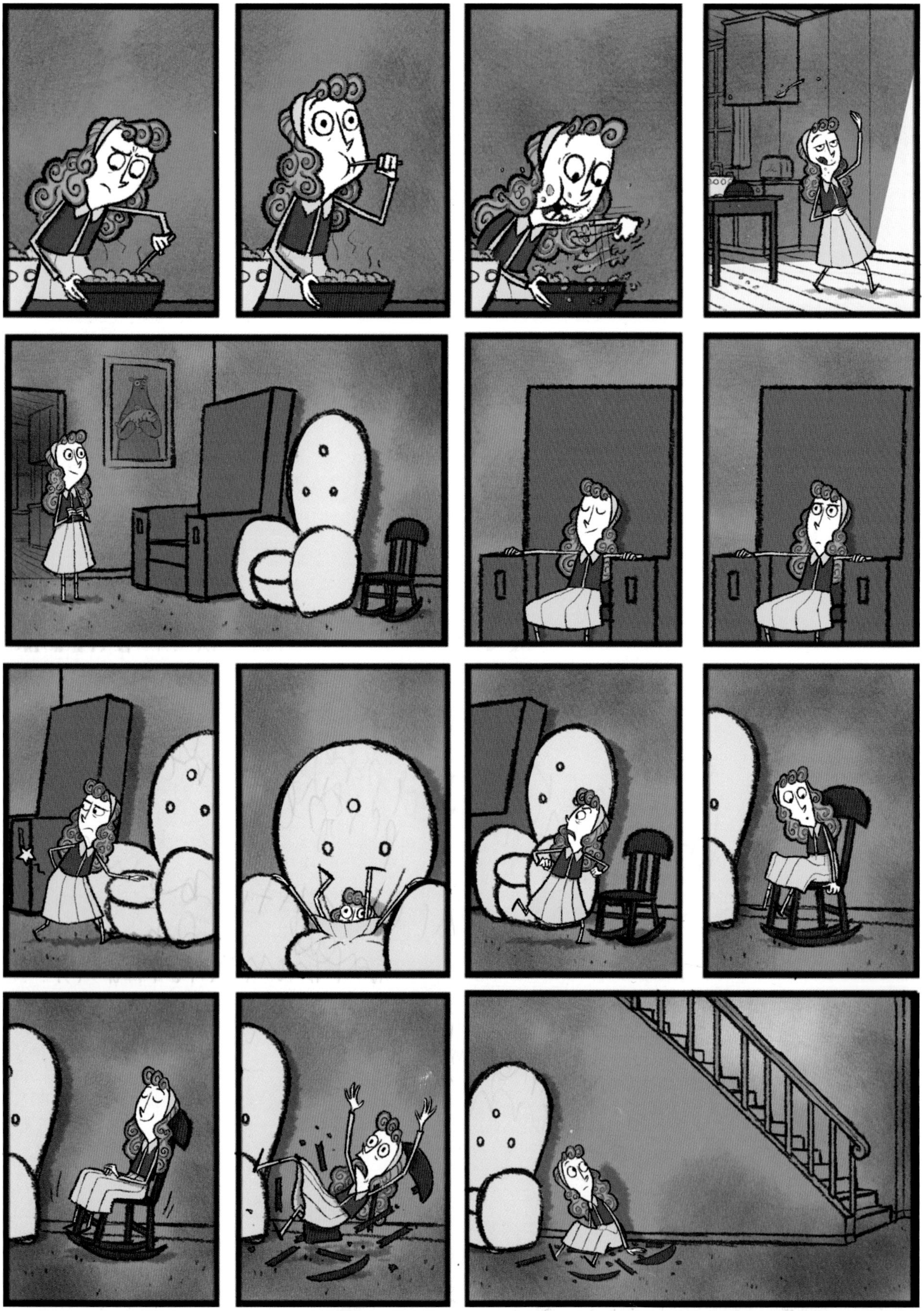

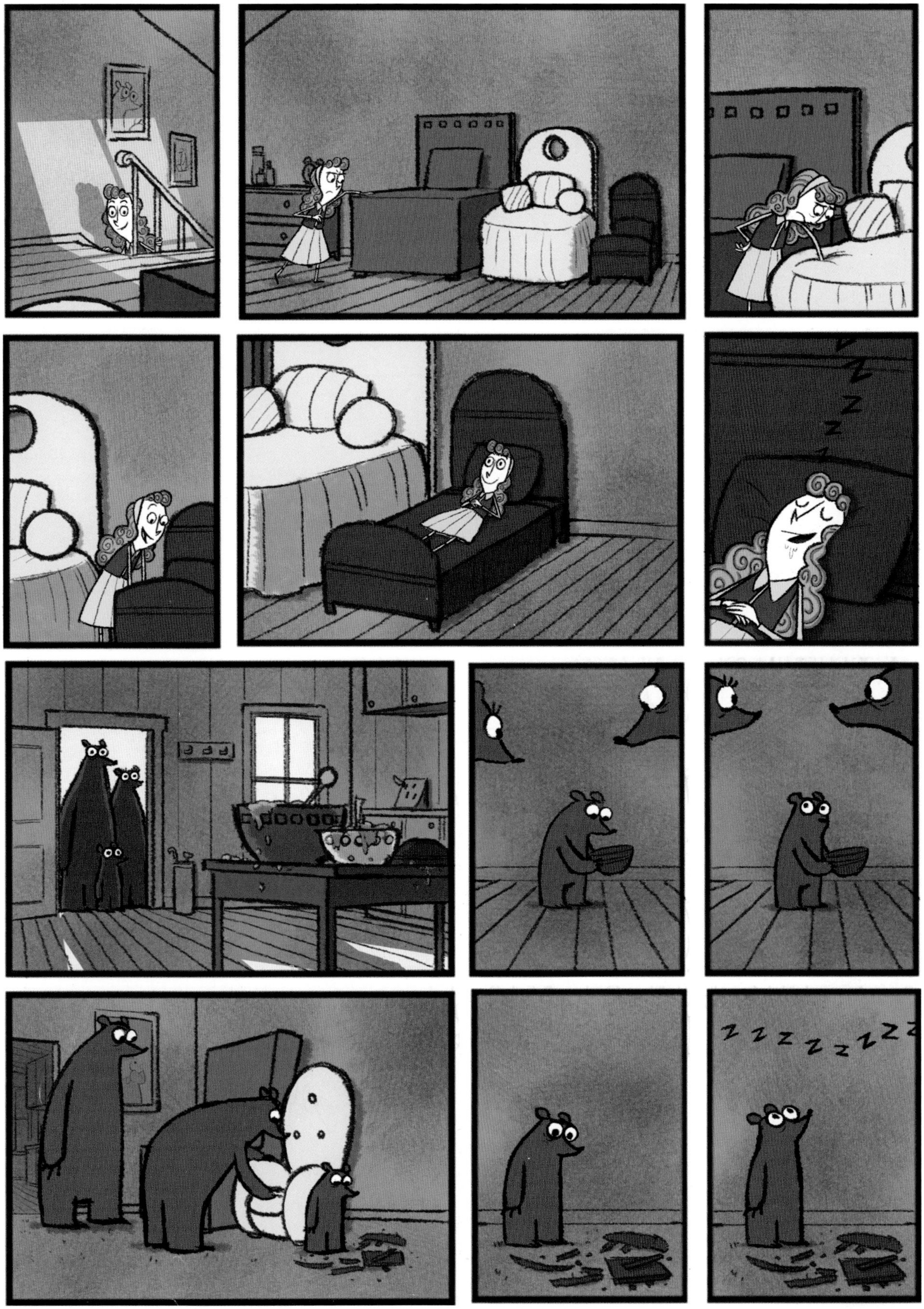

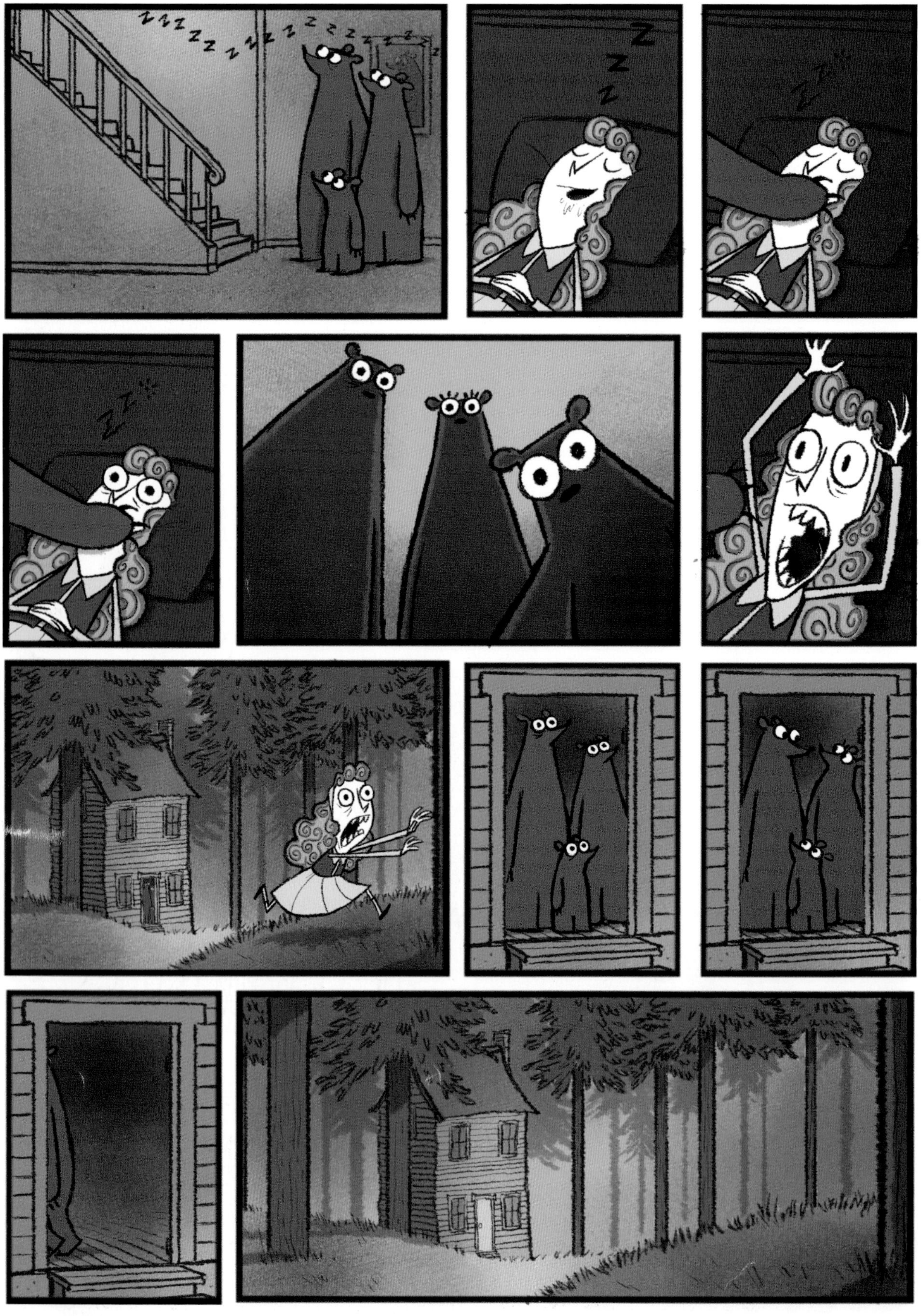
ZZZZZZZZZZZZZZ
ZZZ
ZZ
ZZ

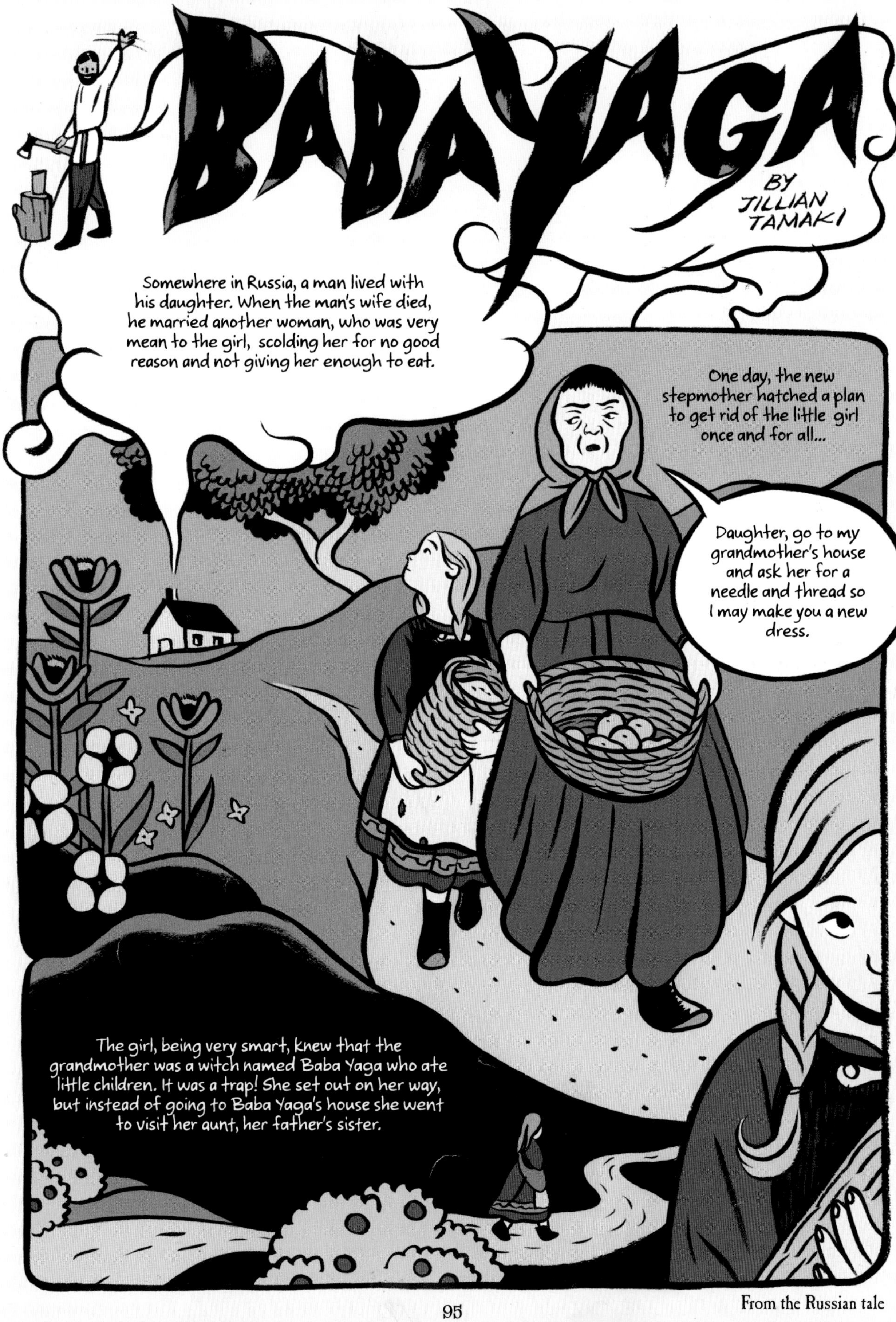

BABA YAGA
BY JILLIAN TAMAKI
Somewhere in Russia, a man lived with his daughter. When the man's wife died, he married another woman, who was very mean to the girl, scolding her for no good reason and not giving her enough to eat.
One day, the new stepmother hatched a plan to get rid of the little girl once and for all...
Daughter, go to my grandmother's house and ask her for a needle and thread so I may make you a new dress.
The girl, being very smart, knew that the grandmother was a witch named Baba Yaga who ate little children. It was a trap! She set out on her way, but instead of going to Baba Yaga's house she went to visit her aunt, her father's sister.




From the Russian tale

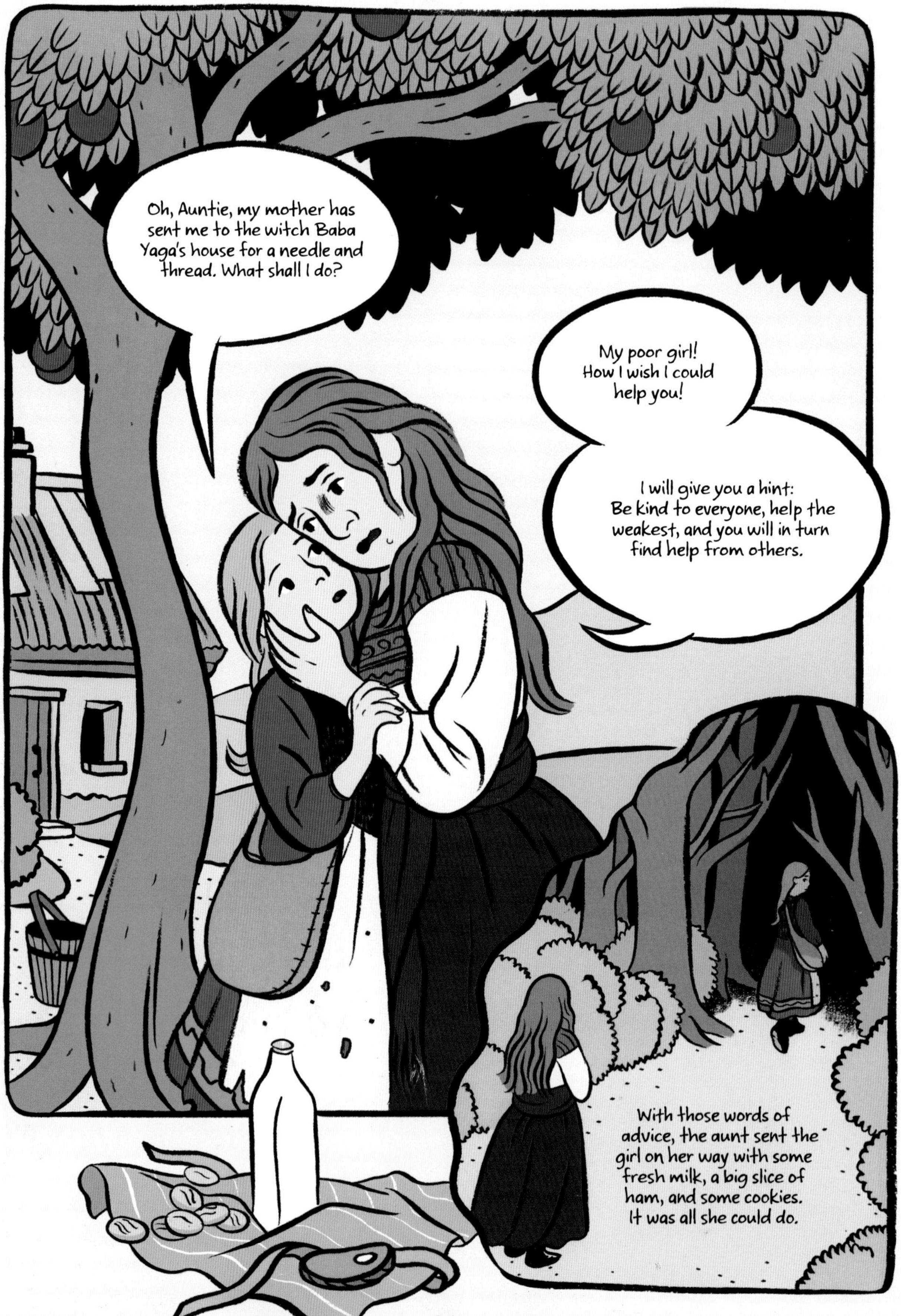
Oh, Auntie, my mother has sent me to the witch Baba Yaga's house for a needle and thread. What shall I do?
My poor girl! How I wish I could help you!
I will give you a hint: Be kind to everyone, help the weakest, and you will in turn find help from others.
With those words of advice, the aunt sent the girl on her way with some fresh milk, a big slice of ham, and some cookies. It was all she could do.

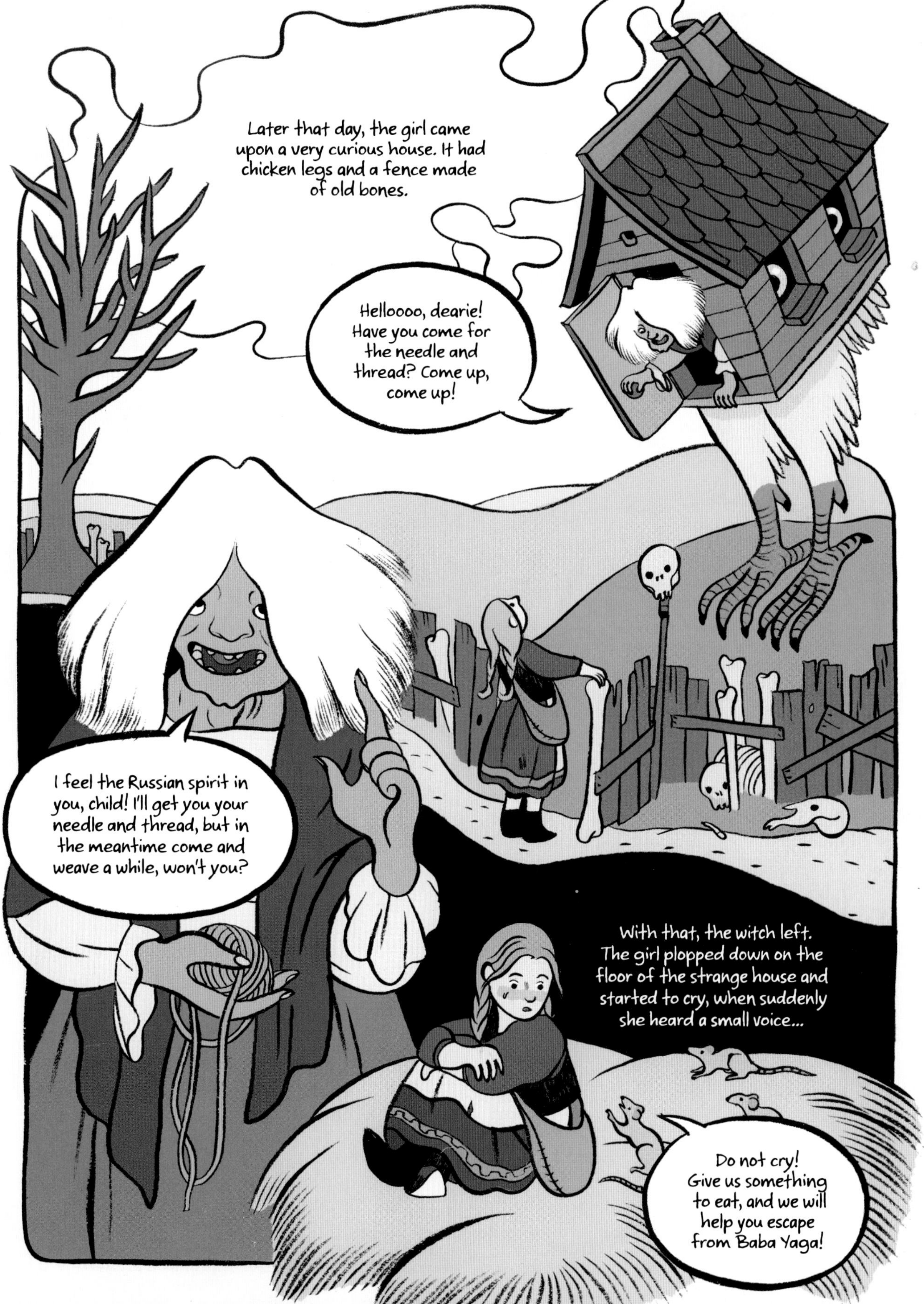
Later that day, the girl came upon a very curious house. It had chicken legs and a fence made of old bones.
Helloooo, dearie! Have you come for the needle and thread? Come up, come up!
I feel the Russian spirit in you, child! I'll get you your needle and thread, but in the meantime come and weave a while, won't you?
With that, the witch left. The girl plopped down on the floor of the strange house and started to cry, when suddenly she heard a small voice...
Do not cry! Give us something to eat, and we will help you escape from Baba Yaga!

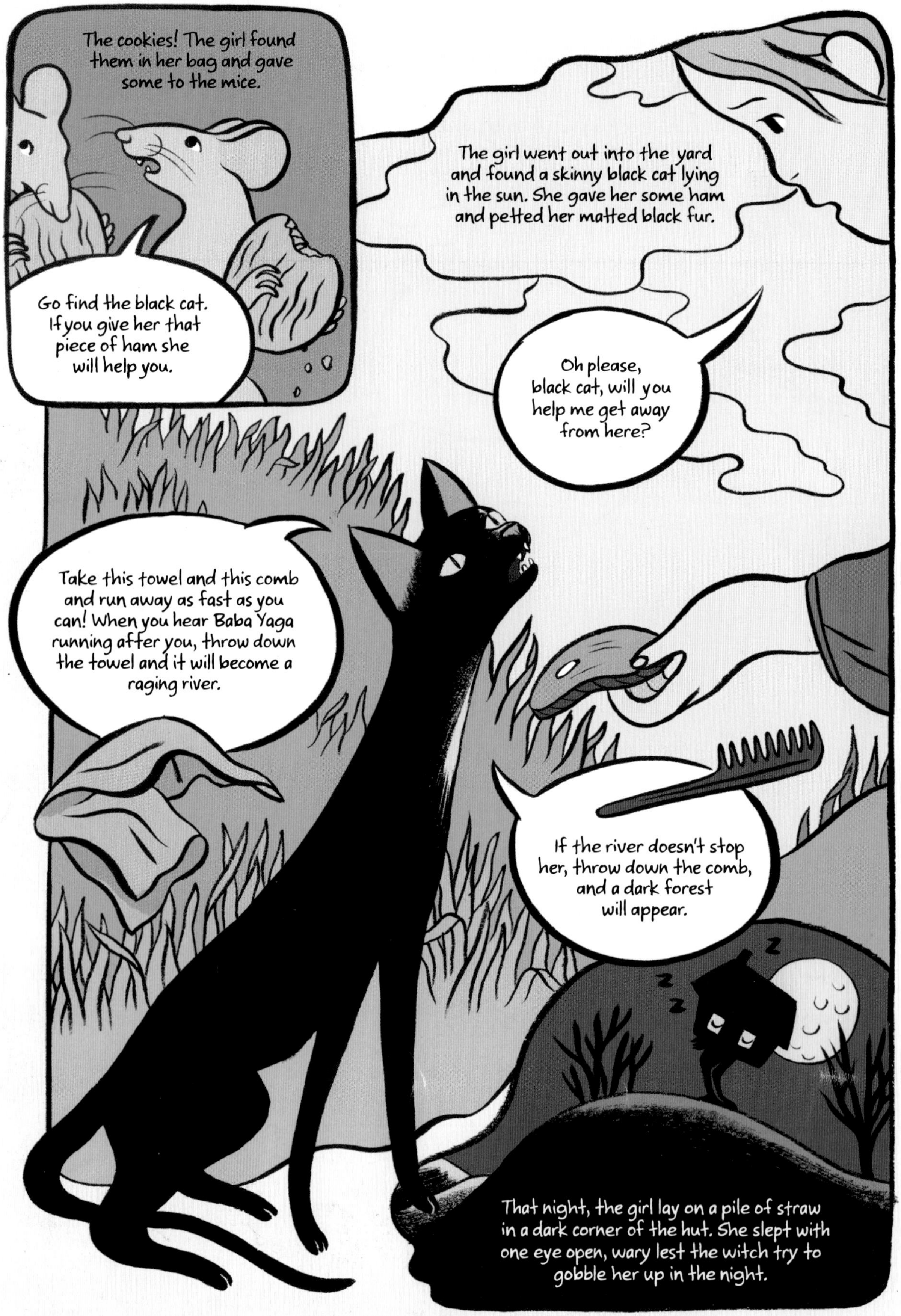
The cookies! The girl found them in her bag and gave some to the mice.
Go find the black cat. If you give her that piece of ham she will help you.
The girl went out into the yard and found a skinny black cat lying in the sun. She gave her some ham and petted her matted black fur.
Oh please, black cat, will you help me get away from here?
Take this towel and this comb and run away as fast as you can! When you hear Baba Yaga running after you, throw down the towel and it will become a raging river.
If the river doesn't stop her, throw down the comb, and a dark forest will appear.
That night, the girl lay on a pile of straw in a dark corner of the hut. She slept with one eye open, wary lest the witch try to gobble her up in the night.

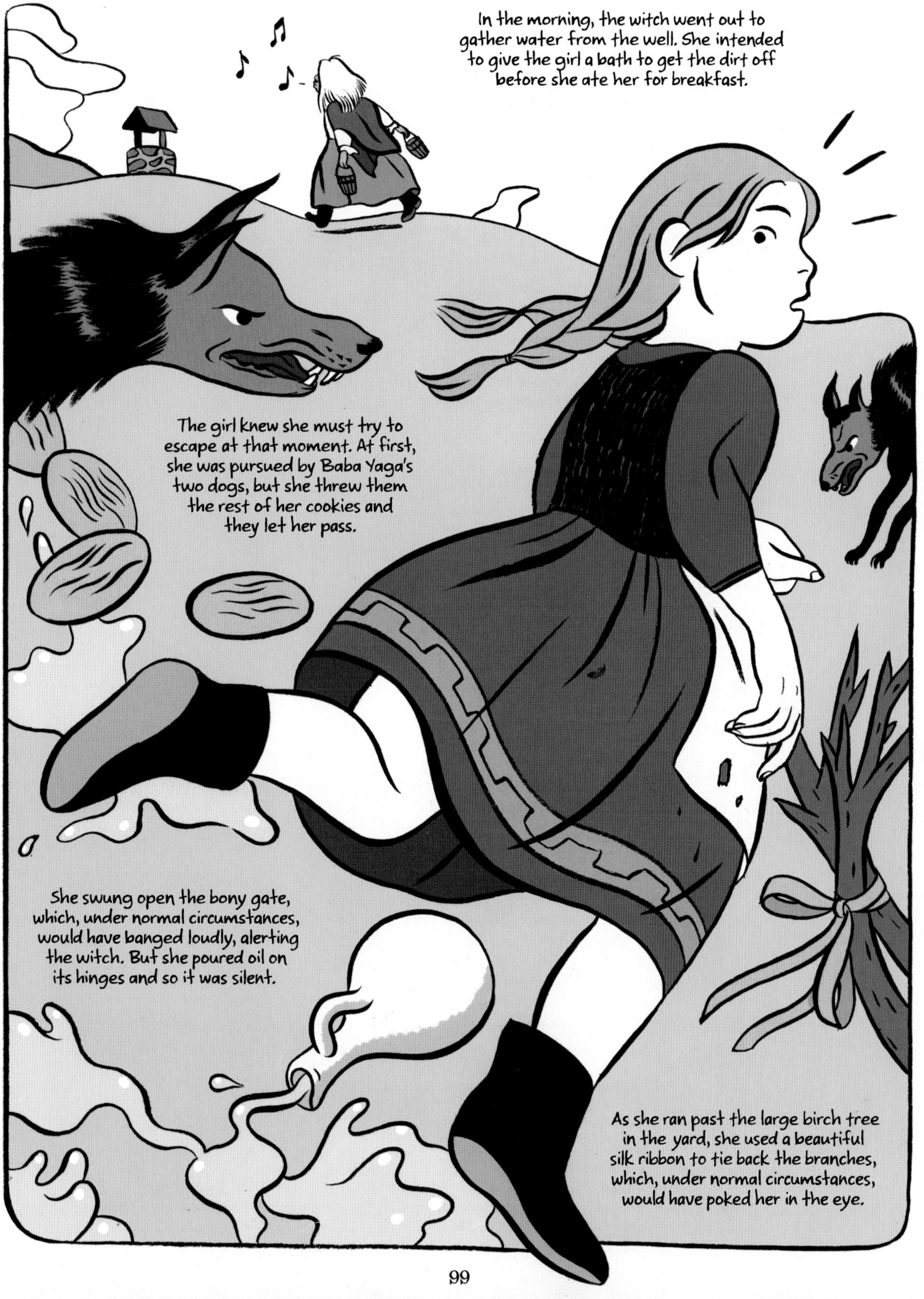
In the morning, the witch went out to gather water from the well. She intended to give the girl a bath to get the dirt off before she ate her for breakfast.
The girl knew she must try to escape at that moment. At first, she was pursued by Baba Yaga's two dogs, but she threw them the rest of her cookies and they let her pass.
She swung open the bony gate, which, under normal circumstances, would have banged loudly, alerting the witch. But she poured oil on its hinges and so it was silent.
As she ran past the large birch tree in the yard, she used a beautiful silk ribbon to tie back the branches, which, under normal circumstances, would have poked her in the eye.

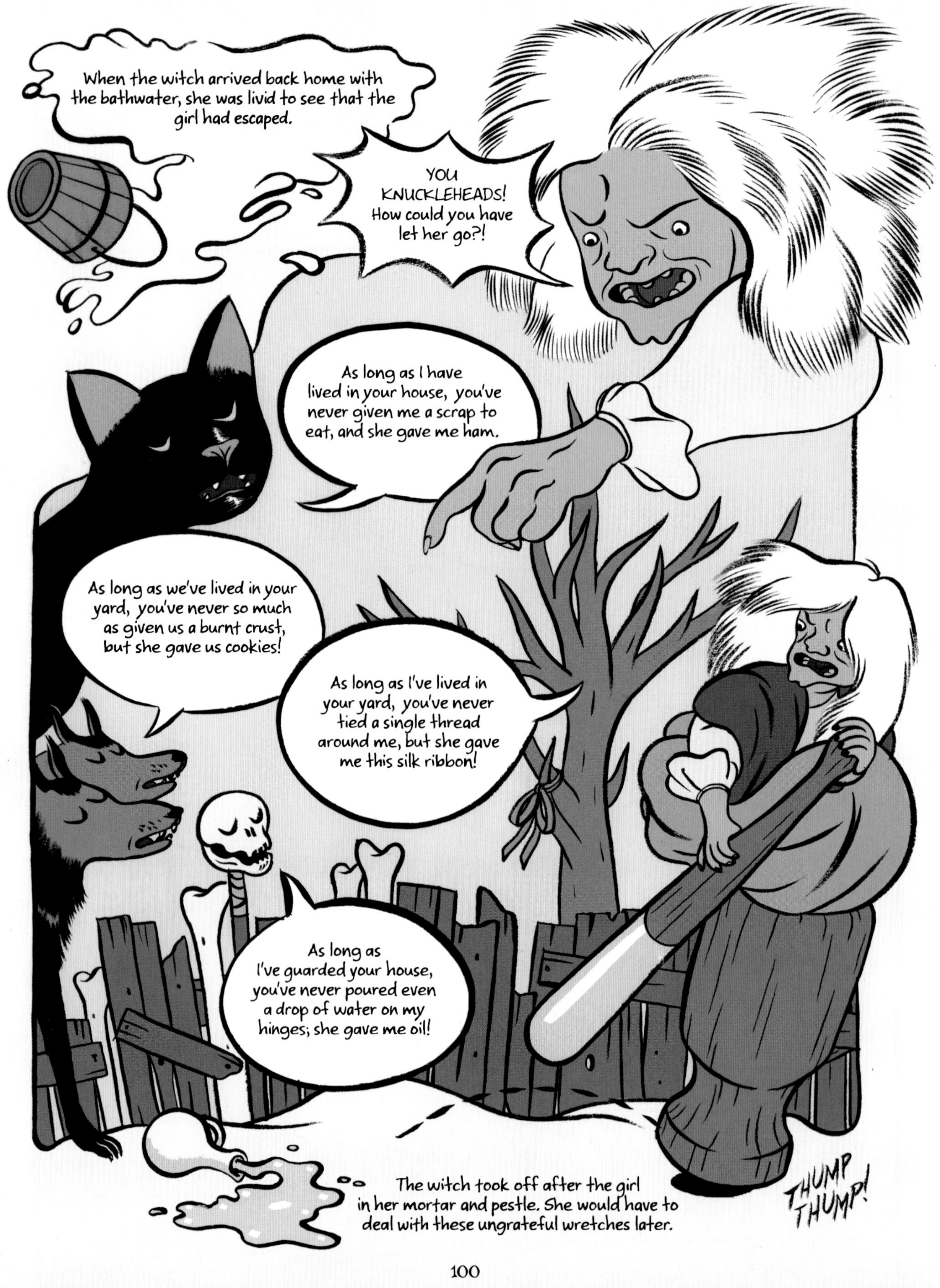
When the witch arrived back home with the bathwater, she was livid to see that the girl had escaped.
YOU KNUCKLEHEADS! How could you have let her go?!
As long as I have lived in your house, you've never given me a scrap to eat, and she gave me ham.
As long as we've lived in your yard, you've never so much as given us a burnt crust, but she gave us cookies!
As long as I've lived in your yard, you've never tied a single thread around me, but she gave me this silk ribbon!
As long as I've guarded your house, you've never poured even a drop of water on my hinges; she gave me oil!
The witch took off after the girl in her mortar and pestle. She would have to deal with these ungrateful wretches later.
THUMP THUMP!

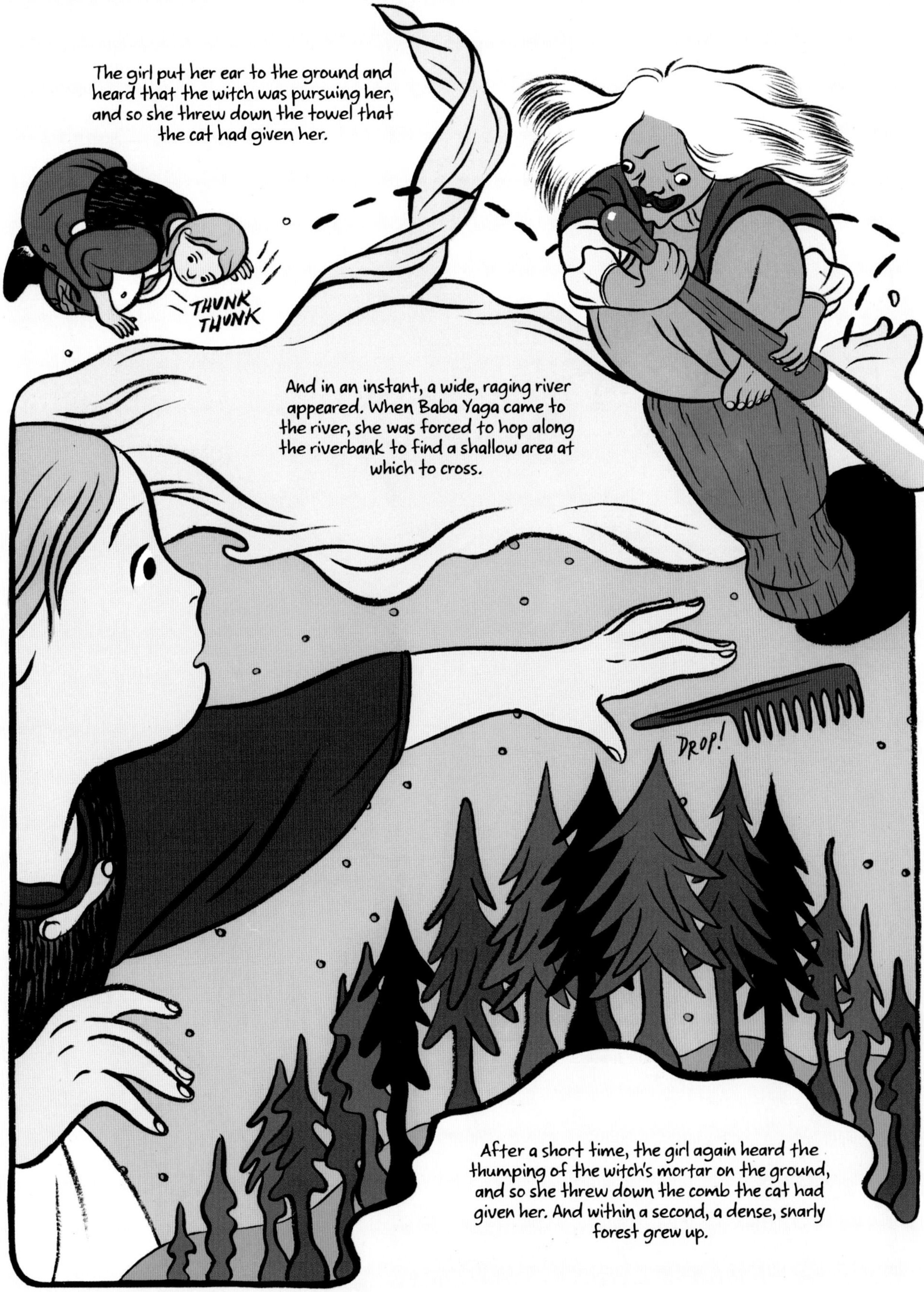
The girl put her ear to the ground and heard that the witch was pursuing her, and so she threw down the towel that the cat had given her.
THUNK THUNK
And in an instant, a wide, raging river appeared. When Baba Yaga came to the river, she was forced to hop along the riverbank to find a shallow area at which to cross.
DROP!
After a short time, the girl again heard the thumping of the witch's mortar on the ground, and so she threw down the comb the cat had given her. And within a second, a dense, snarly forest grew up.

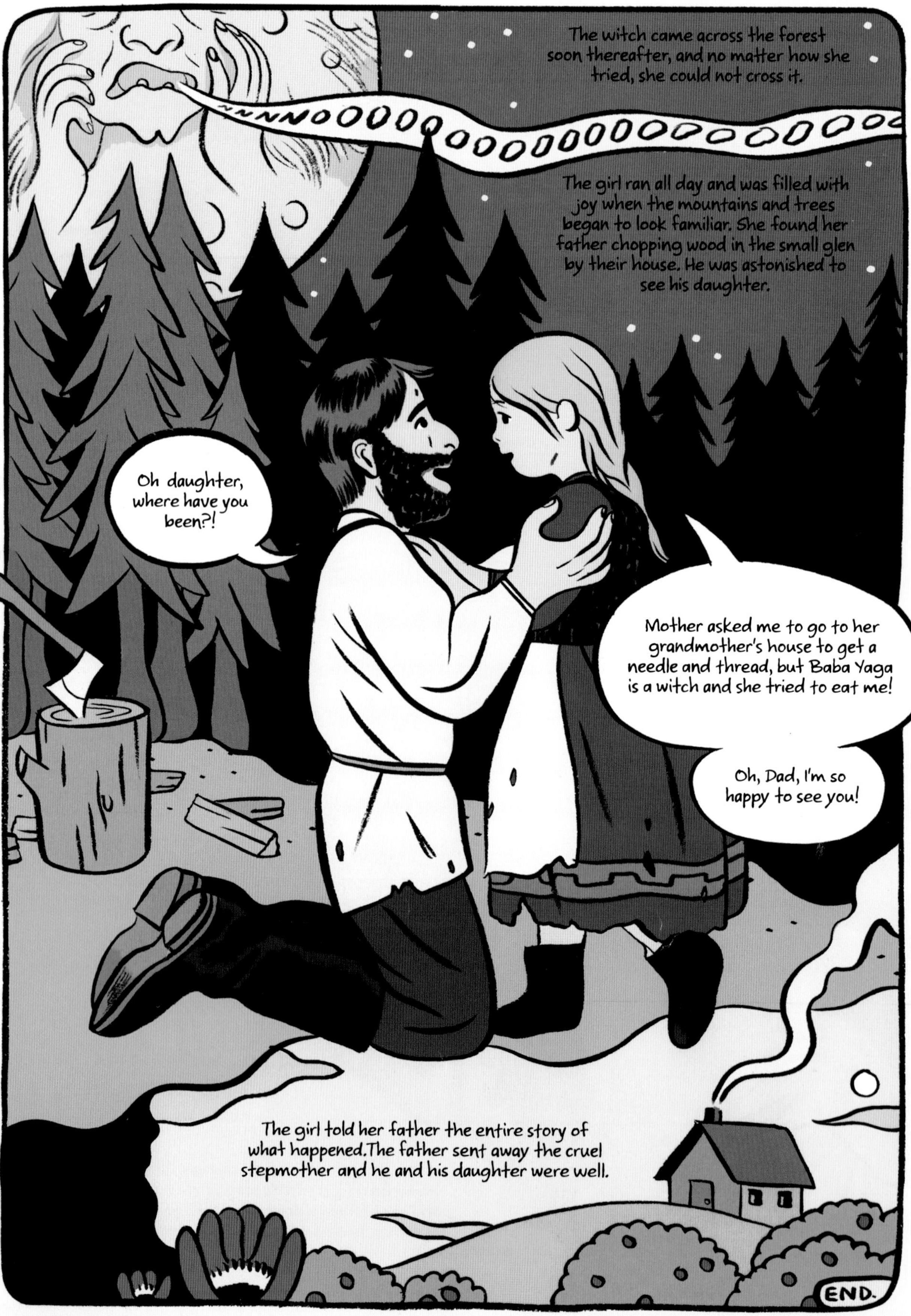
The witch came across the forest soon thereafter, and no matter how she tried, she could not cross it.
NNNNOOOOOOOOOOOOOOOOOOOOOOOOOOO
The girl ran all day and was filled with joy when the mountains and trees began to look familiar. She found her father chopping wood in the small glen by their house. He was astonished to see his daughter.
Oh daughter, where have you been?!
Mother asked me to go to her grandmother's house to get a needle and thread, but Baba Yaga is a witch and she tried to eat me!
Oh, Dad, I'm so happy to see you!
The girl told her father the entire story of what happened. The father sent away the cruel stepmother and he and his daughter were well.
END.

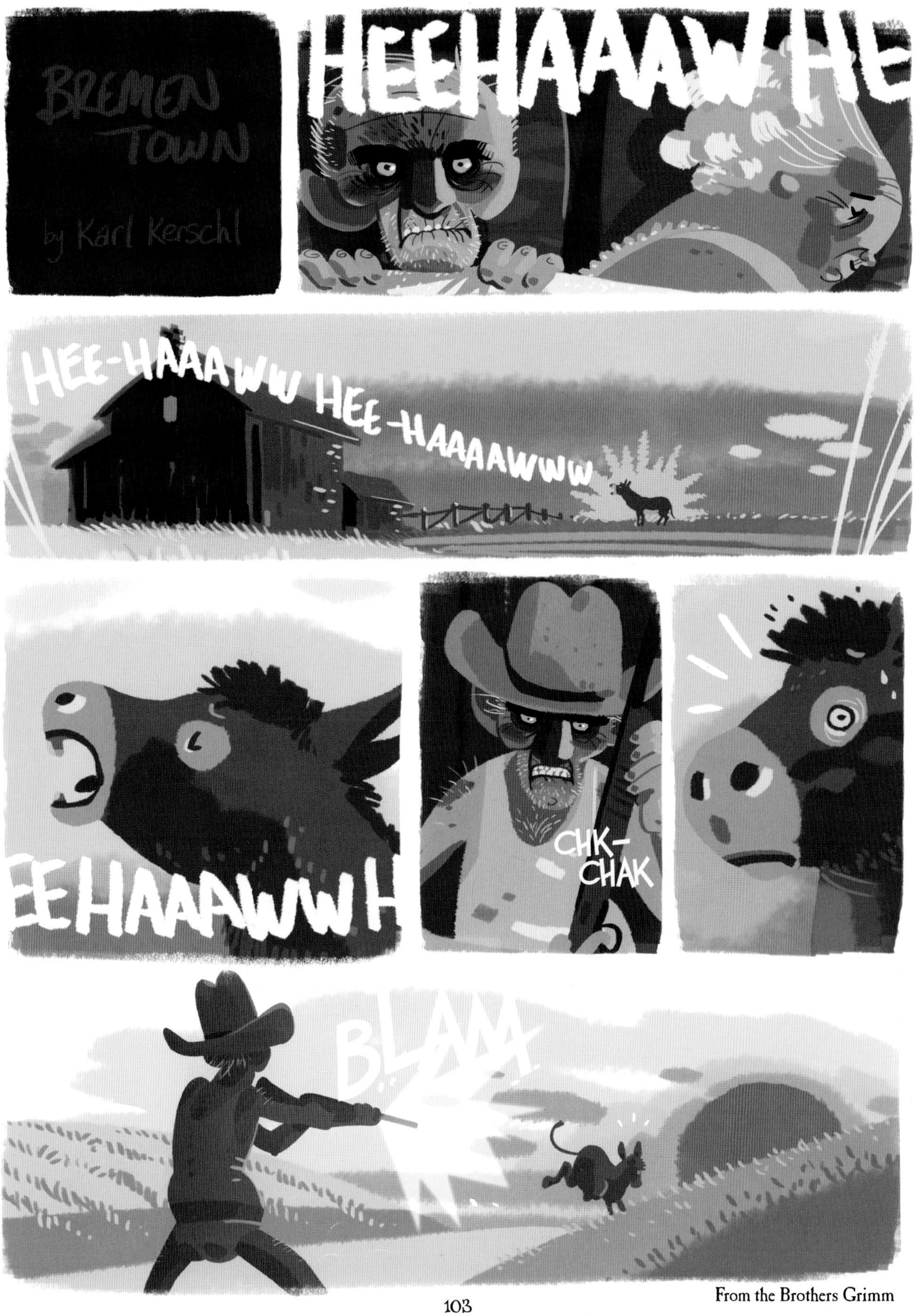
BREMEN TOWN
by Karl Kerschl
HEEHAAAW HE
HEE-HAAAWW HEE-HAAAAWWW
EEHAAAWW H
CHK-CHAK
BLAM

From the Brothers Grimm

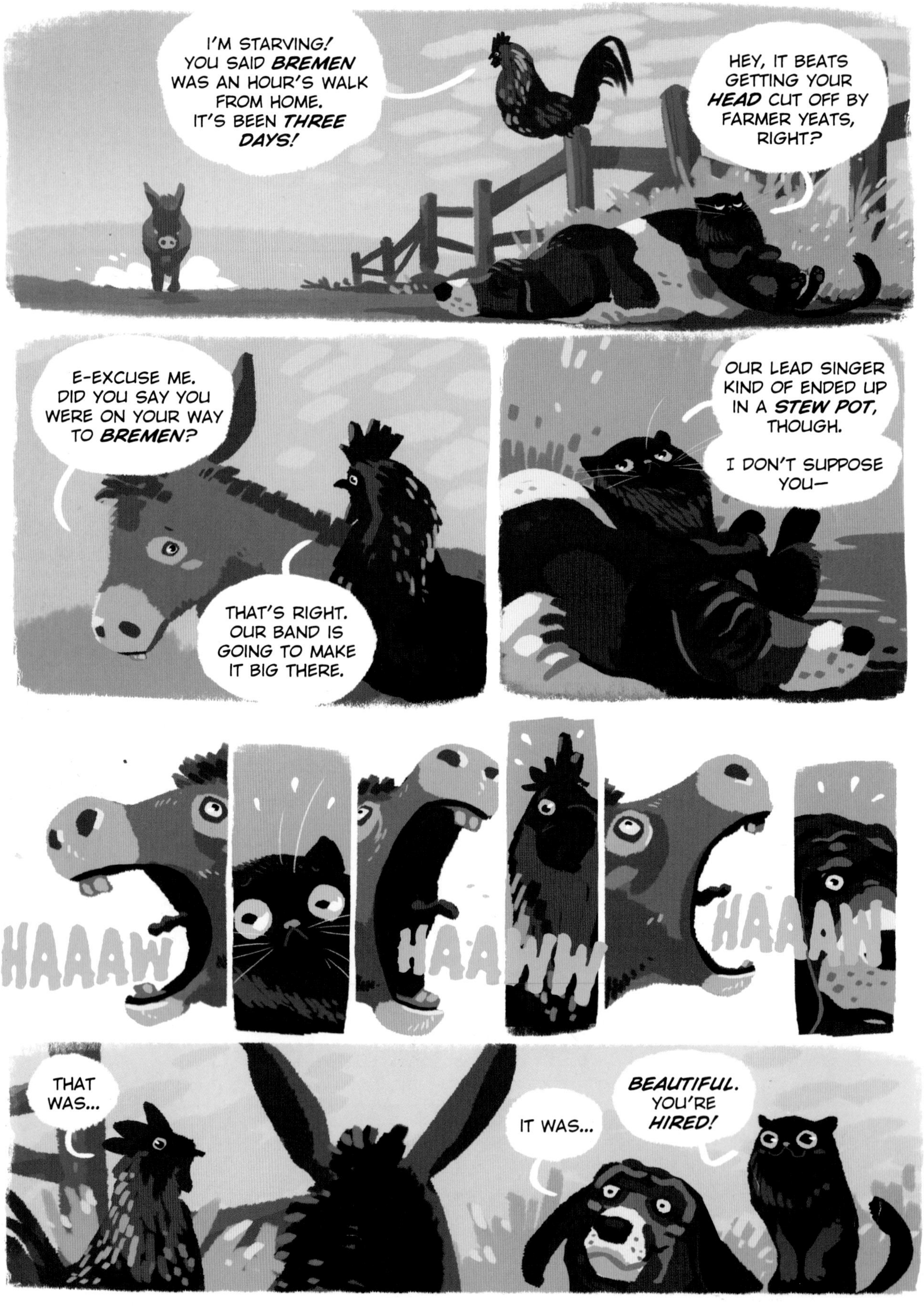

I'M STARVING! YOU SAID BREMEN WAS AN HOUR'S WALK FROM HOME. IT'S BEEN THREE DAYS!
HEY, IT BEATS GETTING YOUR HEAD CUT OFF BY FARMER YEATS, RIGHT?
E-EXCUSE ME. DID YOU SAY YOU WERE ON YOUR WAY TO BREMEN?
THAT'S RIGHT. OUR BAND IS GOING TO MAKE IT BIG THERE.
OUR LEAD SINGER KIND OF ENDED UP IN A STEW POT, THOUGH.
I DON'T SUPPOSE YOU—
HAAAW
HAAWW
HAAAW
THAT WAS...
IT WAS...
BEAUTIFUL. YOU'RE HIRED!

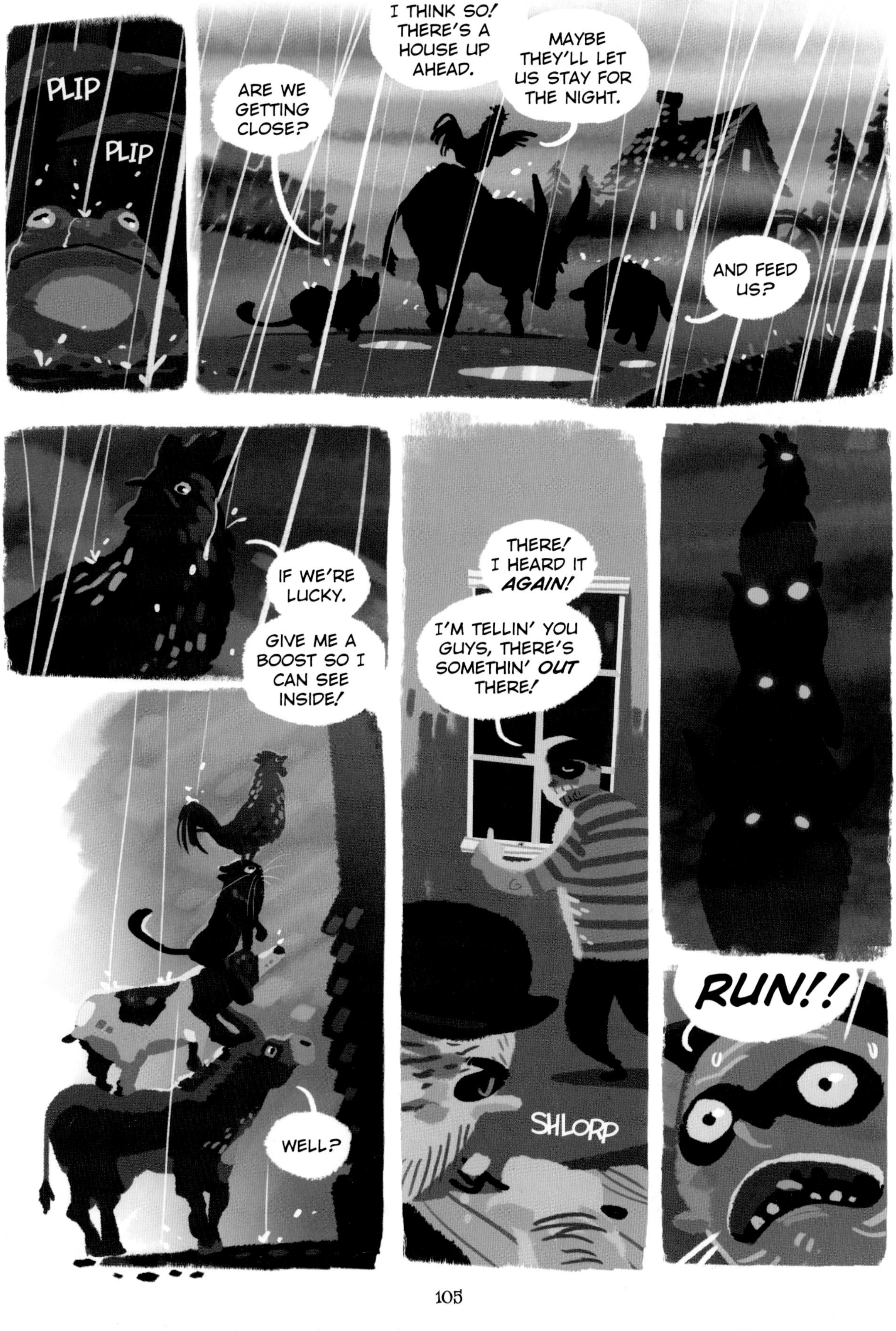
PLIP
PLIP
ARE WE GETTING CLOSE?
I THINK SO! THERE'S A HOUSE UP AHEAD.
MAYBE THEY'LL LET US STAY FOR THE NIGHT.
AND FEED US?
IF WE'RE LUCKY.
GIVE ME A BOOST SO I CAN SEE INSIDE!
WELL?
THERE! I HEARD IT *AGAIN!*
I'M TELLIN' YOU GUYS, THERE'S SOMETHIN' *OUT* THERE!
SHLORP
*RUN!!*

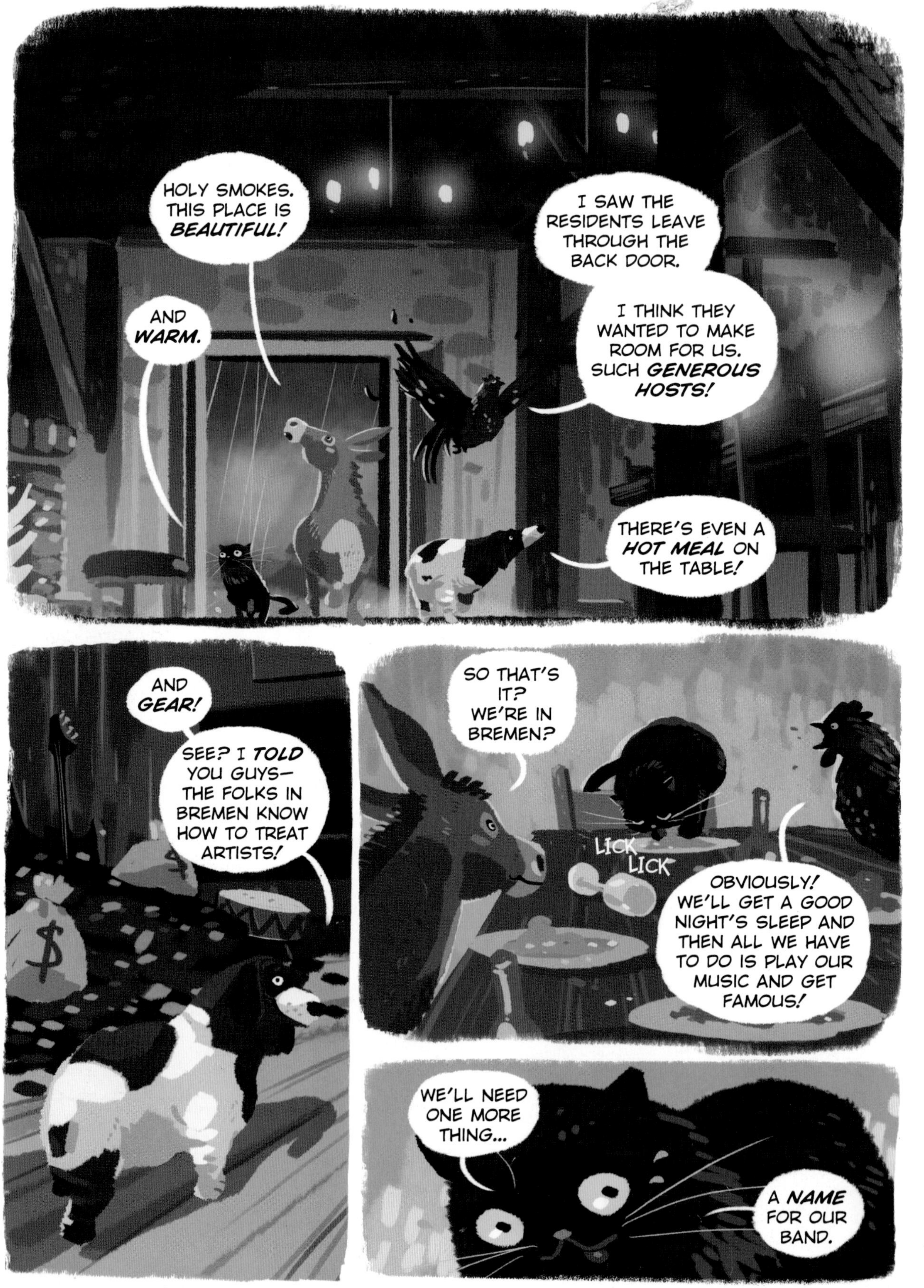
HOLY SMOKES. THIS PLACE IS BEAUTIFUL!
AND WARM.
I SAW THE RESIDENTS LEAVE THROUGH THE BACK DOOR.
I THINK THEY WANTED TO MAKE ROOM FOR US. SUCH GENEROUS HOSTS!
THERE'S EVEN A HOT MEAL ON THE TABLE!
AND GEAR!
SEE? I TOLD YOU GUYS— THE FOLKS IN BREMEN KNOW HOW TO TREAT ARTISTS!
SO THAT'S IT? WE'RE IN BREMEN?
LICK LICK
OBVIOUSLY! WE'LL GET A GOOD NIGHT'S SLEEP AND THEN ALL WE HAVE TO DO IS PLAY OUR MUSIC AND GET FAMOUS!
WE'LL NEED ONE MORE THING...
A NAME FOR OUR BAND.

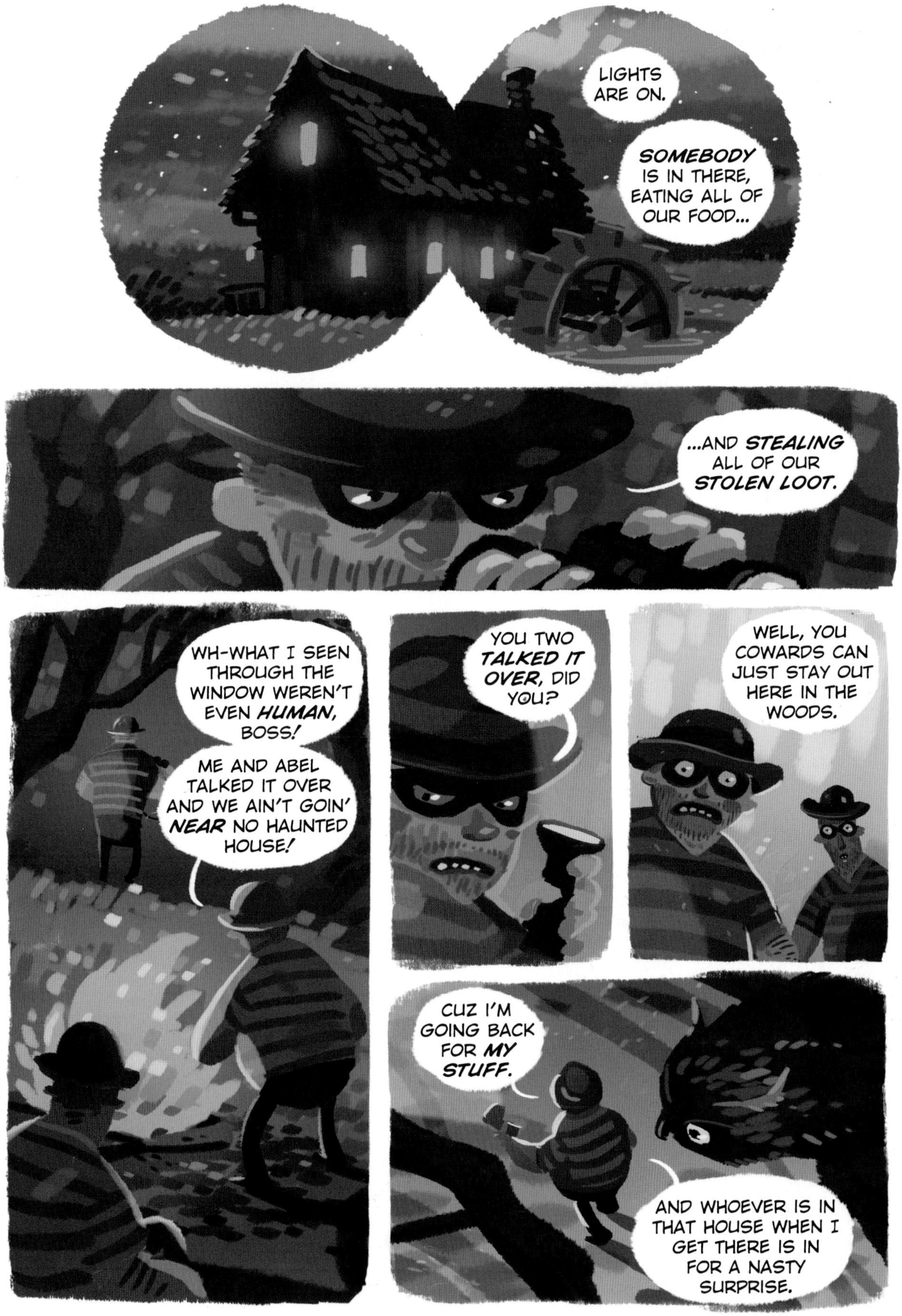
LIGHTS ARE ON.
SOMEBODY IS IN THERE, EATING ALL OF OUR FOOD...
...AND STEALING ALL OF OUR STOLEN LOOT.
WH-WHAT I SEEN THROUGH THE WINDOW WEREN'T EVEN HUMAN, BOSS!
ME AND ABEL TALKED IT OVER AND WE AIN'T GOIN' NEAR NO HAUNTED HOUSE!
YOU TWO TALKED IT OVER, DID YOU?
WELL, YOU COWARDS CAN JUST STAY OUT HERE IN THE WOODS.
CUZ I'M GOING BACK FOR MY STUFF.
AND WHOEVER IS IN THAT HOUSE WHEN I GET THERE IS IN FOR A NASTY SURPRISE.

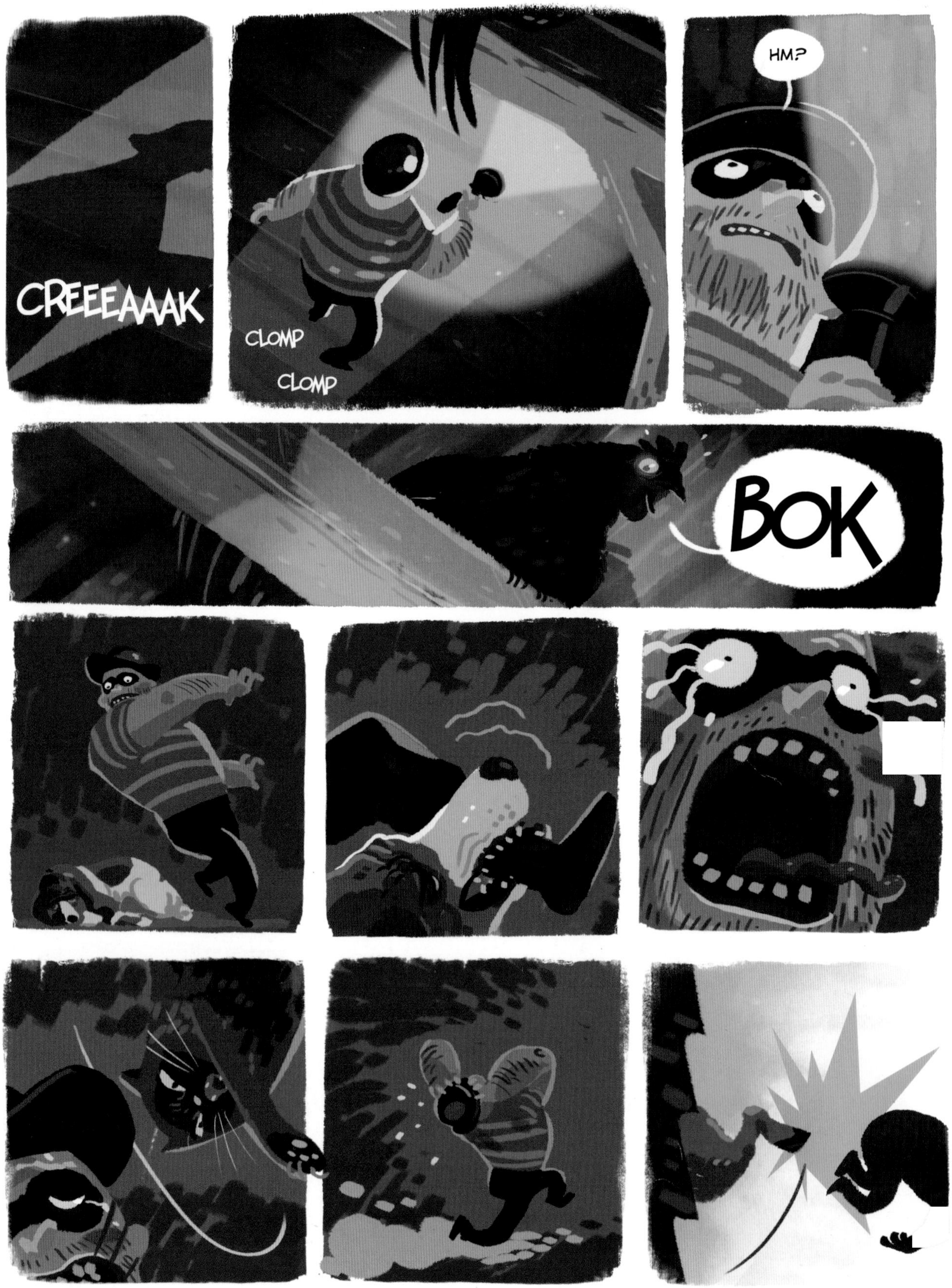
CREEEAAAK
CLOMP
CLOMP
HM?
BOK

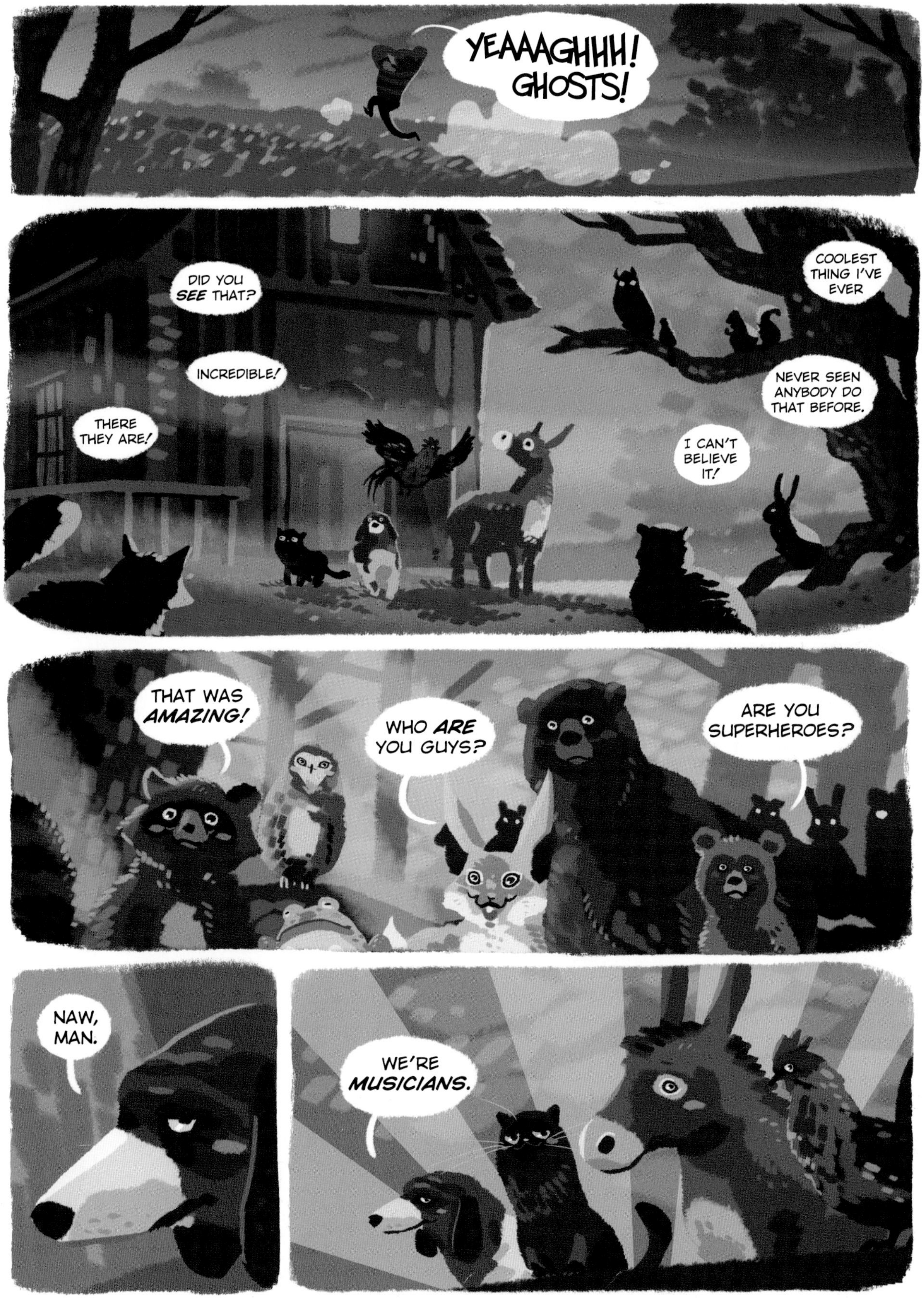
YEAAAGHHH! GHOSTS!
DID YOU SEE THAT?
INCREDIBLE!
THERE THEY ARE!
COOLEST THING I'VE EVER
NEVER SEEN ANYBODY DO THAT BEFORE.
I CAN'T BELIEVE IT!
THAT WAS AMAZING!
WHO ARE YOU GUYS?
ARE YOU SUPERHEROES?
NAW, MAN.
WE'RE MUSICIANS.

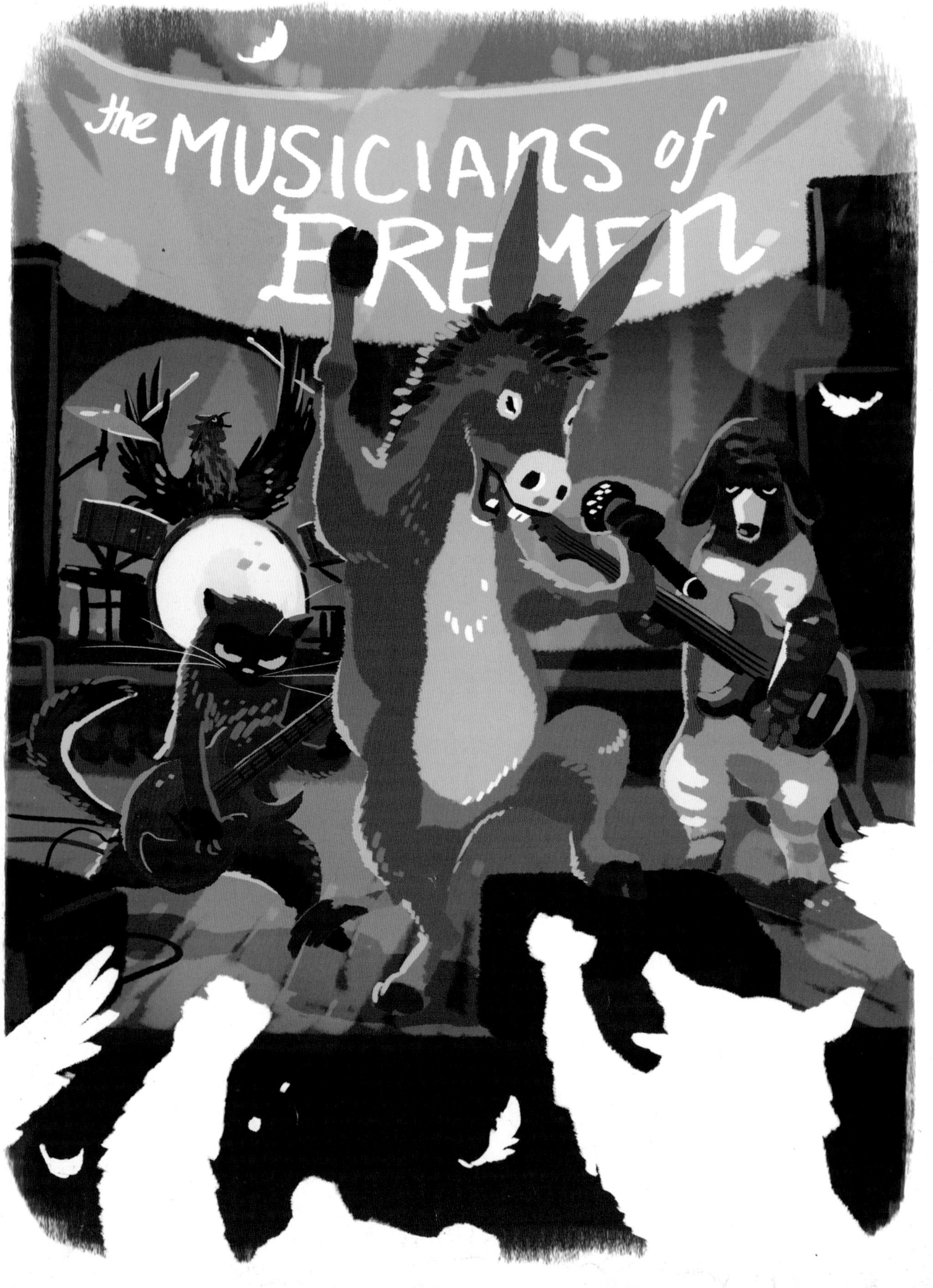
the MUSICIANS of
BREMEN

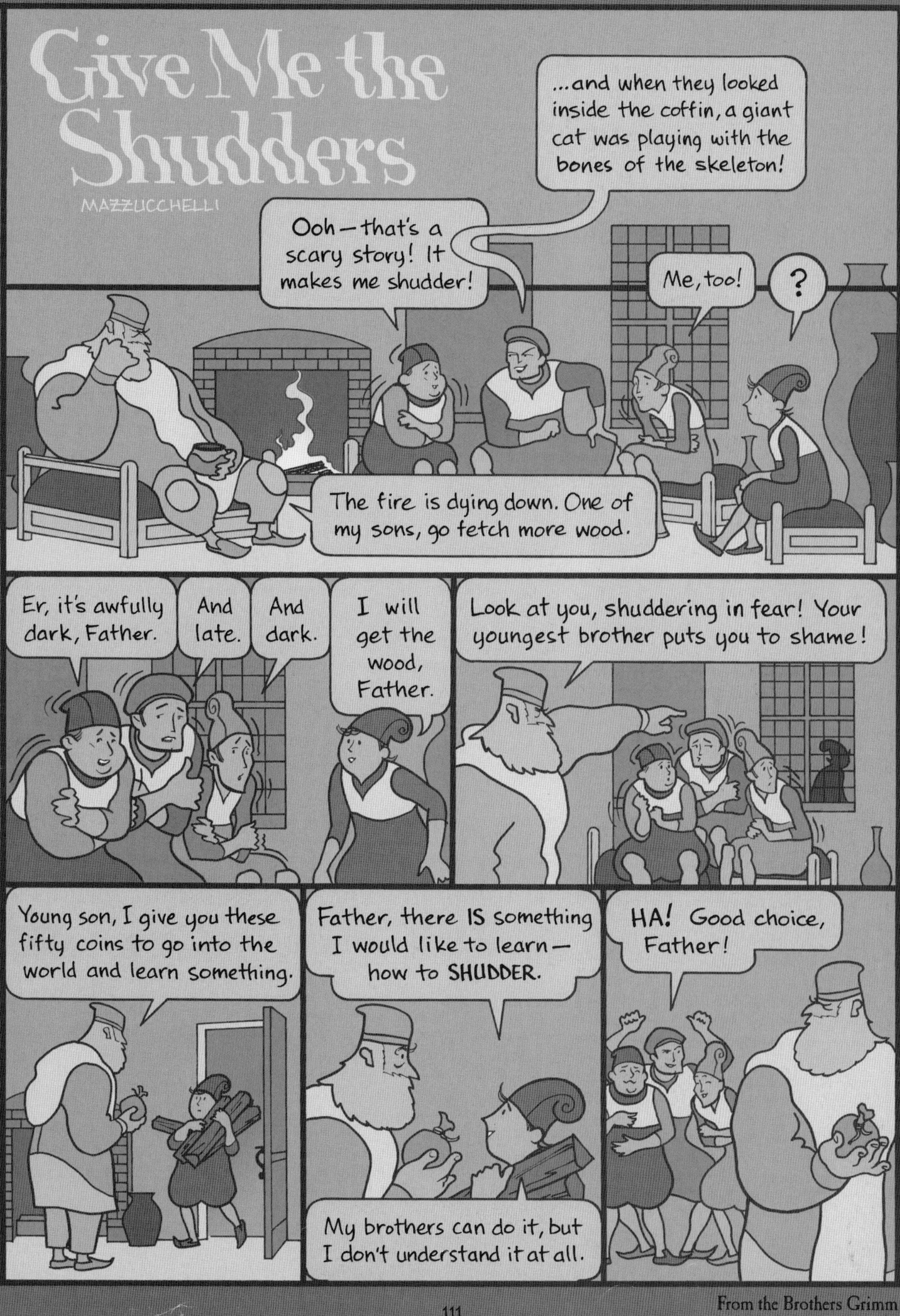
Give Me the Shudders
MAZZUCCHELLI
...and when they looked inside the coffin, a giant cat was playing with the bones of the skeleton!
Ooh—that's a scary story! It makes me shudder!
Me, too!
?
The fire is dying down. One of my sons, go fetch more wood.
Er, it's awfully dark, Father.
And late.
And dark.
I will get the wood, Father.
Look at you, shuddering in fear! Your youngest brother puts you to shame!
Young son, I give you these fifty coins to go into the world and learn something.
Father, there IS something I would like to learn—how to SHUDDER.
My brothers can do it, but I don't understand it at all.
HA! Good choice, Father!



From the Brothers Grimm

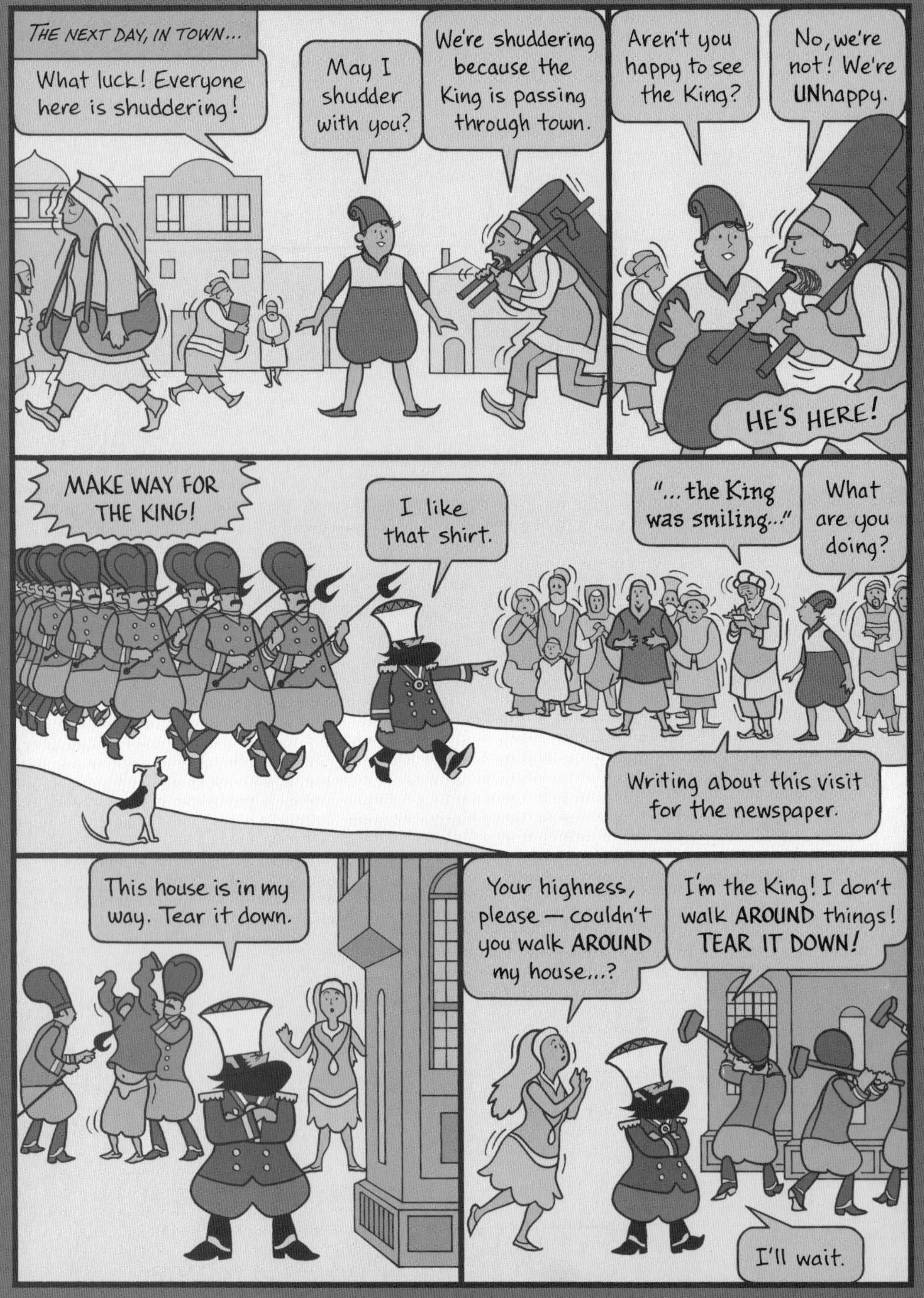
THE NEXT DAY, IN TOWN...
What luck! Everyone here is shuddering!
May I shudder with you?
We're shuddering because the King is passing through town.
Aren't you happy to see the King?
No, we're not! We're UNhappy.
HE'S HERE!
MAKE WAY FOR THE KING!
I like that shirt.
"...the King was smiling..."
What are you doing?
Writing about this visit for the newspaper.
This house is in my way. Tear it down.
Your highness, please — couldn't you walk AROUND my house...?
I'm the King! I don't walk AROUND things! TEAR IT DOWN!
I'll wait.

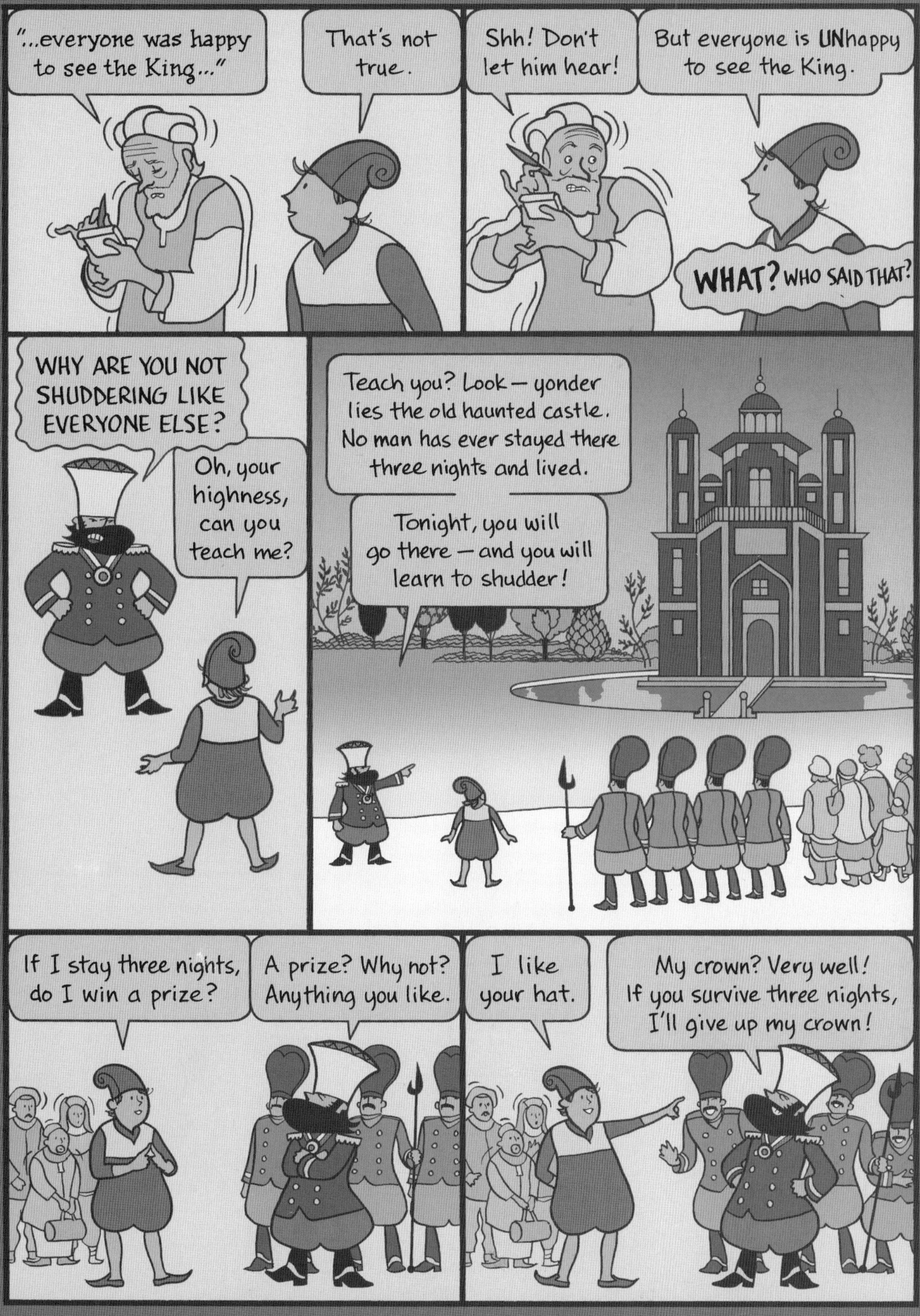
"...everyone was happy to see the King..."
That's not true.
Shh! Don't let him hear!
But everyone is UNhappy to see the King.
WHAT? WHO SAID THAT?
WHY ARE YOU NOT SHUDDERING LIKE EVERYONE ELSE?
Oh, your highness, can you teach me?
Teach you? Look — yonder lies the old haunted castle. No man has ever stayed there three nights and lived.
Tonight, you will go there — and you will learn to shudder!
If I stay three nights, do I win a prize?
A prize? Why not? Anything you like.
I like your hat.
My crown? Very well! If you survive three nights, I'll give up my crown!

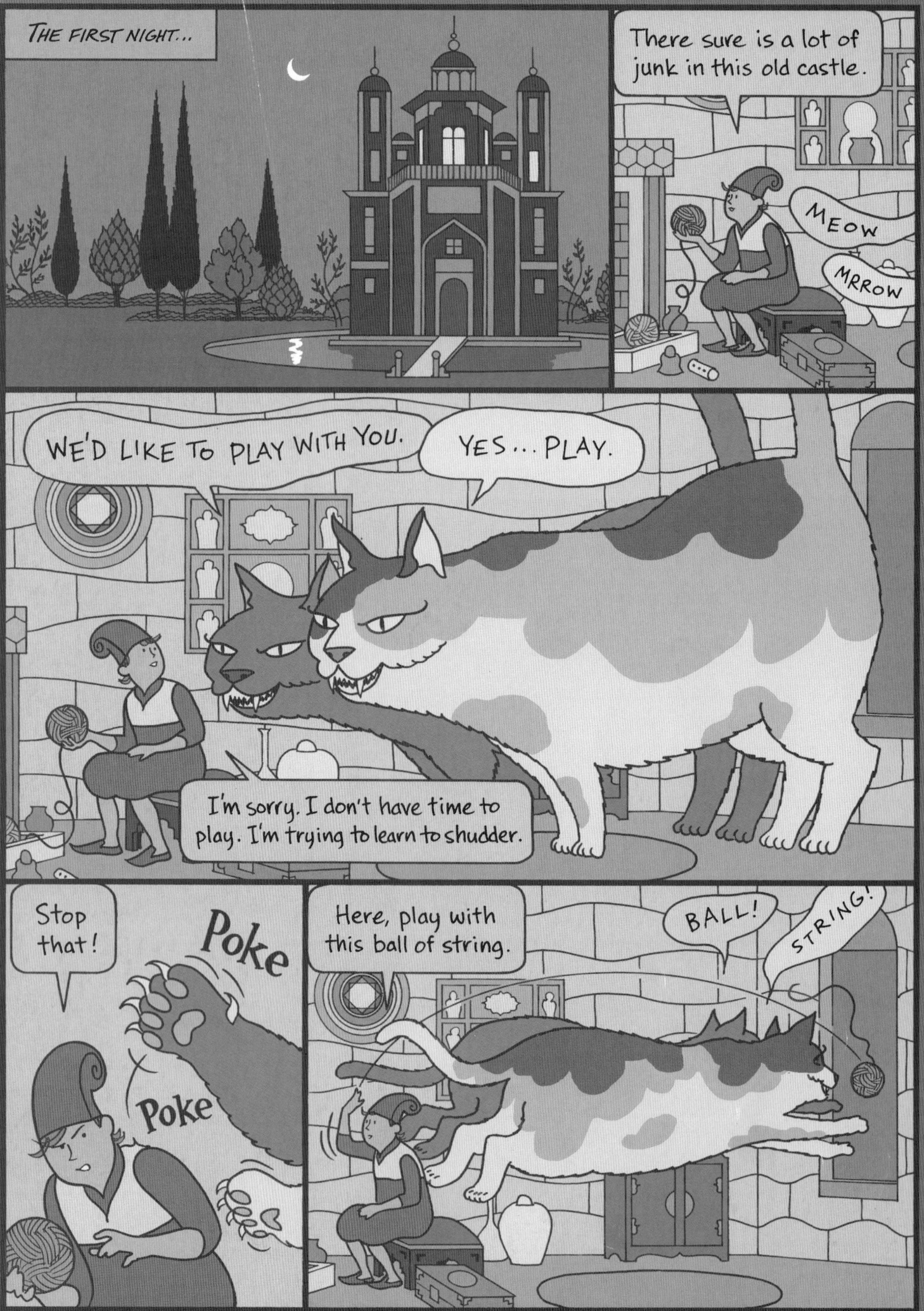
THE FIRST NIGHT...
There sure is a lot of junk in this old castle.
MEOW
MRROW
WE'D LIKE TO PLAY WITH YOU.
YES... PLAY.
I'm sorry. I don't have time to play. I'm trying to learn to shudder.
Stop that!
Poke
Poke
Here, play with this ball of string.
BALL!
STRING!

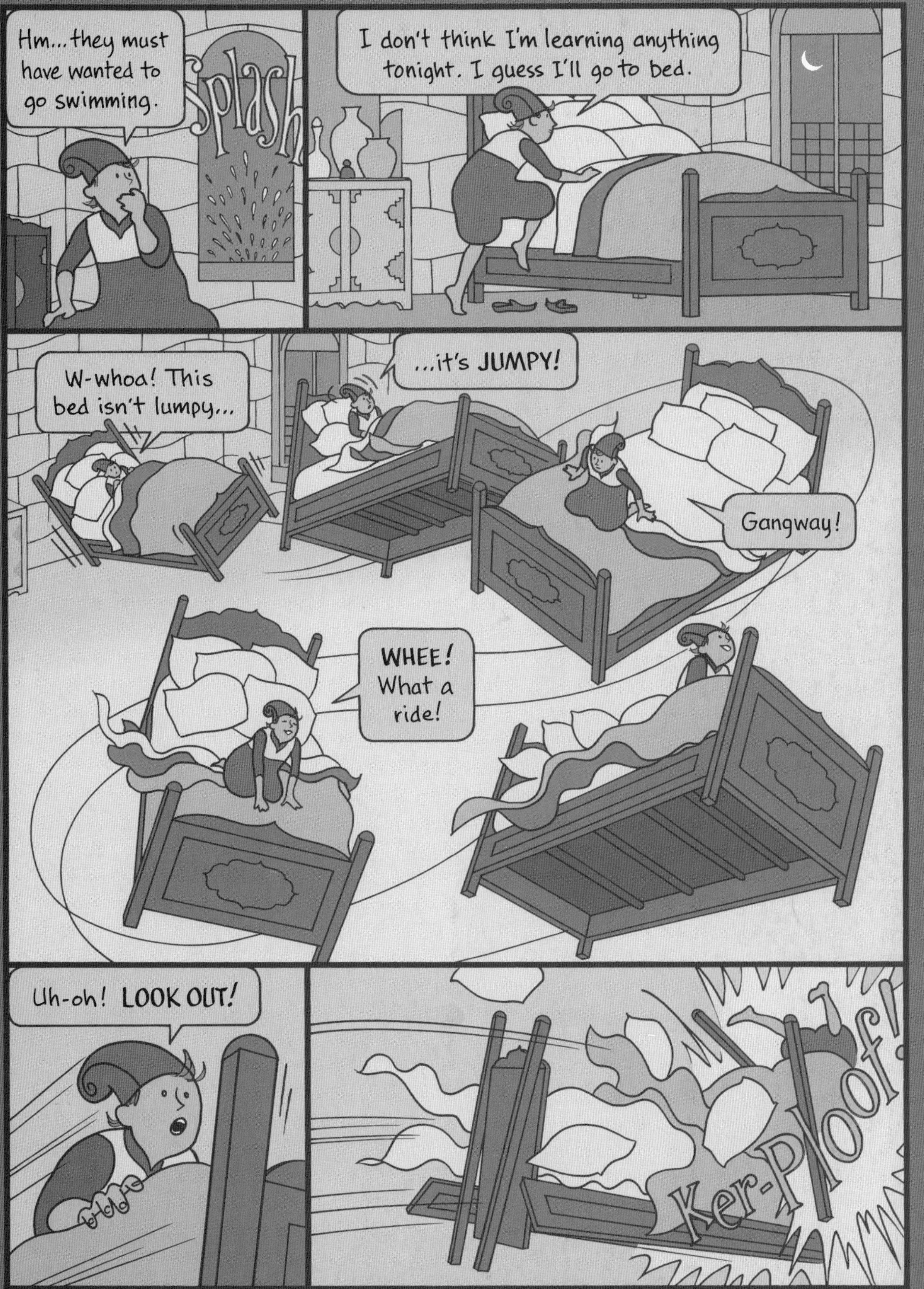
Hm... they must have wanted to go swimming.
Splash
I don't think I'm learning anything tonight. I guess I'll go to bed.
W-whoa! This bed isn't lumpy...
...it's **JUMPY!**
Gangway!
**WHEE!** What a ride!
Uh-oh! **LOOK OUT!**
Ker-Ploof!

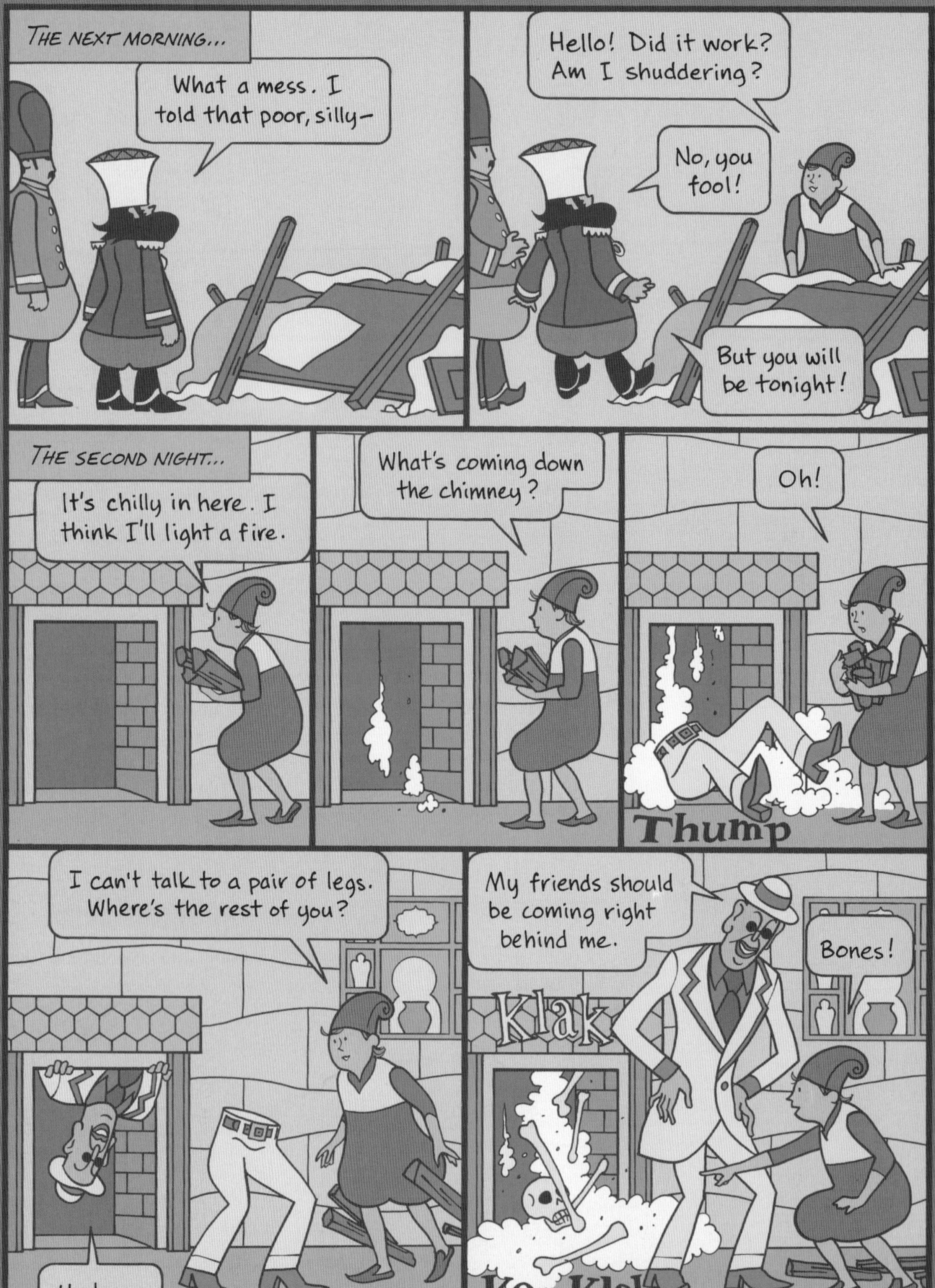
THE NEXT MORNING...
What a mess. I told that poor, silly—
Hello! Did it work? Am I shuddering?
No, you fool!
But you will be tonight!
THE SECOND NIGHT...
It's chilly in here. I think I'll light a fire.
What's coming down the chimney?
Oh!
Thump
I can't talk to a pair of legs. Where's the rest of you?
Up here.
My friends should be coming right behind me.
Bones!
Klak
Ker-Klak

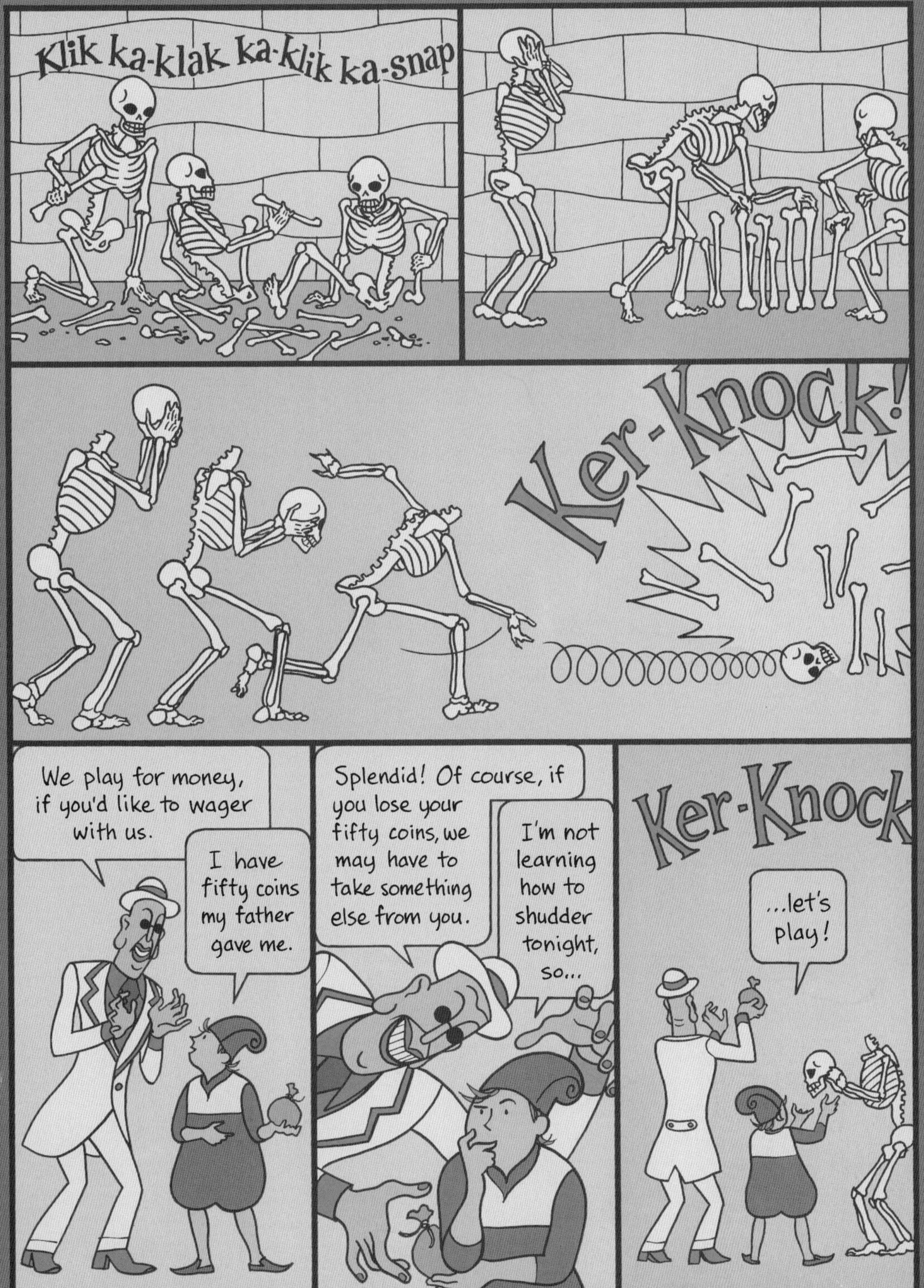
Klik ka-klak ka-klik ka-snap
Ker-Knock!
We play for money, if you'd like to wager with us.
I have fifty coins my father gave me.
Splendid! Of course, if you lose your fifty coins, we may have to take something else from you.
I'm not learning how to shudder tonight, so...
Ker-Knock
...let's play!

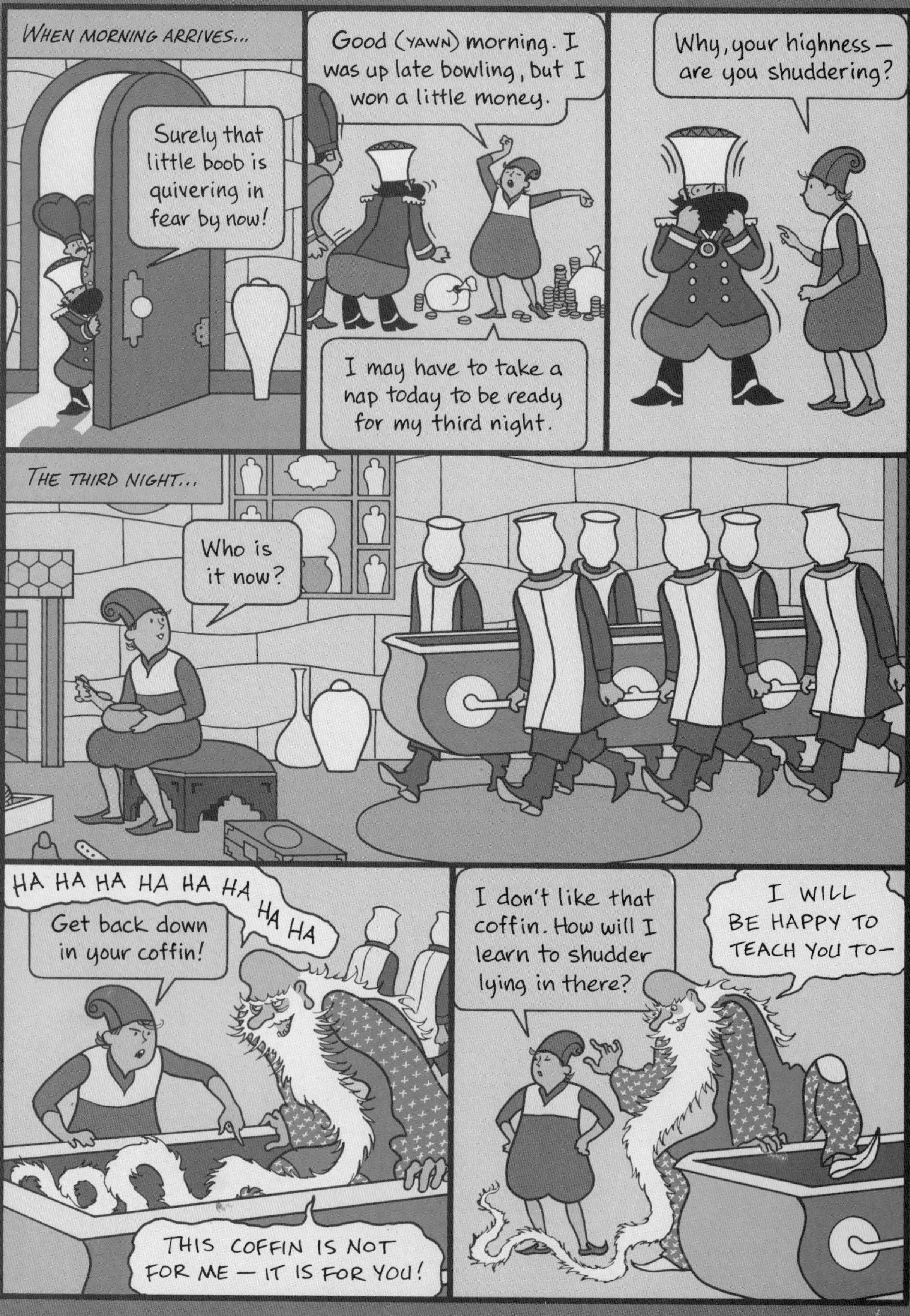
WHEN MORNING ARRIVES...
Surely that little boob is quivering in fear by now!
Good (YAWN) morning. I was up late bowling, but I won a little money.
I may have to take a nap today to be ready for my third night.
Why, your highness— are you shuddering?
THE THIRD NIGHT...
Who is it now?
HA HA HA HA HA HA HA HA
Get back down in your coffin!
THIS COFFIN IS NOT FOR ME — IT IS FOR YOU!
I don't like that coffin. How will I learn to shudder lying in there?
I WILL BE HAPPY TO TEACH YOU TO—

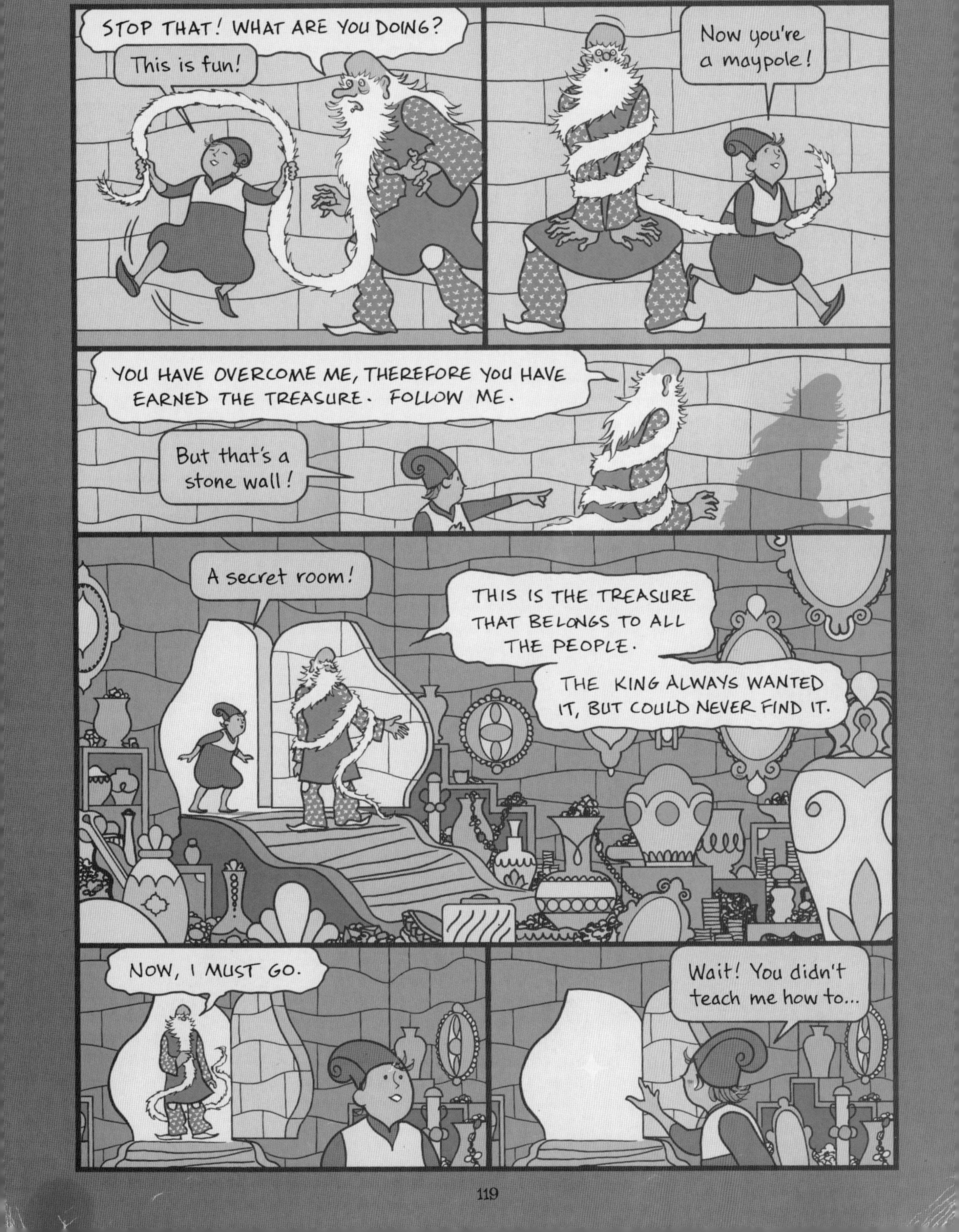
STOP THAT! WHAT ARE YOU DOING?
This is fun!
Now you're a maypole!
YOU HAVE OVERCOME ME, THEREFORE YOU HAVE EARNED THE TREASURE. FOLLOW ME.
But that's a stone wall!
A secret room!
THIS IS THE TREASURE THAT BELONGS TO ALL THE PEOPLE.
THE KING ALWAYS WANTED IT, BUT COULD NEVER FIND IT.
NOW, I MUST GO.
Wait! You didn't teach me how to...

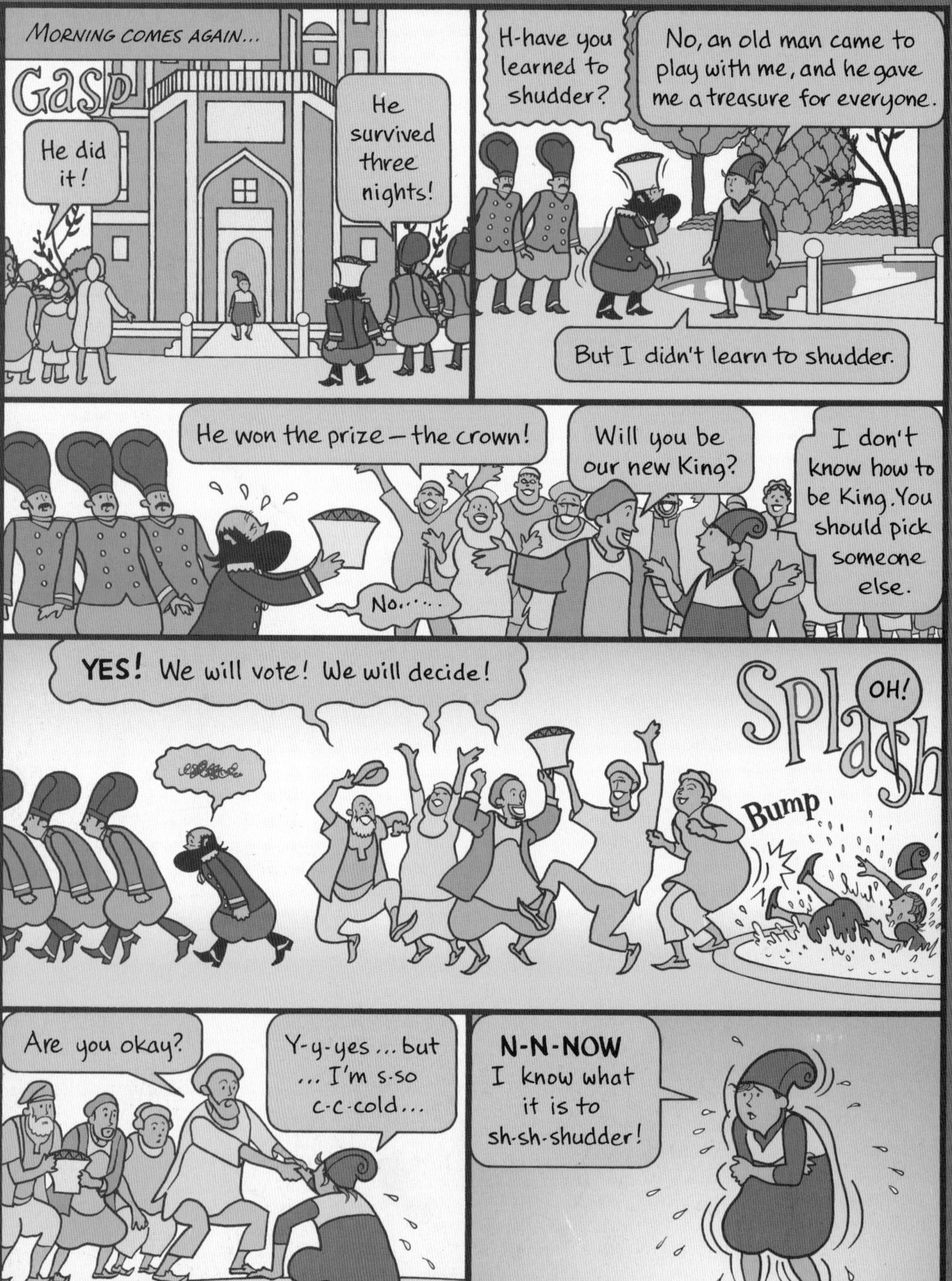
MORNING COMES AGAIN...
Gasp
He did it!
He survived three nights!
H-have you learned to shudder?
No, an old man came to play with me, and he gave me a treasure for everyone.
But I didn't learn to shudder.
He won the prize — the crown!
No......
Will you be our new King?
I don't know how to be King. You should pick someone else.
YES! We will vote! We will decide!
Splash
OH!
Bump
Are you okay?
Y-y-yes ... but ... I'm s-so c-c-cold...
N-N-NOW I know what it is to sh-sh-shudder!

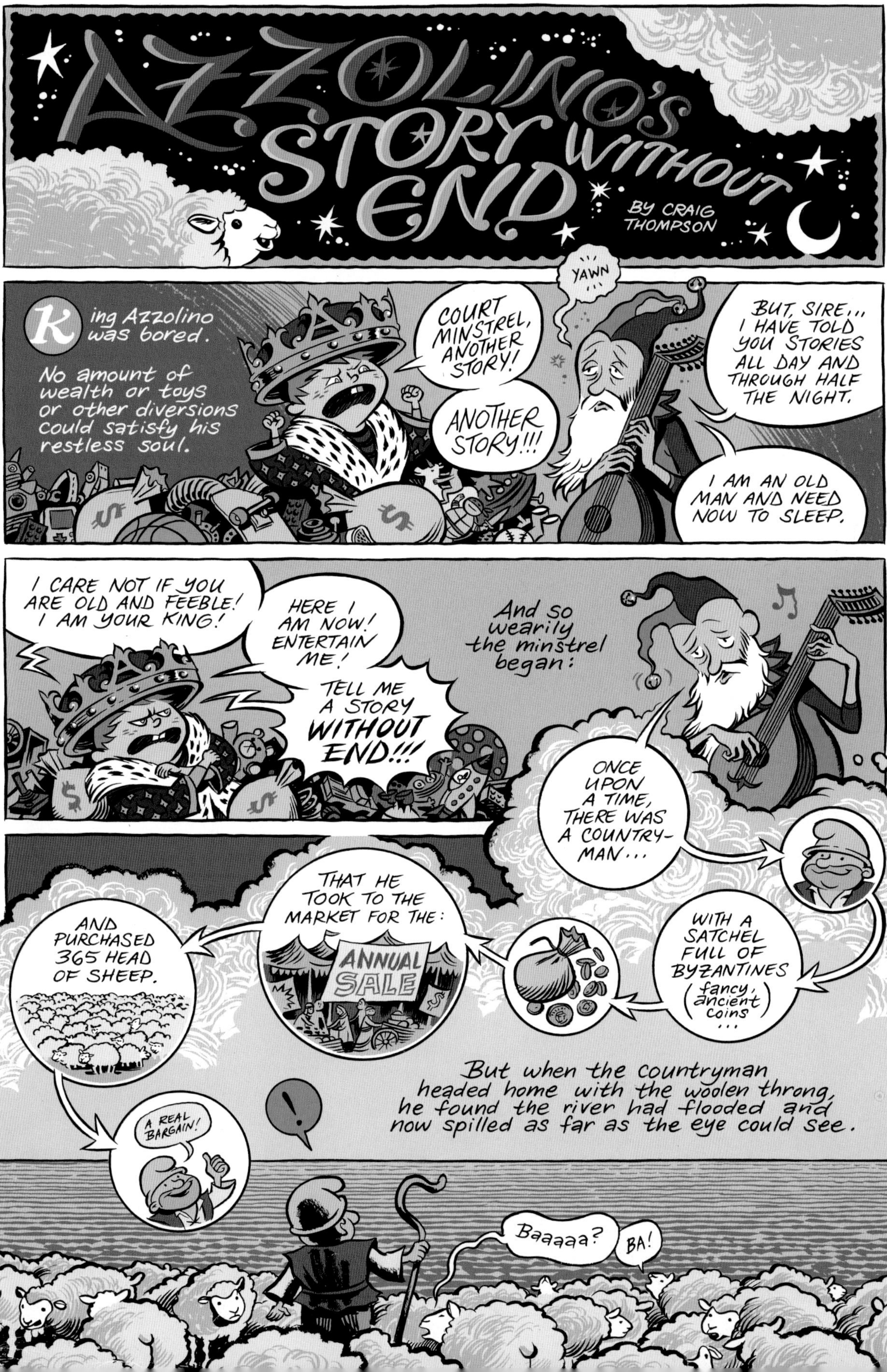
AZZOLINO'S STORY WITHOUT END
BY CRAIG THOMPSON
King Azzolino was bored.
No amount of wealth or toys or other diversions could satisfy his restless soul.
COURT MINSTREL, ANOTHER STORY!
ANOTHER STORY!!!
YAWN
BUT, SIRE... I HAVE TOLD YOU STORIES ALL DAY AND THROUGH HALF THE NIGHT.
I AM AN OLD MAN AND NEED NOW TO SLEEP.
I CARE NOT IF YOU ARE OLD AND FEEBLE! I AM YOUR KING!
HERE I AM NOW! ENTERTAIN ME!
TELL ME A STORY WITHOUT END!!!
And so wearily the minstrel began:
ONCE UPON A TIME, THERE WAS A COUNTRYMAN...
WITH A SATCHEL FULL OF BYZANTINES (fancy, ancient coins)...
THAT HE TOOK TO THE MARKET FOR THE:
ANNUAL SALE
AND PURCHASED 365 HEAD OF SHEEP.
A REAL BARGAIN!
!
But when the countryman headed home with the woolen throng, he found the river had flooded and now spilled as far as the eye could see.
Baaaaa?
BA!

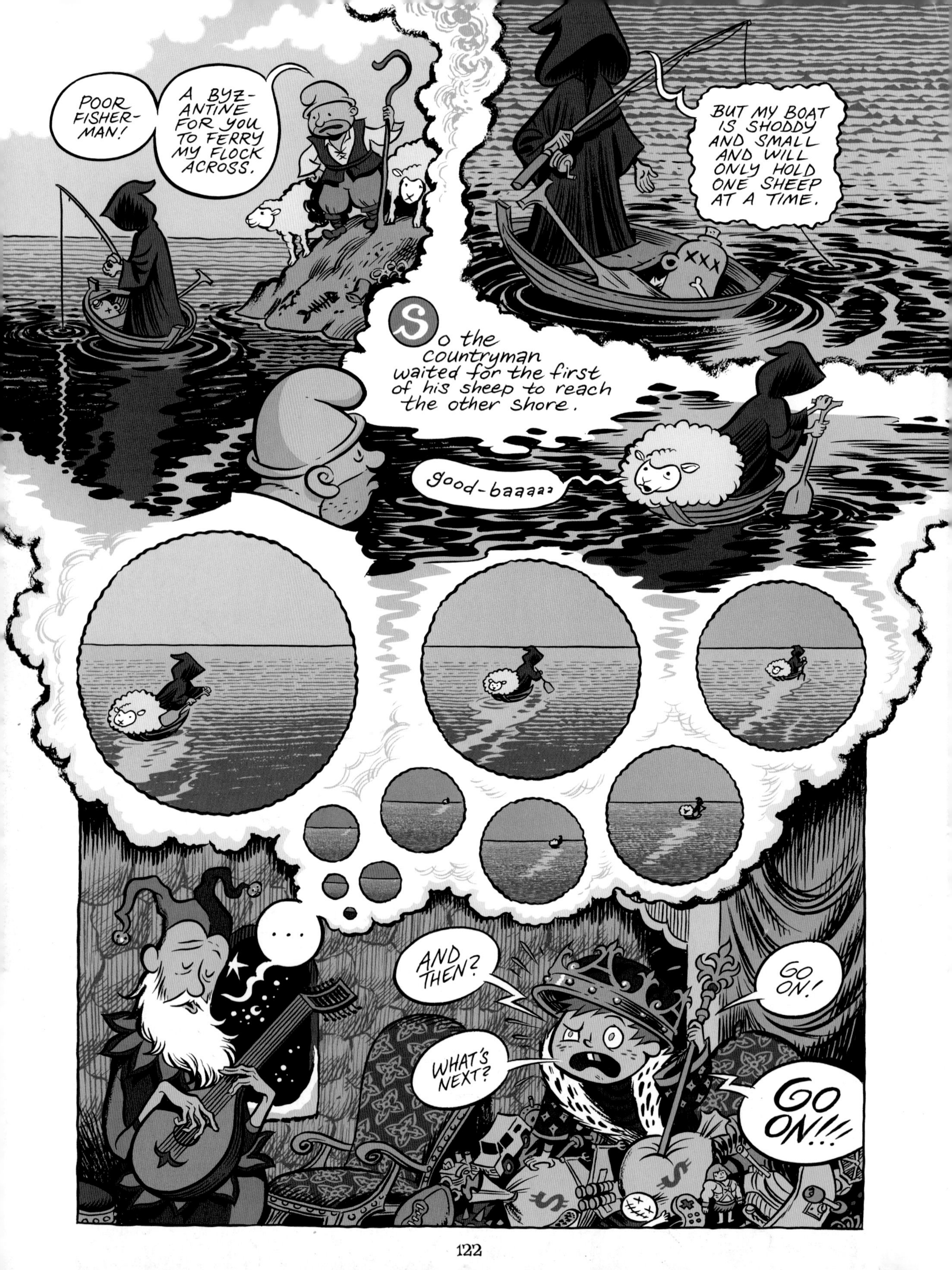
POOR FISHERMAN!
A BYZANTINE FOR YOU TO FERRY MY FLOCK ACROSS.
BUT MY BOAT IS SHODDY AND SMALL AND WILL ONLY HOLD ONE SHEEP AT A TIME.
So the countryman waited for the first of his sheep to reach the other shore.
good-baaaaa
. . .
AND THEN?
WHAT'S NEXT?
GO ON!
GO ON!!!

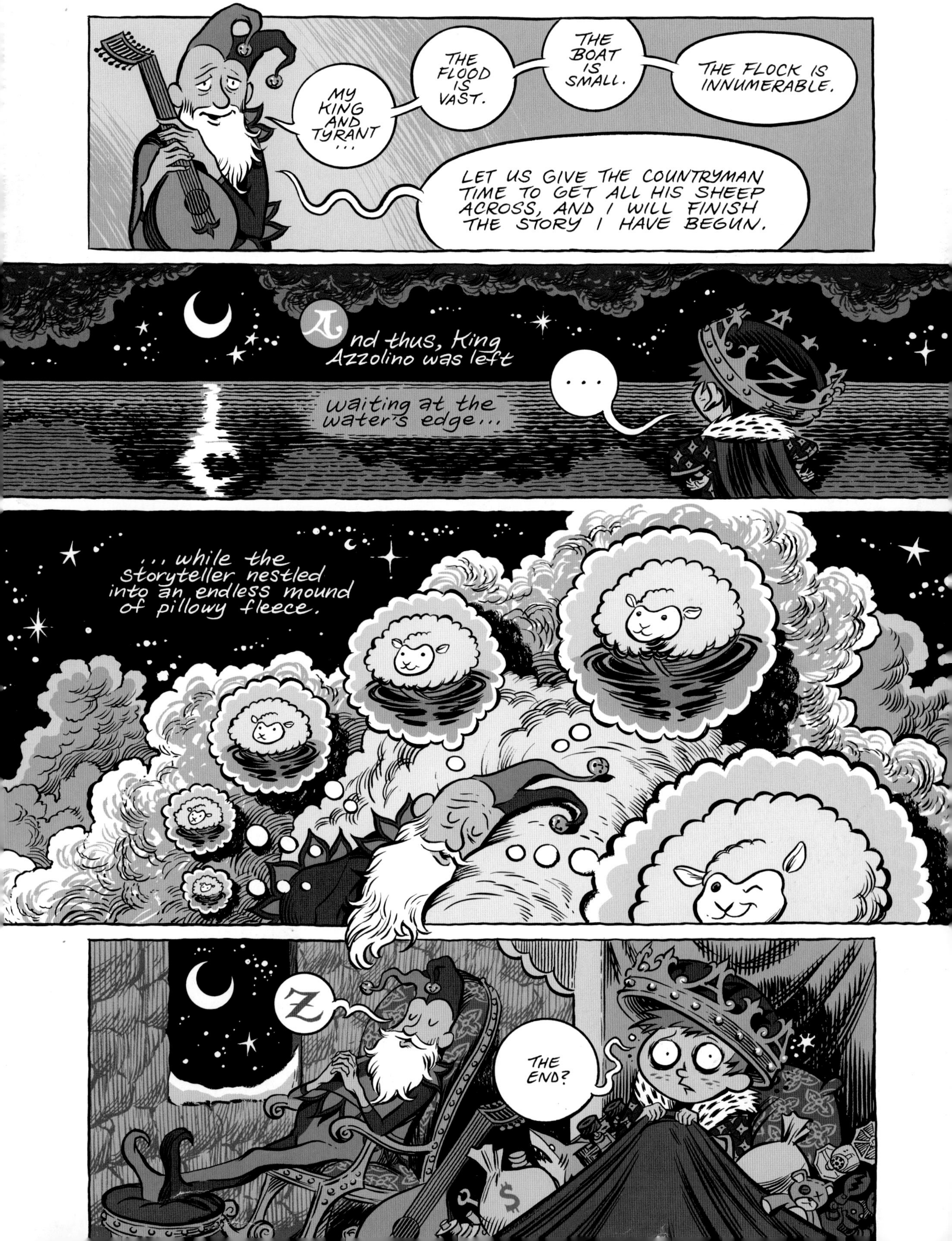
MY KING AND TYRANT . . .
THE FLOOD IS VAST.
THE BOAT IS SMALL.
THE FLOCK IS INNUMERABLE.
LET US GIVE THE COUNTRYMAN TIME TO GET ALL HIS SHEEP ACROSS, AND I WILL FINISH THE STORY I HAVE BEGUN.
And thus, King Azzolino was left
waiting at the water's edge...
. . .
...while the storyteller nestled into an endless mound of pillowy fleece.
Z
THE END?

Choosing the tales for this book involved the best kind of research: reading as many fairy tales as possible in about two months and imagining which ones would make good comics. The only complication: there are too many fairy tales to read in two months, especially if you open up to material outside of the old standbys like the Brothers Grimm and Charles Perrault. Luckily there were some parameters. First Second's senior editor, Calista Brill, and I wanted a mix that included a lot of Grimm tales, a majority of well-known stories, a good sampling of non-European traditions, and a balance of boy and girl heroes. Then came the best part—turning the tales over to our favorite cartoonists and witnessing their comics adaptations defy, hurdle, and otherwise surpass our expectations.

Below are some of the books and websites that I used to get started. Fairy tales make great reading even if you aren't putting together a comics anthology. I can't wait to read more.

*— Chris Duffy*

*Tales from Grimm*, Wanda Gág, University Of Minnesota Press, 2006.
*Cinderella in America: A Book of Folk and Fairy Tales*, William Bernard McCarthy,
        University Press of Mississippi, 2007.
*The Classic Fairy Tales*, Iona Opie and Peter Opie, Oxford University Press, 1980.
*The Grimm Reader: The Classic Tales of the Brothers Grimm*, Maria Tatar, Norton, 2010.
*The Oxford Companion to Fairy Tales*, edited by Jack Zipes (ed.), Oxford University Press, 2000.

gutenberg.org
Project Gutenberg provides a huge online collection of copyright-free works, including many fairy tale books. You can search using the phrase "fairy tales" and the country or region of origin. (For example, "fairy tales, England.")

surlalunefairytales.com
SurLaLune Fairytales is an excellent online fairy tale resource. All the classics are here, and then some.

pitt.edu/~dash/folktexts.html
Folklore and Mythology Electronic Texts is a remarkable compilation of world folklore and fairy tales curated by D. L. Ashliman.

# Contributors

*Graham Annable* (Goldilocks and the Three Bears) is a Canadian cartoonist living in Portland, Oregon. Between storyboarding for feature films and creating the *Grickle* cartoons and comics, he finds time to illustrate a fairy tale every now and again.

*Emily Carroll* (The 12 Dancing Princesses) is a cartoonist living in rainy Vancouver, British Columbia. Her online comics (fairy tale, horror, and otherwise) can be found at emcarroll.com.

*Gigi D.G.* (Little Red Riding Hood) is a Los Angeles-based free-lance illustrator who graduated from Art Center College of Design in 2011. She currently writes and draws *Cucumber Quest*, an all-ages fantasy comic on the internet.

*Eleanor Davis* (cover) is a cartoonist and illustrator living in Athens, Georgia. Her work has appeared in Fantagraphics's *MOME* and *The Best American Comics 2008* and her kids' adventure graphic novel, *The Secret Science Alliance,* was nominated for an Eisner Award. She is currently working on a historical murder mystery graphic novel with history teacher Ann Davis, who is also Eleanor's mother.

*Vanessa Davis* (Puss in Boots) is a cartoonist and illustrator from West Palm Beach, Florida. Her book *Make Me a Woman* was published by Drawn & Quarterly.

*Chris Duffy* (book editor and writer for The Prince and the Tortoise) was in charge of *Nickelodeon Magazine*'s comics section for thirteen years. He also edited First Second's Eisner-nominated *Nursery Rhyme Comics* and is currently putting together the monthly *SpongeBob Comics* series.